FANTASTIC SCHOOLS

VOLUME 3

Edited by
CHRISTOPHER G. NUTTALL AND L. JAGI LAMPLIGHTER

Wisecraft

Wisecraft Publishing

Copyright © 2021 by Christopher G. Nuttall and L. Jagi Lamplighter

ISBN: 978-1-953739-05-6

Edited by: Christopher G. Nuttall and L. Jagi Lamplighter

Cover art by: Tan Ho Sim

CONTENTS

INTRODUCTION

Why do we love magic schools?

Well, I perhaps can't speak for you, but I can speak for myself. I can think of four reasons I find the genre fun to read and to write. Perhaps you feel the same way.

The first reason is relatability. Chances are you've gone to school at some point in your life. And even if you've never gone to school, you've probably seen or read enough stories set in school that you're familiar with the idea and have a strong sense of what it's like.

In other words, school is such a familiar setting that it's an easy comfort zone to snuggle into while we wait for a wild ride into an exciting new adventure to start.

The second reason is wish-fulfillment. Have you ever sat in a really boring class, wondering why it had to be *this* dull, and wishing you could be learning magic instead?

I have!

For me, the worst offender when I was in junior high was history class. My history teacher was one of those types who made everything boring, and I hated the subject with fiery passion.

Ironically, in high school, I had such an amazing history teacher that I became wildly enthusiastic about the subject and ended up minoring in it in college.

Have I ever mentioned that the story of how Charlemagne got crowned Holy Roman Emperor is hilarious? Charlemagne said that he didn't want the Pope to crown him because he didn't need the Pope's permission to rule, thanks so very much. The Pope insisted that yes, Charlemagne did need his permission, thanks so very much, and plonked a crown on his head without permission. This made the Pope look more important, which was the point. Charlemagne was annoyed. Seriously, the Middle Ages is full of true history that would fit well in an epic fantasy book.

Ahem. I digress.

The third reason is conflict. Schools, being highly organized and highly imperfect systems, are rife with familiar and inherent conflicts to weave stories around. There could be social conflicts, such as loneliness or one-sided crushes or bullying. They could be academic conflicts, such as cramming at the last minute to finish a test or trying to figure out what to write a paper on. There could be physical conflicts, such as being forced to play sports in P.E. despite the fact that you have asthma and are clumsy and who cares about where that stupid ball ends up, anyway —

Ah. Not universal? Just me? Well, then.

The fourth reason is worldbulding, and this is where magic school stories, as opposed to school stories in general, really shine.

The thing about a school story set in our world (such as Malory Towers, or Sweet Valley High) is that we already know the rules of the world we live in. We probably know everything the students are being taught. We've taken those subjects; we've learned all those lessons; we've snoozed our way through those boring teachers.

But with a magic school, the author can feed us information in a way that feels natural and interesting, because the reader gets to learn it for the first time along with the characters. A teacher can explain the rules of magic, the history of the culture, the geo-political situation that's going to affect the plot — anything they want to!

Not only that, a good writer is going to excise all the boring parts, which means you're only going to get lectures on *things that matter to you.*

Yesssssssssss!

So, why do we love magic school stories?

Well, all kinds of reasons, of course. But most of all: because they make school fun!

Emily Martha Sorensen
Author of Black Magic Academy

THE WAY OF WIND-WALKING

BY EMILY MARTHA SORENSEN

Mildred's aunts want her to be a bad witch. She wants to be a good witch. When a unicorn shows up to snack on her aunt's garden, she discovers the joy of wind-walking and a new path for her future.

The Way of Wind-Walking

Mildred woke up to find a unicorn poking its head in through the empty space of her bedroom window.

Her mouth opened and closed silently. At last, she managed to say, "Hello?"

In a flash, the majestic creature was gone, disappearing into a gust of wind.

"Oh, good, you're awake!" Aunt Lilith announced, bustling into the room. "We have a busy morning ahead of us. We'll be dusting and cleaning everything in the common areas and bedrooms!"

She proclaimed this as if it were a wonderful gift, which perhaps from Aunt Lilith's perspective it was.

"Even Aunt Hurda's?" Mildred asked with trepidation.

Aunt Lilith was excessively tidy. Aunt Hurda was excessively sloppy. This rarely resulted in goodwill between the sisters.

The youngest of her four aunts was a tremendous slob, and squabbles between her and the second-youngest were frequent. They'd never gotten along, but it was far worse now that Mildred and her aunts were living in a tiny, hidden hut in the forest, rather than the enormous family manor they'd left behind.

Sure enough, Aunt Lilith's face went sour. "No, Hurda refused to allow that, and, in fact, she went out to the forest to collect a bag of live scorpions, which she dumped all over the floor."

Mildred put a hand to her mouth to suppress a giggle. That sounded like Aunt Hurda, all right. She hoped those scorpions weren't for dinner. Aunt Hurda never removed the stingers properly.

"But!" Aunt Lilith said in a grand tone, "Anklistine's cultivated a new kind of berry that will help in our cleaning efforts!"

"Are they flameberries?" Mildred asked hopefully.

If most of the effort would involve sterilization with cleaning fire, she wouldn't be expected to help with the cleaning. She was a wind witch, so she couldn't activate flameberries.

"No," Aunt Lilith said in a reproving tone that implied she knew why Mildred had asked. "They're windberries."

Oh. Mildred sighed. She had known Aunt Anklistine was growing elemental berries, but she hadn't known which kind.

"They're very hard to grow in Restva," Aunt Lilith said proudly. "They prefer the dry soil of Sukanil."

"Well, Aunt Anklistine can grow anything." Mildred shrugged.

"That doesn't make her achievement any less worthy of praise," Aunt Lilith scolded. "In fact, you should go thank her right now. She's in the garden. Get out there! Get!"

She held out her hand to summon a broomstick to swat her niece, so Mildred hastily scrambled out of bed and hopped out the window. She landed in a patch of damp mushrooms that must have sprung up overnight. Perhaps Aunt Hurda had left filth there as fertilizer.

She picked a few and carried them in her skirt to the other side of the house, snacking on them as she went. Aunt Anklistine was weeding by making the earth rise up and spit out any plants that she didn't want among her magical crops.

"Is this poisonous?" Mildred asked, retrieving a purple flower from the weed pile. She liked the taste of most edible flowers.

"I'll check." Aunt Anklistine didn't bother to glance back before she grabbed the plant and tossed it in her mouth. She chewed for a moment. "Mmm. Not a bad flavor. Shame it's useless for brews. Yes, don't eat it; it's poisonous."

Earth witches were immune to natural poisons. Everyone else was not. Mildred was always very nervous to eat Aunt Anklistine's cooking, because her aunt sometimes forgot that small detail when sprinkling in her favorite spices that made everyone else sick.

Not to mention the mushrooms. Ever since she and her aunts had settled in the Forest Beyond to stay hidden from potential assassins, Mildred had made herself an expert on which forest mushrooms were poisonous out of self-defense. Aunt Anklistine grew them all, even the ones that had particularly nasty magical aftereffects. There was one variety that could turn anything, including people, inside out — well, the less she thought about that, the better.

"Where are the windberries?" Mildred asked quickly, trying not to shudder. "Aunt Lilith said you've grown some."

"Oh, right, so you can vacuum-seal the walls to keep unwanted insects out." Aunt Anklistine turned to the left. "They're over —"

She stopped abruptly.

"Where?" Mildred asked, looking off to the left. She saw some nibbled bushes, but no berries.

"Oh, for crying out loud!" Aunt Anklistine exploded. "What kind of animal would be stupid enough to eat windberries?!"

"Are they poisonous?" Mildred asked nervously. If so, she'd be very careful about touching them.

"No, they're not poisonous," Aunt Anklistine said impatiently. "They just kill most creatures that eat them."

"That kind of seems like the definition of 'poisonous' . . ."

Aunt Anklistine stood and brushed dirt off her skirt. Her brow was furrowed, her lips twisted in a sour line. "*You* could eat them without dying, but you wouldn't find much nutrition in a tornado filling your stomach. I'm given to understand some wind witches enjoy the cooling sensation on hot days, though."

"Ohhhhh," Mildred said in realization. "So other creatures would just . . . explode?"

She really hoped Aunt Hurda wasn't going to come home with a bunch of exploded birds. She'd probably pick her teeth with the feathers and use the guts as hair ornaments, and Mildred was tired of hearing Aunt Lilith shriek over her younger sister's lack of hygiene.

"Unless they were magical and connected to wind." Her aunt frowned. "A griffin, maybe? They're known to like windberries, but they aren't native to Restva. And I think I would have heard one crashing through the forest. They don't hunt quietly."

"How about a unicorn?" Mildred asked without thinking.

Aunt Anklistine stiffened and looked at her sharply. "Why do you ask that?"

Mildred backtracked. The last thing she wanted was for her aunts to decide unicorns were garden-munching pests and go out hunting them. "Oh, nothing. Um, it just sprang to mind because they're my familiar."

Aunt Anklistine removed one of her sharp-heeled gardening boots and threw it at her. Mildred tried to dodge, but the boot sailed back and stabbed her shin.

"Yeouch!" Mildred yelped.

"You never — say that — in public!" Aunt Anklistine ordered. "Your familiar is a *karkadann,* and once we get you back to Black Magic Academy, you will prove it to them all!"

They KNOW I have a white magic familiar! Mildred wanted to yell. *That's why I got expelled from the school!*

Aunt Anklistine had a vicious temper. So it was never a good idea to argue with her.

But I'm not going back, Mildred thought with angry determination, accepting the herbs Aunt Anklistine handed to her to take in to the kitchen. She wouldn't fight back, but that didn't mean she'd agree. *I'm done forever with school.*

All they ever taught at Black Magic Academy was ways to hurt people. How to be cruel.

Aunt Anklistine had graduated. Aunt Hurda had been expelled. Aunt Lilith had never been admitted in the first place.

Mildred knew exactly which aunts she wanted to be more like, and which she didn't.

Without windberries, a very put-out Aunt Lilith set Mildred to work doing her usual chore: vacuum-sealing fresh ingredients in packets for winter so that they wouldn't spoil before then.

"If we'd had windberries, you could have sealed up the walls," she kept saying. "We could have even had you build a trap to kill Tractia!"

Mildred was sick and tired of hearing about the windberries.

She was even more sick and tired of hearing plans for her to kill High Witch Tractia, as if that were something she wanted to do.

There was a tradition at Black Magic Academy that if an expelled student managed to personally kill the High Witch who'd expelled her, she would be readmitted into the school. Only two girls in hundreds of years had ever managed that, for unsurprising reasons.

But Mildred's aunts had fixated on the idea that there was a way for her to go back to the most prestigious school in the world and finish her education. Despite the fact that Mildred had said over and over again that she wouldn't do it.

After hearing Aunt Anklistine scold her for hiding the book on building death traps instead of reading it, Aunt Lilith scold her for sweeping dust into corners instead of capturing every single speck, Aunt Anklistine scold her for not remembering anything from her Menacing Spells classes, and Aunt Lilith scold her for labeling five packets of winter spices incorrectly, Aunt Hurda returned.

She tracked filthy mud across the inside of the house with great relish, hung dead flies from greasy strings in every window, and then grinned in pleasure, displaying her filthy teeth, as Aunt Lilith exploded about how impossible to live with she was.

Mildred took that as an opportunity to slip out of the house and go for a walk on her own. On days when her aunts were nagging, and those days were frequent, she appreciated that they lived in the middle of a forest, so it was possible to make herself scarce.

Wild mushrooms weren't the most dangerous thing in the forest, and she'd had more than a witches' dozen of close calls where she'd wound up crouching, terrified, inside invisible wards she'd hastily cast while some Forest Beyond monster snarled around the edges, trying to figure out how to get through and eat her.

But there were some things you just had to do, and getting away from your nagging aunts was one of them.

She was carefully avoiding a parasitic glassberry vine protruding from a tree it was feasting upon, making sure she got nowhere near the vine's curved slivers of thorns, when she heard a sound behind her and turned.

The unicorn was there. The one from this morning.

Mildred gave a sharp intake of breath.

The unicorn didn't move. He just watched her.

Slowly, she moved closer towards him. He didn't run off. She reached him and touched his side. He didn't flee.

"I've heard unicorns are skittish," Mildred said quietly. "But you're not running from me. Is it because I have a unicorn familiar? Do you recognize me as one of you?"

The unicorn swished his tail, brushing a fly off his back.

She wished the unicorn could talk. But animals didn't talk, not even the magical ones. Not in words that humans understood, at least.

"Where are you from?" she asked anyway. "What brought you here?"

As far as she knew, unicorns didn't live in the Forest Beyond. They were native to Sukanil, a country further south. The flat plains of their climate were more conducive to windstorms, which unicorns loved, and the frequent droughts didn't faze herbivorous creatures who could make suffering plants flourish just by tapping them with their horns and healing them.

The unicorn didn't answer, but he did whoosh into wind and blow around her, then return to her side and nudge her with his nose.

"I don't understand," Mildred said, feeling foolish. "What are you trying to say?"

The unicorn snorted in evident exasperation.

"Can you show me?"

The unicorn vanished into a gust of wind, then returned.

"Oh!" Her eyes widened. "I've heard of that! It's called wind-walking! Is it something unicorns do?"

He snorted and shook his mane. Mildred could tell he didn't understand her words and was getting impatient.

She inhaled nervously and patted the front of her dress. Her familiar talisman lay underneath, displaying its gentle relative to the dangerous *karkadann* that much nastier and therefore more socially acceptable students at Black Magic Academy sometimes received.

"You want me to wind-walk, don't you?" she whispered.

She'd never tried to use her familiar for anything. Her aunts had always made her feel ashamed of being quiet and kind instead of vicious and vengeful.

But here . . . here was someone who was just like her and who valued that about her.

Okay, Mildred thought, swallowing. *I'll try it.*

She focused on the magic of her talisman, telling it to lend her the magic of the creature that symbolized who she was inside, and pulled it forward, focusing on what she had just seen the unicorn do.

She blew into a wind that circled the unicorn, gusting his mane and tail through the air.

Mildred staggered as her legs formed again, laughing giddily. She loved that! She hated flying on a broomstick—she got airsick—but with no stomach to get queasy, no bristles to grip with sore and sweaty fingers, and no wooden stick to dig into her rear while she tried to balance on it, blowing through the wind was a pure pleasure.

It felt like joy.

It felt like freedom.

The unicorn blew around her again and then reformed next to her, swishing his tail to hit her arm. He still seemed quite impatient.

Mildred grinned. *Okay! I don't know where we're going, but I'll trust you.*

She joined with the wind, as did he, and he blew to the south, towards Sukanil. She followed close in his wake, swishing through branches and sending leaves spiraling every which way.

As they neared the southern edge of the forest, moving as fast as any witch on a broomstick could, the unicorn reappeared and trotted forward, absently touching spindly branches and cracked roots with the tip of his horn. The drought-damaged trees immediately started budding forth fresh green leaves.

Mildred dropped out of wind-walking, too, examining the trees with interest without touching. She didn't know some of these species, and she had long since learned from Aunt Anklistine that touching unknown trees in the Forest Beyond was just asking for a cauldron full of trouble.

"Ah, there you are," said a woman's voice.

Mildred's head shot up in alarm. A stranger in a purple dress, wearing a matching set of armbands, was stroking the unicorn's nose while he nuzzled at a bag by her side, clearly expecting a treat.

Traitor! Mildred thought furiously.

"You're Drakin's daughter, right?" the woman said, pulling a handful of velvety red flower petals out of her bag and holding them out. The unicorn gobbled them down. "I heard a rumor you got expelled, but nobody seemed to know why. Your classwork was excellent; you'd made plenty of enemies; and your familiar was a *karkadann*. There seemed to be no reason why Black Magic Academy would expel you. Unless, of course . . . your familiar wasn't what it seemed."

Mildred swallowed. She thought about fleeing, but the unicorn was clearly the woman's friend, and he was far more experienced at wind-walking than she was.

"What do you want?" she asked, her voice shaking.

"I want you to come to my school," the woman said, shutting her bag. The unicorn butted his nose against her arm aggressively, clearly upset about this. "I'm High Witch Dal of the Sukanil School of Magical Studies. I think you'd be an asset."

"No!" Mildred burst out, shaking her head. "I'm done with school! I'm done with competing! I'm done with making enemies! I'm done with all of it! I just want to be left alone!"

"And your school isn't going to cure her of any of that irritating meekness," Aunt Anklistine's voice said from above. An instant later, she landed between them, catching her broomstick as it fell. Earth witches couldn't be injured by falling. "Hello, Dal. When Mildred mentioned a unicorn, I wondered if that meant you were sneaking around. That pet of yours is very fond of windberries."

"He is a bit of a pig," the woman said amiably, patting his nose.

"Mildred is *not,*" Aunt Anklistine said emphatically, "going to your school."

"Shouldn't that be her decision?"

"Your school teaches nothing but useless white magic!"

"We also teach black magic. We're not as prejudiced as your alma mater is. We see the value in understanding everything."

"You *barely* teach black magic!"

"It's barely of value," High Witch Dal said calmly. She looked over at Mildred. "I think you'll find that if you want to survive in witch society—and I do mean that literally—you're going to need an education. By all accounts, your death-enemy is one of the most powerful witches of your generation. It would be wise to learn how to defend yourself, in case she comes after you after she graduates."

Mildred swallowed. That *was* true.

"Yes, and your school is hardly known for its Deadly Spells classes." Aunt Anklistine folded her arms. "Go away, Dal."

"Not until she answers." High Witch Dal folded her arms, too.

Mildred took a deep breath and stepped hesitantly forward. If the High Witch of the school had a unicorn for a pet, the school couldn't be so bad. And anywhere would be better than Black Magic Academy. If she needed to learn to defend herself, she may as well go. "Well . . ."

Aunt Anklistine's cloak billowed outward, and a massive snake lunged from behind her, stopping with its fangs posed right beside High Witch Dal's neck. The snake seemed to be attached to Aunt Anklistine's lower back, like some kind of tail.

"My familiar is a chimera," Aunt Anklistine said sharply. "These fangs are poisonous. I'm sure you think your unicorn can cure any poison, but trust me: I'm fast with this tail. I'll kill it before it tries. Now leave. Now."

No! Mildred slammed her hand against her aunt's back, using the same spell that she used to vacuum-seal ingredients for winter. Aunt Anklistine clutched her throat, air gone from her lungs, and High Witch Dal spun out of her reach and hopped up on the unicorn's back, which held his horn posed against her aunt's heart.

There was silence for a moment. Then Aunt Anklistine turned her head to look at Mildred. There was a faint smirk on her lips. "So you've finally learned to do something useful."

"Don't threaten other people!" Mildred said heatedly.

"And you're finally showing some vague resemblance to a fighting spirit," Aunt Anklistine said with satisfaction. "It's about time. All right, Dal. I'll tell you what. You can take her as a student—as long as she's required to take every single class on black magic you offer."

"Deal," High Witch Dal said immediately.

Mildred's face screwed up. "I don't want—"

"I don't care," Aunt Anklistine said snidely. "Do you want to go or don't you?"

"Yesssss . . ."

"Fine." Aunt Anklistine tossed her broom off to the side, where it hovered. She sat on it, holding on to the bristles with only one hand. "I'll go get Lilith and Hurda, and we'll figure out what background story and assumed name you'll need to use. Obviously, you can't go as yourself, or you'll be a target for assassins from Black Magic Academy. The two of you, stay put unless you want me coating the forest with inside-out poison to find you. Because if you make me, I will."

Mildred shuddered. Why did Aunt Anklistine's threats always have to be so gruesome?

She watched her aunt fly up above the trees and head back the direction they'd come.

"So how many black magic classes am I going to have to take?" Mildred asked, resigned.

"Zero."

Mildred blinked and looked over at her.

"Joke's on her," High Witch Dal said casually. "We don't offer *any* classes specifically on black magic at the Sukanil School of Magical Studies. Students are allowed to study it if they must, but we don't go out of our way to teach it."

Mildred was startled.

The High Witch folded her arms and smirked.

Mildred spurted out a laugh and stroked the unicorn on the nose as he bumped the side of his head against her.

She was going to like this school.

Emily Martha Sorensen writes clean fantasy adventures with clever characters, fun plots, and lots of humor. She thinks the world needs more happiness and laughter, so she goes out of her way to create stories about them.

Probably her best books to start with are *Black Magic Academy,* which is about a good witch who gets sent to a school for wicked witches; *The Keeper and the Rulership,* in which forbidden magic may be the key to building a new magic system; and *Aquarius, about a married* couple fighting to conquer a terrible curse.

She also has two webcomics: *A Magical Roommate,* which is complete, and *To Prevent World Peace,* which is currently updating.

You can learn more about her here: http://www.emilymarthasorensen.com

SUMMONED

BY JAY BARNSON

Virtual Reality can seem almost magical in its ability to seemingly transport a user to another world. For Ethan, it seems like a fun escape from his lonely life in upstate New York. However, when he tries an exclusive game called "Nyrlim Magic Academy," the technology seems too good to be true. Is he really just playing a game, or is there something else happening in this virtual world of magic and conspiracies?

Summoned

Ethan willed his feet up each step of the stairway to his second-floor apartment. The threadbare dirt-colored carpeting barely padded his heavy steps. Ten hours of JavaScript debugging had never exhausted him like it did now, in the year of the pandemic. He hated being isolated in a near-empty office manned by a mask-wearing skeleton crew. He hated being isolated in his empty apartment just as much. While he had never been gregarious, he missed being able to talk to people face-to-face without a mask or a computer screen in the way.

Three years ago, he thought his life was finally about to begin. He had graduated a semester early with hardly any student debt and had landed a decent programming job upstate in a town that was neither too big nor too small. He'd even found a small apartment of his own without the kinds of useless roommates he'd spent his college life dealing with. Now he missed those guys, with their stupid habits and their weekends of alcoholic excess. Anything was better than returning to an empty apartment in a world afraid to socialize.

He slow-yanked himself up the last step by pulling on the metal railing, risking tetanus from the painted-over rust. It was an old habit, especially when he was tired, but the bit of whole-body exertion woke him up a little. He rounded the corner and spotted the package in front of the door. The brown box was over two feet long, about 18 inches wide and deep. Ethan did most of his non-food shopping online, so packages at his front door were a regular sight, but he'd ordered nothing recently. Certainly he would have remembered something this large.

Ethan unlocked and opened the door to his dark, chilly apartment. He brought the box inside, finding it surprisingly light for its size. He switched on the lights with his elbow and closed the door with his foot as he examined the box. The return address label was unfamiliar.

He set it on the floor of his barely furnished living room, and opened the package. It contained yet another box, this one a sleek gray box emblazoned with the glossy but otherwise unassuming "Klendistone" logo.

Now he remembered. He'd considered canceling his order several times over the year, as the boutique company had failed repeatedly to ship what once promised to be a massive leap in Virtual Reality technology. He'd held out, mainly because he'd been too busy to make the effort. They'd sent him a questionnaire two months ago to see if he qualified for beta access to the software with the first batch of hardware. He didn't remember hearing back from them, but he'd received a few emails from them over the last year apologizing for delays, and he could have ignored a shipping confirmation.

Ethan glanced over at the clock on the microwave. He'd come home late, but there was still time to set up the hardware and try out one of the promised virtual worlds. Right now, the idea of visiting any place but here sounded too good to be true.

Thirty minutes later, he'd finished setting up the system and making sure his meager furnishings were moved out of the way. He strapped the Velcro bands to ankles and the strange controllers over his hands, lowered the headset over his eyes, and switched on the power. After going through some exercises to calibrate his body and the room, the system gave him a virtual tour of the equipment, and then offered him a chance to try a VR web-store or an exclusive pre-loaded title called "Nyrlim Magic Academy."

If Ethan had received one of the very first units shipped, he'd be one of the first people outside the company to play their exclusive game. He had low expectations, as he doubted the tiny company could have had much money to pour into developing the title and the hardware. Still, it would be fun to check out a game that hardly anyone else had played yet. He'd grown up with fantasy stories dealing with special schools for people with supernatural abilities, and a VR game about a magic school sounded fun.

The game opened with him standing in the courtyard of a stereotypical castle-like structure. The graphics would have been unimpressive on the latest game console, but the feeling of immersion more than made up for it. A gentle breeze wiggled the grass in polygonal uniformity, but it was enough that he could almost feel the wind on his skin. The morning sun peeking over the castle walls might err on the side of cartoonish rather than realistic, but it was still thrilling. His feet moved a little strangely but still followed his movements, and his hands and fingers seemed to move perfectly. Besides hand movements, the buttons on the controllers provided additional input.

A woman materialized in an explosion of particle effects, wearing a skintight black dress that defied the laws of physics as it clung to the curves of her skin. Her black-peaked hat completed the image of a "sexy witch's costume" for a Halloween party. Her glassy eyes turned to him without focusing.

"Welcome to Nyrlim Academy," she said in a sultry voice. Her mouth movements did not synchronize perfectly with her voice. "I am Vera, and I will teach you the basics so you may excel in your training at the Academy to master the magical arts!"

The effect was in some ways laughable, and her narration of the tutorial sounded like community theater, but after fifteen minutes he'd performed basic tasks like moving around the courtyard, picking up objects and moving objects with his virtual hands, and using the in-game interface.

"We were told you have considerable control over a handful of top-tier spells already," Vera said with exaggerated gravity. "Show me what you can do, and we at the academy will teach you to build upon them."

With that, she gave instructions to cast five spells. They involved pressing a button, moving the hands a particular way, and speaking three or four nonsense syllables. The first spell created a ball of fire, which he threw at a straw target dummy nailed to a post. It erupted into flames so impressive he could almost feel the heat. A tiny text message appeared at the edge of his vision: "Aptitude registered."

Next was a magical shield which he used to deflect some dart-like magical attacks that Vera shot at him. Once again, he saw the "Aptitude registered" message. Next came a spell to move weights at a distance. After moving the heaviest of the weights, he received the message again. The fourth spell weakened or erased an existing magical spell. Vera tested him by creating an illusionary monster and having him dispel it. The movements felt natural to him, and he succeeded on his first try.

The final spell was conspicuously unnamed by Vera. "This is a defensive spell that should be used with great care, but it is the most powerful spell in your arsenal. Be warned that if you use it more than once, it will be much weaker until you have fully rested."

She demonstrated the words and hand motions to cast it. He followed the instructions as the others, but nothing happened to the replacement targeting dummy. The "Aptitude registered" message came up, just as with all the other spells, but nothing else happened —no special effects, no sounds, nothing.

After his third try, Vera said, "Excellent! You have demonstrated your potential, and I know you will excel here at Nyrlim Magic Academy. Proceed through the doors, and you will be guided to the dormitories. I expect to see great things from you, wizard."

The double doors she indicated remained closed.

Ethan sighed and spoke aloud. "Thanks a lot, Vera. It looks like your game is buggy right from the get-go."

"I do not think you are casting the spell correctly," Vera replied.

"I'm not casting a spell, I'm complaining about your buggy game."

"I do not think you are casting the spell correctly."

"So much for this," Ethan muttered to himself.

"I do not think you are casting…"

The world went black except for tiny letters that appeared in space in front of him. "System registered. Klendistone comm protocol 201 executing. Screenshots disabled."

Ethan hesitated before pressing the exit button. The words hovered there like a prompt, promising nothing but endless black from a crashed game, and the darkness gave him a feeling of vertigo.

As the seconds ticked by, the image subtly changed, with splotches of dark gray emerging from the darkness. Eventually, a scene resolved itself, and he found himself standing in a stone room lit by candles. The walls were partly covered by shelves of loosely-bundled papers and a handful of books. A chalk circle crowned with strange symbols surrounded him, and three people in robes stared at him wide-eyed.

The people were younger than him. One, a blond boy with a slight acne problem, seemed the oldest at maybe twenty years of age. He was flanked by two girls that seemed to be in their late teens. The one to Ethan's left had light skin and long hair that seemed impossibly black and glossy and seemed to be a little older than the other two. She stood just in front of a bucket of water with a mop inside it, the mop handle leaning against a shelf.

The girl to the boy's other side was blue-skinned, as if she had argyria—silver poisoning. Her braided golden hair enhanced the effect. Of the three, she seemed the youngest, maybe sixteen years old. That made the argyria surprising, as Ethan thought it only occurred after years of silver exposure.

The young man swallowed, his Adam's apple bobbing. These were not the plastic characters of computer graphics. Everything Ethan looked at, from their facial expressions to the tiny candle flames, seemed photo-realistic, as if he was looking at a movie on a 4K TV in full 3D. It was seamless, perfect, limited only by the screens and lenses of his headset. The company must have pre-recorded the footage from live actors.

The boy stared at Ethan open-mouthed. "We did it! We actually did it!"

"Now what?" the blue girl asked. "What are we going to have it do?"

"I don't know," he answered. "I really didn't expect this to work."

Ethan grinned. "I gotta say, I'm impressed," he said to himself. "This is really incredible."

The three characters flinched at his words. The blue girl stifled a shriek with both hands.

"You can talk?" the boy asked.

Ethan laughed. The photo-realistic characters went far beyond any video game he'd seen with their ability to react with perfect timing.

"This is cool as hell," he muttered.

The blue girl started shaking. "Hell?" She turned to the boy, grabbing his arm with both hands. "Oh no, Dane, we summoned a devil from Hell!"

Did the characters key off of what he'd said, or was that a coincidence? If it was the former, the game was far more sophisticated than Ethan could have imagined. Sure, voice recognition was pretty common these days, but having characters respond to his statements in such a lifelike manner was beyond cutting-edge.

The young man—Dane—looked down at Ethan's feet. "Eve, are you sure that you got the binding spell right?"

Ethan followed Dane's gaze and examined the circle. A staple of fantasy and supernatural horror stories, circles like this were supposed to cage supernatural creatures stuck inside. Was he supposed to be playing some kind of summoned monster? It didn't mesh well with the storyline of the tutorial. However, being stuck in the binding circle could be a clever design trick to limit the amount of the world he could view. Would it let him escape? He had to try.

He manipulated the hand controls to instantly move, as he'd been taught in the tutorial. The view in the headset wavered, and he found himself outside the circle, behind a shocked Dane. The disorienting effect gave Ethan a brief sensation of vertigo and nausea, but it soon passed.

The teenagers gasped. Their reaction was convincingly realistic, unlike any game he'd ever seen, even on the latest consoles. He reached up and lifted the headset to peek at his apartment just to make certain the real world was still there. Reassured, he addressed the three young people. Even with the latest AI, 3D graphics and animation, there were limits on how well they could respond.

"Who are you?" he asked.

"Please, don't kill us!" the blue girl cried out. "We're sorry!"

"What?" Ethan raised his hands in what he hoped was a friendly gesture. "I don't want to hurt you. Don't attack me, and we'll get along fine." If the game forced him to fight these three, he was going to be pissed. Aside from the blue skin of the one girl, they seemed like kids he'd gone to high school and college with not too long ago.

Dane sighed in apparent relief, but the girl with the black hair seemed unconvinced. She folded her arms and said, "I'm Alicia Stormhand. This is Dane McDougal and Eve Delaney. We're students at Nyrlim Academy of Magic."

"And who do you think I am?"

Dane held up a sheet of paper. "Spirit entity zero-zero-zero-zero-zero dash zero two six. We, uh, summoned you. We invoked the Right of First Summoning, and the binding ritual..."

"Which was supposed to hold me inside that circle? Did you screw it up?"

"We're sorry!" Eve cried out again.

Alicia glanced sideways at Eve. The candles in the room reflected in silky orange pools in her hair. "That, or you were far too strong to be held by the simple binding spell we used."

Ethan guessed the game-makers intended the latter to make the player feel special. "So what's this first summoning thing?"

Dane answered, the answer sounding semi-rehearsed, as if he was answering a question on an oral exam. "Spell casters summon entities in one of two ways—with or without a name. Without using a name, any entity may be called that meets the criteria of the spell. These are usually weak, although there is a danger of a more powerful entity appearing and overwhelming the summoner. Calling a specific entity by name increases the summoner's control over it. This control is much stronger if the summoner is the first living spell caster to summon the entity. This is why unused names are so highly sought after. It is also why..." He glanced at Eve and then returned his gaze to Ethan. "That is also why summoners with the first rights to powerful beings are targeted by their rivals."

"So summoners are basically slave owners, is that what you are telling me?" Ethan asked.

Dane stammered, and Alicia came to his rescue. "It's not like that. Not usually, anyway. Most summoned spirits are not really free-willed entities. And the named ones usually make bargains for their services."

The game was getting interesting right off the bat. Honestly, he couldn't see how a title of this quality could have garnered an exclusive with a little boutique VR manufacturer, no matter how cool and next-generation their hardware might be. The realism of what he was seeing was a quantum leap beyond the tutorial. "Uh-huh. And who did you guys kill to get first rights to me?"

"We wouldn't!" Eve said. "That's why we summoned you!"

Dane, regaining his composure, answered. "Your original summoner was Theodore Callister, a professor here at the Academy... and my... never mind. We took your name from his office. We summoned you to ask you who murdered him, or at least tell us who his enemies were."

"Sorry, I have no clue who you are talking about."

"Professor Callister? He was the wizard who summoned you before."

"Uh, nope. This is the first time this has happened to me." Ethan played along.

He had been expecting a high-fantasy adventure with this game. Was it now turning into a murder mystery? Add that to a growing list of mysteries around the game itself. He threw some more wrinkles at the game characters and see how their canned responses would work.

"Besides, that number isn't my name. My name is Ethan. I am not a spirit, I'm just a guy with a new Virtual Reality game I wanted to try. You are characters in my video game."

It hurt to say this, as it felt like the closest human contact he'd experienced in weeks. It felt like he could just reach out and touch them—yet it felt real enough that he didn't want to be rude, game or not.

Alicia was the first to respond. "Ethan, is it?" She inclined her head slightly to one side. "I hate to be the one to tell you this, but you are clearly not human, and this isn't a game."

The response, and the humanity in her voice, was absolutely convincing. He looked at his hands, which glowed white in the air, disconnected from a body. "This isn't my body. I'm actually standing in the living room of my apartment right now." Once again, he lifted the visor to reassure himself. He lowered it back into place over his eyes and shook his head. "This all looks so real."

Dane stared at him, as if trying to make sense of his words. Alicia raised an eyebrow again, and bit on her lower lip. Eve opened her mouth in shock, but instead of voicing fears, she said, "Could this be like astral projection? A magical device to project your spirit into this avatar?"

"Huh." Ethan thought for a moment. "It's not like I'm unconscious in the real world."

Eve looked at Dane. "If what he says is true, he could control this form like a puppet. It would explain why my binding wasn't strong enough. I used the wrong spell. If I'd known..."

Dane patted her shoulder. "It's okay. We knew that was a risk, and he doesn't seem hostile. I think we're okay."

Alicia folded her arms again, frowning slightly. "Summoning a human would be unprecedented, and offer frightening implications. Especially with binding. However, many spirits are known to lie, aren't they? Especially if they aren't properly bound." Her eyebrows lowered as she looked Ethan over.

Ethan laughed. "Seriously? You are actually asking me to prove I'm human? How would we do that?"

Both the girls looked at Dane, who shook his head. "We never covered anything like this in any class. I have no idea. Maybe we can summon it again, with a better binding?"

"No, we've already used up the Right of First Summoning," Eve said. "Maybe a far more powerful spell would work, but especially if it is a human, there's nothing more I can do. I'm sorry. We should dismiss it and clean this up before we're caught."

Ethan eyed the bucket and mop. Out of curiosity, he moved toward it and grabbed the mop handle. The mop moved clumsily, but with a bit of effort he was able to control it as he mopped at the circle on the floor. For the most part, the mopped section turned into a swirling puddle of chalky sludge, but there was something fun about a tedious chore when done in the context of the game.

Dane snorted. "That's the worst mopping I have ever seen. If that's an attempt to prove you are human, I think you failed."

Ethan laughed. "Hey, it's my first time doing it in VR. I've got to get the hang of it."

Eve eyed the door. "We need to go soon. We're going to get in trouble. If we're caught..."

Alicia waved at the door. "You two go. I'll handle the dismissal and finish cleaning up."

"Are you sure?" Dane asked.

"I can dismiss a summoned spirit. I'll be fine."

Dane opened the door a fraction, peeking outside. "Okay, it looks clear," he said.

He took Eve by the hand, and the two slipped out, quietly closing the door behind them. Ethan kept mopping, and Eve knelt down beside him and grabbed from rags that had been draped on the side of the bucket to help.

"So I guess you are all three studying to be wizards," Ethan said.

"They are." She shrugged. "Eve is one of the most powerful student spell casters in the school. Dane is Callister's nephew, and a very gifted summoner."

"What about you?"

She shook her head and scrubbed a little harder. "I'm good at the academics, but I'm not powerful enough to go far as a wizard. I've already been here two years longer than usual to try to get my practicals up, but I turn twenty-one next month. I won't be allowed to stay after that."

"What, they kick you out at twenty-one?"

She nodded. "Professor Callister was putting together a graduate program based on some new research and had invited me to be a part of it. With his death, I don't think anyone else will sponsor it. I'm going to have to choose another career field with magic as a secondary skill."

"I think I understood most of that," Ethan said. "So where are we, exactly?"

"The school? It's near Vissos in the Kingdom of Aligia. What about you?"

"Never heard of that. I'm in New York. Upstate, not the city. Uh, in the United States."

"I have never heard of any of those." She glanced up at him, arching an eyebrow. "It sounds made up. Is there an Old York to go with it?"

Ethan snickered. "Just York, yeah. Back in England. I've never been there. I've never been much of anywhere, really. I'm only about sixty miles from where I grew up." He dipped the mop back in the bucket and set back to work mopping the floor.

"Are you also studying to be a wizard?"

"No such thing here. I graduated from college a couple of years ago. I'm a software engineer."

"I understood most of that," she said. "I don't know what a software engineer is, but it sounds like applied science."

"That's about right. Do you have computers in this world?"

"People who do mathematical calculations?"

"Machines."

"Ah. Some counting devices, yes." She squeezed the rag into the bucket. "I think we're done here. I should dismiss you now."

Ethan peeked under the headset at the glowing LEDs of the clock on the microwave. "I should have gone to sleep a half an hour ago. I didn't realize how long I've been playing. It's time for me to go."

"I will cast a dismissal spell. It's not too powerful, but if you are willing to leave, it won't need to be."

Ethan shrugged, but the expression didn't really translate to his avatar. "I can just exit the game here and save you the trouble, you know."

"I still don't know what you mean by game. But even if you are telling the truth, I don't want any of your puppet lingering around." She made a circular motion with her hands, gesturing at him. "For what it's worth, I'm sorry for the inconvenience. We didn't know we were summoning a real person."

Ethan laughed. "Actually, this was an extremely interesting night."

She smiled at him. "You are an interesting person, Ethan. I enjoyed meeting you."

"I was glad to meet you, too, Alicia. And your friends. I look forward to seeing you again."

Her smile dropped. "I... I think that is unlikely. But maybe." She spoke a short nonsense phrase while gesturing at him. The screen went black again, except for a message that read "Klendistone comm protocol 200 executing. Screenshots re-enabled."

He exited the game, turned off the headset, and then plugged the VR system in to recharge.

He went to bed after a quick meal of dry cereal, but it took him two hours to fall asleep, thinking of Alicia, Dane, and Eve. He just couldn't convince himself that they were only characters in a game.

The next day, Ethan called his boss to say he'd be working from home. These days, that was a non-event. Most of his coworkers did the same, almost every day, including his boss. He really didn't have much need to go into the office at all, except that it gave him a change of scenery.

But the game had done that even better, hadn't it? Even if he'd only seen the courtyard and a storage room, it had been a new place. At least, it felt that way.

As he worked, he glanced at the virtual reality gear sitting on the shelf near his tiny desk. Nyrlim Academy was only a few feet away. He resolved to take a real lunch break today and visit the school once more. Maybe he'd see more of it than a storage room. He thought about the things he wanted to talk about with Alicia, and then mentally chided himself when he caught himself.

"You're losing it, Ethan," he said out loud.

She wasn't real. None of it was real. Nyrlim Academy was just a game.

When lunchtime rolled around, Ethan wolfed down a microwaved meal and threw on the VR gear. He swore in annoyance as he launched Nyrlim Magic Academy, and a patch notice came up. As he waited, he looked over the patch notes and saw a warning that anyone who had played the game earlier should start a new game, as their current save state might be corrupted.

"For the very few players who have received the first batch of Klendistone VR kits and who played the unpatched version, we apologize."

It was too late to abort the update. When it was complete, Ethan took his chances and loaded his game from the previous night. He didn't want to lose what had happened in the storeroom. Not yet, at least. Re-playing it again would shatter the illusion, and part of him *wanted* it all to be real.

He found himself standing in the tutorial courtyard again. This time, the doors to the castle stood open. The scene seemed like the set of a high school play compared to the storeroom the night before. Sexy-witch Vera, in her cartoonish glory, stood beside him.

"Uh, hi. I'm Ethan," he said.

"You have completed the tutorial," Vera said cheerfully. "You may now enter Nyrlim Magic Academy. If you have forgotten how to cast the spells, I can help you."

Ethan took the hint. It had been late when he'd played, and he hadn't spared a thought for the spell system. He remembered how to cast all the spells except the one to move the weights around the courtyard. When he consulted with Vera, she spoke of only four spells. The bugged spell was missing, which was not surprising. However, the magical shield spell was also missing, replaced by a spell to "stop someone's heart." He practiced it until he had it down against illusionary monsters that Vera conjured, but this seemed like a strange selection for a game about young students at a magical school. This was a darker game than he'd imagined.

After one last drill to make certain he could cast the spells he'd learned, he walked through the doorway, anticipating another trip to an extremely realistic location.

Instead, he walked into a chamber where a plastic teenager wearing robes vaguely reminiscent of the ones Dane, Eve, and Alice had worn before approached him and volunteered to show him to his room. An arrow appeared in front of Ethan, showing the direction he should move to follow his guide, who helpfully waited for him and droned on in a monologue tour of the academy as they made their way to the student wing. The student's robes sometimes clipped through the floor or their arm as they gestured and walked. It was nothing like his experience the night before.

"Hey, can you take me to a student named Alicia?" Ethan asked.

The student character ignored the question and droned on as they walked. They came to an empty parlor, and the student pointed to one of five doors along the hall. "This is your room. You will find all your belongings have already been unpacked for you. There will no doubt be other students in the parlor from time to time, so be sure to visit it frequently. I have to go greet other new students, so excuse me!"

With that, the student vanished in a poof of special effects.

Ethan saved the game again and quit, frustrated. He took off the headset and stared at it, wanting to yell at the inanimate object. Where were the people he spoke with last night? Where were the graphics that were as real as a live-action HD TV show? What had happened to his game?

As he stared at the headset, he noticed a shiny metal plate on one side with tiny laser-etched writing. He brought the headset closer to his eyes to examine it. Amid the government labeling and model number and some microscopic symbols that might have been logos or kanji writing, there was a box with a serial number which read, "#000000-026." The same number that Dane had recited from the piece of paper the night before.

———

He worked until late into the evening again. He grew irritated every time he caught a glance at the VR equipment sitting on the shelf. At one point, he closed his laptop and was determined to spend the rest of the day at the office to avoid looking at it. He felt like he had fallen for a bizarre bait-and-switch.

He took short breaks to look for reviews of the game, but none were available. Some journalists mentioned the game in passing or had brief previews, but the headset and the game were so new that only a handful of people had played it "in the wild" yet.

The experience the night before now took on the flavor of a dream in his mind. Maybe that was all it had been. Could he have fallen asleep while playing it? Maybe he'd gone to bed and dreamed about the experience, the dream being so vivid that he consciously couldn't distinguish it from his memories.

None of these theories made explained everything. He'd glimpsed a place that felt real, and spent time with people that felt real. If it had all been a delusion, what did it say about his mental state? What did it say that his interaction in the game felt more real than anything else he'd experienced in weeks? The more he tried to push it from his mind, the more the Klendistone VR set seemed to taunt him.

He logged off his work network, heated a frozen pizza for supper, and tried to browse some videos for the night's winding-down activities before going to bed. He browsed forums about Nyrlim Magic Academy, and found one post that had gone up in the last hour.

"I found a secret area of the game, I think. Some dude told me I had to gain aptitude in magic to unlock the rest of the area and sent me back. Tried to get a screenshot, but it didn't work. The graphics were much better than the rest of the game. It was like a recorded video."

Comments included the obligatory "Pics, or it didn't happen" post, someone complaining about the return of "full motion video" in VR games, an unanswered question about how he found the secret area, and a half-dozen posts from people complaining about how they weren't included in the first batch and hadn't even received notice that their Klendistones had shipped yet. Had another player seen something? Could Ethan's experience have been real after all? Ethan closed his laptop and grabbed the headset and controllers off the shelf.

He'd seen the "screenshots disabled" warning before he'd appeared in the storeroom. Maybe the developers didn't want the secrets of the game leaked before the full release of the hardware? However, the built-in headphones were connected by a standard jack. He had a splitter cable and could route the audio to his phone. While the change in graphics was massive, the conversation with the three students had intrigued him the most, and he'd wished he could have played that back during the day. Besides, he could hold his camera up to the lenses of the headset and take a picture. He wasn't interested in proving anything to the rest of the world, though. He only wanted the proof for himself.

Once his phone was set up with a cable and ready to record, Ethan put on the headset and started the game. Everything was where he had left it at lunchtime. He stood in a living area of some part of the student dorm area. The door to his dorm was only a few feet away. The visuals were nice, but not realistic. The full 3D presence made them more believable, but they still fell far short of what he'd seen the night before.

"Hey, is anyone here?" Ethan called, not loud enough to wake up his real-life neighbors. "Dane? Alicia?" After a moment's hesitation, he called, "Eve?" Even the blue girl would be a welcome sight—proof that he hadn't just dreamed the whole thing. Thinking back, he tried to cast the buggy spell three times, just as he had the night before. Nothing happened. In frustration, he cast the fireball spell, but the game disallowed it.

"Casting such a destructive spell in this environment would result in instant expulsion," Vera's disembodied voice whispered in his ear.

Ethan sighed. Maybe he should just play the game the way he was supposed to. He moved to the door to his dorm room and put his virtual hand on the door handle.

The world went black. In the corner of his vision, a message read, "Klendistone comm protocol 201 executing." Ethan's heart leaped. It was a shorter message than he'd seen the night before, but the effect was the same.

The darkness resolved into an impossibly-detailed view of a large academic office. An oak desk bigger than Ethan's kitchen area dominated the room, covered with papers, books, and even some old-fashioned scroll tubes. It was surrounded by equally-impressive oak bookcases overflowing with books, documents, and jumbles of objects that would have easily tipped or broken lesser shelving. A man stood at the other side of the desk in flowing blue robes adorned with piping along the shoulders and sleeves. His perfectly groomed beard matched the steel gray of his eyes and hair.

Ethan gasped and fumbled around half-blind in the real world to pull out his phone and start the recording. Once he had confirmed it was working, he returned it to his pocket and re-adjusted the headset.

"... Startle you," the man was saying. Ethan had missed the first part while he was messing with his phone. The robed man glanced down at a paper on his desk and said, "This is a, ah, bonus stage. You will be allowed to explore it once you have demonstrated your magical aptitude and proficiency."

Ethan looked down at the floor. A magical circle was drawn there, more complex than the one in the storeroom. The man stammered. "Oh, I see you note the circle. That's a precaution... Never mind. You completed the tutorial?"

"Yes," Ethan said. "Twice."

"Oh. Failed the first time, then? Well, let's get this over with. Let's see your fireball skill, then."

"Um, here?" Ethan glanced around. "This place looks pretty flammable."

"Ah, you are that confident you can pull it off?" Was it just Ethan's imagination, or was there a glint in the man's eye? He pointed to a coatrack beside the door, where an overcoat and what looked like a derby-style hat hung. "There's nothing of great value there. I will make sure nothing goes out of control. Begin!"

Ethan followed the instructions from the tutorial, making the motions with the controllers and repeating the phrases Vera had taught him. A sphere of white-hot light shot out from his outstretched hand, striking the door beside the coat rack and bursting into a short-lived explosion.

"I missed, sorry!" Ethan said.

"It's quite alright. That door is protected against magic, flame, axes, and just about everything else."

Ethan nodded. "I was just thinking about what would have happened if someone had come in just now."

The man shook his head. "The door is locked. We have complete secrecy here. Now, I take it you were trained in the spell to stop a heartbeat?"

Ethan nodded. "Yeah. Just a few minutes ago."

The man smiled. "I think you meet my qualifications, so let's get on with this. I have a task—sorry—" He glanced down at the paper on his desk. "I have a quest for you. Complete this quest, and you will be given access to all new... er, content." He continued in a wooden voice. "Three demons have infiltrated our school, disguised as students. I need you to find these demons and destroy them, without being seen." He picked up a metal object and placed it on the side of the desk. "I will give you this bracelet, which allows you to move unnoticed through the school so long as you avoid the instructors and direct contact with any of the other students."

"Why avoid the instructors? Aren't they helping to hunt down the demons?"

He waved his hand dismissively. "They don't know who the demons are. As I said, they are disguised as students."

"Then how do I find them?"

"I have ascertained their identity. They murdered an instructor only days ago, but they left evidence behind."

Dane and the others had been seeking the identity of the killer, too. This tracked, but the man in the robe wasn't convincing. Was he hiding something, or was this shoddy acting? Whatever the case, Ethan handled it as if it was happening in real life. Worst case, he'd re-start the game.

No, that wasn't the worst case. As impossible as it was to his logical mind, it felt real. If by some bizarre reason this was actually happening, he had to choose his actions carefully.

"Have you brought this to the attention of the authorities?"

"What?" The man scratched his head. Ethan almost chalked it up to a video game filler response, but then the man answered, "We have to solve our own problems here, as the actions of wizards and demons may be beyond what the conventional authorities can handle. We need your help."

"So who are these demons?"

"They go by the names Dane McDougal, Eve Delaney, and Alicia Stormhand. I have melainotypes of each one that you should study so you can positively identify them. It would be easiest if you were to eliminate them in their dorm rooms, away from any prying eyes."

Ethan felt his body grow hot, and he hoped there was no technology reading his expression. He took a moment to bring his voice under control. "What is your evidence against them?"

"That is not your concern. You will do the school and the students a great service..."

"Who are you? What did they do to you?"

"What? I'm Harold Klendistone, the assistant principal of the academy. These students are... No, they are demons. That's all that matters. Complete this quest, and you will be rewarded with access to... whatever you want. Oh, content!"

"You murdered Callister, didn't you?"

Several expressions flashed across Klendistone's face, finally settling on raised eyebrows and a frown. "How did you know? Callister summoned you first, didn't he? Damn it! Well, he's dead, and I have the Right of First Summoning now. I order you to say nothing of this to anyone, in this world or your own."

Ethan felt like someone gripped him around the throat, a sensation physically possible with the VR gear. He lifted the headset part way, but there was no one else in the room with him. As he replaced the visor, he noticed how the circle now glowed.

As he had the night before, he tried to move out of the circle. The vertigo was far worse than it had been before, and he felt his vision swim and darken. He staggered, coming into contact with his desk in the real world, and leaned on it for support. Inside Klendistone's office, he was still trapped inside the circle.

Klendistone laughed at his attempt. Ethan stared down at the circle and then made the motions he'd learned the night before—the ability to erase magic. The glow of the circle wavered, and Ethan lurched forward, out of the circle, hoping he wasn't about to hit a wall in the room in his own home.

Klendistone's eyes widened. "How is this possible? Callister is dead! I have the Right of First Summoning."

Klendistone wiggled his hand and spoke words to a spell Ethan hadn't been taught. Ethan was already reacting with the "shield" spell when he recognized it as the "dismissal" spell Alicia had cast on him the night before as he exited the game.

The shield appeared in the air and shimmered as Klendistone's completed his spell. The wizard growled. "That was a mistake, alien! My spells can find you in your own world. Even when you take off that infernal device."

"So you and Callister created the VR gear?" Ethan asked.

"That is what you call it?" Klendistone seemed to be in no hurry. "We provided our agents in your world with the information and resources they needed. Callister saw it as an experiment and was blind to the possibilities of thousands of newly summoned entities. Summoners spend years finding the names of fresh entities to summon, and here we had an almost unlimited supply! He lost interest earlier this year, which was fine by me, but his plans to move bodily between our worlds would have disrupted this project, and he objected to my use of compulsion spells and bindings on aliens. He threatened me if I carried out my own experiments. As you are about to learn, you never threaten Harold Klendistone."

Klendistone made another unfamiliar gesture, and Ethan countered it again with the shield. This time, arcs of electricity bent around the shield, and the pain felt like a thousand hornets stinging all at once.

Ethan cried out in pain. Klendistone laughed and followed up with another spell. Ethan barely formed the shield in time. Icy mist curled around the phantom barrier, cold biting Ethan's fingers and forearms with pain like a fire. He couldn't keep this up. If he took off the headset, would Klendistone still be able to hurt him, or was the wizard bluffing about that?

Somehow, it didn't feel like a bluff. A wrong guess would be instantly fatal. Not that the spells being thrown at him felt like they'd be anything less than fatal if his shield failed. Ethan took the offense and cast the fireball at Klendistone.

Klendistone caught the sphere in his hand, and it faded with a muffled pop. "Is that what you are trying? Are you going to attempt to stop my heart next?" He snorted. "Where do you think those spells came from?"

Again, this didn't sound like a bluff. Rather than going for a direct attack, Ethan cast the object-moving spell on the bookshelf near the wizard. Klendistone glanced up too late, as the enormous bookshelf toppled onto him, burying him in books. The mahogany desk broke its fall and kept it from pinning Klendistone.

The assistant principal crawled out and snarled at Ethan. "I have had enough of you."

He began chanting and gesturing with something more complex than Ethan had yet seen. While he was inexperienced with this world of spell casting, Klendistone's fury was plain to read. Ethan doubted his shield spell would do much to deflect whatever the wizard was creating.

In desperation, Ethan used the bugged spell from the tutorial. It did nothing in the game, but would it actually do something here, in this alternative world? He spoke the words, pressed the button, and made the required gestures in the air. A shimmering wall appeared, not unlike the shield, but this seemed to have a translucent presence, a mirrored surface.

A moment later, Klendistone unleashed his spell. For an instant, Ethan saw the reflection of his own 'face' in this world against the surface of his defensive spell, a slightly glowing orb with vague mannequin features. Just below that, Klendistone's blurry face stared through the distortion with a look of horror. The air flashed as Klendistone's spell reflected from the mirrored barrier back onto the wizard, and the barrier shattered.

Klendistone shriveled into a gray statue of himself, kneeling on the floor surrounded by his books and treasures. Then the gray form collapsed into a pile of dust on the floor.

Some dust filled the air, giving the room a smoky haze. Ethan was grateful that he was breathing in his apartment, rather than filling his real lungs with the remains of the assistant principal. Someone pounded at the door, followed by muffled shouting from several people. It had been a noisy battle, hadn't it?

For a moment, Ethan considered exiting the game and taking off the VR gear. He still hurt from Klendistone's spells, and he was in real danger from angry wizards. But then he thought of the three students, particularly Alicia. What would happen to them? Would they be blamed? Would anyone learn what really happened to Professor Callister?

Ethan worked the lock and opened the door. Four adults in robes spilled into the room, immediately surrounding Ethan.

"Where is Klendistone?" one of them, a woman who looked to be in her early sixties, demanded.

"He's that pile of dust on the floor," Ethan said.

"You murdered him!"

Ethan shook his head. "No, I defended myself. I only... Well, let me explain. Actually, even better!" He reached into his pocket. "Let me play back a recording for you."

Ethan rushed up the stairs to his apartment in the early evening, heavy grocery bag in hand. He'd grabbed another microwaveable meal in his lightning-fast shopping trip, but he wasn't interested in heating it right now. Instead, he opened one end of the bag of salt, and carefully poured it into a three-foot circle on his living room floor. He'd have to vacuum it up. Eventually.

He removed the charging cables from his VR gear, turned it on, and started Nyrlim Magic Academy. It had been two weeks since his initial visit, and three days since he'd last been summoned to the strange world where the real academy existed. Verifying that his avatar was standing in the simple courtyard of the game, he took off the headset and controllers and placed them on the floor inside the flour circle, and waited.

A minute passed, and then a glowing figure rose from the floor, lifting the VR devices with it. The shining image coalesced into the form of a girl.

"Alicia! You are actually here!" Ethan said.

"In the flesh. Kind of," Alicia said with a giggle, raising the visor over her eyes. Her body looked solid, but there were moments where she seemed to shimmer and waver, as if she might vanish in a heartbeat. She glanced quickly around the room, but her eyes rested on him. "So this is your apartment?"

He grinned. "You are the first girl I've ever invited in here."

She laughed. "Okay. Before you get too many bright ideas, I have two reasons for this visit. First, it's to verify Dane's effort to expand on Callister's work. The Professor had almost solved the problem of sending people and objects between our worlds fully."

Ethan nodded. "Klendistone wanted slaves, not trade and travel."

"Yes. And that brings me to the second reason for my visit. The faculty has chosen to go ahead with Callister's plan for a graduate program."

"You're in?"

"Of course! And... so are you, if you are interested. We have talked to people from the company that made your device, but we don't know who to trust out there. But you have already helped us immensely, and you have an aptitude at magic. We could compensate you..."

"Yes."

She arched an eyebrow. "I hadn't finished my offer."

He grinned at her. "Sorry. You can keep going if you want. Can I take magic classes, too?"

She rolled her eyes. "I'll ask them if they can make an exception for you once you get here. Besides that, while I was never great at the practicals, I've been told I'm an excellent tutor."

Jay Barnson gets to work with Virtual Reality by day, creating high-tech simulators for training. By night he creates virtual worlds through words. One might question how much he actually lives in the real world. He is the author of the Blood Creek Witch fantasy series set in the backwoods of the Appalachian Mountains.

LAB PARTNERS

BY FRANK B. LUKE

Another world lies hidden alongside outs, invisible to most. Those few who can cross into it rediscover themselves as knights, rogues, clerics, and wizards. It runs along a very specific set of rules that exist in our world as a game, Legends & Lore. This story takes place before the story "Crucible" in the first volume of this collection.

Karen and Sally expected a short trip into the wetland for their Magical Ecology class. They only needed to interview a magical creature. The first monkey wrench came when a third mage joined them. He was Evil. Karen, being Good, couldn't stand him. The Neutral Sally just wanted to complete the assignment! But of course, Dr. Graff's assignments never have only one hitch...

Lab Partners

Karen Hahn parked her white economy car in the little offshoot next to the wetland. It was a pleasant fall afternoon. The white-robed mage exited the car and waited for her college roommate to get out.

Wearing a red robe decorated with golden stars, Sally climbed out. "Well, you have no style in this thing, but I'll give you credit for the miles-per-gallon aspect. I don't think the gauge dipped at all with this trip."

Karen grinned and tied her brown hair back in a ponytail with a blue tie. Then she waved a hand over the car. "Just a little magical amulet in the fuel injection system."

Sally sighed. "So it's not something we can patent and sell to the mundanes. Too bad." Then she smiled. "No matter. I'm sure we can find a magical creature to interview in these parts."

"We'd better," Karen replied, changing her regular boots out for mud boots. She could clean the robes, but her white boots might be ruined by the mud. "The report is due Tuesday, and we've come up dry everywhere else. What do you think is out there? Imps, fairies, pixies?"

"Oh, I hope not pixies," Sally said with a grimace as she put her red sunglasses in her purse and back in the car. She fished a couple of butterfly nets from the back of the car and held one out to Karen. "Their brogue is hard to understand, and I didn't prepare anything for interpreting it."

Sally was already wearing mud boots.

Before the girls could take another step to their search area, an old, black motorcycle came over the hill and parked right behind them.

"Ho, ladies. I need to join you," the rider said, not asking for permission before exiting the bike and coming to them.

The new arrival wore black robes with a blood-red belt. The grease in his hair made it seem blacker and shinier. He had not worn a helmet but carried a butterfly net like the girls did. He chewed on a toothpick.

"You need us, Nathan Hagard?" Karen asked, disturbed by his sudden appearance. She did not like Nathan at all.

They were widely-separated in the alignment grid. She was Lawful Good, while he was Neutral Evil. Sally was True Neutral. "We don't need you."

"No, but you have to take me," he smirked and held out a glass disk with the flat side up.

An image of their teacher, the red-robed Dr. Graff, appeared. "Miss Hahn and Miss Orman, Mr. Hagard's lab partner for the class has fallen ill after trying to summon a small basilisk for extra credit. Luckily, the creature was too immature to kill him. However, he will need time to recover from the venom. I have instructed Nathan to join you. I apologize for the inconvenience and short notice."

Karen tapped her foot. "Sounds like we have no choice in the matter."

Sally's blue eyes were bright. "I don't mind. Three people doing the work can't be a bad thing."

The new arrival pointed with his butterfly net. "Then let's go into this swamp."

Sally rolled her eyes. "That's a bog. You haven't paid a bit of attention in class all trimester, have you?"

Nathan cocked his head and gave her a lecherous grin. "Oh, I pay attention. Just not always to the teacher."

"Okay," Karen said, letting her annoyance be heard. "The sooner we get in there, the sooner we can catch a critter."

"*Find Living Thing*," Sally said, tapping a compass while invoking a spell. "Follow me."

The trio set out behind her, Karen in the middle. She knew the compass would now find the kind of creature that Sally had been thinking of when casting. They would have no indication of distance, just direction.

"Can we triangulate?" Nathan asked. "Move, say, 20 yards to the right and see how the arrow changes? Math can then tell us the distance."

Sally shook her head and showed them the needle already wobbling. "Whatever I got, it's moving. We need to hurry."

They followed her into the bog, walking carefully on the spongy ground. The ground shifted under them with each step.

Sally lectured, "The dead, green matter here is not firmly attached to the earth. Instead, excess rainwater has collected underneath it, or, I should say, the plant matter collects on top of the rainwater below. It's very acidic below. That's what makes this a bog."

The trio spread out a little to distribute their weight. The plants were mostly pines, other evergreens, and flowers that could also handle the acidic soil.

Beautiful, Karen thought as she felt the moss growing on the pine nearest her.

"*Rope Friend,*" Nathan said behind her.

Before Karen could stop, a vine at her feet raised up and tripped her. Trying to regain her balance, the white mage fell sideways into the water. She grimaced and bit back harsh words. Behind her, the deep voice chuckled.

"Nathan," she said, climbing to her feet without even an offer of help from her black-robed partner. "That was not nice. My robes look atrocious!" Her pristine white robes were covered in mud now. Even the bright blue trim on her lapel and cuffs was spattered with dark mud. Only her mud boots looked the same as before.

"Karen!" Sally shouted, rushing back to them. With only a look at the two, she knew what had happened. She gave Karen a hand getting out of the muck.

Karen glared up at Nathan, fists on her hips. He towered over her by a head and had a strong jawline and chin. His deep black hair was wavy and curled on top. His eyes were brown pools of chocolate.

He smirked back and twisted an onyx ring back onto his finger. "Oh, come on. That little joke was nothing."

"Nothing to you, but the noise probably scared any creatures away." Her blood pounded in her ears and closed in on her vision. She struggled to keep her voice at a natural level. She didn't want to frighten away anything that was still nearby.

Nathan rolled his eyes. "Sally will surely find one first. She has enough talent with the wild, I'm surprised she didn't cross over the

Veil as a druid." He snarled and pulled his red belt tighter. It was the only splash of color on his black outfit.

"No use for druids?" Karen asked.

Nathan raised an eyebrow. "I have no use for any divine casters, or the divine for that matter. And I haven't for some time."

The tone of his words chilled Karen, but she didn't press on. "Whatever. I'd like to finish this assignment so I can study for my exams in the other school."

As Karen said this, she felt the weariness of being in two schools bear down on her. Her major back in the regular world demanded much of her time. The magic school on this side of the Veil took the rest of it. All the extracurricular clubs she had planned on being part of in college had gone by the wayside. Magic was a harsh mistress.

Sally glared at Nathan. "Take a hike." Before he could protest, she continued, "I'm not telling you to go home. Karen needs to dry off."

He nodded and disappeared back the way they had come.

"*Grasping Hands*," Karen said, undoing the belt on her robes.

Two invisible hands took hold of the robe's shoulders and held it up between Karen and Nathan.

"I don't trust him. You know how his alignment works." She took off her necklace and hung it on a nearby tree branch. A winged chameleon flapped away into the next tree.

Sally nodded and stated, "A Neutral Evil person will do anything to attain their own goals and satisfaction without regard for laws and others."

The red robe twisted the ruby on her only ring until a gentle heat wafted out from it. She pointed it at her roommate.

Karen stood there in her bra and panties, letting the heat dry her off. "My hair will have to wait until later. Can't we just send him back for this?"

"Karen, it's a prank. Nothing more. He's Evil, but..." Sally bit her lip to hide a smile, "...ruggedly handsome, if you ask me."

"I didn't ask you, and you aren't the one he pushed into the water."

"You were in no danger. The bog's only a couple feet deep here. He's right that you *are* rather uptight."

Blinking at her roommate's accusation, Karen pressed ahead. "He said that to you? When?"

"The other day during a break in Intermediate Scrollwork." She looked away. "My hand was cramped, and he rubbed out the soreness."

Something in Sally's voice made Karen ask, "Sally... are you going to date him? He's Evil!"

"And I'm True Neutral; he's no more outside the box for me than a Neutral Good, and you'd have no problem with that! We're going out tonight once we finish the assignment."

"But he's not a Christian! We should only become romantic with our fellow Christians."

Sally rolled her eyes. "Don't tell me you never thought about dating the bad boy in hopes of converting him?"

Karen shrugged. "Did that once. Doesn't he have a girlfriend that hasn't crossed over?"

Sally nodded. "We'll go somewhere she for sure won't see us. Probably use a transportation spell to get there."

"You'd help him two-time a girl?"

Sally replied, "Look at it this way. He's already been vetted and approved."

Shuddering, Karen gave up. "Still. I don't like Nathan."

"Is there any black robe you like? And I don't mean that romantically."

Karen thought for a moment. She replied, pointedly, "Actually, not a single one."

"That bastard!" Sally shouted and pointed at a floating crystal eye. She grabbed a rock and threw it.

Calling her now-dry robes over, Karen let the invisible hands dress her. "What?"

"Nathan sent a spying eye!"

The two women fumed. "Nathan! Get your lousy butt back here!" Karen yelled.

Nathan sauntered back into view, the crystal in one hand and a smirk on his face. "Problem, ladies?"

"You were spying on me undressed!" Karen shouted, not caring if she scared any creatures away. "Go! Go home! We won't work with you!"

Nathan feigned great pain. "I'm hurt. A couple of jokes, and you want to call off our partnership?"

Sally agreed with Karen. "I'm with her, and don't worry about tonight. The date is off!"

Karen stomped over to him and looked up. He towered over her. "Yes. The second wasn't a joke. It was an invasion of privacy. I've never let anyone see me like that!"

"Oh, please. I bet you've shown more skin at the beach. Pink is your color," he snarled.

Cheeks red with rage, Karen balled her fists and thought about her prepared spells. Only second level, she didn't have many. Sally and Nathan were the same level. A more advanced caster could have sent multiple eyes, but Nathan's level allowed only one. A red haze covered her vision. "Just go. I'm sure Dr. Graff will side with us when we explain what happened."

Before Nathan could respond, Sally interrupted. "Karen! A fairy is stealing your necklace!"

"Stop! Come back with that, you little thief!" Karen shouted as she took off after the lithe, blonde fairy flying away from the branch upon which Karen had left the necklace. Nathan and Sally were right behind her. The cross on the end of the necklace had been handed down from her grandmother.

About a foot tall, the tiny thief wove back-and-forth over the forest path, just out of reach. The necklace trailing behind her, she giggled with pleasure!

Karen jumped over a fallen log and ducked under a low branch. The bog ground shook under their feet.

Four translucent wings sprouted from holes in the fairy's black dress and kept her away. She tossed fairy dust at the trio.

Karen pushed on, rubbing her eyes with one hand and reaching for the fairy with the other. The dust clouded her thinking. She wished she'd grabbed her butterfly net before starting the chase!

Beside her, Nathan elbowed past. He had his net! With a single swipe, the fairy was in it!

The tiny woman thrashed inside, trying to reach the opening. Nathan grabbed her legs just as she reached the top.

"Give me back my necklace!" Karen said, snatching the necklace from the fairy. "Why did you take it?"

The fairy did not answer.

Nathan snorted, "She wants to ask us something but couldn't just come up to us, for some reason."

The fairy stopped fighting and nodded. She had a cute face, crystal blue eyes, and short-cut hair. It bobbed around her strong jawline. Her eyes widened. "How did you know?"

The black robe rolled his eyes. "You didn't fly through any brambles when trying to get away from us. You stayed over the path even as it twisted between the trees."

Her shoulders slumped. "You figured it out."

"Only had to think a little. Now, name?"

"Kendi," she replied, looking at Karen.

"Why did you take it?" the white robe asked.

She looked up at the trio, tears running down her high cheekbones. "Alfred. My clan needs help against Alfred."

"Who is Alfred?"

"He's a wicked cleric of Loki who's been kidnapping fairies." At their look, she shouted, "Don't worry. He's old, but only crossed in the last few years. Low level."

"Sounds like you'll get along real well, Nathan," Sally snapped.

"I don't know," the man replied. "Clerics of Loki tend to be Chaotic. We might ally for a time, but our paths would part sooner or later."

"How can we help?" Sally asked, her face full of empathy. "Let her go, Nathan. Tell us what you know."

Kendi let out a sigh of relief as Nathan released her. Her little wings beat to keep her in the air. "We don't know why he's taking us. We do know that he takes captured fairies to his cabin not far from here. He lives there with his cat, Grimm. I can show you."

The black robed mage shook his head. "Evil clerics need a reason to act. Maybe you curdle his milk? Turn over the cat bowls?"

She glared at him and put tiny fists on tiny hips. "That's another clan here in the bog. We're nice fairies."

Karen held up a hand. "He may be low level, but I guarantee we are lower. Eight spells a day for each of us, all of them low-powered. Sally used one when we entered the bog. We have items, too, but..." She spread her hands.

"I burned two slots already this morning before we got here," Sally said, raising her hand.

Brow knotted in irritation, Karen snapped, "I've told you to save slots for when we need them."

"Who's to say I didn't need them?"

Karen then whirled on Nathan, her eyes aflame. "And I know that you've used at least one today!"

"Can the three of us handle the cleric?" Nathan asked Kendi, ignoring Karen. "Party of three lowers our average level for figuring challenge ratings. Can you guess his level?"

The fairy bobbed her head. "Level four, we think. You'll have fairies with you," Kendi insisted. "Remember that his cat is as evil as he is, maybe more so."

"I brought a Mind Call scroll in case of emergency," Sally said. "Since we're in a quest now, no cell phones allowed."

The young woman in red removed a scroll from her robes. Closing her eyes and clutching it, she said, "*Mind Call*. Dr. Graff. Cleric of Loki in Northampton Bog kidnapping fairies. Require assistance. Please come or send another."

The scroll glowed brightly for a moment then turned to dust.

The mages waited. Kendi whispered to Karen, "What does this do?"

"The spell allows a message of twenty-five words or less to be communicated telepathically. The recipient can then respond with a new message of the same limit."

"Shouldn't he have answered by now?" the fairy asked.

"I would think so."

Sally opened her eyes. "It failed. He must be traveling on another plane."

"Of all the times for a natural one," Nathan said, shaking his head.

Kendi fluttered up. "Can you try to contact someone else at your tower?"

Sally shook her head. "I only brought one scroll."

The fairy led the trio of mages deep into the bog until they reached a ring of toadstools. "The fairy home!" Sally shouted, excitedly.

Other fairies flew out to meet Kendi. All were about a foot tall and wore tiny clothing made from the fur and plants. A dark-skinned fairy with hair of flames flew up and greeted Kendi.

"You're looking hopeful, my friend."

"Perth is coming back!" Kendi then turned to the trio. "Perth is my husband. He was one of the first taken. Six who live here have been stolen."

Kendi led them to her tribe's chief. Only young fairies flew near the human settlements. This one was old with gray hair and a long beard. His wings were wilted and torn. Four fairies held up his chair. Another behind him nudged him awake. Karen approached slowly and knelt before him. Thanks to Kendi's instructions on the way, she knew what to say.

"O great one, your servant has told us of your village's plight. We will help in any way we can."

The other two knelt on either side of her. Nathan added, "We pledge our most valiant effort but cannot promise to succeed."

The chief chuckled from his air-borne throne. "The gods rain down blessings on us when most needed! Let the festivities begin!"

The tribe whooped and began to dance in the air. Fairy dust rained down as they glided and spun. They danced in pairs and in fours. Dozens of fairy children, small enough to fit several in a human hand, flew in circles as well as impressive and complicated patterns. Adults hovered to make sure they flew correctly. Other adults brought out a sheet of fabric filled to overflowing with fruit and berries. Water and juices were provided.

Kendi had pointed out the mates of the other kidnapped fairies. They all danced, excited that their mates would be coming home, but she sat underneath a tree by herself.

Sally nudged Karen. "Someone has eyes for Kendi."

A male fairy in blue and yellow flew up to her, asking her to dance. Obviously, it wasn't meant to be romantic since the other stranded mates were dancing, but Kendi shook her head. As he asked again, and she repeated her actions, Nathan moved closer.

After the fairy asked a third time, the mage asked his own question. "Are you deaf, blue boy? Kendi doesn't feel like dancing."

The little blue fairy flew off after one last moonstruck look at Kendi.

Sally shared a look with Karen. He *was* interested in her romantically. Dr. Graff had covered small parts of fairy culture in class. The way the fairies held up marriage as the ideal, it surprised them to see one of them so obvious and public in his attempts at adultery.

Kendi settled down on a toadstool and cried.

"Hey, no tears," Karen said. "I'll get your husband back, and then he can chase off the man in blue! You'll have your happy life together."

She cried harder. "No, we can't. You see, we've been married ten years and have no children. I'm not even pregnant and have never been pregnant."

"I feel for you," Sally said. "Maybe we can get a cleric to come here."

The tiny woman shook her head so hard her hair was flying from side to side. "No, you don't understand. Moke was wooing me because when Perth is returned, we will be forced to divorce!"

"What? Why?" the girls' eyes widened.

"Because after ten years with no children, it is obvious that the gods have not blessed our marriage. I don't know what upset the goddess of childbirth, but all my sisters have many children and all his siblings do, too. The chief will break our bonds and free us for others so the tribe may grow."

"I've never heard anything like this."

She looked down at the ground. "Marriage is the foundation of family. It's meant to provide a place for the children to be raised. The gods give children. If a couple has no children, it means the gods don't bless the marriage, and we married against their will. Without strong families, we don't have a strong tribe."

Nathan opened his mouth. "Now I've heard everything. It can't be because one of you is infertile. You have no children because the 'gods,' who you say love your people, won't grant a simple request. Why ten years? Why not five?"

The fairy cried harder.

Sally motioned for Nathan to hush. "We'll do what we can."

The cute fairy flew up to Karen and hugged her. Her tears dripped on the robes.

"Don't worry," Karen said. "I'll pray to God. He'll grant a child."

Karen could see Sally dig her elbow into Nathan's side as the man snorted in derision.

Kendi flew up and tapped the end of Karen's nose. "Will he? You humans are so big. Are your gods bigger, too?"

"I suppose so. Have you met many humans before?"

She shook her head. "You're the first I've really met." She lowered her voice. "You big guys scare me; I could get squished. Even dwarves are huge compared to me! If it weren't for Alfred, I never would have approached you."

Butting in, Nathan said, "Of course, we can't work for free."

Kendi nodded and motioned for other fairies to come close. "No. You can't. Name your price."

With another elbow in Nathan's ribs to keep him quiet, Sally interjected, "We just need to interview a fairy for our magical ecology class back at the Tower of the Moons."

"That's all?" the fairies asked in unison.

"Surely you want more than that!" Kendi said.

"It is all we need. Though if we are wounded and you have healing potions afterwards..."

"Of course! No potions here, but we have magic to help."

"Alfred may need more than we do," Nathan grumbled, grit in his voice.

She giggled. "I like that. You sound determined."

"We are, but we need more than determination," Karen said.

The fairy nodded. "I agree. If determination was all it took, I'd have a dozen children by now."

Surprised at her statement, Karen carried on. "We need a plan to put into action."

"If plans and actions were all that mattered, I'd still have a dozen children."

Blushing, Karen wanted to change the subject, Kendi looked to be early thirties, but the math didn't work for humans. "How long is a fairy pregnancy?"

"Exactly four new moons." She waited a moment, hovering in front of Karen's face. "Aren't you going to ask what we need along with determination, plans, and action?"

"What?" the white robe asked, her voice quavering with trepidation.

"The blessing of the gods."

The three mages sighed in relief.

Along with several fairies to guide them and help them, the trio set out for the cleric's cabin.

Karen stalked along, fuming. She couldn't wait for this adventure to be over and turn Nathan in to the tower for what he did to her! While the head of the black robes would find it amusing, her own mentor wouldn't. Mistress Janey, the head of the red robes, would probably vote for disciplining Nathan as well. She didn't know what they would do. The school's discipline manual didn't cover all situations but left the administrators with leeway.

In front of her, Sally asked Nathan, "You said something today that made me think you were a Christian at one time, at least not an atheist. Is that true?"

"Yes," Nathan answered, softly. "I used to be a Christian, but I found out that my pastor for years had been having affairs."

"So you became Evil?"

"Bite your tongue! Then I'll kiss you and make it better. It wasn't a one-bad-day situation. I realized this man who had pastored me and counseled me had been a duplicitous scoundrel. He wasn't in it to help us—he was in it for himself. From that day, I started looking out for number one, first and foremost. Over time, Good became Neutral. Then Neutral became Evil. I still don't think of myself as Evil. I prefer Assertive."

Karen felt a whisper of pity for Nathan but only for a moment. His invasion of privacy made no apology possible.

Kendi landed softly on Karen's shoulder. Her lightness surprised Karen. Oh, Karen knew that fairies had hollow bones to make flying easier, but to know something in your head was different than experiencing it.

"Can you tell me something, Karen?" Without waiting, the fairy continued, "You called your school the Tower of the Moons, but there's only one moon! Unless you mean moon as a measure if time, the way we use it."

The brunette shook her head. "We recognize three types of the one moon, one for each color of robe worn by the moon mages. New moon for black, full moon for white, and red moon for half moons."

"Interesting. You wear white, so you do white magic?"

"Exactly, and after I face the Trials, my might will wax and wane with the phases of the moon. Nathan's power will wax opposite of mine. Sally will be most powerful on the half moons and least on the full and new."

"When do you test?"

"A few months from now. I'm level two and have to have the experience for level four. I'm trying to space it out."

One of the fairies flew down to them. "Hush. We're getting close."

They proceeded in silence the rest of the way to Alfred's cabin. Soon, Karen saw the blue-gray rock walls next to a single, dead tree. A whiff of smoke rose from the chimney emerging out of the thatched roof, and lantern glow shone through the windows. Iron bars in the windows would keep fairies from escaping or entering.

A fairy sentinel complete with tiny sword descended to Kendi. "He is in there with Grimm. He usually goes hunting about this time. We sense no traps or wards."

"The big people will go in there once we distract him," she said.

Nathan told the fairies, "Just make it look good."

A few minutes later, Alfred emerged from the ramshackle house with Grimm at his heels and a net in his hands. The human cleric wore a ragged, black cloak with bright red boots. He walked hunched over, had a bulbous nose, and had only a fringe of black hair. "Let's go, Grimm, you miserable cat! We'll check the traps first for little folk. Ha ha!"

As he walked away one of the sentinels emerged from the trees in front of Alfred and sped off just above head height. Alfred and Grimm took off after him!

Kendi whispered, "Two minutes, then we go in."

Karen counted the seconds in her head until they went in. She, Sally, Nathan, and a couple of fairies slipped in. Other fairies remained to watch out for Alfred.

The room inside the cabin was stuffed with equipment and lined with shelves. A shelf to the side held glowing bottles of golden liquid. Karen estimated three dozen jars holding fairies. "Holy cow! Kendi, you said six!"

The fairy's gaze whipped around the room, her hair flying.

"The others are from other clans. Help them if you want, but you have to get ours out." Kendi fluttered in front of a jar with a male fairy. He beat on the glass.

"We're coming for you, Perth!" the little fairy said. Overcome with excitement, she grabbed hold of the jar lid and screamed. "Iron lids! Oh, he's evil."

Nathan quipped, "Iron lids is a sign of thinking ahead, not evil." He smiled, grimly, "But it is what I would do."

Sally took the jar and screwed off the lid. "I don't know if we'll have time to open them all! Alfred might catch on and come back!"

"Breaking the jars might hurt the fairies. We can't carry them all. We have to try. Oh, I wish I could cast a *Mass Opening* spell!"

Karen and Sally set to opening the jars. Nathan looked at the work bench and picked up a bottle identical to those on the shelf.

"Nathan! We're here to free the captives!" Karen hissed at him.

"Dr. Graff will know what this is. It must be important!" He slipped it into the pocket of his robes then set to opening the prison jars.

Satisfied, Karen opened two more then heard a wolf whistle.

Flabbergasted, she spun around and snapped at Nathan. "This is hardly the time or place!"

"Twasn't me, Miss Goody Two Shoes! That was the signal he's coming back! Life isn't all about you!"

Sally shouted, "Just open the jars!"

They hurried, opening every jar they could.

With a yowl, Grimm sprang into the cabin. Orange with darker orange stripes, the cat looked feral and dangerous. The freed fairies zipped around the cat, trying to distract him.

Grimm paid them no mind. His yowls almost sounding like chuckles, he held up one paw and extended the claws from it. He leaped at Sally's face.

The red-robed mage shouted, "*Bedazzle Monster!*"

"Hurrh?" Grimm growled. As his eyes crossed, he thumped into Sally.

She threw him to the ground.

On their side of the room, Karen and Nathan rushed to open more jars.

Grimm struggled to his paws and leaped onto the lab bench. His tail knocked over a lantern. Oil spilled out and flames spread across the table.

"Karen! Fire!" Sally shouted.

The mages hurried to open the last jars. Just as the flames flared high and lit the roof, they opened the last one.

The grateful fairy lass gave Nathan a kiss on the cheek as she flew past.

The three mages hurried outside, a singed Grimm padding after.

His mouth agape in horror, Alfred watched the fairies he had captured fly away into the night. Several stayed with their rescuers to help them.

"No! You've ruined everything!" Alfred shouted, trying to grasp the fairies in his hands. Failing, he looked at the trio. "I'll get you!"

The cleric lunged for Karen. As he touched her arm, he shouted, "*Take Moderate Wound!*"

Pain radiated from Karen's arm throughout her body. She crumpled to the grassy bog ground, writhing.

Alfred spun and kicked Sally's legs out from under her. The red robed mage fell.

Nathan dug sand from his spell pouch. "*Sleep!*" he shouted, throwing the sand in Alfred's face.

The cleric scrunched up his face and furrowed his brow. "Ha! I made my save!"

While he was looking at Nathan, Karen grabbed his ankle and pulled him to the ground. Nathan took the opportunity to stomp the cleric in the face.

The fairies swooped down and did their magic on the moaning Alfred.

The red robe took her turn, throwing a pinch of colored sand into the air. "*Rainbow Cone!*"

A cone of multiple colors erupted from her hand, striking the cleric and knocking him unconscious.

"It won't last long," Sally said.

"It'll last long enough." Karen climbed to her feet, looked down at their foe, and waited for him to open his eyes. Finally, he did so. "Do you surrender?"

Alfred closed his eyes again and nodded, weeping.

Karen and Sally lowered their hands and stepped away. They turned to the fairies who had stayed to help.

Kendi and another fairy flew in close. The little blonde woman beamed with joy. "Karen, Sally, this is Perth, my husband."

"A pleasure to meet you," Sally said.

Before Karen could give her own greeting, she heard Nathan shout, "Watch him! *Certain Hit!*"

As she dove for the floor, a wet thunk came from behind her.

The two women turned back to Alfred only to see Nathan laying beside his corpse, hand on the black-hilted dagger embedded in Alfred's chest. Yowling, Grimm vanished into the bog.

"Nathan..." Karen wasn't sure what she felt.

"He was preparing a prayer to strike you in the back, Karen." His face was grim, no sign of glee or satisfaction.

The black robe knelt beside the dead cleric and picked up the sacred medallion hanging around his neck. "Loki, just as they said." His eyes glazed over, and his jaw went slack.

"Nathan! Nathan!" Karen said, rushing over and shaking his shoulder. Sally was right beside her.

Blinking, the black robe shook his head. He dropped the medallion like a hot potato and rose to his feet, shaking.

"Fire and steel," he muttered.

"Fire and steel? What does that mean?" Sally asked.

Like a switch being thrown, Nathan's expression turned to iron. "Nothing. I saw nothing."

"Saw? We didn't ask if you saw anything. We asked what you meant," Karen argued.

Wordlessly, Nathan headed for the trail back to the fairy village.

Sally shrugged and set out after him.

Confused, Karen followed.

Back at the tribe's land, fairies danced in the air to fairy music. A bonfire burned brightly, lighting up the night and throwing sparks. The three humans sat off to the side with Kendi and Perth.

"I think that's enough for our report," Sally said, putting away her pen.

Kendi fluttered back up in the air with a giggle. Perth would not leave her side.

"We thank you so much," Perth said, "Even though our reunion will be short."

Sally whispered, "Come with us, the two of you. No one will need to know about you and Perth."

Perth replied, "We'd know."

Karen shook her head. "What will you do?"

Tears streamed down Kendi's cheeks. "Not much we can do. Two weeks from now will end our time together." She took his hand as Perth stared down at the ground, his other hand clenched in a fist.

"Pardon me, Kendi, Perth," said a fairy they had rescued. "I see you are hurting. Why? This is a celebration." This male had the sagging jowls of middle age and a pot belly.

Kendi shook her head and said nothing. She just waved for the fairy to leave, but he remained.

Nathan took the direct tack but kept his voice level. "She's sad because *your* tribal tradition says she and her husband have to divorce since they don't have any children yet."

"Oh, that's terrible!" he said, fluttering close to the humans. "Divorce is such a terrible thing!"

Sally shouted at him. "We agree! Now, if we could just get your chief to relent, we'd be set, but he won't overturn tradition."

The fairy shook his head. "Not my chief and not my tradition. I'm from another tribe. We don't force divorce."

Perth's head shot up. "You don't?"

Kendi looked up at the new fairy, too.

"No, we don't. I'm Den, by the way, from the Charst tribe."

Perth said, "In the cabin, you said they're from north and east of here, right?"

"Far to the northeast. I got captured during our annual migration over this bog."

Kendi shook her head and squeezed Perth's hand tighter. Tiny rays of hope crept into her voice. "We won't have to divorce."

"But you will have to make changes," Den said. "We don't worship your gods in the Charst tribe."

Perth let go of Kendi hand and slipped an arm around her slender waist. Somehow, they kept flying. "The law of our gods will separate us forever. Why should we stay? Den told me of their single god in the cages. He is just and not capricious."

"But the god of my tribe may not bless you with children, either. Would you then just abandon him?"

"No," Kendi said. "We will serve your god for our lives, if he lets us stay together."

The newcomer explained, "Please understand, we expect you to become one of us. Where we go, you will go. Our god will be your god. Your own tribe will reject you, and forbid you to return. You will never pray to any god except ours. You will only serve the Father, Son, and Spirit."

Karen's jaw dropped.

Kendi and Perth flew high up in the air and shared a kiss. They floated down gently to the humans' eye level. "Well, you know we'll be leaving tomorrow for parts unknown!"

"We wish you the best," Karen said, cheerily.

Perth kissed Karen and Sally on their cheeks.

"Perth!" Kendi giggled and playfully slapped her husband.

"What? It's the fairy way! I won't mind if you say thank you to Nathan."

Kendi flew close to the black robe, hovered near his cheek, then backed away. "Nope. Can't do it. Sorry."

Nathan smiled at her. "It's okay."

Laughing, the human trio began the trip back to their vehicles at the edge of the bog.

About halfway there, Karen said, "A good day."

"It could have been better," Nathan said.

"Oh, you'd have preferred an evil day, I suppose," Sally quipped.

"Not what I meant." He stopped and took a deep breath. "I behaved very badly today, Karen. My spying on you was inexcusable. I invaded your privacy and caused you pain and embarrassment. I am sorry."

Karen raised her eyebrows in surprise and glanced at Sally.

Sally grinned and nodded encouragingly.

"I accept your apology, Nathan."

Sally nudged her and said, "And I think we should not tell Dr. Graff that part of today. Nathan was a big help, without him we couldn't have freed the fairies. Still no date, though."

Grudgingly, Karen agreed. "But understand this. Girls talk, and if I ever hear you do such a thing to anyone else, no matter her alignment, we will band together and hunt you down like the Evil pig you are."

Taken aback, Nathan nodded. "As you say. Who wants to type up the report? I'm all thumbs on the keyboard."

"I'd better do it," Sally said. "I acted as scribe, and no one else wants to decipher my chicken scratches."

"How did you make it through Madam Stacy's scrollwork class?" Writing spells on scrolls required very precise lettering.

"With a penalty of -1 to every attempt."

The trio laughed and walked out of the bog.

———

Frank B. Luke grew up in Oklahoma, met his future wife at seminary in Missouri, and now resides in Iowa with her. They have two young boys who keep them busy. They are associate pastors at a small church outside Knoxville, Iowa. While he earns a living as a web developer, she takes care of the house and boys. He writes fantasy and science fiction to explore God's truth in fantastic ways. He finds such story-theology connects with readers on both cognitive and emotional levels.

Other stories in Night Candle setting are forthcoming. More about Frank B. Luke's writing can be found at https://frankluke. wordpress.com/published-in/

TED TALK

BY KARINA FABIAN

Everyone knows trolls can't do magic...except Gurlurk, who has heard one Ted Talk too many. When he discovers there's more to it than believing in oneself, he doesn't take it well. When chaos ensues, it'll take a dragon to save the day. Will Vern give up his comfy napping place and "just do it"?

Vern's many adventures are told in the *DragonEye, PI*, books and stories by Karina Fabian. Gurlurk makes an appearance in *If Wishes Were Dragons*, where the two face the consequences of that fateful day when Gurlurk discovered that "digging deep" sometimes means deep trouble.

Ted Talk

Ted Rawlings left the "You Too Can Be a Motivational Speaker!" seminar with a spring in his step and hope soaring in his heart. He could do it! He could use his words and the fire in his spirit to inspire hundreds—no, thousands!—of complete strangers. And make money at it, too.

He just needed to get the cash for the $600 down payment for the "Can-Do Circle" before all the slots were filled. He'd take a shortcut through the atrium to the cash machine and be back before the break was over.

His eyes on the garish convention hall carpet and his mind already planning his first motivational talk, he didn't notice that the "doors" to the atrium were glowing, and the garden beyond was a mystical forest.

Gurlurk crouched on one side of the quarry, grabbing boulders and hurling them at the other side while he sulked. The impacts made a soothing counterpoint to his grumbling.

"Stay home, Gurlurk."

Crash!

"Know your place, Gurlurk."

Bam!

"Do duty, Gurlurk."

Crack!

From behind him, a voice said in an odd accent, "Uh, excuse me?"

Gurlurk whirled, a beachball-sized rock in his hand, ready to hurl it at anyone his royal parents had sent to drag him back to the home-caves. Instead, a puny human in weird clothes cringed and held up his hands defensively.

"Please!" the tiny one cried. "I come in peace! I'm terribly, terribly lost! I was walking across the hotel, looking for an ATM and..."

The small one chattered on. Gurlurk understood about one word in three, and piling on more words did not help, but the human kept at it, anyway. It somehow made Gurlurk feel even more depressed.

"Go away, manrunt," he said. "Gurlurk got own troubles." He crouched back down and resumed throwing rocks.

After three boulders met their doom against the side of the quarry, he heard light footsteps, and then the manrunt was sitting beside him.

"You seem sad," he said.

Gurlurk understood these words, at least, but he didn't know how to answer. Even if trolls had the vocabulary to describe the long, dark night of the soul, he wasn't going to admit his existential ennui to a complete stranger. If ennui was the right word. Probably not; it sounded too elvish. Instead, he shrugged and threw another stone.

The human set a hand on his arm. "Come on, big guy. You can talk to me. What's wrong?"

"Stupid parents. Stupid rules. Not want be fighter. Want different. Want..." He sighed. Who was he kidding? He couldn't have what he wanted. Yet, he'd defied his father and his king. Now, he was stuck with a puny human as a companion, and he was out of rocks.

"What?" the human pressed. "What do you want?"

Gurlurk shrugged.

"Oh, I bet you know. You just have to dig deep."

"Dig? Me no dwarf!"

The human yelped. "Sorry! I mean, look inside yourself. No, not actually! Not... Whoa. Stop, stop! Dang, you're limber. Sit, sit. Now, close your eyes. Imagine yourself doing exactly what you always wanted. The thing that would make you the happiest and best you possible."

Gurlurk had never had a human talk to him in such a friendly manner before. Usually, they ran screaming or shouted threats. The surprise as much as anything made him sit obediently and close his eyes. He let his mind drift as the human nattered on.

What would make him happy? What would be his dream come true?

He remembered his father taking him to see a traveling show of faerie performers. They'd hidden behind an outcropping on a hill, looking down at the marvels—dancers draped in brilliant clothes, acrobats swinging from ropes, and a mage. He'd loved the mage. Magic was common enough among the faerie folk but unheard of in trolls. Plus, there was something about the elf magician's showmanship, the way his audience cheered at the simplest trick...

Later that night, as they made a meal of the performers, he'd begged extra portions of the mage. He thought he felt the magic flowing in him with every swallow. For days after, he imagined each belch was proof of the magic fermenting inside him. He had felt happy and unique. If only...

"I see from the look on your face that you know what you want," his companion singsonged.

"Want be mage." Then he opened his eyes. Reality returned in the form of broken rocks and a puny, weirdly-dressed manrunt.

"So?" the manrunt asked. "Do it!"

"Can't. Trolls no be mages."

"You can't think like that, friend. Listen, if there's one thing I learned this weekend, it's whatever you can conceive and believe, you can achieve. You just have to believe in yourself."

Ted had no idea how he'd ended up in this bizarre forest talking to a 16-foot, 800-pound...troll? He hadn't known you could get flashbacks from pot. Kristie had said it was medical grade... Anyway, he'd decided to just go with it.

And it was actually going pretty well. He'd met Gurlurk "where he was," established a connection, found his pain point... Two hours later, the troll rose to his feet, cheering.

"Yes! Ted talk true! Gurlurk be mage. Gurlurk believe! Gurlurk go Hermes Magical University now."

Ted wanted to cheer, too. His first time out as a motivational speaker, and he'd convinced a troll to go to college! That had to be some kind of record. "I believe in you, Gurlurk! Really. Anything I can do to help. I am here for you."

That's when Gurlurk hit him over the head with a rock.

It was a testimony to the kind of week the HMU admissions counselor was having that, when a 16-foot troll with dirt on his feet and old meat chunks on his shirt walked in and demanded to become a mage, his first thought was, "Is it really only Wednesday?"

It's because I'm multilingual, the gnome thought with a sigh. *Never mind that he could squash me with one stomp. I just had to take those extension classes in guttural languages.*

"Mister Gurlurk," Piccs began.

"Prince Gurlurk!" the troll thundered reflexively. Then, he got a curious scowl on his face and amended, "No. No want be prince. Want be mage."

Fighting an internal sigh, Piccs skipped the honorifics altogether. "Gurlurk. Piccs apologizes. Gurlurk no be mage. Trolls no be mages. Trolls no can use magic."

"Gurlurk can! Ted say! Ted say, 'Believe and achieve.' Gurlurk believe. Gurlurk do magic."

"Ted, who? Ted, where?"

Gurlurk looked at his stained shirt guiltily.

I don't get paid enough for this. Piccs met the troll's eyes. "Make deal. Gurlurk prove do magic, Gurlurk become student."

When the troll stood there, dumbfounded, the little gnome made shooing motions with his hands and returned to the pile of paperwork that no amount of magic seemed to reduce. At least, it was Hump Day.

Gurlurk wandered the edge of campus, the only troll in the chaos of magical and magic-using creatures. The entire student body seemed to be in the courtyards and streets celebrating something called "pledge week." Gurlurk didn't hear any vows being made, only laughter and song, catcalls, and encouragements to drink.

And spells. All around him, people were using magic in ways profound and base, from filling the sky with ethereal images to pantsing an unsuspecting victim. Some people cheered or groaned, but there was so much magic happening, most people went their own way, taking it for granted.

What was he doing here? He didn't belong. Trolls don't—

No! A little voice that sounded like Ted said in his mind. *Don't give up on your dreams! Believe and achieve!*

But how? Now, he wished he'd waited to eat the manrunt until he had this figured out. What would Ted say?

"Believe and achieve"—but he'd been believing all day, and nothing magical had happened. "Just do it"—but that didn't seem to help, even when he did the squatting and hand thing. "Imagine your best self, then fake it until you make it"—he hadn't tried that yet.

He stopped in front of a house where mages were making rainbows to slide down into a huge vat of ale. This was as good a place as any. He closed his eyes and let himself go back to his childhood, where all the world was possibilities and food. He imagined the taste of the mage, let himself feel the excitement. He would fake the magic fermenting inside his guts until he made it real!

He belched.

When the thunder of his gaseous outcry ceased, he realized everyone had gone silent. He opened one eye to find them all staring at him.

Then they all applauded.

"That was amazing," a drunken human in a draped sheet said. His friends raised flagons and hollered in agreement. "Get over here and do it again!"

Gurlurk's heart skipped as he lumbered to the house. The human who invited him handed him a flagon, and he downed it in one swallow, then belched, earning more cheers and another flagon.

After his third one, however, he realized there was no magic issuing from his mouth. He scowled at the drink, then at the gaggle of males that surrounded him: humans, elves, a dwarf... They all wore togas, and they all grinned at him expectantly. He looked past them at the banner with the words "Phi Iota Tau Sigma." Was it a spell? He tried to sound it out.

"Phi Iota Tau Sigma," the males cheered and clicked glasses, then drank.

"It spell?"

"No!" The dwarf paused to burp, then continued. "It's us! Phi Iota Tau Sigma, the greatest magical fraternity in HMU and the world!"

"Huzzah!" his brethren yelled and clicked glasses. The gnome reached so high to touch his to the others that he lost his balance and toppled off the table he'd been standing on and into the vat of ale. The rest broke into song:

Phi Iota Tau Sigma, May our magic live foreva
May our friendship long endure
For magic, friendship is!
Together, we can all excel
We plumb the depths of every spell
Phi Iota Tau Sigma, may our magic carry on.

Together, Gurlurk included, they dipped their flagons into the vat, fishing out their gnome brother, and they toasted, drank, and belched. Gurlurk sighed contentedly. He had found his tribe.

"You teach Gurlurk magic now?" Gurlurk said.

There was a pause, then laughter.

"Trolls can't do magic!"

And that was when Gurlurk lost his temper.

———

On a hill not far from Hermes Magical University, Vurnerrah, a dragon of Faerie, an awe-inspiring creature of fire and might, had splayed out on a hill and was trying to nap.

It was a nice hill, flat, and bare of trees where a dragon could get the best afternoon sun. And when said dragon was the length of a football field with a wingspan to match, it was not easy to find the perfect hill for sunning. Thus, he was doing everything he could to relax, enjoy the warmth on his scales, and ignore the screams and crashes coming from the university below.

However, when he heard the gaggle of mortals ascending the hill, grumbling and rolling something with them, he knew his moment of peace had passed. Of course, someone had seen him land, and of course, they wanted some favor.

He settled himself into a more regal pose and waited, judging their progress by their cursing and vomiting. He hoped it was out of their system by the time they reached the summit. At least, they were coming from downwind.

Finally, they broke the tree line and paused, wide-eyed. He waited.

They gathered into a tight knot, debating. He heard, "No, you do it," in several languages. Someone said something about someone else wanting to be a bard. There was agreement, and one hapless human was thrust from the Circle of Safety. He stumbled toward Vurnerrah, gulped, and with a visible effort to regain his composure, straightened his tunic and fraternity pin and approached, feigning confidence. Vurnerrah gave him points for not soiling himself.

The human threw his arms wide in supplication. "Oh, great dragon! Great and..."

"Beautiful," Vurnerrah prompted.

"Yes. Uh, beautiful and magnificent. And merciful! We of the Sacred Fraternity of Phi Iota Tau Sigma—"

"PITS? Are you being hazed?"

"—implore you, the great protector of... Um, what?"

Vurnerrah stretched languidly, mostly to show off his beautiful and magnificent wingspan. He hadn't felt the "bard" was appropriately inspired. "It's just that I didn't demand that lunch be brought to me, and I prefer my meals a little less pickled. So, either this is a hazing, or you're trying to butter me up before asking a favor."

Relieved of having to come up with a speech, the human relaxed visibly, which told Vurnerrah everything he needed to know about the human's career potential as a bard.

The man said, "Well, you see. There's this troll."

"Wait." He gestured for the others to bring the cask of wine. He popped the cork with one sharp claw and took an experimental swallow. Light, fruity, a hint of pixie oak... Acceptable payment for his attention.

In the valley, there was an explosion. The Piotas exchanged worried glances. Mortals.

Vurnerrah smacked his lips and recorked the cask. "Now, what about this troll?"

Ted had told Gurlurk not to let negativity hold him down. "Just crush all that negativity—really crush it!—and push away the people who would hold you down. Then, you'll find yourself surrounded by people who will support you in your goals."

Gurlurk was trying to do that. He really was. So far, he'd crushed the Phi Iota Tau Sigma frat house, destroyed the lobby of the admissions office, and ripped up a couple of dubious-looking trees for good measure. He'd flung away the nay-saying Piotas (those that hadn't run), and when Piccs demanded he leave, he'd stomped on him.

But no one had stepped up to fill the void with positive support, and it was starting to annoy him.

"Gurlurk want be Piota!"

He ripped up an oak tree and flung it roots first through the wall of the admissions building.

"Gurlurk want learn spells!"

He grabbed the centaur charging him and flung him into the advancing squad of security officers.

"Gurlurk want do magic!"

Suddenly, the sky darkened. Gurlurk cheered. He'd done it! He'd made weather magic!

Then huge claws grabbed him by the shoulders and lifted him into the air. It wasn't weather magic. It was a dragon blotting out the sun. He howled in disappointment and struggled.

The dragon spoke to him in perfect Trollese. "What wrong with you? Trolls no do magic. Trolls no do magic; magic no hurt trolls. That deal. That deal since alwaystime."

"No! Not this time. Gurlurk believe. Ted say, 'Believe and achieve.' Gurlurk believe."

"Who Ted?" The dragon twisted its neck so it could look at him. It sniffed his clothing. "A Mundane? You took life advice from a Mundane?"

Gurlurk's uppercut caught the dragon in the jaw. The dragon yelped and dropped him, then caught him with his tail.

"Be thankful you don't go with a sweet zinfandel. Behave or I eat you," the dragon warned, then spoke more calmly. "Mundanes no understand trolls. Ted no know trolls no do magic."

"Ted different! Ted 'get' Gurlurk! Ted understand."

"Really? Ted know you plan eat him?"

Gurlurk thought. Ted had seemed rather surprised when he hit him with the rock. "Nooo...."

"Ted Mundane. Ted no know trolls. Ted no know trolls eat people. Ted no know trolls not magic. Ted idiot."

Gurlurk beat on the dragon's tail. "No! Ted smart. Ted say Gurlurk do anything Gurlurk believe!"

"Listen, Meat..."

"Prince Gurlurk. No, wait. Mage Gurlurk, Gurlurk the Great!" That had a nice sound to it.

"Prince? Prince Gurlurk need go home. Need rule caves. Need make troll babies."

"Dragon sound like Dad!"

───────────

As expected, Prince Gurlurk did not see reason. Even worse, he had caught a piece of Vurnerrah's tail and was trying to bite through the scales, which didn't hurt but did involve a lot of drool. Time for Plan B.

Vurnerrah rose above the clouds and hovered, waiting while the troll realized it was a long way to the ground and screamed until he passed out from the thin air. Then the dragon headed to the entrance of a cave where the Piotas waited with sturdy ropes and a large donkey-drawn cart. They quickly bound the unconscious troll and wheeled him into the cave and down into the dungeon. Vurnerrah used magic to shrink himself small enough to follow.

They took a meandering path through the halls, some of which were still under construction, until they came to a large room filled with oddities: ropes, wheels, gears, a couple of banged-up lab tables, and the components for spell-making. At one end of the room, a pair of 20-foot doors opened into a smaller but still large closet.

A half-dozen Piotas, now partly sober, swarmed about, discussing strategies and making preparations. Some were creating lights in the closet while others were piling food and blankets into it. Still others giggled as they discussed a spell.

The leader of the Phi Iota Tau Sigma fraternity greeted Vurnerrah with open arms. "Welcome to the Dungeon of PITS, where would-be brothers face tests of the heart and mind!" he boomed. Then, his voice lowered to a more casual tone, and he said, "It's a good thing, too. This room is where pledges are supposed to create a spell to keep the doors magically sealed before the troll can break them or open it from his end. What a coincidence, huh?"

Dragons can't raise their eyebrows, so Vurnerrah tilted his head curiously at the Phi Iota Tau Sigma leader.

He shuffled his feet. "Well, we weren't going to use a real troll, just a magical facsimile."

They dumped the moaning Gurlurk into the closet and untied him while Vurnerrah made himself large enough to fill the room, just in case the troll decided to come to fighting. They dashed out as Gurlurk sat up.

Vurnerrah stuck his face close to Gurlurk's. "Gurlurk been bad troll. Do much damage. Kill many people Gurlurk not eat. Gurlurk in Time Out now. Stay calm. Think about place in world."

He saw the troll tense and bared his teeth in response. "Time Out, or I eat you."

Gurlurk glared at him, then went to the blankets and shoved

them into a nest. He pulled one around his shoulders and squatted. "Gurlurk hate dragon!"

He wouldn't be the first mortal to say that. Vurnerrah backed out, and the Piotas shoved the doors closed. While a group of them started working a spell, he spoke to the leader.

"I'll go to his village and tell his parents where he is and explain the situation. They'll come to fetch him after they think he's had time to calm down. In the meantime, my payment?"

The Piota leader touched his fraternity pin. It was a nice pin, white gold, with the letters surrounding a dragonstone chip embedded in sapphire. Some dragons were all about the gold coins and precious gems; but Vurnerrah leaned toward crafted items with unique stories, and this was a story worth remembering.

The leader grinned apologetically but spoke with the conviction that had earned him the title of Piota Prime. "I'm afraid we can't just give you the sacred jewelry of our order. We'll need to induct you into the rolls. Will you swear to be loyal to your fellow brothers and obedient to the rule of the Sacred Order of Phi Iota Tau Sigma?"

"No."

He shrugged. "Well, you can be an honorary member, then."

Piotas dressed in ceremonial robes began filing in from the hallways, singing the fraternity anthem. In the meantime, the students working the spell finished their last touches. Ropes glowing with magic swirled over the door, twisting and knotting themselves until they resolved into a combination of runes and Greek letters. They read: *Phi Iota Tau Sigma. We plumb the depths to reach new heights.*

In the closet, Gurlurk picked up a rock and threw it against the wall. It was a tiny stone and made a puny little sound.

"Believe, Gurlurk."

Plink!

"Achieve, Gurlurk."

Clink.

Karina Fabian is Vern's much-harassed biographer. In between writing his stories—and hearing him nag about her not writing his stories—she writes science fiction, fantasy, and horror. To pay the bills (because Vern's broker than she is), she writes product reviews for Fit Small Business. Learn more and check out Vern's adventures at http://karinafabian.com

TROLL IN THE GARDEN

J. F. POSTHUMUS

Mundane substitute teacher Harold Sylverson has introduced much to his magical pupils, including his love for tabletop gaming. At the begging of his students, he brings in enough dice for his classes as well as the books and sheets required to play the fantasy roleplaying game. But not all his students are thrilled with him bringing the Mundane to the Magical. When one of the parents of the school's bullies arrives to deride Harold for his teaching methods and the fact the game is nothing like reality, chaos ensues when the father brings a troll from the book of monsters to life. Now there's a troll in the garden, and Harold, with his fellow instructors, have to figure out how to get rid of it!

"Troll in the Garden" is the third story featuring Harold Sylverson; the first can be found in *Fantastic Schools Vol. 2* and the second can be found in *Cracked: A Chicken Anthology*.

Troll in the Garden

Chapter 1

"Master Sylverson! Did you bring it?"

"Can we see it now, Master Sylverson?"

"Who wants to see that boring stuff the Mundanes play with, anyways."

"Get stuffed, Wesley! I saw him bringing the boxes in and it looks *cool*."

"Students, please calm down." Howard Sylverson instructed in a calm, if bemused, tone. "To answer you, in order; yes, I brought it. No, first we have attendance and homework review to do. No one is required to look at or interact with anything I have brought from the non-Magickal sections I've lived in. And Ashley? Watch your language. Master Westerford has a right to his opinion."

He paused, dropped his chin so that his bright eyes twinkled over the rims of his glasses. He dropped a wink in the direction of the last student he'd addressed.

"Absolutely spot-on, Ashley. It *is* cool."

Most of the classroom's occupants cheered. Howard Sylverson, who taught World History in this classroom five days a week, smiled at his students. Even at Wesley Westerford and his small pack of brooding sidekicks. He knew Wesley was a bully, and his company of five other students here at Hogsback Creek Academy were empowered by him to act just as vulgar and entitled as he did.

Hogsback Creek Academy, School of Magecraft, here in scenic Virginia. Howard silently reflected. *Home to the Fighting Bumblebee, witches and wizards of all levels. I came here by mistake, and was asked to stay on after my first week as a substitute.*

Staying was precisely what he had done. His so-called ordinary life of streaming entertainment, texting, overpriced coffee to go and microwave meals in between substitute teacher gigs? That had been turned completely upside down and front to back in the course of a single phone call and car ride up Hogsback Mountain. Old road signs that he was apparently not supposed to be able to see led him when the cell phone service and GPS failed. He'd parked, asked to be shown his assigned room, and then the world stopped making sense. The world he had known, at least.

That was six weeks, or a figurative lifetime, ago.

Since then, Howard had been given full-time teaching privileges by the headmaster of the school, Angus McMillan. He had living quarters complete with running water that he used at the Academy. On weekends, he often returned to his apartment within the Mundane, or non-Magickal, community.

The majority of his students had taken a quick interest in "Sylverson's life as a Mundane". Once it was established that he did, in truth, have no knowledge of the Magickal that existed all around? The questions and requests seemed never-ending.

What do you have on your portable phone thing? Does it even work here?

How do you keep from being bored all the time if you didn't see all this stuff?

Is it true that Mundanes don't read from paper or parchment anymore?

Why can't Mundanes know about us? Because they don't understand us? We have to learn Math! I don't understand that at all!

On and on it went from the first day. Howard didn't mind it, though. He had so much to learn about their lives, so their questions gave him a chance to teach them about his.

"Students, please get to your seats and raise your wands. Flares up, if you would." He instructed the gathered crowd. Groans of disappointment, followed by the loud shuffling of bodies into wooden desks.

The thirteen students each held up a carved wooden stick in one hand. Sparks or small flames of various hues began sputtering from the tips. Howard had learned early on to employ this method of counting his charges. Some of these children had advanced enough skills to project illusions of themselves or others, albeit temporarily. In the first fortnight of his time here, there were several times that truant students had evaded being detected as absent until he had been educated by other instructors.

Howard verified that all of his students were in class. He smiled to himself once this was accomplished. No surprise that they were all here, even Westerford and his lackeys.

Today was the day that Howard had agreed to bring all the materials for his favorite teen-years activity. Thirty years' worth of Medieval fantasy role playing table top games and all the silly beloved junk that he'd acquired to go with it. The books, adventure modules, maps, figures and of course the dice.

Enough dice for each student to have a set to play with. *Okay, Howard* silently admitted, *enough for each student to have four sets to play with. I admit I have an obsession!*

"Thank you, everyone. You may lower your wands, and pass forward your homework."

Most of the homework came to him via parchment scrolls. There were a surprising number of assignments that came to him today on ruled paper, written with number 2 pencils. More and more of his students were adapting to "his" way of writing down work.

Howard knew some of his students would never try the Mundane practice of paper and pencil. That was fine. He couldn't get the hang of using a quill and ink to save his life or dignity.

Once all the homework had been gathered, Howard turned the pages of his handbook to the answer portion of the assignment he'd given. This was his routine. After everyone had turned their work in, he reviewed the proper answers to the class. He had tried to accommodate his former method of reviewing before students turned in their work, to give them a chance to change incorrect answers. That had changed when he had been offered to stay here, full-time.

He no longer had to worry about giving students easy "A's" so they wouldn't whine to parents and guardians. Which would make his ability to return to a school for more work difficult.

Granted, he hadn't had to worry about dodging fireballs, noticing sleeping potions next to his packed lunch, getting literally cursed or dozens of other unexpected tribulations, either. At least he considered his life to be vastly more interesting as a result.

As Howard looked up from the handbook, two things made him

pause. The first was the heavy, pregnant silence in the room. The second was the wide, expectant stares of most of the students.

"I get the impression that few of you are interested in the homework's answers. More so than usual." He added the second sentence as a joke. No one responded.

"You are *that* curious about an old game based on the imagination of Mundanes? Or dice that don't roll themselves or do anything besides show numbers?" Howard proposed.

The energy in the room felt immediately thicker, and he swore he could hear it humming all around him.

"I'm not," Westerford declared flatly. Some of his group grunted in agreement.

"Master Sylverson?" A lad with long strawberry blonde hair and twinkling brown eyes spoke up. "Can we use Wesley's homework as the example for last night's assignment?"

"That is a fine suggestion, Xolyn." Howard replied with a little more cheer than he should have. He moved towards the pile of scrolls. His eyes kept Wesley Westerford in the peripheral so he could enjoy how rapidly the bully's face blanched.

It was not disappointing.

"Fine, get your dumb game," Wesley grumbled. Snickering came from all around the classroom. Young Westerford looked like he wanted to curse every person he could see.

"Well, since we have your illustrious blessing in the matter," Howard said while making a dramatic flourish with his left hand, "I shall do just that!"

Cheers erupted.

Chapter 2

Some of the students helped Master Sylverson move the boxes of gaming materials out of the closet and onto a summoned grand table. Since Master Sylverson was unable to summon so much as a cup of coffee, the student who was best at casting such spells did the best she could. Katherine Butler, the student in question, managed just fine. A table of requirement appeared even as the first boxes were being brought out.

The table was long enough to seat all the students and the teacher. As more boxes were brought out and the contents moved around, the table's width expanded to accommodate. By the time the maps, books and other paraphernalia were spread out for all to see, the table took up half the classroom.

Howard was grateful that his students could command the chairs and desks to stack themselves against the walls to make room. He'd had to use Mundane methods to rearrange classrooms plenty of times before. The class might have had five minutes to look over everything before time was up if it wasn't for Magick being used.

In addition to getting to watch something as nifty as furniture walking and stacking themselves, there was still plenty of time to do this particular "show and tell."

While the helpful students had been busy, Howard noticed Wesley and his group huddled together. There seemed to be some chatter happening, although he could only see Wesley's lips moving. A mental note to be on the watch for some extra trouble was made.

"Master Sylverson? What's *this*?"

Howard was brought out of his pondering by the voice of a cheerful, eager student. He located the source and smiled.

"Ahhh, good catch, Daphne!" Howard said earnestly. "That is The Great Book of Monsters! It's an illustrated listing of the different races and creatures you encounter in the game."

"Really?" Daphne's eagerness seemed to double immediately.

"It says great book of monsters on the spine, dummy," interjected Shaun. He and the rest of Wesley's group were approaching the table.

"Yes, Daphne, and it's a pretty cool collection," Howard replied, as if the other student hadn't spoken.

"Is this supposed to be a dragon on the cover?"

Howard nodded, and added, "Yep, that's how some Mundanes imagine dragons look like." He pointed to the book cover's illustration. "And that's supposed to be a dwarf getting ready to fight it."

Daphne glanced once more at the illustration and burst out laughing. She began to show it to the students closest to her.

And the questions started coming from all around.

"Why does the dragon's face look like it's part horse?"

"Can you fight dragons in the game, too?"

"Are you *sure* that's supposed to be a dwarf, Master Sylverson?"

"Show us how the game works?"

"I've got a book that says '*Spells*'? Did the Mundane people get any right? Can I look inside?"

"What are these for, Master Sylverson?"

"You're going to let us play the game, right, Master Sylverson?"

"Why don't these dice do anything besides roll?"

"Can I stay here after class?"

Taking in a deep breath, Howard prepared to answer the questions.

At that moment, the door to the classroom swung open. Even though Howard had never met the person in the doorway, he knew the man's identity. The features were too much like the son's, right down to the haircut. Overpriced robes and gold filigree along the sleeves spoke volumes about how much this chap wanted to impress and intimidate. Lessons he'd taught his offspring.

The oft-mentioned but never met William Weatherford, in the flesh.

Mister Weatherford strode into the classroom like a celebrity at the opening of a film with their name at the top billing. Howard expected smartphones and paparazzi to suddenly appear and blind them all with photographic flashes.

When the senior Weatherford spoke, he even sounded, to Howard, like an actor taking the stage to begin a monologue in a lousy Shakespearean production. One that couldn't afford a classically trained thespian.

"So... this is what McMillan pays a Mundane for: Rubbish instead of history."

"I know, right?" the younger Weatherford replied in an eager tone.

A part of Harold's mind told him there was a time to put a parent in their place, to respect the classroom. And that time was not now. This was a fully trained wizard, and one that obviously expected his words to carry weight. Possibly even wanted to make an example of whomever failed to pay felty to his supposed greatness. Someone Harold had no clue how to properly deal with.

Of course, that part of Harold's mind got promptly booted to the far corner.

"You must be the janitor," Harold said. "So good to see you. I've been asking for the windows to be cleaned for weeks, now. Get along with it, and don't interrupt my class."

Somewhere in the ensuing silence that followed, one of the students dropped a single die on the table. It rattled and rolled loudly in the empty air. Harold was pretty sure it was a twenty-sided die. He wondered what number had come up when it ended its journey.

Energy crackled in the room. Harold felt the fine hairs on his neck and arms start to stand up. Mister Weatherford swore violently in Latin even as his left hand dove into the folds of his robes. There was movement all around Harold, but he dared not take his eyes off of this newly made nemesis. He braced himself to move as soon as the wand came out of Weatherford's absurd outfit.

"I thought I smelled you on the grounds," a thickly accented voice growled. "Shall I presume you're about to show Master Sylverson your favorite card trick? Mayhap astound him with a trained dove or two?"

A few of the students snorted with laughter. Weatherford the elder spun back to the doorway, hand still buried beneath his clothes.

Olan Kram, professor of herbology, leaned casually against the door frame. His head brushed the top of the frame, giving full view of his impressive height and considerable scowl. The flaming red hair which was normally captured in a long ponytail lay across his broad shoulders.

"Kram," the older Weatherford muttered. More than a little contempt in that voice.

"I'm waiting, Billy boy," countered Master Kram.

Slowly an empty hand came out of the robe and came to a stop at Weatherford's left hip.

"Well, damn. I was hoping to see if you could guess my card," Kram said with a deadpan expression. "It's the Ace of Spades, incidentally."

Harold took a moment to look behind him at his students. Emily, Andy, and Jackson were trying to stuff their wands back into their robes. The rest were concentrating on the confrontation at the front of the class. Some looked stunned. Most looked eager.

Bless those three, Harold thought, *they were going to try and defend me.*

"Shouldn't you be squeezing tubers or boring children with your technique for extracting thorns from roses?" Weatherford's adult voice brought Harold back to the situation.

Master Kram chuckled. "By your granny's beard, Billy boy, you are feeling mighty bold today, aren't you? Did the wife let you have an extra cookie?"

Silence held for a long moment, Weatherford finally turned away, walked to the large table, and snatched up a book.

"I suppose you approve of this drivel?" Weatherford the elder asked over his shoulder to Master Kram. "Our students being taught the ignorant ways and beliefs of the non-Magickal?" He began flipping through the pages of the book he'd taken.

Harold noticed it was the Great Book of Monsters, volume two.

"There is plenty to know if any of *our* students wind up living or working among them." Master Kram countered. "As for today, the faculty were notified that Master Sylverson was bringing these materials in. Mostly as an educational entertainment for his classes."

"Exactly!" Howard interjected, "It's all rather silly stuff. Even more so when you see how wrong we mundane beings are about so many species. I mean, the fact that most deny their existence is amusing enough, but how we imagine their appearance is just-"

"Look at the pictures of the *unicorns*, Father!" Wesley interjected. He began flipping pages violently in the book his parent held. With a triumphant sneer on his face, he suddenly stopped, smacked a page. The older Weatherford scowled.

"Oh, how pretty!" Mister Weatherford said. He balanced mockery and contempt quite well with his voice and facial expression. "I suppose this abomination also defecates flower petals and grants wishes to children!"

"Rainbows, actually, depending on the mythos you follow," Harold automatically corrected. "And they're supposedly only fond of young female virgins!"

Harold knew he was attempting to make light of the unicorn mythos he was familiar with. It took no time at all for him to see the effort was wasted on the Weatherford males. The younger looked as if he were a giant toad who watched a fly come just a little too close. The elder was scowling even deeper than before. Red color was rising in his face.

"Bad enough that mundanes encourage their children to think a terrifying and xenophobic species is fair to behold, but they make them pedophiles as well? Is there any end to the ignorance?" Mister Weatherford demanded.

"Best pay attention," Master Kram called from the doorway. "If Billy boy is calling anyone ignorant, he'd certainly know. Can smell his own kind, after all."

And then, Master Kram made a more than passable imitation of a goat bleating.

A rather loud imitation, to give an honest account. Complete with his forefingers pointing up to indicate tiny horns at the side of his head.

Harold couldn't help but bark laughter. Which gave many of the students the courage to join in.

Upon later reflection, that may not have been the best response.

Chapter 3

"What other atrocities is this mundane teaching the children?" the elder Weatherford roared. His eyes were too wide, his face rigid. He flipped a few pages in the book. So roughly that the action ripped the bottom of at least one page.

"I suppose this ridiculous depiction of a troll is supposed to be intimidating? Or frightening?" he continued. "At least it barely resembles an *actual* troll!"

The younger Weatherford had been standing rather close to the elder. With his father's rage really coming to the foreground, Wesley had begun to edge away. His hands fidgeted near the inner pocket in his robes. The robe, although neatly pressed and spotless, was standard issue for all students, as was the inner pocket. That was where most students kept their wands.

Isabella, a favorite student of Harold's, stood up. Her long black hair, which normally fell down her whole back, was cascaded across her entire torso. Complete with her lowered brow and angry body language, she made her teacher think of a Japanese horror film creature.

"Master Sylerson told you this is all for fun! None of it is supposed to be taken seriously or as how anything looks or acts!" she said with all the dignity and steel of an angered adolescent.

Mister Weatherford did not acknowledge her directly. He did raise his voice as he began to read from the book.

"*Trolls often carry simple weapons such as clubs. If they are found carrying more sophisticated weaponry such as swords or axes, the weapons would have been scavenged from trolls' victims, or, quite possibly, a former meal. They can only attack once per melee, and are prone to confusion.*"

He put the book down on the table with a bang. It stayed open to the pages he had been looking at. As he lectured in his loud, booming voice, Weatherford looked back and forth to his son, other students, and Master Kram. He made no eye contact with Harold, or any of the students who had made any effort to defend their mundane teacher.

"What if the troll council saw this? They would be livid! This generation will be clueless how to engage or keep negotiations with any other species if they are taught this rubbish!"

Making a mental note to ask Olan Kram about troll councils at a later time, Harold cleared his throat and tried to get through to the older Weatherford. The younger one looked petrified.

"We mundanes make up for knowledge with a great deal of childish imagination, Mister Weatherford. I don't deny that. We usually can't manage negotiations with each other! Attempting to do what you or other Magickal persons do would be, absolutely, ludicrous. None of what you're concerned with is what is actually happening here, however."

Just as Harold was prepared to go on with his attempt at de-escalation, William Weatherford stomped over to his son. Wesley cowered. His father yanked the boy's wand out of his robe pocket, tearing the cloth.

"I will *show you all* how wrong these books are!" promised Mister Weatherford. He pointed his son's wand at the open book.

Olan Kram charged from the doorway.

"Billy, you idiot!" he yelled. "Don't!"

There was the sense of pressure building in the air just before the flash of light obscured the book, the wand, and most of Mister Weatherford. A second flash came right after as Kram shot the wand out of Weatherford's hand with a bolt of energy from his open palm. As the students were trying to understand what happened, Kram tackled Weatherford. The two men crashed to the classroom floor.

All of the students were in a frenzy of confusion and excitement. Harold clapped his hands together. The sharp sounds brought the chaos to an end. The collective adolescents stilled, found chairs to sit in or places to stand on. The sole exception was Wesley, who seemed torn between going toward his father or finding someplace else to be. Harold was about to address him, when his eyes fell upon the open volume of the monster guide.

"Ummm... the picture of the troll is gone. From my book. Can someone explain why there is a big blank space in my book?" Harold asked no one in particular.

"Because Billy the goat-fucking idiot just embued it with life," Master Kram grumbled from his place on the floor.

He and Mister Weatherford were both rising up onto their feet.

Several feet separated them, but neither man looked ready to attack the other. Both looked disheveled, irritated, but kept their eyes to their own feet.

Two students snorted brief laughter. But Isabella spoke up.

"He used Magick to make the picture come alive, Master Sylerson. It's a restricted spell, because people use it badly."

"Wait, that can be done?" Harold asked, aware that he should close his still-hanging jaw.

"It's only temporary," Mister Weatherford tried to sound nonplussed. "The spell only grants a limited life span. But you'll all see it's nothing like an actual troll."

"*Only temporary?!*" barked Master Kram. "A creating spell from a well-worn witch or wizard may live as long as a century, and might resist being disapparated! Now we have one made by a pandering fool with no impulse control!"

That's when the "troll" smashed the windows from the outside.

Chapter 4

Harold instinctively put himself between the flying glass fragments and as many of his students as possible. He didn't know what was going on. Until he opened his eyes and looked at the eight-foot-tall creature walking out of his childhood imagination and into his classroom.

The book troll was having to pull itself in through the broken window frame by its abnormally long arms and claws. The legs were half the length of its arms. A black loincloth was the only garment. Black hair, the only hair that this troll appeared to have, hung from the ape-like face and down its chest. The skin was a mottled green. Claws on both hands were at least six inches long. Red eyes scanned the room and occupants.

"*Cachu,*" Master Kram swore. With a movement like throwing a heavy object, Kram thrust his fist in the direction of the book troll. A cloudy shape that looked like a war hammer ejected from the knuckles, flew with astounding speed to strike the creature in the chest.

The spell struck the book troll hard enough to push it back out the broken windows, plus another fifty yards away. The large mass hit the back courtyard with a wet crunch, rolled for another few yards, and came to a stop.

No movement came from the book troll's crumpled form.

A wiry student with shoulder-length dirty blond hair and sharp blue eyes spoke up.

"Well, Wesley's dad was right. That looked more like a goblin with lousy hygiene than any troll I've ever seen."

From behind him, Harold heard Ashley reply, "Just shut up, Alfred!"

"See?" Wesley blurted out, his swagger seemingly restored. "Like my dad said, not going to be a problem!"

Without realizing he was going to say it, Harold declared, "None of you have watched movies, have you?"

The troll started to get to its feet.

Harold would later reflect that this day was the one with all the long, pregnant silences. Another occurred while the occupants of the classroom watched the book troll stand and begin to walk towards them again. The monstrosity looked more like it had woken from a nap than been physically thrown a considerable distance.

Grabbing William Weatherford by the neck, Master Kram demanded, "Are you going to keep gawking, or get rid of your little creation?" before pushing the man towards the shattered remains of the windows.

After keeping himself from fumbling over his own feet, Weatherford the elder pulled out his wand. It was as eye catching and full of frippery as his robes. Gold leaves wrapped around the wooden shaft. Some dark scaled hide made up the bottom of the wand like the grip of a sword. An ornate uppercase W was carved at the bottom.

Weatherford raised the wand toward the advancing creature.

"Disperse!" Weatherford commanded.

Another brilliant flash, similar to the one he had caused with his son's wand, burst out.

And the book troll was still coming.

Now may be the time for me to dismiss the class so we can all run, Harold reasoned.

"TROLL IN THE GARDEN!"

That panicked declaration came from the open doorway of the classroom.

Harold looked to the hallway, where the voice had actually come from. Announcements were made via Magick, so they sounded like they came from everywhere. This was a voice from somewhere down the hall, coming this way.

An older school master ran by the opened door. He was holding his robes up with both hands to prevent tripping. He yelled again as he continued moving away, so it sounded like: "TTTR-RRRROOOOOOOOOOOLLLLLLLLLLLLLL INNNN THE GAAARDEEEEEN!!!"

A moment later the sound of someone colliding with something far more solid, such as a door or wall, was heard, followed by a thump. Harold looked to his students. They looked to be as confused as he was. The troll, which wasn't even a real troll, was in the courtyard. It was almost back in the building! The garden was past the courtyard, in the opposite direction.

With an uneasy tone in his voice, Master Kram explained, "There's one that lives in the woods near the garden and hedges."

"A...real troll," Harold replied.

"Yes."

"Why the hell didn't Daddy Dipshit just take us out there and hold the picture in the book up next to it?" Harold screeched.

"He."

"What?"

"The troll that lives off the grounds. Male. Not an 'it' unlike the sexless thing that Billy boy made," Kram said, before adding, "Daddy Dipshit. I will need to remember that one!"

"Why wasn't Weatherford able to get rid of the uh, book troll?" Harold asked.

Kram blinked for a few moments before answering. "My impulse is to say that wands are a crutch, and therefore he lacks the ability to disperse a creation with or without one. Certainly his choice of crutch is more fashionable than practical, but that makes little difference."

"Any opportunity to insult me, eh?" William Weatherford grumbled.

"All that aside," Kram continued, ignoring Weatherford, "I'm not sure what element is keeping the bugger- aw, hells!"

Harold was pushed aside by Kram. The book troll was finally back at the window. The herbology teacher pulled his hands together, raised them to his lips. As he opened the hands palms upward, he blew across them. Harold had the slight sensation of his skin reacting to energy in the air just before wind erupted just ahead of Kram and slammed against the book troll. Loose fragments of wooden frames and cracked glass flew past the troll, as it was picked up and pushed twice as far as the hammer-shaped spell had sent it.

"Pardon my asking," remarked Harold. "But if your 'magic hammer' spell didn't kill that, why did you just hurricane it past the courtyards?"

Kram shrugged but regarded Harold with a quick smirk before saying, "Because I could? It gives us a little more time."

Harold nodded his understanding and turned back to the class.

"Class dismissed! Please get to safety!" he ordered. The students began to disperse in a not-quite-panicked manner. All except for Jackson and Ashley.

"We can help!" Ashley insisted.

As Harold was about to rebuke his well-intended students, they pointed their wands at the collection of gaming materials. Realizing what they were about to do, Harold grabbed up the second volume of the Great Book of Monsters. Just as he did, the rest of the materials began filing themselves into the boxes and other containers they had been in before the start of class. In a matter of seconds, it was all put away and floating to the closet.

"I'm not complaining about using Magick instead of good old-fashioned labor this time," Harold said to Ashley and Jackson, "but I must insist you leave now! Go find someplace safe!"

The two said "Yes, Master Sylverson!" before bolting out the door. He looked back to Olan Kram.

"Now what?" he asked, before realizing Kram was punching Weatherford the elder repeatedly. "Olan, is *now* the best time for this?"

His fellow teacher replied by connecting a sharp uppercut to Weatherford's jaw. The punch lifted William Weatherford off the ground about an inch before Weatherford collapsed to the floor, eyes closed, not moving.

Kram ran to the broken windows and peered out, anxiety on his features.

"Dammit. Rendering the spell caster unconscious did *not* end the enchantment," Kram observed. There was bitterness in his voice.

"Oh, so that's why you pummeled him."

"That," Kram retorted, "is the official reason, yes."

"Now what?"

An inhuman bellow cut the conversation short. Both teachers looked out towards the courtyard, and beyond it.

The real troll had moved from the garden, making its way toward the book troll. Only twenty yards separated them at that moment, and the book troll seemed oblivious.

Harold observed, "Oh. That's what a real troll looks like."

The true troll was ten or eleven feet tall, perhaps twelve if he stood without a hunch. His skin was grey, reminding Harold of the color of old boulders. The arms were proportioned only slightly longer than human. Certainly not the exaggerated limbs that went past the knees, which was noticeable on the book troll.

Dressed in breeches that had obviously been crafted for someone of his stature, the real troll was obviously male, as the mashed lumps in the trousers attested. Both trolls were flat chested, but the book troll's loincloth had no true definition. Neither had body hair. Harold decided, like his student named Alfred, he could no longer look at the book troll's long matted hair and not think it was a poorly tended mane, or perhaps a wig. The real troll was bald, with no eyebrows.

The final argument for the difference between the trolls was, to

Harold, the large and well-made weapon the real one carried. Again, well crafted and designed for a being of considerable size, the scythe was casually slung over the larger troll's left shoulder. Someone in the troll species had made that, and with some measure of skill.

"Perhaps we should just let them fight it out?" Harold meekly suggested.

"Oh, that would certainly end well." Kram's tone did not suggest he actually believed his comment.

Headmaster McMillan's voice came from everywhere:

"All students and guests, please move to the main lecture hall at the front of the academy at this time. Faculty, this is a safety protocol. Please get to your assigned duties."

As the headmaster repeated this announcement, the real troll moved the scythe from his shoulder and swung it back to cleave the book troll in two. The booming voice of the headmaster had startled the book troll, however, and it had begun to look all around. So it saw the larger being coming, and dodged the attack.

The blade of the scythe struck the ground and sunk several feet into the soil. Before he could pull it free, the real troll had to release his grip and move back to avoid the slashing claws of his chosen nemesis. Each lurching step backwards made a heavy thudding sound.

Finally, the larger troll decided he had given enough ground and moved towards the intruder. Moving in between the long arms of the book troll, the male swung a fist at his enemy's torso. As he did, the book troll tried to move away, and the two became entangled, fell, and finally rolled away from each other.

Planting its curled hands on the ground, the book troll launched itself feet-first at the real troll. The feet struck at the jaw and nose, clearly breaking something in the real troll's face. As the book troll landed nimbly on its feet, the real troll staggered back, dazed and barely able to stand.

The booming sound of gunfire rang out twice, The real troll gave out a yipping sound while his massive hands grabbed at his backside.

Buckshot pellets tore at the book troll's face. It flopped back against the ground, and writhed.

Gamekeeper and Grounds Mistress Laelothryll Araloth, known to Master Harold Sylverson as "Later", stepped into view.

Impressive enough on her own, today she carried a massive double barrel shotgun that looked right out of an American Western movie. The sight was odd to Harold, but he remembered that as the former leader of The Wild Hunt, she was familiar with all kinds of weapons, as well as what they would be most effective against. She kept the magic and mundane creatures away from the castle, and subsequently, the staff and students.

Later was also now loading fresh shells into the shotgun's breech as she calmly strode towards the trolls.

She was always a vision to Harold. He watched the wind carry her unbrushed chestnut hair around her stoic face. Felt the earth move with every step of her hiking boots. Relished the way her legs scissored as she walked in blue jeans. Thanked deities he didn't believe in that she was wearing the lightweight blue jacket that showed off her figure instead of the bulky black leather one.

"Go on! Get out of here! Nothing here for you to worry on! Go on!" Later yelled at the real troll. He looked uncertain at her approaching, and grabbed at his backside even harder. As she raised the shotgun, the real troll decided he had better places to be, and ran off.

Gamekeeper "Later" Araloth lowered the shotgun and shook her head, She began moving towards the still quivering heap of the other troll.

"What in the nine Hells is that supposed to be?" she asked Harold.

"Uh, a troll. From one of the games I played as a kid," Harold replied.

Then he realized that he didn't need to yell for her to hear him. He had walked out through the broken windows, into the courtyard and was halfway between Later and the book troll without noticing he had even begun to move. After that revelation, Harold noticed enough to hear Olan Kram calling him an idiot and much ruder things in Welsh, and the herbology teacher's voice was getting closer.

"That thing is supposed to be a troll?" Later sounded dubious, and her face was one large frown. "I thought someone cursed a dead musician from the Eighties, and it wound up wandering the grounds!"

"Heh," Harold replied with a laugh. "Zombie metal head. That's even better than the goblin with bad hygiene."

The Gamekeeper looked past Harold and asked, "What is he talking about? Did the troll or this undead headbanger fetch Harold a blow to the head?"

Kram replied, "I wish. Then I could excuse this damned *cariad taro* fool from walking into danger with only his questionable wits and dumb luck to save him!"

"Oh, I suppose I would have saved him," Later said with a tired smile. She looked down at the almost motionless heap of book troll and asked, "Now what am I supposed to do with this? Throw it in a cage? How did it even get here?"

"It was conjured from a mundane book that Master Sylverson brought to class," offered Kram.

Later looked startled. She looked at Harold.

"You conjured this? Or one of your students?"

Harold shook his head.

"No, it was a visiting parent. William-"

"Weatherford. I should have guessed he was around. The flowers are wilting," grumbled Later.

"What is everyone's gripe with Wesley's father?" Harold interjected. "I mean, it's obvious that—"

The book troll leapt to its feet. No visible damage could be seen on its face or torso. The creature lunged at the Gamekeeper.

The Gamekeeper promptly struck the book troll across the face with the shotgun, kicked it away from her, then emptied both barrels into the creature's stomach. It collapsed to its knees, clutching the wounded area.

"I doubt that's going to do much more than shooting it in the face did," warned Kram.

"Any idea what might?" Later snapped. "I come ready for most contingencies, but I don't want to run through all of them to take this abomination out!"

As if to underline her point, Later put the shotgun on the ground. That freed up her hands to remove a small sack from her pocket. The sack looked big enough to hold a smartphone, wallet and keys, maybe some pocket change.

If Harold hadn't seen such before, he wouldn't have believed it was possible when she was able to plunge her arm to the elbow into the sack without changing its shape. As the lower half of her limb reappeared out of the magical bag, her hand was holding a full-sized cross hilt sword that looked right out of an Arthurian legend. Her free hand put the sack back in the pocket. He wondered, not for the first time, what else she had tucked into that sack.

"Step aside," Later said casually. Harold and Olan obliged, in time for her to swing the sword down into the left shoulder of the rising book troll. It screeched, but used the undamaged arm to shove Later away.

She recovered her balance quickly. While she brought the sword into an en garde position, all three of the adults watched the book troll get to its feet. The deep cut in its shoulder was already knitting back together. Later charged, swinging for her adversary's neck.

The troll smacked the blade aside, ignoring the lacerated palms and severed fingers that the defensive gesture had cost it. Without losing a breath, the troll shoved its weight into Later's torso. She fell back again, this time losing her balance.

Harold made a move to help Later get off the ground, only to be intercepted by the troll. The enormous being moved fast, easily getting between Harold and Later. Harold had forgotten the high level of dexterity the Monster book had described the trolls as having. His mind tried to latch onto another bit of information from the book, until the troll came for him.

The sword that Later had been swinging moments earlier pierced out of the troll's chest. The troll teetered away. Long arms and talons were trying to get a hold of the weapon now protruding through its torso.

Later had thrown the sword, from her prone position on the ground, to get the troll away from Harold. She was getting to her feet while desperately digging into the magic sack.

Olan Kram used a spell to shoot thick webbing against the troll's legs and feet. The oversized spider silk dropped the creature to the cobblestone walkway. The scene looked like a massive spider was trying to make the troll stay for dinner.

Harold had always been afraid of spiders.

Kill all the spiders! His childhood voice rang in his brain. *Kill them, kill them with-*

"Fire!" Harold blurted as the memory clicked into place. "These trolls are susceptible to fire, Later! Got any?"

Later gave Harold a wolfish grin. Out of the small sack she produced an odd golden tube. She pointed this tube at the book troll.

"Fire in the hole!" Harold heard her say, just before he felt Kram yank him back.

A gusher of flame poured out of the tube. More than could have come from a full-sized flamethrower, let alone a tube that seemed to be less than nine inches in length. Also, the flames were tinted with green and purple, in addition to the traditional reds, yellows and orange.

The book troll was incinerated in seconds.

With a satisfied smile, Later put the tube back in her pocket. She looked at Harold, who was more than a little stunned.

"If fire could hurt that, I figured Dragon Fire would finish it," she said, as if that explained everything.

"Now where did you get that?" Harold heard Kram ask.

Later shrugged.

"Well, I know a guy, who knows a guy."

Kram chuckled, He patted Harold on the shoulder.

"Come on. We need to give Headmaster McMillan the all clear so he can recall everyone. And we can file a formal complaint against

Weatherford. How about dinner? I know a proper pub around here that serves a wicked pepper steak. We can tell Harold here all about our formative years with William Weatherford," suggested Kram.

Later nodded in agreement, and the idea thrilled Harold. He heard himself say, "Can we not reprimand Wesley? And let me talk to him? I recognize the fear I saw in him when his dad was getting more and more out of hand. I, uh, dealt with a similar situation."

Kram came into view and gave Harold an odd look. Then Kram looked at Later, who also had an odd look. They both looked back at Harold.

"Certainly, Harold," Later said in a soft tone. "Olan and I will arrange that with the Headmaster."

Harold nodded, and the three of them headed toward the back door.

"Um, Olan?" asked Harold while they walked. "I didn't think you really liked me."

Olan Kram smiled and gave Harold a wink.

"I just didn't have anything in common with you. Not until Billy boy started making your life miserable."

"Oh."

"Don't worry, now you'll hear so much from me, you'll miss when I avoided you."

Harold really doubted it.

Wife and a mother of five, **J.F. Posthumus** is an IT Tech with over a decade of experience. When she isn't arguing with computers and their inherent gremlins, or being mom to the four younger monsters (the eldest has flown the nest and doing quite well on his own), she's crafting, writing, or doing some sort of art. An avid gamer, she loves playing Dungeons & Dragons, and a variety of other board games with her family and friends.

She's also a hopeless romantic, thanks to all the fairy tales she cut her eyeteeth on. They were what J.F. Posthumus learned to read before she discovered the *Boxcar Children Mysteries*. From there, she fell into the rabbit hole that's reading, where she discovered a love for mysteries, fantasy, and the occasional romance. Since writing was a favorite subject, she naturally incorporated her love of murder, mysteries, and fantasy into her works.

A CONFLICT OF CONSCIENCE

BY ROGER D. STRAHAN

Sha-Ri a' Alean de Camlin, now Sherill 'Sherry' Lynn Martin, had been transported through her use of magic from her world to New Orleans, only to find that magic there had been sealed off for millennia. Once there, to save her friend, she was forced to rip open the seal, opening the powers of magic to the world. But that had consequences beyond just opening the door to magic; it released beings that had been in a state of slumber, as well as infusing the humans of the world with the ability to work with this newfound power. In response, Sherry created what became known as the Queens School of Magic, a place of refuge as well as a school to teach others how to use their powers.

But to the politicians, the powerful, those who had held the reins of power for decades or longer, facing the possibility of a people, a group, who would refuse to follow their dictates, the fear of that loss of power became a driving force. So, when Sergeant Donald Drake, U.S. Army, was discovered to have the ability to use these powers, the shadowy forces hiding in the government ordered him to infiltrate the school, to see if the school was, indeed, a threat. But, as Drake found out, there was more than one agenda behind his orders. The question he had to face was, could he follow his orders like a good soldier...or not?

A Conflict of Conscience

Prologue: Earth had many stories and legends about magic, fairies, elves and other magical beings, but there was no evidence that they existed. However, all that changed when Sha-Ri a' Alean de Camlin was jerked from her world of magic, castles and kings and deposited in New Orleans, Louisiana. As far as she knew at the time, she was the only person who had any magical ability but she had quickly found out that magic, at least in a limited amount, still existed on Earth. She found out that magic had been as prevalent, as powerful as it existed in the world she was from, but had been sealed away back in the time of King Artur to stop an invasion through a spatial portal.

Since arriving, she had found friends, she had found opponents, and, most importantly she had found what she thought she would never have: a lover and consort; and in the process, she had ripped open the seal that had held magic away from this world for millennia. For better or worse, magic had returned to Earth with all its promise and threats. So, to meet this threat, this promise, Sha-Ri a' Alean de Camlin became Sherry Martin and started what would ultimately become The Queen's School of Magic in New Orleans. This became especially important to the humans who were affected by 'magic'.

***

It was dry; it was dusty; there were flies everywhere. In other words, it was a typical summer day in Iraq. Staff Sergeant Donald 'Duck' Drake, U. S. Army, was riding shotgun in the Humvee, leading his armored platoon on a routine patrol. The platoon, mounted in five Strykers, rolled through the irrigated areas of Iraq south of Baghdad. Drake, twenty-seven, 6'5" and 240 pounds, and heavily tanned from the desert sun, was in his third tour in the Sandbox. As such, he had both the physical presence of a leader as well as the rank and experience. To him, this was no different than any other patrol he'd led over the last few months. The thing was, the patrols over the last few months had been different. He had been able to anticipate IEDs and insurgent attacks far more accurately, to the point that his CO was taking note. To Drake, that wasn't necessarily a good thing. A good NCO was supposed to do his job without getting noticed, and being noticed was not always a good thing in the Army.

So far, the patrol had been uneventful, which was the way he liked it. Ordered to check out the irrigated farmlands south of the city, they had rolled south, crossed over the river and had headed back up towards Baghdad along the other side of the river. A few miles south of Baghdad, Drake had begun to relax; they were on the home stretch. Suddenly, alarm bells went off in his head. He abruptly sat up in the Humvee, and told the driver to stop. As the Humvee came to a halt, he keyed his radio, telling the troops to dismount and set up a perimeter. At that moment, he didn't know why, but he knew something was wrong. Again, his senses were working overtime. Over the last few months, just based on his instincts, he'd pulled his platoon out of more than one bad situation with either no casualties or very low casualties, so he had learned to trust his feelings.

The troops quickly set up a perimeter, taking cover in the low ditches running along the edges of the road as the gunners in the Strykers and his Humvee started scanning the surrounding irrigated farms. Standing beside the vehicle, Drake found his attention being pulled towards a small hummock alongside the road some fifty yards ahead of the vehicles.

But, before he could investigate the hummock, his head whipped around, almost as if it was being pulled by some unexplained force. He found himself looking at a low wall, the type used to corral the goats that were ubiquitous in this area. As he looked at the wall, it was like he was looking *through* the wall. There, hidden by the wall, were armed insurgents and it was very clear his unit was the target. Without turning his attention from the wall, he pulled up his sling-mounted M4, bringing it to bear on the wall while stepping back to take cover behind the Humvee.

"Action right! Insurgents behind the wall!" he shouted. Even as the order passed down the line, the troops took aim while the Strykers swung their heavy weapons around to face the wall. Drake knew they couldn't drive on down the road with the IED ahead, and he was betting that a similar one was just now being set behind them. The only action was to take out the ambush, then clear the IEDs, while trying to avoid casualties.

The insurgents, seeing that their ambush was blown, started popping up above the wall. At the same time, the IED ahead of the patrol was triggered. Moments later, there was an explosion to the rear of the platoon. The road was temporarily blocked, but there were no casualties. The insurgents had succeeded in trapping the patrol on the road, but that was a fatal mistake. Even as the shooters began opening up on the patrol, the Strykers began ripping the wall with a combination of .50 caliber machine gun rounds, 7.62 mm Gatling guns and 40 mm rapid fire grenades. The wall was shattered along with the ambush by the combination of heavy fire coupled with accurate aimed fire from the troops. Some tried to run but were quickly cut down. In a matter of a very few minutes, except for the rumble of the vehicle engines, the sounds of battle faded away.

Drake looked around at the patrol. No one had been injured. At his command, two three-man teams advanced on the wall, with Drake following along with a support team. There was a sudden burst of fire at the far end of the wall, followed by the explosion of a grenade. Then all was quiet again. Weapons ready, Drake and his team stepped around the remains of the wall. There lay approximately fifty dead insurgents, most torn up by the heavy weapons. A corporal walked up with his team.

"There was one that was injured," the corporal explained. "As we approached, he tried to pull a grenade. We shot him, and the grenade rolled away from his hand and went off, which is what you heard."

Drake looked around at the bodies. Even now after so many patrols, so many battles, the smell of death, the torn bodies, the futility of the fights still assaulted his senses. He shook his head and sighed. At least none of his troops were injured or worse. "All right, load up and let's get home. We'll let the Iraqi troops clean up this mess."

As he led the patrol away and around the crater in the road, all he felt was relief that he and his troops had survived one more fight that meant nothing in the grand scheme of things. The only good thing was that the end of this tour was in sight.

Once they rolled into the base and the platoon dismounting to their barracks, Drake sat down to do the paperwork. Even in war there was paperwork, and in this case, the After-Action Report. After thinking about what happened, he carefully prepared a very sterile report. It wasn't quite as short as Caesars' "I came, I saw, I conquered," but it was concise and to the point. As he summarized what happened, he was determined to leave out the details as to how he came to realize that there was an ambush. He didn't want to open that can of worms. However, that didn't stop the members of his platoon from talking.

It was two weeks and three more uneventful patrols later that he was called into the office of Captain Reynolds, the company commander. As Drake stepped into the office, he noticed the civilian sitting in a chair to one side. He was very nondescript, wearing a short-sleeved shirt, khaki slacks and laced-up boots. Focusing on his captain, he came to a halt, saluted, and barked, "Staff Sergeant Drake reporting as ordered."

Reynolds waved an off-hand salute in return and motioned at a chair in front of the desk. "Sit. I've got some questions for you. They're going to sound odd, but I want straight answers, no evasions, no equivocations. Understand?"

Drake nodded even as he felt sweat breaking out on his forehead. *What the hell is going on?*

"All right. Here is the main question. How in the hell do you keep avoiding getting caught in ambushes? How do you keep avoiding IEDs? Your platoon has the highest rate of any unit under my command in terms of not being caught in an ambush, and, instead, turning the tables on the insurgents. Your platoon hasn't had a single IED hit a vehicle in months, and the casualties are the lowest. Now, this can't be an accident, so spill it. How are you doing it?"

Drake glanced around at the civilian who was lounging in the chair, head leaning to one side, chin resting on his hand. Whatever was going on, this person was involved.

"Ignore him, Drake," Reynolds barked. "Answer the question."

Drake closed his eyes for a moment. "I'm not real sure how to answer it. I know what I see; I know what I feel, and I trust it; but I am going to have a hard time explaining it."

Reynolds leaned back in his chair, hands clasped across his chest. "As I was taught a long time ago, you start at the beginning, walk through everything one step at a time, and stop at the end."

Drake nodded. "Yes, sir." He paused in thought and then began. "I call it a feeling, a hint. The best example is the recent patrol where we encountered insurgents and an IED. As we approached the location of the IED, it wasn't that I saw some indication of the IED; rather, I *felt* that something was very wrong. I've learned to trust these feelings over the last few months as they've never been wrong; and when I first began having them, I found out the hard way that to ignore the feelings would result in bad things happening."

"So, I halted the patrol and dismounted the platoon, who set up a perimeter around the vehicles. I found my attention drawn to a low wall some fifty yards distant from the road, set among some scattered trees and a wadi. It was if I could see the insurgents hiding behind the wall. I directed the troops to engage the insurgents, which they did. While the insurgents added an additional IED to block us for retreating, when the IEDs were activated by the insurgents, we were well away from them and suffered no damage or casualties. As we were aware of the attack as opposed to being caught off-guard, we were able to effectively ward off the attack with no casualties."

"Does that answer your question, Captain?" Drake concluded.

Rather than responding, Reynolds looked over at the civilian. "Mr. Jones, is that what you were looking for?"

Jones stood up, walked over, and, placing a hip on the desk, placed his hands in his lap. He looked down at Drake. "Sergeant, when did these 'feelings' start taking place?"

Drake thought back and considered things. "I would guess about March, more or less. It wasn't like 'boom, they're here' but just sorta began happening."

Jones nodded. "That makes sense." Jones looked up towards the ceiling, and then back at Drake. "What do you know about all this stuff people are calling 'magic'?"

Drake's eyes opened wide. That was not a question he'd expected. "I haven't paid it much attention. I know that some troops have had to intervene in tribal actions where they're trying to kill some of its members for using sorcery, even to the extent of relocating the people to one of our bases." He paused for a moment. "The odd thing is, I know of more than one case where our platoon relocated a family or individuals, but when we went back to check on them, they had disappeared from where they were resettled."

"Fine," Jones continued with a dismissive wave of his hand, "but what do you know about what is happening in the U.S.? Specifically, about the person called the Witch of New Orleans?"

Drake shook his head, wondering where this was heading. "Not much. I think I've seen a couple of things the family's sent me, but that's about it. I've been watching baseball, reading, doing my extension studies, that sort of thing in my off time. I haven't been out on social media except to talk to the family from time to time."

"Well, let me bring you up to speed," Jones replied. "What people call magic, or power, or 'the force' if you will, the ability to do things with their minds which are not natural, this ability to manipulate this power, actually is a fact. Now I'm not talking about pulling a rabbit out of a hat. I am talking about real, honest to God, blow a hole through a wall power. We have seen evidence of portals, individuals capable of creating shields invulnerable to bullets, even doing surgery without opening up a person. Real 'oh my GOD' stuff. And on top of that, we have solid proof of mythical creatures returning to this world. Elves, gnomes, flying horses, well, you name it. If it hasn't appeared, it doesn't mean that it won't. And to top it off, this so-called

Witch has been acclaimed Queen by all these beings, along with a bunch of people who apparently can also use this thing they call 'magic'. She's bringing them into her enclave outside of New Orleans for training."

"Now, the President has assigned a White House assistant as a go-between between him and all these beings. But," Jones held up a finger, "there are those in various agencies who have reasons to believe he may be compromised, that he may not be providing all the data needed to make solid decisions. So, our analysts have given us two options regarding what may be taking place; one, that these people can be an asset, or, two,..." and he looked straight at Drake. "They are a huge threat to our country."

Jones glanced around at Reynolds, who reached over to a folder on his desk and pulled out an envelope, sliding it across to Drake. "Here're your travel orders. You're headed to New Orleans. There, you'll be contacted with your operating orders. You would normally stay at one of the bases in the area, but for this, you are going as having just ended your tour of duty and have been honorably discharged. There's even a DD-214 in there, but don't get excited, it's a fake. There is also a cell phone that will be used for people to contact you and for you report in, along with two credit cards in your name that have already been activated. There's not a credit limit, but don't go crazy; you will have to provide receipts." Drake groaned at that while Reynolds grinned. "So, go pack and turn in your weapons. Your flight leaves in three hours." Reynolds stood up and extended his hand across the desk with Drake standing up and shaking it. "Good luck, Sergeant."

As he walked out of the company headquarters, Drake looked down one more time at the orders which he'd been handed by Captain Reynolds. They didn't make sense. He was supposed to go on detached duty. And not just any detached duty, such as a rotation at the Pentagon or to assist another unit. Nope. He was supposed to become a spook for this Jones guy. He didn't know who he was, but whoever he was, first, his name wasn't Jones and, second, he worked for some three-letter agency out of D.C.

Instead of going straight back to the barracks, though, Drake found an out-of-the-way corner where he could watch the Captain's office but not be readily noticeable. After a few minutes, Mr. 'Jones' walked out, hopped in a car, and headed towards the base entrance. As he drove away, Drake noticed a U.S. embassy tag on the car. Nodding to himself, he headed back to Reynold's office. Nodding to the aid at the desk outside his office, he stuck his head back in the door. "Captain, do you have a few minutes?"

Reynolds looked up from the paperwork on his desk. "I figured you'd be back so I told them to let you in. So, haul up a chair and we'll talk."

Drake looked once more at the orders. "So what do you think is going on?" he asked, sitting down in the indicated chair.

Captain Reynolds clasped his hands in front of him on his desk. "As you probably realize, all this is courtesy of one of the intelligence agencies. There's been a lot of back-channel talk about recruiting people from our forces who have been affected by this so-called magic, and what you did, what you saw, tends to fall into that category." He held up one hand. "Now I'm not calling you a magician, but you smelled out that ambush that would have caught virtually any other patrol flat-footed. So, someone up the command chain called someone else, probably in the NSA, and, bingo! You get to go back to the world, specifically New Orleans."

"Yes, they want you to spy on what is going on in that school, enclave, whatever they call it. But, be honest about what you see. Tell them the good along with the bad. And, find another secure site to save all your reports to. These people *always* have an agenda beyond what they tell you. They may want an honest report, but they may want to have an internal enemy to support their actions. You never know unless you are on the inside, and," Reynolds pointed at Drake, "you're not privy to whatever is going on inside."

Drake shook his head. "So, do my job but cover my ass. Is that what you're telling me?"

Reynolds nodded. "You got it in one. From my situation, I'm losing one of my best men. At the same time, you're getting to go back to the world. Now, one more thing. PTSD is always an issue. If you have problems, find help, either in this group or from one of the psychologists attached to the VA hospital. In any event, don't let this job add so much stress to you that you break down. What you are dealing with in terms of what you have done here, coupled with both the changes taking place in you and the stress of what you are being asked to do, it may break you. So, if it gets to be too much, don't be afraid to bail. Understand?"

Drake looked down at his orders once more. "And my unit?"

Reynolds smiled and nodded understandingly. "You know the drill. You feel responsible for your troops and a bit guilty of leaving them." Drake nodded back as Reynolds continued. "Almost every soldier who has ever commanded a military unit feels that when they receive orders sending them off to another job. But, turning over command is part of following orders, whether you are a squad leader or a commanding general. So, you've got your orders, and I've got to find a replacement for you, hopefully one as good as you. Now, get out of here," Reynolds finished with a grin and a wave of his hand, "I've got work to do."

Drake sighed as he nodded. Standing, he gave a picture-perfect salute to Reynolds and then spun in place, and left, headed for the barracks. There was a lot to consider, but the good thing is that it was New Orleans, with Bourbon Street and a lot of loose women. He grinned. It was time to go to work.

***

Two weeks later, Donald Drake found himself wandering down Royal Street in New Orleans. During the day, the French Quarter was quiet, with shops and bars open; but most people were looking for places to eat at some of the famed restaurants, like the Court of Two Sisters. Drake, instead, was following some esoteric orders. The orders he'd received over his phone were somewhat bizarre. Instead of going to an office or meeting someone at one of the bases, he was told to show up at Ryan's Irish Pub on Decatur at 11:30 a.m. Once there, he was to order lunch, and someone would meet him.

So, at 11:30 sharp, he'd walked into the small pub. Like so many of the older spots, it was narrow and deep, all dark wood, with a bar running along the left side, and a scattering of tables on the right, restrooms and kitchen at the rear. The small sign at the door said 'seat yourself' so he found a table about halfway back, up in the shadows of the lighting and sat down. Glancing around, it was either early, or the locals were still asleep, since the bar was pretty much empty; there were only a couple of men nursing long-necks at the bar. He expected one of those to approach him, but no one paid him any attention, focusing instead on their drinks and a rerun of a baseball game on the TV over the bar.

Following the recommendation of the waiter, he ordered the rack of dry-rubbed ribs and a glass of tea. When they came out, the odor of the ribs made his mouth water after months of military food. Tearing into the rack of ribs, he had to admit that, even though this was an Irish pub, they had great food. He was halfway through the meal when a female voice asked, "Can I join you?"

Donald looked around and found a thirty-ish dark haired woman standing across the table from him. She was wearing a Mardi Gras t-shirt, shorts and sneakers, a small purse over one shoulder. Donald glanced around and saw that most of the tables were still empty; still... "Sure, haul up a chair." As the woman sat down at the table in the chair next to him, a waiter came over with a menu and glass of water. With just a glance at the menu, the woman ordered a burger and a beer, sending the waiter on his way.

Donald looked over at the woman, his meal forgotten for the moment. "Okay, I'm Donald, and you are...?"

The woman smiled at him. "Yes, you are. You're Staff Sergeant Donald Drake, on detached duty from your unit in Iraq." Donald raised one eyebrow. He'd expected to be contacted but he figured some guy in a suit, not the woman setting across from him.

"You still haven't given me a name," he replied.

"No, and I don't need to, but you can call me Mary if you like. It's not my name, but think of me as an old friend, not your clandestine contact, at least for now. Unlock and hand me your phone for a moment. I'll put my contact number in it under that name," she said.

It was clear to Donald it was a command, not a casual request. Donald slid his phone across the table, where Mary entered a number and name in his 'Contacts' file. That done, she slid it back across to him. He noticed that there also was a second contact, one titled 'Mr. Jones'. *Now that's interesting,* he thought.

As he picked up the phone and put it in his pocket, Mary's burger arrived, so for a few minutes, they concentrated on the meal. As Drake finished his ribs, she put down the burger and leaned his way, elbows on the table, but with her head turned away from the bar and other patrons.

"Here're your orders. They're short, but here is some background that you need. What do you know about magic; and I don't mean the stage magician type, but what has been taking place recently?"

Donald paused in thought. "I got the short briefing before coming here. Beyond that, I've seen some things I can't explain. I did some research over the last couple of weeks and social media has stories almost every day. Now, we did stop some villagers from killing a family whose children were being accused of having evil spirits. According to the parents, the children were showing abilities that were, well, considered magical. We just shrugged and bundled up the entire family and sent them into a safe zone in Baghdad. But no one in my unit has shown any unusual abilities."

Mary cocked an eyebrow at Donald. "No one?"

Donald sighed. "Okay, so you must have read my after-action report from a while back."

Mary nodded while taking another bite on her burger. She took a pull on her beer and then looked back at Donald.

"Your story was quite interesting to a lot of people in Washington. That's why you're here, and here's what you're to do. You don't believe you have any powers and yet unusual things have happened around you. Right?"

Donald nodded back.

"So, what we want you to go out River Road, to that magic school. I think it's being called the Queen's School of Magic now. Once there, you are going to get trained in whatever form of magic, of power, that you have. But, as your verbal orders said, you are also going to report on what is going on.

"You see," she continued, "there are a lot of people in government who are very concerned about what is going on there. Is it a cult? Do they have real magic? Are they a *threat* to the country? We need to know. And the only way to know is if we get someone inside the school, someone who can report back to us."

Donald's phone chirped, showing it had received a message.

"That will be a message with a link to a web site. They're very internet savvy; enough so that we can't penetrate their firewalls. That's why we need someone inside. When you go to that web site, you'll find it lets you ask to come to the school for training. That particular site is very open, almost like you're applying to college. So, sign up, go out there, and find out what's going on. And then report back. If we find that it's benign, then fine, we'll work with them. If we consider them a threat, well, we do have a lot of military." She held up one finger. "And when you are on line, pull up the videos of the so-called 'Witch of New Orleans' and her school. You really, really need to know what you are going into. There're a whole lot of creatures there that are not human, but are highly intelligent. Just be diligent in your research, just like anyone else that would be thinking about the school."

Donald considered what was being asked of him. Finally, he asked the main question that was hovering in the back of his mind.

"You're thinking a Waco situation, aren't you?"

Mary sighed. "That's a possibility, but that was the biggest screwup ever. We definitely don't want that situation if we can avoid it, but we can't avoid it unless we know what is going on, and you're our 'in' as regards to getting information about what is going on in that place. So, any questions?"

Donald leaned back and, taking a pull on the beer bottle in front of him, closed his eyes and considered what he was being asked to do. He wasn't in the intelligence business, although he had done some work in that area while in Iraq; but it wasn't anything like what he was being asked to do. On the flip side, it would give him the training for whatever was happening to him. He nodded to himself. He'd sworn to protect the U.S. from enemies both foreign and domestic, and if this was a cult of personality that was a threat to the U.S., then, yeah.

He opened his eyes and looked across at Mary. "I'm in. Now, how do I get messages out as they'll be monitoring phone and internet usage?"

Mary nodded. "We thought of that. When you open your phone, you'll see an app with an 'S' on it. That is a special app. Your phone connects like normal to the local cell towers. But, it will also connect securely to a 'Stingray' tower we have set up across the river from the school. To do that, you click on the Stingray app," Mary explained. "That changes the signal to a scrambled one that only connects to the Stingray tower." She smiled at Donald as he stuck the phone in his pocket.

"Good. Now," she raised her hand and motioned the waiter over. "I'll take care of the checks. It's the least...or most I can do. Good luck, sergeant."

Later that day, back in his hotel, Donald opened his laptop computer and went online to the web site. He looked at it, and from the first moment, it was clear that it was very professionally done. The graphics were sharp, the forms were easy to fill out and submit, which he did. It had to be an automated site because as soon as he submitted the forms, he got an immediate email giving him the directions to the school.

He clicked back on his computer and double-checked his application to the school. Nope, no mention that he was an active member of the military, just his basic data such as address, and so forth, and what changes he was experiencing. Okay, *so I'll go in as a former member of the military, discharged, and was planning on going back to college when this stuff started.*

Then a second email arrived from 'Mr. Jones' with an attachment. He opened the attachment and began reading. The more he read, the more worried he got. It centered around the fact that the people on this property had crowned someone named Sha-Ri a' Alean de

Camlin as their Queen. There was even a link to a video. As the video played, Drake leaned back in the chair, amazed at what he was seeing. There were all sorts of beings as well as a lot of people kneeling in front a young red-haired woman standing under a huge oak, a woman who was being crowned as a sovereign leader. The U.S. didn't have any royalty; it had been thrown out during the American Revolution. Yes, there was a form of royalty but they were the music and movie stars with no more real power than the fanbase influence. But these people, they were following her as someone with real authority, which could create a huge schism between this group and the U.S. government.

Donald froze the video, focusing on the tableau on the screen. He shook his head. *I think this is going to be more complicated than I originally thought.*

***

Drake spent another day just being a tourist while picking up a couple of regular suitcases along with a full non-military set of clothes. While he had some civilian clothes, ninety percent of his stuff was what he would wear around a military base. He stripped all the tags, and then found a laundromat and ran everything through the washers and dryers so it didn't look like it was just off the rack. Finally, he added these to his existing civilian clothes to complete the look of someone just out of the military. He kept a couple of pairs of camo fatigues and his boots, just like any other veteran would do; the rest he put in a closet-sized storage unit. The only thing he had to remember was to relax around others. He had to drop his shoulders a bit, relax his stance and not bark an answer to any questions.

The next morning, he tossed his suitcases into the backseat of his car and, following the directions he was given, drove west out of New Orleans to River Road and Plantation Row. The traffic on River Road was heavier than he expected for a narrow road in a thinly populated area. He drove past a large number of the old plantation homes, some restored while others were in severe decline. Then he suddenly hit a traffic backup on the road as he came up behind what was clearly a tour bus. Diesel fumes from the bus forced him to roll up the windows as the traffic inched along. Finally, he came upon a fenced property on the right. Standing along the edge of the road were a bunch of people with protest signs calling for, among other things, the arrest of the Queen, the registration of all magic users, and even the imprisonment of all magical users and beings, as if that was even possible.

He grinned when he realized that this must be the edge of what was now called the Queen's enclave. He finally reached an entry drive with a sign identifying it as the Queen's School and turned in, stopping as a guard waved him down. As Donald showed the guard his acceptance email, other guards were paying close attention to the nearby demonstrators. As the guard handed back his identification, Donald asked, "What's with the people with the signs?"

"We've tried to keep a low profile out here," the guard explained. "For a while, the main thing was people trying to take photos of the facility, of the folks here, which still happens. But, recently, there was an attack on the facility."

"An attack? What happened?" Donald responded. He hadn't heard about that.

"A team tried to penetrate the grounds and kidnap people. Luckily, one of our trainees reacted quickly and we, well, actually the trainee by herself, managed to take them out. And we are having to send out recovery teams to bring in threatened people. Recently, a tactical team had to go to Los Angeles and save a clan of elves from being sliced and diced by some corporate lab. That made all the papers."

"Wait a minute. You've had people being kidnapped and treated like lab rats?"

"Yeah. You need to be aware of what is going on. These nuts," the guard continued, motioning at the shouting protestors, "are being paid by someone. We managed to corral one and get him to talk. They're a bunch of paid agitators, paid by some big money outfit to stir people up against us. So, just keep your eyes open. Anyway, head on up to the main buildings and park where the other cars are."

Donald nodded and headed up the drive which ran beneath rows of huge oaks that completely overhung the road. As the trees opened up, another guard waved him to a parking area already packed with cars, pickups and vans.

Climbing out of the car and, leaving the suitcases for now, Donald walked towards the restored and impressive plantation home. But, as imposing as it was, the other beings walking around the property, training, and so forth were still a shock. Even being prepared by the videos, the reality was almost overwhelming. There were the flying horses with horns, *Pegasi,* he thought. In the distance he could see elves training with humans everything from martial arts to high powered magical arts. Even as he walked towards the front steps, he had to stop suddenly as several kids, both human and elven, along with three Pegasi colts went charging past. Bemused, he headed on up, stopping at two guards in tailored green and gold light-weight uniforms standing in front of the steps to the main building. What really got his attention was that the two guards appeared to be *elves.* When he told them he was new and checking in, one of the guards welcomed him to the school and gave him directions to the main desk. Thanking him, Donald mounted the steps and entered the school.

Walking through the doors, he found himself in an immaculately maintained and decorated entry room, a room that was probably a formal parlor in the original home. There was a desk at one side manned by a young mixed-race woman, apparently in her twenties. That began a whirlwind of movement that momentarily reminded him of the times he had changed units in the army. When everything was done, he'd received a key to a single room, a folder with the basic rules, wi-fi passwords, meal times, and a map of the facility. Even as he finished the paperwork, the young lady at the desk looked sharply at him.

"Something is bothering you. You're concealing something. Spill it."

"Excuse me? I'm not hiding anything," Donald replied.

"I'm Stella, and I'm an empath. Something is there, buried in your mind. I know people try to hide things in their mind, but around here it's virtually impossible. There are too many with empathic or similar powers. So, spill it. You'll have to anyway."

Donald sighed. He'd hoped that he wouldn't be challenged so early, so he pulled out his story about being a recently-discharged veteran and was having to deal with both PTSD and some weird powers that let him feel when something was wrong. He gave Stella a quick summary of his patrol, intimating that it was at the end of his tour in Iraq and he'd been given a medical discharge as the doctors couldn't figure out what he was talking about.

Stella looked across the desk at Donald, and then, to his surprise, she stood up, came around the desk, and gave him a big hug. She stepped back with an understanding smile on her face, her hands still on his arms. "I get it. I've had to deal with hearing other people's thoughts, their feelings ever since that weird night. Here, I'm learning control; how to focus on one person, how to dial out what is best described as 'noise' of everyone around me. It was literally driving me crazy. Now, have you tried to do anything, like creating light or fire?" Donald shook his head.

"Good, and *don't try* it. There've been way too many deaths from someone trying to use their newfound power, usually trying to call up fire. They set themselves and, sometimes, people around them on fire. These powers can be very beneficial, but they can be very dangerous, so let our teachers work with you. Okay?"

Donald nodded again.

"All right. It's coming up towards lunch, so go grab your bags and find your room; it's on the east side of the buildings. You'll hear the lunch bell and it is served in the dining area on the back side of this main building. Today, just get familiar with the facility, and tomorrow morning after breakfast, head for the rear porch. Someone will find you. Welcome, and good luck," Stella finished, giving Donald one more hug.

Shaking his head, Donald walked back out, grabbed his bags, and then started wandering through the building. He found the stairs easily enough and he found his room on the top floor. Opening the door, he pocketed his room key and then tossed his bags on the bed.

He nudged the door shut, and then, pulling the phone out, clicked the Stingray app and, pulling up Mary's contact number, opened up a text window. *I'm in,* he sent. And then, after looking around the room, began unpacking. *This is going to taking some getting used to,* he thought.

***

The next morning, Donald walked out back and stood on the rear porch, watching a wide range of people training to use their powers. What amazed him is that the powers appeared to be extremely varied, both in type and in power. One high school-aged girl was exercising her powers to punch holes in a thick piece of steel. Off to one side, there were people; well, he thought they were people. They were a combination of animals and humans. *Shapeshifters* came to mind. For some reason he found himself attracted to a woman who was a human-like lion, complete with full body hair and a tawny mane. Dressed only in a workout bra and shorts, she was tossing her opponent, a male werewolf similarly dressed, around like it was nothing. They looked to be evenly matched but there was something in her approach, her muscle memory, her movements that reminded him of the special forces members he'd run across. He couldn't help but smile. As the two separated and caught their breaths, the woman's head jerked up and she spun, looking straight at Donald. She stood there for a moment, and then smiled at him and nodded. Taking a deep breath, she turned back to her opponent to go again.

Drake turned back to watching the others. *Damn. I must have reached out with my mind to her. That's the only way she'd have known. Gotta be more careful...but...*he glanced around at the woman again. *I thing I'd like to know her; yeah. Definitely.*

He was jerked out of his thoughts when a man walked up to him. Just slightly shorter than Drake, there was an aura of power around him. "Hi. I'm Rafe McMahan. Stella says you are dealing with some form of mental powers."

Donald nodded and extended his hand, which Rafe shook.

"Yeah. I seem to be able to detect when something's wrong. And..." he paused for a moment, considering telling Rafe about what just happened. Mentally, he shrugged; *gotta learn control, anyway.* "And I was watching the shapeshifters working out over there and, honestly, found myself very intrigued with the lioness. I'm ex-military and can really appreciate what she is doing."

Rafe laughed.

"And probably how she looks as well. Right?"

Drake nodded with a grin.

"Yep. You got me there. But the thing is, I think she felt me looking at her; at least, that is the feeling I got when she turned and looked at me."

Rafe grinned. "Don't worry. Her name is Lynda Pence. How she got here is her story to tell, but you should know, she's a warrior. And," Rafe looked at Donald through slightly narrowed eyes. "Since you're a warrior yourself and you've been on the sharp end, when you get a minute, why not introduce yourself? She's had a hard time since she came into her powers, but she's happy here, being accepted for who and what she is, and not having to hide any longer."

Rafe motioned towards some chairs sitting beneath one of the huge oaks. "Come on, let's talk"

The two walked across the chairs and sat down. After a moment, Drake began telling his stories, how he protected his platoon from attacks. Rafe nodded, and then focused on Drake. Donald sat there and then suddenly heard in his mind, *Do you hear me?*

Almost automatically he mentally replied, *Yes.*

There was a moment and then he heard in his head, *Good. Yes, you have power, primarily mental powers, like I do. You'll get training so you can learn to use these effectively, as well as to be able to mute them or hide them as necessary.*

Rafe paused and then continued, this time just talking normally.

"You will also get trained in powers you probably don't realize you have. For example, you should be able to 'shield' yourself; that is, generate a wall of power that will stop an attack, even to the point of being able to stop gunfire. And then there are the basic powers of controlling light, controlling fire, and so forth." He grinned at Donald. "You're going to work very hard, because if you don't pay attention, if you don't learn to control your powers, you can kill someone by accident, or even kill yourself. You're ex-military; think of where you are at with your powers as the same as giving a loaded firearm to a kid with no training."

Donald nodded to McMahan, understanding the point he was making. Even as he sat there, he noticed McMahan's eyes flick somewhere behind them. Donald closed his eyes and focused his mind behind them to whoever was there. He relaxed for a moment, and then smiled.

"Hi, Lynda," he said, not looking back.

"Darn. I was hoping to sneak up on you," a woman's voice responded. The tawny-haired muscular woman, now in human form, walked past and around him to stand in front of him. "You seemed very interested in me, so I thought I would say 'hello'."

Donald stood up and extended his hand.

"Hi. I'm Donald Drake. And you are Lynda Pence?"

Lynda glanced over at Rafe.

"You cheated. You told him who I am," she accused him with a grin.

"His powers tend to the mental, so there's no real hiding from him. You felt him looking at you, didn't you?"

Lynda nodded.

"See, he needs training so that his powers don't bleed over and don't impact others while being able to actively control them."

Lynda looked at Donald while addressing Rafe.

"Well, it's lunchtime, and you're not going to be able to really get started training until this afternoon, so, Don," she said, focusing on Drake, "are you going to invite me to lunch?"

Drake grinned.

"Since I don't have to pay for it, absolutely. So, would you care to join me for a bit of lunch?" He stepped up beside Lynda and took her offered arm, and the two headed off towards the large dining area.

***

The next month passed like a whirlwind for Donald. He worked in the morning learning to control his basic powers. There he found out his ability to shield himself was very strong, but other powers were weaker, which, he found out, was not unusual for someone whose powers went to the mental side. The afternoons were spent learning to control his mental powers. It would be common to train with either elven warriors or the security team commanded by Gunner Williams. The more he worked, the more he became impressed with what they were putting together. As he listened to the people talk, he didn't hear any talk of declaring war on the U.S. However, there was a growing worry that the law as it was didn't recognize all these intelligent beings as being 'human' under the law. This was being reinforced since rescue teams were being forced to going out more and more often to recover magic users and other beings that had kidnapped and used for experiments. And more than once, the recovery teams had come back with people that looked like they had been imprisoned at concentration camps or, even worse, dead.

Evenings found him walking outside, often with Lynda. She was a warrior, which attracted her to Donald. One evening, they were sitting under a large magnolia, occasionally swatting at a mosquito and talking. Donald had told her about his background, but so far she hadn't opened up. For a while she had just sat there, quietly enjoying the companionship. Finally, she looked over at Donald through hooded eyes.

"You need to know who I am, and how I got here."

Donald just nodded for her to continue. She looked away across the lawn as fireflies flitted through the dark.

"It was in Miami. I'd graduated law school, passed the bar and had literally just accepted a marriage proposal. We'd left the restaurant and were walking to a club to celebrate when a man came out of an alley, grabbed me, and put a knife to my throat." She shuddered, the memory of that night still raw. "He pulled me into the alley, demanded my fiancé's billfold, and then told me he was going to rape me, threatened to kill me."

She paused for a long moment.

"And then, something happened; something clicked inside me. In moments, I became the lioness, complete with claws, growing in size and ripping my dress. I grabbed the hand with the knife, crushing it, and proceeded to rip his throat out." She shook her head as she shared the horror of that night. "I'm standing there in my lion persona. I remember turning to face Spencer; that was his name. Anyway, I'm standing there, drenched in the man's blood. I remember tasting it on my lips."

She paused, clearly lost in the memory, and then continued. As she did, Donald realized just how traumatic that must have been for her.

"The taste of the blood..." She shook her head. "The lion inside me seemed to growl in satisfaction. I smiled at Spencer, glad to be alive while all the time ignoring the dying gasps of the rapist. But Spencer...he couldn't handle it. He turned and ran, leaving me there alone with the body. I made it back to my apartment on foot, only to find the police there. I gave them a story about taking the knife away from the man and using it on him. They accepted my story even though the police knew there were huge holes in it."

She sighed. "Anyway, Spencer and I split, and I tried to go on with a normal life; well, normal for what I had become. I had accepted a job at an attorney's office so I used the time between the attack and reporting to work to learn how to control my changes. I also learned what to wear under my clothes instead of normal underwear." She looked at Donald and grinned. "When I change wearing normal clothes, that often means they get shredded, which can be embarrassing. Anyway, it turns out the lawyer I was working for was moving money for a South American mob. They got spooked and decided to eliminate any loose ends, and that included the attorney and me. The mob sent three shooters and, well," she shrugged. "I killed them."

Donald looked across at her, amazed. "You took out three armed killers single-handed? And didn't get hurt?"

"Oh, one bullet grazed my arm," she replied, "but I heal fast. Anyway, I knew the cops weren't gonna buy my 'oh poor me' story. I mean, I had crushed the throats of two of the men and sliced the third one's throat. And besides, I'd have to show my lion form, and I didn't want to end up in some lab somewhere being experimented on."

Donald nodded; he'd seen the results as the teams had recovered people and beings from labs.

"So, I headed here," she continued. "But," she held up a finger. "Things were about to get real weird; well, weirder than what had already happened. As I drove into New Orleans, I felt something pulling me to a park just off Canal. I stopped, went into the park, and ended up seeing Sherry and some other magician hammering each other, with other magicians, cops and security people following Sherry. The magician she was fighting noticed me and grabbed me. Now, he's threatening me, using me as a hostage." She gave Donald a wry grin. "I decided then and there that I wasn't running any more, that I was going to control what happened to me."

"So you killed him," Donald surmised.

"Oh, yeah. I ripped him from belly button to breast, and then tore his throat out."

Donald grinned. "That'll do the job."

"Yeah," she replied. "Anyway, Rafe and Sherry called some high-powered attorneys, got me cleared from the mess in Miami, and, now, I'm here. I'm getting licensed in Texas and Louisiana; Rafe wants me to serve as their in-house legal officer." She leaned back and smiled at Donald. "So, do I scare you?"

Donald stood up, reached down and raised her into his arms. "Not one bit. You are a warrior, strong and proud. So am I. What's there to fear?"

***

On evenings, when Lynda was tied up elsewhere, Donald would be found walking around the yard, talking with one of the Pegasi or elves, or sometimes watching the children, both human and inhuman, chasing fireflies. What would have been unimaginable a couple of months ago now had become just another part of his life. For possibly the first time in his life, he was at peace with where he was.

But late in the evenings, alone in his room, he was starting to have concerns about what he was being ordered to do. He was still in the military and was used to following orders. But, the more he reported, the more he learned about what these people were about, the more he wondered if he was doing the right thing.

It had become clear that these people did not pose a threat to the U.S., or, at least the government hadn't made them turn against it. Rather, it was becoming apparent that the politicians and unethical people in various position, both in the corporate world as well as governments, were a threat to all these people, be they mythical beings come to life or a magic user. His reports continued to describe exactly what was happening; how he was being trained, along with the events that were taking place. Nowhere did he say they were a threat to the government.

What was getting him nervous was the pushback he was receiving from his handlers. More and more pressure started coming down on Donald, disabusing him of the idea that his handlers wanted an impartial report of what was going on. Rather, it became obvious that they had a different agenda and, after stronger and stronger hints, one evening their agenda had come across crystal clear. That particular evening, after he sent up his daily report by text, he got a phone call from someone identifying themselves as 'Mr. Jones', even though the voice was different. That was just one more indication that his handlers weren't being honest.

When he answered the phone, rather than a conversation, he got a lecture.

Okay, Drake, we didn't send you down there to enjoy yourself, to have a vacation in New Orleans. We know that these people are a threat. There are people that are pushing the Attorney General to declare them a terrorist group and we need the data from you to support that. Now listen; if you don't play ball and give us what we want, you can kiss your Army career goodbye.

Donald had spent the rest of the evening trying to decide what to do, how to comply with the orders he had been given. He'd been taught to obey orders, no matter what. As a sergeant in the army, he wasn't paid to make strategic decisions, just implement the orders to the best of his ability. But now, he was facing a crisis of conscience. If he followed the orders to the letter, he would be lying: lying to his superiors, lying to those around him, and lying to himself. What was he to do?

The next day, he'd begged off his training, saying he had to figure some things out. Given his background and experience, the others figured he was dealing with his PTSD, and, in a manner of speaking, he was; except the PTSD he was facing was the conflict in his soul. Did he give the spooks the fabricated data they wanted, or did he turn his back on his career and be truthful to the people he had met, the beings he considered friends, and, especially, to Lynda?

He wandered away from the home and into the woods that ran from behind the home down to the Mississippi levee. There, under the oaks, he checked the ground for fire ants and then sat down and leaned against one of the aged trees. The problem he was facing chased itself round and round in his head. The more he thought about it, the more unsolvable it became, and was really giving him a headache.

As he sat there, contemplating what how to solve the problem, he heard a voice in his head: *You are troubled, Donald. Can I help?*

Donald looked up to see Ramon, the huge black Pegasus, standing in front of him. "You followed me?"

Oh, Donald human, I could feel your distress as you walked past the herd. For that matter, the entire herd felt your pain. I don't know what is bothering you, but perhaps talking to me will help you decide what path to take in solving your problem.

Donald looked up at the Pegasus, his deep blue eyes seeming to peer into his soul. He sighed. "I am being asked by someone to lie, to satisfy their agenda rather than to adhere to the truth. If I fail to follow their orders, my whole career is gone. I will have sacrificed so much of my life for nothing."

For nothing? Donald, I know your story. I know that you have put your own life on the line for your comrades. I know that you have stood between evil and those who simply want to live their lives quietly and peacefully. And, from what you say you are thinking, if you obey your orders, what-

ever they are, you do not feel that you will be able to forgive yourself for whatever happens after that.

Ramon paused and then shook his mighty head. *There is a passage in your people's religious book along the lines of what does it matter to gain the world but lose your soul.*

Donald's head jerked up. "You've read the Bible?"

Ramon snorted and shook his head. *Oh, Donald. My people were there when much of it was written. There were monks and priests that accepted that we were an intelligent people and felt it their duty to tell us of what they felt were the truths in these writings. This particular passage stuck with me because it forms the basis of morality. In simple terms, you can take one step towards evil, which makes the second step easier. You can lie once, and then twice, and then lying becomes what you do without even thinking about it. You can betray those who you feel responsible for once, and then twice, and then the next betrayal becomes much easier. And each time you do these things, you sacrifice a piece of who you really are. You give up your morality, your soul, all that makes you, you.*

If this is what you are facing, think about the consequences, not so much for others but the consequences to you, to your soul. Is it worth preserving what you had if you give up who you are? I just ask you to consider this. Now, I have hints from your mind as to what you are being asked to do, but I will hold that in confidence as you have trusted me in the past, as we have walked and communed in previous days.

At that, Ramon turned and walked back towards the main buildings, leaving Donald pondering what Ramon had said. It all boiled down to one simple fact, the fact that he had to be true to who *he* was. Not what the Army thought he was, not what his handlers wanted him to do, but who he was and wanted to be.

It was mid-morning and Lynda was involved in her training when she saw Donald walk away from the buildings, climb in his car and drive away. Late that afternoon, he returned, carrying a briefcase and a gym bag. She looked around for him at supper but missed him. When she asked around, Gunner Williams told her Donald was down at the shooting range. She thought it was a bit odd as he hadn't been down there before, but he was ex-military and she figured he just wanted to get some practice in. Mentally shrugging, she didn't think anything else about it.

**

Mr. 'Jones' answered the scrambled phone on his desk.

A voice on the other end began with no preliminaries: "Your source is not giving us what we need. For that matter, we believe that he is becoming a liability. If he rolls on us, we will be disavowed by the powers that be, and we definitely don't want that. This is your mess. Clean it up." The phone disconnected, leaving 'Jones' staring at a dead phone in his hand.

Damn. Why couldn't Drake play ball? All he had to do was just give us something we could use, but, no. He had to play it straight.

'Jones' shrugged. It wouldn't be the first time he had to eliminate a potential source of trouble. He picked up the phone again and started making calls.

**

It was Saturday. Donald had asked Lynda if she wanted to go into the Quarter and have supper and then visit some of the Bourbon Street clubs; she readily agreed. So as the sun creeped down, they drove out of the entrance to the school. As he tried to turn onto River Road, his car was momentarily stopped due to a few straggling protestors crossing in front of him. Watching the people crossing in front of him as well as traffic, Donald didn't notice when one of the protestors stuck a tracer bug to the rear of the car. As they drove away, the protestor pulled out his phone and hit a contact number.

It was an easy drive into the Quarter, where they parked down on Decatur. As they were going to a dressy/casual restaurant, Lynda was wearing a frilly sleeveless top and leggings, while Donald was wearing a short-sleeved shirt, slacks, and a leather vest, which was a bit unusual for him. A quick walk into the Quarter on Bienville led them to a seafood restaurant, where they had wonderful dinner.

With a few drinks and good food in their bodies, they started down Bienville towards Bourbon Street, planning to start hitting the bars. Suddenly, Donald's internal alarm started going off. He stiffened, his head starting to swivel. Lynda, her hands around his right arm, glanced at him, clearly concerned. Without stopping, he moved her from his right side to his left, freeing his arm.

As they approached Bourbon, a young dusky-skinned girl came bounding up to them. Donald and Lynda stopped as she looked up at them. What got their attention was that her eyes were *white.* "Hey, mister. I don't know who you are," she began, "but you've got people following you that want to kill you."

Donald's eyes grew wide, and he heard a growl from Lynda.

"Just chill," the child continued. "They won't do anything with me here. I've seen that. But when I walk away, that's when they'll try to kill you. Don't let them. You've got things to do."

Lynda looked at the child. "Just who are you, young lady?"

The girl grinned.

"I'm Sharon, Sharon Broussard." She blinked, and the white eyes were replaced by her normal dark eyes. "It seems that I can see into the future sometimes. It has to be for people or things that are important, and I can't see my future. But I can see a few minutes into the future. If I hadn't stopped you now, you might or might *not* have survived the attack. Now, the odds are in your favor. You, mister, use your powers; you can see the bad guys. Now, I gotta go."

As she turned to go, Lynda called out. "Sharon, when this is over, come see us at the Queens' school."

Sharon grinned, waved, and skipped off, ducking around the corner on Bourbon.

Donald took a deep breath and felt the power come over him. He pulled up a powerful shield around the both of them and then reached out, letting his 'feelings' take over. "There's two back up Bienville from us, two across the street and two down at the corner of Bourbon." He glanced at Lynda. "Do you think we can take them?"

Lynda just grinned at him and nodded. "You take the two back up the street. I'll take the two across the street. Those two across Bourbon will have to navigate the crowd, so that will give us the advantage. So, what are you waiting for?"

Donald replied with a feral smile, "Nothing. On one...two..." Donald spun, pulling the concealed Glock with a suppressor from the shoulder holster concealed under the vest. Even though his targets had already eased their pistols out, Donald had learned his craft in the hardest arena possible, the battlefield. He'd been in similar situations so many times, he couldn't count them. In less than two seconds, he'd taken them both out with double-taps each, one to the chest and one to the head.

Even as Donald spun towards his targets, Lynda ducked and dodged between two of the parked cars, screening herself from the two across the street. She shifted into her lion persona in moments, accelerating beyond normal human speed and dove towards the parked cars on the other side of the street. The two shooters had ignored her, thinking she was just Donald's date and not a threat. That was a fatal mistake. The men were firing at Donald, the rounds impacting harmlessly against his shield. Bewildered, they continued to fire, focused entirely on Donald, oblivious to their surroundings... and Lynda. Lynda glanced through the car windshield and out the side windows to where the men were standing just a few feet away. A jump and she hit the hood of the car and cleared the car's roof, ripping into the two would-be killers. In seconds, they were down.

By now, the tourists on Bourbon had started screaming and running in all directions, making it hard for the final two shooters to get a shot at Drake. They were trying to work through the crowd, but were definitely being delayed. Donald saw them coming and considered shooting them, but the problem was the crowd. It would be so easy for a round to miss, to hit someone by accident.

Shaking his head, he holstered his pistol and, strengthening his shield, just waited for them, his powers now focused on the two men. Amazed and somewhat worried, the two came to a halt some ten feet from Donald, glanced at each other, and then began firing. Once again, the rounds impacted his shield and fell uselessly to the ground. Lynda, meanwhile, was working her way around behind them. Donald caught her eyes and shook his head, raising one hand to stop her.

Focusing his mental powers, he reached out and took control of their minds. Donald could see that they were aware and yet unable to move. That was fine; he just needed a couple of minutes. Keying his cell phone to record, he put pressure on one, then the other. "Tell me," he demanded. "Who ordered this? WHO?"

Unable to resist, the two spilled out the name of their boss, his address, everything they knew. The mysterious Mr. 'Jones' was no mystery anymore. One more push with his power, and both men had sudden, fatal brain aneurysms. He wasn't going to leave them alive, not after trying to kill him and Lynda.

Lynda walked up, glancing down at the two as she walked past, and then up to Donald. He looked her up and down. "No blood," he remarked with a smirk.

"Nope, just broke their necks. Didn't want to mess up this blouse. I just got it, and it survived the change," she replied, grinning. She sobered up. "We need to go before the cops get here."

Donald saw the flashing lights as the police car crossed Bourbon on Bienville. "Nope. Too late. Just relax." He reached into his back pocket and pulled out a folding billfold, flipping it open to the ID and badge, keeping both hands clear as the police began storming the scene.

One of the officers walked up, pistol drawn but pointing away but wary of the two standing in front of him. Before he could ask, Donald handed him the ID. The officer looked at it, and then did a double-take. His head jerked up, looked back at the ID, and then back at Donald. The ID said, "Special Agent; Office of the President of the United States" with the Presidential seal. The badge matched the ID.

"Uh, sir, I'm going to have to get my lieutenant here." The officer paused and then handed back Donald's ID.

Lynda glanced around at Donald. "Office of the President? Special Agent? What the hell?"

"I'll tell you later. For now, just go with the flow," he replied softly. Lynda raised an eyebrow but nodded. He raised his voice, addressing the policeman.

"That's fine, officer. I think our night on the town has been pretty much ended, but not how we wanted it," Donald replied. "We'll be right over here," motioning at one of the cars. They eased over to the car and leaned against it. As they watched, crime tape was being strung, first on the side where they were, and then across Bienville when other officers found the bodies of the other two men.

"I'm sorry, Lynda," he began. "This is absolutely not how I wanted tonight to go."

"Don't apologize, Don. After all, this is the most excitement I've had in months." She gave him a sultry smile. "And besides, the night is still young."

More and more police showed up along with detectives, and then a lot of phone calls were made by various police officials. Finally, a detective came up to the two. "It took a call to the White House, but someone there verified that your ID is real."

Donald nodded and pulled out his cell phone, opening up the recording. "I'm the first agent, but I won't be the last. Now, pull out your pad. Here's who set this up," he began, starting the recording.

***

Mr. 'Jones' was busily shutting down his office. He hadn't crashed the computers yet; they were still sending the last of his data to his boss' system, located in a nondescript office building in the D.C. suburbs when the door crashed in. "Hands up! Step away from the computers!"

His head snapped around, and his hands reached for a command preset to destroy all evidence but he was spun away as several bullets hammered him, leaving him dead, the computers available for the authorities to analyze.

***

Later that evening, Lynda was snuggled up next to Donald on the back porch. Her head leaning on Donald's shoulder, she sighed.

"Okay, 'secret agent man', out with it. What's going on?"

Donald leaned over and kissed Lynda on the forehead. "A couple of things you need to know. First, I'm not ex-military; I'm still in the Army, on detached duty. Yes, they wanted me to be trained, but they also wanted me to find out what was actually going on here in the school. Some people are very antsy about all the changes, the powers that people have, the beings that have come into existence again."

"Now," he continued. "My handler started putting pressure on me to lie about what was going on, so his boss could push the government to declare Sherry, the school, and everyone here a threat to national security. I couldn't, in good conscience, do that, so I made some calls and got in touch with Robert James, who is the Director of the Office of Magical Beings, Actions and Analyses and works directly out of the White House. One thing led to another, and, ta da, I'm a Special Agent working for the office of the President, assigned to James' office."

He sighed. "I'm sorry that I couldn't be straight with you on my background, but..."

"You had your orders," she finished. "Look, you know my background. So many others have similar experiences, so you're not unique." She paused for a moment, the only sounds being the cicadas singing in the trees. "Do Sherry and Rafe know?"

"Yeah. I sat down with them back when I got back from New Orleans after getting with Director James and explained everything. They're cool with the situation."

Lynda reached up and turned his head, giving him a deep kiss. As she drew back, she asked the question Donald dreaded.

"So, what happens with your position in the military?"

"I've been moved to the Army Reserve. Oh, by the way, I got a promotion. As a federal agent, I now hold the rank of Captain. As far as the other goes, I'm now a federal employee, assigned as a permanent agent working with Director James, as well as Sherry," he finished.

With Lynda snuggled into his shoulder, Donald looked out across the yard, lit from the stars and the moon. Even this late, people and magical beings moved around. Fairies were visible, flitting around the trees. He thought back on his life. He'd joined the Army right out of high school since he couldn't afford the ridiculous costs of college. The military would pay for him to get an education, so that was his answer. In his career, he'd fought beside some of the strongest and best men and women the Army had to offer, all in what was effectively a millennia-long civil war in Iraq and Afghanistan. He'd seen what the Islamists did to those who rejected their viewpoint, but in the Army, he couldn't do a lot to stop it; there were too many politicians with differing agendas to do what was really necessary.

But here, he was needed. He'd found that out tonight. He'd found a fellowship among the other beings, the other magicians, and even the people with very minimal or no overt powers who had come to the facility. For the first time since high school, he had found a home. And, just perhaps, working with the people here, he might be able to do more to clean up the messes the politicians routinely left for the military to clean up.

So, *now,* he thought, *my conscience is clear. I can fulfill my oath to the United States as well as my individual oath to protect those who need protecting, those who are now around me.*

He turned and pulled Lynda into his arms, kissing her deeply. After years of moving from one place to another at the whim of the military, he'd found a home.

Roger D. Strahan has lived a varied life. A real estate appraiser and broker, he has also performed on stage, been a semi-professional lighting designer, written scripts for technical lighting productions, and written several books. His most recent series is *The Witch of New Orleans,* which follows the exploits of Sherry Martin through the city of New Orleans.

A native Texan, Roger now lives with his wife, Paula and pups in Port Charlotte, Florida. He can be found on his website, roger-d-strahan-author.com, or by email at author@roger-d-strahan-author.com.

HOW JON CAME TO PUT CHICKENS ON THE CEILING, AS TOLD BY MASTER MAGICIAN ROBERTO THE WISE

BY BARB CAFFREY

This story takes place in the Elfyverse, a place of enchantment and multiple universes. This is a prequel story to the two novels of Bruno (né Jon) and Sarah, AN ELFY ON THE LOOSE and A LITTLE ELFY IN BIG TROUBLE. The name "Elfy" comes from the fact that these magical beings are shorter than the Elfs. (Yes. They're Elfs in this universe, because "elves" is a swear-word in their language. Long story.)

Author's note: I'd always wondered how Bruno (then named Jon) put the chickens on the ceiling. (It's referred to by Lady Keisha, and discussed in passing later by Bruno and his love, Sarah, in the two extant Elfy books.) Now I know...and you're about to find out. – Barb Caffrey

---

How Jon Came to Put Chickens on the Ceiling, as Told by Master Magician Roberto the Wise

"Dammit, Keisha, I want to pull my hair out." Roberto, called the Wise by his students and others, sighed, and sank into one of his sister's cozy chairs in her lavish private apartment set just apart from the rest of her priestly order.

"Why?" His sister, the renowned priestess-Adept Keisha *Madhrogan*, stared at him. "Oh, settle down, brother. I've never seen you this upset about anything. What's wrong?"

"The school. What they're having me do to the kids, especially young Jon who just lost his parents a few, short years ago...it's disgraceful, sis! I swear, they mustn't want the poor child to grow to be an adult. And they've got him thinking he's so much younger than he is, too..."

"Spells?" Now his white-haired sister perched alertly on the edge of her seat, like a bird checking for crumbs. "Are they Dark?"

"Possibly. But they *say* not. And if I speak up, I'll lose my place." He sighed again.

"You could go anywhere," his sister said, bluntly. "Any school would love to have you. But I know you want to stay at Robin Good-fellow...and I'm guessing young Jon's a part of why."

Roberto nodded and wished his sister couldn't read him so accurately.

"Someone has to look after the lad. As it is, every time Jon shows a spark of magic, they have me douse it. I have to tell him he's doing it wrong, and I *hate* it. I swear, the boy's going to be an Adept-class, and you know—far better than I, sis!—that Adepts work magic far differently than the rest of us."

"We can, yes. It depends on a lot of things. But the boy was replicated, wasn't he? To have that age difference, and him not know?"

"Yes," Roberto admitted. "But even if they allowed me to, I couldn't tell him. He thinks replicas are the lowest of the low."

Keisha twirled her white hair, and thought. "They've completely bollixed things up. He's potentially quite strong, they're afraid of him, and they've had you get in his way."

"Yes. It's surprising that he remains so good-hearted." Just thinking about how Headmaster Carlito had mistreated young Jon this past year made Roberto want to spit nails. Flaming ones, even—directly at Carlito. "The worst part is, because he thinks he's much younger than he is, he won't be prepared when he hits the Age of Ascension. And soon that's exactly what's going to happen. They'll throw him out, saying he's too old, and he'll be bewildered, angry, and hurt, with no place in the worlds at all! That's why I need your help."

"Calm down, brother. Of course, I'll help." She twisted her ring of office, a small onyx dragon, 'round and 'round her finger. "I can at least look for a way to save him, to get him away from the School. That should allow him to find his talents and grow into manhood unscathed."

"Would you? Please? I swear, this kid is good, but he's been so squashed...he only has one friend..." *And that Leftwich is no prize. Though he does have a cheerful heart, and a cute dog, too.* Hellfire, Jon even liked Leftwich's dog Annbess, even though Jon was the one who, most of the time, had to walk the poor thing, as Leftwich kept getting thrown on punishment detail and couldn't. Jon, at least, had been spared *that*, mostly because of the sinister hints he'd given to Head-master Carlito.

Too bad the rest of them hadn't worked, he thought. That's why he'd come to talk to his sister, one of the most powerful women he knew in any Realm. If she couldn't help Jon, no one could.

"You do know who his parents were?" Keisha asked idly.

"Not really. They were high muckety-mucks, or Jon wouldn't have been able to be replicated. Much less sent to St. Robin Goodfellow's School."

"I love the school's name," Keisha said, snickering.

Yes, the full name of the school was "St. Robin Goodfellow's School for Scions of the Nobility and Other Unfortunates." Some-times Roberto wondered if he, himself, was one of the unfortunates, especially as he'd been educated there himself, many years ago.

Keisha broke into his thoughts. "I know who they most likely were, if you want—"

"Don't tell me, sis. My head hurts enough as it is. No one should be treated this way. Not a ditch-digger, not a street rat...no one. His parents aren't relevant. At least, not yet—right?"

"I agree." She frowned, and drummed her fingernails on her oaken desk. "So, you're here. You must have some ideas for the poor lad. What do you think you should do, and more importantly, what do you want me to do?"

"I'm going to do whatever I can. But I'll need backup, sis. He's in big trouble. Headmaster Carlito hates him. Most of the boys follow Carlito's lead, and play nasty tricks on him. And as almost all of his magic up until now has been doused by me, or 'redirected'—" Roberto hated that word with a passion "—he can't even respond! It's wrong. Can't you help?"

"I can. But it may not be easy." She thought for a minute, wrote something down, and then smiled. "Have you ever had any visitors from the Human Realm at the School?"

"We do every year. Why?"

"I want to send someone in specifically for young Jon. Someone talking about Northern California—"

"Where your good friend lives."

"Lived. Yes. She's dead now, is my sworn-sister Jelena, but she has relatives there. And I think one of them might even be Jon's age..."

"Anything would be better than what young Jon is facing right now, Keisha." *Hells, he's almost certainly an Adept-class, being mistrained, picked on and abused...how much worse can it be for the poor lad?* "Even going to the Human Realm to visit your late friend's relatives has to be better than this."

"Then we'll get him there. Somehow. But for now—" she gave him a pointed, long look "—you have to find a way to properly train him. At least, part of the way. So he can access his magic and fight back."

"How? Carlito won't let me do a blessed thing!"

"Let me work on Carlito. And if he doesn't bow to me, well, maybe he'll like life as a slug."

Roberto puffed a laugh. Yes, there were reasons you didn't want to get on Keisha's bad side.

His sister's face grew pensive. "I wish Hallvard was still alive. He'd definitely make Jon interested in the Human Realm, could I but get him here."

Roberto had liked Keisha's Human husband very much. Hallvard had been a good, level-headed man, with a strong Earth sense and a great counterpart for Keisha.

"I do, too. But as he's not—" Roberto broke off, because he didn't know what else to say. He'd always been bad with emotions, anyway.

"I will find a way. And I will talk with Headmaster Carlito. Anything else?"

"Just…I hope we find a way to spend *Ba'altinne* together this year, sis. Or at least one of the major holidays. It's been too long since we shared a good meal—" Even today, he'd managed to carve out two hours, no more, before he had to be back at Robin Goodfellow to teach astronomy. Magic was later in the evening, which had never made any sense—astronomy was far more fun when it was dark— but Roberto didn't make the rules.

He only found ways to get around them.

"I hope we do, too, dear brother." Keisha's smile lit up her violet eyes, and he felt warmed even though they hadn't physically touched. "If I can, I will. Count on it."

And Roberto left it at that.

A few weeks later, Roberto was teaching magic in his favorite class-room. Everyone was seated at desks. The cauldrons, mortars, pestles, herbs, and other accoutrements of magic were put away, as this was to be a theoretical lesson only. Jon excelled at these, so, of course, he was paying attention. But aside from him, only his friend Leftwich seemed awake.

Had Strohan taken them all on a long run again? Physical training was supposed to be only every other day, but Strohan liked to give what he called "snap quizzes" while running, and could make nearly anyone run. Not Jon, for some reason but just about anyone else.

Well, it didn't matter. All that did matter was that this gave

Roberto his excuse to let all of 'em go but Jon. And then start telling Jon more about the Human Realm, all while conversing in English, which he'd been teaching Jon for the past several weeks since he'd last talked with his sister. Keisha had managed to make the headmaster back off, but hadn't managed—as of yet, anyway—to get a Human visitor into the school. She had, however, managed to send a Trader in, and young Jon had been fascinated by the Trader's tales. Especially as the Trader had actually traded with the Humans, as well as the Elfs, the Trolls...she had entranced the whole class when it came to her quick escape from the Orc Realm, but Jon had paid most attention to the Humans and Elfs, as he ought. Roberto had been fiercely proud of him.

Roberto still had to let the kids in his class go, though, before he could talk with Jon at any great length. But he refused to make it easy on any of them as he truly was displeased. He looked at red-haired Pyotr, who'd put his head down on the desk and was snoring away.

"Putting you to sleep, am I?" Roberto purred.

"Um, no sir!" Pyotr snapped out, sitting bolt upright.

"You can write me a five-thousand-word essay on the problems a distracted magician might face while dealing with a Dark Elf for tomorrow morning, then." He ignored Pyotr's downcast face, and looked at the rest of the class. "The rest of you can write me a one-thousand-word essay on the same subject. Class dismissed!"

As usual, Jon hung back to talk with Roberto. (Had he not, Roberto probably would've had to stun the poor kid with a spell, and then try to talk with him in the middle of the night. Bad business, that.) "I'll have that essay for you by tomorrow, sir—" young Jon said. His earnest face, his every-which-way brown hair, and his thick glasses had made him a laughingstock when he'd showed up at Robin Goodfellow four years ago. But there had been something about the lad that called to Roberto, and until this year he'd been able to help Jon find his own way despite the absence of parents, prestige, or any vestige of friendship except for Leftwich. Then Carlito had become headmaster, and everything had gone to the Hells...

"That's all right. I'm sure you'll do fine. But I have something else to talk with you about now." Roberto schooled his face, and did his best to look encouraging but as if he weren't trying too hard. Boys could sense that, and they'd run from it. Even Jon.

"What, sir?"

Yes, young Jon was unfailingly polite. Maybe that was one reason Roberto liked him so much. But that was beside the point; he'd best get to getting.

"I've been remiss in saying this, Jon, but there's more to life than just St. Robin Goodfellow, you know."

"You mean…girls?" Jon looked scandalized.

"Well, yes, but that's not what I meant." Trying to suppress a smile, Roberto went on. "There are many places for a magician. Some of them, like the Human version of Earth, don't seem to use much magic, but magic still exists there. With subtlety, you can do a great deal; with additional power, which you have—"

"But the kids all say I have nothing! That I'm no one! And that—"

"That's absurd." Roberto loaded his words with certainty. "You are Jon, and you are important because of that. No other reason." Roberto glared, and Jon had the sense to shift from foot to foot. "You are a smart young man. You know better than that!"

After a pause, Roberto went on. "Besides, you are a much stronger magician than you realize." Before Jon could butt in and say he wasn't, Roberto pointed to the blackboard. "Could you wipe that board clean for me?"

Jon waved his hand, and the board was clean.

"See? No one else in the class could've done that."

"You could." Jon gave him a long, level look. "I've seen you do it before."

"Well, yes. But I'm an adult magician with full command of my powers, and am considered a reasonably strong Master. No one else in this class has my potential—except you, and you are far beyond me."

Jon started to stammer, but Roberto would have none of it.

"Why do you think we're talking in English right now? Why do you think I taught you English? Why do you think I want you to realize that you have value and worth?"

Well, that third question didn't have much to do with the others, but he hoped Jon would catch his meaning.

"I thought it was because you were encouraging me in my scholarship," Jon said, very quietly. "I know I'm smart. I learn quickly. And I had thought of being a scholar. Like you."

Roberto felt warm, somewhere deep inside. He truly wished Jon was his son at that moment, because no one could've paid him a bigger compliment. But this wasn't about him. It was about Jon. He redirected the conversation, and got back to business.

"I invent things," he told Jon. "And yes, I am learned, and yes, I am a scholar. But there are more ways to serve yourself than that. And your talents, Jon, are as big as the ocean, as wide as the worlds, and as deep as the Void itself."

"I didn't think the Void was deep so much as it just *was*," Jon said, puzzled.

Roberto inwardly rolled his eyes, knowing full well as a teacher he couldn't show his frustration. "That may be so. But my point is that you, Jon, can do as much as you put your mind to. You have many strengths, talents, and gifts to draw upon. And you can use them in different ways than most."

"How?" Jon asked him.

"Well, look at the blackboard," Roberto said. "Look what you just did! You waved your hand, and the words were gone, right?"

"Yes, but...that's how you do it."

"Wrong." Roberto looked closely at Jon. "I first draw upon images that I learned long ago. And then I use those images to get at my power. And that shortcut allows me to use the wave of my hand to get rid of the words. That isn't what you did, is it?"

"No..." Jon thought. "I just waved my hand and told the magic to remove the words."

Yes, this youngster had power, all right. To do that without altering the chalkboard itself was a heavy and sophisticated piece of magic for most. But Jon had done it, easily, without any strain at all. And obviously didn't see the significance of it.

"Well, that's something very few magicians can do without practice, and lots of it," Roberto told him, as gently as possible. The Hells with mis-training this boy; it was time to tell him some home truths. "I think you have a lot of talent, Jon, for magic. But you aren't like the other boys here. And the curriculum they have set up doesn't suit you at all."

"Then what can I do?"

"Find your own way, child." Roberto reached out and dared to ruffle Jon's hair. "You can do it. Just use your imagination."

Then, hoping that gave the youngster something to chew upon, Roberto packed up his stuff and went to his quarters.

The next day, Roberto took in all the various essays—Jon's, he scanned quickly, and was inwardly delighted with the clarity and cogency of Jon's arguments. That young man was going to go far, if only he could be brought to some semblance of his actual talents and worth—but he had to teach the rest of the dullards before he could talk with Jon again. And as there was a full Moon tonight, Roberto had thought they might head off to *Geadheil Mebrugud*—or at least close to it—as no one else would dare the magical portals there with the extra energy thought to be granted to them by the Goddess at the full Moon as they might cause grief to lower-ranked magic users than he and Jon. They could talk in private, and he could maybe show Jon just a few of the spells he'd put together, and see if Jon could learn how to improvise on the fly.

Several hours later, Roberto paced inside his small suite of rooms. It wasn't quite moonrise, so he didn't want to give away anything to Headmaster Carlito. Technically, he wasn't supposed to leave the grounds except during authorized furloughs or legal holidays. Doing so was grounds for immediate dismissal. *To Hells with that,* he thought impatiently. *Jon needs my help, and he's going to get it. If Carlito sees me, I'll just stun him and move along. I know I'm more powerful than Carlito ever was...and Keisha will back me even if Carlito figures it out.*

He didn't like thinking about politics, but there it was. Roberto knew Keisha was powerful. Even if he, himself, was not an Adept, he also could be a power...and it was time to let Carlito know it. Quietly, if need be; forcefully, else.

But hopefully that night would not be tonight.

He wished he had a way to get a hold of Keisha, but his urgent message hadn't gotten a reply. That's how he knew she must be closeted with some high sticklers somewhere; anything else, she'd at least send him back a message (maybe even by passenger pigeon; they'd recently brought them back using frozen genetic material). He knew she'd have helped, providing she wasn't taken up with her other duties. That's why he'd gone to her in the first place. He knew his sister hated those who abused their power, especially over children, even more than she hated the Dark.

She knows this is necessary, he thought stubbornly. *Jon's an Adept-class mage, or, at least, he should be. He has to have help. He has to start realizing who he is and right now. And he must start to use that creative brain of his to start thinking of solutions, sooner rather than later.*

He sat down to think and wondered just what, if anything, he could use to spark Jon's creativity. Not to mention give him the idea that yes, indeed, he could do magic and lots of it.

Then his backpack chirped. It was midnight. Time to go.

He went to Jon's room, where, once again, Leftwich was snoring away merrily. (Sometimes Roberto thought the only reason Leftwich liked Jon was because of how Jon tolerated his snoring.) But Jon, himself, was studying—not surprising, that.

"Want to get away?" Roberto asked him.

Jon just laughed.

"Take my hand, then. And we'll go...elsewhere." In an eyeblink, thanks to the spells Roberto had set up all day, they'd landed just outside *Geadheil Mebrugud*. He thought it was too risky to go in there before he'd talked to Jon; magicians had fallen so deeply into their meditations before, in that place, they couldn't come out of their trances. That would not help Jon, if it happened to him, and it was more likely than not considering how much magic Jon had coupled with his overall lack of proper training.

Despite the lack of the sun, it was easy to see here due to the starlight, moonlight, and other-light...for some reason, the magic here illuminated things, just outside of *Geadheil Mebrugud*. The pale blue light of the magic was unearthly, but Roberto had gotten used to it over the years.

"Wow!" Jon raised his eyebrows. "Blue light? Where are we?"

Roberto told him, then said, "We don't have a lot of time, but we have a few hours. I wanted to tell you—then maybe *show* you—a few tricks my mentor showed me, years ago." It had taken Roberto a long time to figure out just what was going to work, and this should; besides, his mentor really had given Roberto a ton of help, years ago, and it was good to think of old Fenris for a change.

Roberto hadn't brought any of his new "thinking backpacks," because he hadn't wanted to complicate the issue. But he had brought a regular backpack with magical supplies, things that might help with transfiguration...and a bit of chicken feed, as he enjoyed feeding the birds and knew Jon did, too.

He decided to start there. Even though it was late evening, with Jon's talent, Roberto figured a simple summoning spell should draw at least a few birds to them. He asked Jon to recite it (as this wasn't a spell that worked well by instinct), correcting the errors other tutors had drilled into Jon along the way; finally, the spell was ready, and Jon cast it.

Within a minute, there were at least thirty birds—common swallows, most of them—converging on them. "Throw them some bird seed, now!" Roberto commanded. "And if you know of a way to multiply it, go ahead and do it!"

More birds were coming (more swallows, a few cardinals, and perhaps a spotted owl or two), too, and he knew the bird seed he had wouldn't be enough. Fortunately, Jon had grasped the concept; when he'd thrown the bird seed into the air, he'd mumbled something, and the bird seed had expanded seven-fold.

Neat trick, Roberto thought. *I'll have to ask him how he did it.*

As soon as the birds settled down, Roberto asked Jon to cancel the working to make sure no more birds would show up. Jon did something—Roberto wasn't sure what—and the air was still again. The birds that were already there grew quiet, a few still picking at a bit of bird seed here and there.

"What was that supposed to teach me?" Jon asked, with a quizzical look on his face. It was rather endearing, Roberto thought... oh, if he only could've been this boy's father!

But Jon was waiting for an answer, so Roberto had best come up with something.

"I wanted to see if you could match your magic to the situation. And you did! It was wonderful. You somehow created more bird seed than I had brought, and every bird got to eat; you called over thirty birds within a minute, and I don't know how many after. I couldn't do that, not on my best day."

"I've always been good with animals, though," Jon said modestly. "They like me, and I like them. And I didn't want them to be hungry..."

"Of course not. But you rose to the occasion, see?"

Roberto could see that Jon didn't. He tried again, starting with a home truth he hoped Jon would take to heart.

"Every single tutor, with the exception of me, has tried to dampen your ability."

Jon just looked at him, shocked.

"It's true. You can do many things without studying or learning from books, and that's much more typical of someone who's likely to become an Adept-class mage in the future than not. The rest of us have to learn a different way; we have to build things up, step by step. But that's not what you do, is it?"

"No..." Jon thought. "I asked the Goddess to please multiply the grain, and She did. And with the birds, I just asked if any would come...and they did."

Roberto felt no spiritual energy around, and he would know if Jon was headed for the priesthood by now. Keisha's Order had come in several times to Robin Goodfellow and talked with all the lads, and while a few were likely to join, Jon had never been among those candidates.

"You may well have asked the Goddess, but what you did came from yourself," Roberto said flatly. "You have a gift, Jon. You can do things by instinct that other people can't no matter how long they study. And what you did just proves that."

Jon still didn't seem to understand.

Roberto tried one, last time. "If you think about it, you will realize that you have a way to defend yourself now. You can call birds out of the sky, even at the darkest time of night when most are asleep; you can multiply the amount of food they have. And I'm betting if I gave you something to transfigure—" He tossed Jon an apple. "—you could turn this into bird seed, too. Couldn't you?"

Jon looked at the apple, held it, held some bird seed, closed his eyes...and magically, the apple became more bird seed.

"See? I could not have done that."

Jon's eyes were round behind his thick glasses. "I did that?"

"You certainly did. And there's more where that came from, too."

For the next hour, Roberto worked with Jon on his transfiguration skills, and even taught Jon how to create useful things from pocket lint. (Roberto had always wanted to use that spell, but he'd never had quite enough magic to carry it off. Jon had it, though, and to spare.)

As he wound up the lesson, he told Jon, "Just remember one thing. You have the right to defend yourself. If someone attacks you, or is abominably rude, you can and should defend yourself. But be clever, be smart, and make sure you don't hurt anyone; that's the best way to get their goats."

Jon laughed but said nothing.

They teleported back to Jon's room, where Leftwich continued to merrily snore away. Annbess was a bit more wary; she raised her head, and Jon gave her a good scratch behind the ears. Roberto raised his finger to his lips in the universal signal for quiet (apparently even the Trolls did this, which Roberto found puzzling considering how little the Trolls actually spoke, but whatever), and teleported back to his room for good measure.

All that teleportation had given him a headache, but it had been worth it to see the light in Jon's eyes. Roberto was sure, now, that Jon would be able to use his magic to better advantage. Providing he just believed he could, that is; he'd have to continue to work on the boy's sense of self-esteem, no doubt.

Fortunately, I'm a good teacher, Roberto thought in satisfaction as he started to drift off to sleep. *And Jon's a very good student. He really deserves better than this school.*

The next day started the same as always, for Roberto. He broke his fast, drank as much coffee as he could hold as he wasn't as good on little sleep as he used to be, and prepared to teach his various classes.

About midway through the day, right before he was about to head to lunch, he heard a shout. "Master Roberto! Emergency! Come quick!" Leftwich ran up to him, and pulled at Roberto's sleeve.

Roberto's class had left ten minutes ago, so he didn't have to worry about them. And he didn't want to waste time asking Leftwich, who was panting with the effort (as Leftwich, like most of the boys, had never gotten the hang of the levitation spell for general purposes— and using it was even harder in a crisis), what was going on. He simply let Leftwich lead the way, and prepared to use whatever magic he could as he was sure it would be useful.

Still, he felt no urgency ahead. He felt...laughter? A long-delayed comeuppance, perhaps? And maybe some frustration on the part of the tutors, though his spells to mimic the empathy he didn't truly possess sometimes didn't get things right.

Once he got to the clearing beside the school, though, he understood.

The chicken coop was open, which wasn't usual for this hour. Jon stood before the chicken coop, too, and looked like he was concentrating hard. The usual tutor for natural magics, Farish, was half-in, half-out of the coop. And from what Roberto could tell, Farish was doused with chicken guano.

Leftwich pushed him to the coop and looked at Jon, without malice, but with surprise.

Ah, so Jon's figured out how to do something...I wonder what...

Then Roberto knew, as he saw the coop's ceiling. With birds running about, as if they were on land, clucking and chasing each other as if they were on holiday...except they were doing so on the ceiling.

No wonder old Farish was doused in chickenshit!

"Can you stop it?" Leftwich whispered.

"Did anyone ask Jon to do so?" Roberto asked, not whispering at all.

Farish turned to him in startlement. "Jonny-wonny did this? How?"

"Jon—" Roberto emphasized his name, as Jon, like Roberto, did not believe in the current Elfy convention of rhyming nonsense "—will have to explain that for himself. But he's surely concentrating. Take a look!"

Farish, unwillingly, looked back at Jon and swallowed hard.

"What did you say to him?" Roberto couldn't help but ask this, as he had to know what had finally broken Jon out of his rut. "Did you tell him he couldn't do magic? Again?"

Farish's face said it all, at least, before another daub of chickenshit landed on his nose.

Serves the bastard right, Roberto thought. *How dare he try to mis-train Jon?*

"Never mind. You can tell me later." Roberto went over to Jon, who still was locked in concentration, and gently spoke. "Jon, whatever you're doing, you've made your point."

"He told me I was useless!" Jon grated out and kept doing whatever it was that had defied gravity and allowed the chickens to run on the coop's ceiling. "He told me he didn't even know why I was at Robin Goodfellow!"

"He was wrong," Roberto told him. *Obviously!* "Now, can you reverse the spell? Safely? Without the chickens falling on anyone's head?"

Farish looked as if he had swallowed a live trout. A huge, live trout. But he said nothing, which was just as well. Roberto would've throttled him, else.

Jon made one small, arm motion. He closed his eyes, and Roberto turned back to the coop only to see the chickens slowly descend to the floor, turning right-side up again midway down. Somehow, Jon had thought of everything, though Roberto was sure Jon had no idea such a spell was considered impossible.

An anti-gravity spell. That's what it is, Roberto thought. *And they think this boy has no talent?*

Then he looked at Farish again, and shivered. The man's eyes were panicked; his pupils, huge. A fight-or-flight reflex.

Roberto took Jon in hand and said, "I think we'd better go talk to Headmaster Carlito, Jon. Right now."

And if Farish thought Roberto was doing it for him...well, Farish had another think coming.

Roberto led the way to Carlito's office. Fortunately, as it was lunchtime, Carlito's secretary had gone for her break. One fewer person to watch as Jon was chastised—unnecessarily—was all to the good as far as Roberto was concerned.

Carlito grimaced as they walked in, and spoke. "Roberto? Farish? Why have you brought Jonny-wonny to me this time?" His voice sounded world-weary, but his eyes were hard. It was obvious he'd caught how disheveled Farish was but wasn't about to say anything.

"Jon," Roberto said, "did something unprecedented. He put chickens on the ceiling."

Carlito laughed. "You're kidding me, right? Jonny-wonny, our failed apprentice-mage, did something like that? How? He doesn't have the power!"

At that, Jon threw something at Carlito without moving a muscle. Roberto felt it as Jon did it, of course; so did Farish. But Carlito was caught unawares as a huge snare, akin to a fish net used for a particularly large trout, covered his whole body. Then the trap got tighter, and tighter, until Carlito's lips started to turn blue.

Farish looked as if his world had been turned upside-down since breakfast. This latest spell that Jon—now revealed as a prodigy—had cast apparently was the last straw. He took one look at at Roberto, then at Jon, and fainted.

It figures, Roberto thought, disgusted with both Carlito and Farish. *I always have to clean up after these bastards. They'll never admit they're flat-out wrong to anyone, if they can help it.*

"Jon, as much as I understand—"

"But you don't, Master Roberto! He told me I don't have any power, and he'd never tell you that." Jon scowled. "And it's not the first time he's said that. But it will be the last, because I'm sick of hearing it." He moved his hands, just slightly, and his magical net picked Carlito up, suspended him in the air, then reversed his polarity.

Being suspended in air didn't exactly do Carlito any favors, because between the shock of being turned upside-down, and the continued constriction of his airway, he, too, passed out.

"Jon," Roberto said gently, "by this point, you have to know they're mistaken. Farish is incorrect regarding your abilities; Carlito is, also. The other kids, save maybe Leftwich, couldn't be more wrong about you. You have power. Lots of it. And you deserve better than this school."

Jon turned toward Roberto. His face, Roberto now saw, was flushed bright red, and angry tears had fogged up Jon's glasses. He didn't look like he'd ever let Carlito down, and if Roberto couldn't talk Jon out of this mood, Jon might get into a whole lot of trouble unless Roberto could cover it up.

Roberto tried again. "You don't *need* to hurt Carlito. You've made your point. You have tons of power. You can let him go. I'll deal with him." He gave Jon a long, meaningful look, and hoped that would do the trick.

Jon looked like he was considering all this. "It's not that I want to hurt him. I just wanted him to be quiet."

"I sympathize, truly I do, but you can't go around doing things like this. It's bad for your reputation." Then, Roberto played what he felt was the winning card. "You need to go to Earth, to talk with those folks, the Humans. They have magicians there. They mostly revere Elfys. And you could do quite well there, you know."

"They'd accept me? Even as short as I am? I'm at least two feet shorter than the average Human woman, much less the average male Human."

"Not every Human will care about your height. And really, Jon, there are interesting people there. They speak English, at least where we'd send you—Northern California—and I think you'd appreciate being there. Nice climate. Warm year-round, by our standards. And think about your opportunity to study comparative religions, sociology, history...it's a treasure trove of information! They even have something there called the 'Internet' where you can look up what you need, far easier than anything we have here..."

"Hm." Jon looked struck by this. "And I could study to my heart's content?"

"You certainly could. And I'll help you get there—but only if you let Carlito go. Now."

At that, Jon dropped his hands, and the net floated gently to the ground. Carlito, unfortunately, was still upside-down. Carlito's head gently hit the floor first, before the rest of him followed.

Roberto made a privacy bubble, just in case Farish or Carlito—or worse, both—came back to consciousness anytime soon. And continued to speak in English, as well, just in case Farish or Carlito could get through his spell, as neither of them spoke English nor wanted to learn. It also was an unspoken pledge to Jon that Roberto would back up what he'd said and find a way to get Jon to Northern California.

"I'll never say Carlito didn't deserve this. Nor Farish, either. But you have to realize that after you get a bit of your own back, it's time to move on. They ultimately aren't going to matter. You'll be out of this school soon—" *And just as well,* Roberto thought wryly "—and you'll probably never see them again."

Jon took his glasses off, used his black plaid flannel shirt to wipe them off, and then put them back on again. It was obvious to Roberto that Jon was using every trick Jon knew in order to get his temper under control.

"They told me, again and again, that I am a failure." Jon said this unemotionally, almost robotically.

"They were, are, and ever shall be erroneous." Roberto loaded his words with as much certainty as he possibly could. "You will prove them to be idiots, as you grow older."

Then he banished the privacy bubble and sent Jon on his way.

Five minutes later, Farish woke up. He looked Roberto full in the face, and said, "I don't want any part of this. You can handle it from here." And he took himself off.

Roberto puffed a laugh. Farish was a bigger coward than he'd thought.

It was even possible, Roberto supposed, that Carlito had brain damage from Jon's magical choking spell, much less getting suspended in the air by his feet. If so, Roberto for one wouldn't shed any tears...but how could he cover this up?

I don't blame Jon for any of this, he thought. But...

There had to be a way to keep Carlito from blaming Jon. Perhaps a stunning spell would induce temporary forgetfulness; if it didn't work, he could always call on Keisha and ask her to turn Carlito into a slug after all.

As he laughed, he cast the spell. Carlito's features, already still, somehow seemed even more remote, even more empty. The stunning spell would only last for an hour or so, but while it was in use, it should damage Carlito's memories just enough to keep Jon's name out of the fire.

He sent a quick spell-message to his students, saying all afternoon classes were cancelled. And prepared to deal with Carlito, one way or another, once Carlito woke up.

An hour went by. Carlito's secretary had poked her head in, at one point, and Roberto had sent her on her way, too. She muttered something about this having happened to Carlito before, which Roberto didn't understand, but at least was happy to take the half-day off with pay. Roberto knew he could make it happen, especially as Carlito's memory was likely to be malleable for an hour or two after he woke up.

After an hour, Carlito started to stir. Gently, Roberto helped him up, babbling about how he'd sent the secretary away and hadn't called a Healer because of Carlito's well-known orders (the man was vain, and he would hate to be known as a fainting idiot, even though he was). But that he'd stayed with Carlito until...

"I get the point," Carlito said irritably, waving him off. "But it's night now. Wasn't it just the late afternoon? Something to do with Jonny-wonny..."

"You really should see a Healer," Roberto put in earnestly. *Yes, especially as any spell residue should be gone by now,* he thought savagely. "It has been at least an hour since you passed out." *Lady of Light, please don't let Carlito remember what happened!*

Carlito grunted. "I've been on a weight-reducing regimen. This isn't the first time I've passed out."

Roberto just stared at him. Was it truly going to be this easy?

But Carlito had gone on. "The Healers told me to take it more slowly. They even reminded me I could use glamours—glamours, when everyone with any magic can see right through them without even trying!"

"Though it's considered rude to do so," Roberto murmured.

"Even so. I'm the Headmaster of this school. I need to present the proper image. A glamour won't do!"

Roberto nodded, even though he felt the entire conceit was silly. Carlito had never struck Roberto as being overweight, not that Roberto cared about such things anyway.

"If you didn't eat today, you really should eat something before you head off to take your rest," Roberto said, reaching out to pat Carlito lightly on the shoulder.

"Yeah, yeah, I know." But Carlito seemed touched that Roberto hadn't called the Healers, and Roberto let that erroneous reasoning stand.

After he made sure Carlito got to his room, Roberto sought out Jon. As Roberto had half-expected, the boy was still awake. His eyes grew round, especially after Roberto cast a privacy bubble spell. (It was better to be safe than sorry, and while Leftwich was snoring at the moment, Roberto absolutely didn't want Leftwich waking up to hear any of what he was about to say.)

"There will be no trouble with Carlito going forward," Roberto said flatly, leaving the whole subplot about Carlito's weight-loss journey to the side as was fitting. "He doesn't remember what happened. And Farish isn't about to bring it up, because he's been deeply embarrassed."

Jon looked chastened, but a hint of relief was in his eyes. "I hadn't wanted to stun the Headmaster, sir. I just wanted him to see that I do have talent. I do!"

"Yes, son, you do," Roberto agreed, ruffling Jon's hair again. It got easier with practice. "But my advice now is very simple. Get away from Robin Goodfellow. Go to Northern California. Learn all you can, and keep on learning...and don't let anyone tell you that you have no power and don't matter."

Jon's eyes filled with tears, which Roberto pretended not to see. "You really think those Humans will accept me?"

"I truly do," Roberto said, nodding his head in the Human way for emphasis. "And I can't wait to see just what you end up doing once you're there."

On that note, Jon's near-future plans were settled. He'd go to Northern California, and use the English Roberto had taught him to learn and grow as a person...and as a mage.

And if Jon needs me, Roberto thought, *he can get a hold of me at any time by using the Emergency Book I'm about to give him. But what could possibly go wrong on the Human version of Earth, anyway, that would require my help?*

Barb Caffrey is the author of *An Elfy on the Loose, A Little Elfy in Big Trouble*, and *Changing Faces*. She wears many "hats," as she's also an editor and a musician. She is also one of the biggest Milwaukee Brewers baseball fans on the planet, follows the Green Bay Packers during football season, and keeps an eye on the Milwaukee Bucks during basketball season. (Yes, she's from Wisconsin. Why did you ask?)

She is rarely without a book in her hand (or on her Kindle), and has kept up a blog for nearly eleven years. Find her at https://elfyverse.wordpress.com, and tell her you read her story!

(She'll get a kick out of that.)

KIDNAPPED

BY GEORGE PHILLIES

Adara Triskittenion is a student at Dorrance Academy, her society's equivalent of a technical university, In her first few weeks as a student, she survived three serious attempts by the resident bully to kill her, as recounted in Practical Exercise, a tale found in Fantastic Schools, Volume I, She has now advanced to her second year at the Academy, where life is about to become more interesting.

Kidnapped

It was a beautiful late evening. The ocean breeze was cool, carrying the burnt sugar scent of katsura trees now starting to gain their fall colors. I stared across my desk toward the Pelnir Sea, into which the crescent of Ausonius, the third moon, was sinking through the twilight sky.

The evening's beauty was ruined by the note I'd found mixed with my graded Diagrammatics homework. "Adara Triskittenion. At next Lecture, you will see me after class. Young lady, there are certain anomalies in your work that need explanation. Aspen, Instructor."

On the bright side, it appeared that Serene Master Aspen actually wanted to see me, not throw me out of the course onto my under-padded backside, the way Serene Master Brennan did last year. Nor did Aspen accuse me of anything improper or quote rules at me.

I checked one last time. Homework sets due tomorrow were ready to turn in; homework sets due three days hence on Eightday were mostly complete. I briefly remembered certain classmates of mine, astonished that I started on homework sets well in advance. Start at the last minute? What if something went wrong? They were a bunch of idiots!

Lecture notebooks were in a neat row on a book shelf, the foolscap in-class sheets from which they had been generated lying in separate notebooks next to them. I'd done the readings and taken notes matching tomorrow's lectures. A vigorous swim and jog back from the beach had certainly set my pulse pounding, even after a cool shower.

My townhouse was up on a ridge, so from my top-floor view I could look across much of Dorrance Academy. Most Academy build-ings are only two or three stories tall, those stories starting down on the Academy Plain, so I could peer over polychrome tile rooftops as far as the New School and the high surf breaking at the far end of the bay. In the distance the goldenstone granite of the Great Library was tinged with sunset bronze. The last rays of the setting sun reflected from facets of the quartz towers of the School of Theology, painting the towers with bright diamond speckles.

I had the work I needed to do, prep for the Eightday exam in Diagrammatics II, and the work I wanted to do, comparing carefully Marchanti's *Metaanalysis* with Kaspar's *Triangle Diagrams*. Duty first. I'd read *Triangle Diagrams* one more time, looking for things I'd missed in the first careful read, then read carefully the chapters from Serene Master Aspen's textbook, and finally start working problems – the ones for which he gave worked solutions – from his book.

Well after dark, I'd made a last pass through *Triangle Diagrams*. I'd spotted a few bits I'd missed on the previous read. Marchanti's triangle homework problems seemed much easier now that I'd slogged through a few square diagram problems for Serene Master Aspen's homework. Supposedly it is easier to reduce a diagram, shrink the number of sides and combine interior nodes and lines, than it is to expand a diagram, turning a hex diagram into a sept diagram. That claim seemed to be true.

My stomach growled. Loudly. It was well past dark. The refectories had all closed, but the three all-night bars were open. "Bar' was a misnomer; they all had fine full-course menus. I slipped into my enchanted clothing, not quite armor but inconspicuously hardened. My *gnothdiar* went under my cape. Most of my fellow students would say I was going way overboard on obeying the arming rule. Most of my fellow students did not have an unresolved Death-Pride-Honor duel with a combat duelist. Harold Fourbridge might be banned from campus, but if I walked over to Harmony, at least once a month I found myself being followed by three or four guys. They were not very good stalkers, and fled if I turned to approach them, but they kept showing up.

***

Rainbow's Rest was my usual late meal spot. Some of their prices were a bit steeper than others, though they clearly made their money on the alcohol I did not consume. However, when I said I wanted my steak well done, they delivered it well done. When I wanted lamb chops so perfectly done that the meat was falling off the bone, they delivered. I didn't see anyone I knew, but was happy to sit by myself and eat. Tonight, I settled for clam chowder loaded with clams and stir-fried vegetables. Then it was back home to study.

The exam Friday matched another four chapters of Serene Master Aspen's textbook. I'd already skimmed the earlier chapters as prep. A good hour before bedtime, I'd worked through the first chapter and started doing his worked problems, the problems with the detailed solutions in the back. Working problems is a totally terrible way to learn anything – your knowledge ends up being a patchwork cloth full of holes – but it is a wonderful way to check that you have learned what you read. First you work the problems that have solutions, without looking back in the book. Then you look in the back of the book at the worked solutions, and see what you did wrong. Some of Aspen's solutions are baroque in their complexity. There seem to be much easier ways to get to the same answer. However, the strange solutions introduce really cool tools for problem-solving.

***

I took my breakfasts in Standard Hall with the Army Houses' recruits. Usually I sat with the folks from Violent House. These were mostly first- and second- year students, people like me. However, all the Army Houses had the same rule. If you tampered with your unaging spells before you moved into a House, that being year three, you were out, no longer a recruit. You'd given up on casting powerful spells. Breakfasting with guys (and more than a few gals) who were for sure not sizing you up for tampering with your unaging spells was a lot more fun than eating at the General Magic table. Also, they reacted with respect rather than covert smirks when they discovered I generally wore armor-enchanted clothing and carried a *gnothdiar* to satisfy my weapon requirement. Besides, I could get in line, take my tray, say 'Army House Standard Breakfast' and find it was a lot cheaper than eating elsewhere.

"So, Adara," Gwendolyn Norville asked across the Violent House breakfast table, "have you considered joining us for morning martial skills training?" The Army folks all did combat magic drills before breakfast.

"A little early for me, thanks," I answered. That was true, even if I was being polite. I can get up at half past dark, but I don't like to. A bit before dawn is more my style, just before the sky changes color, made easier by the very long days, close to twenty-eight hours, of the Academy. Also, I'd joined them a few times. They did great warmups, but then they skipped the high-energy drills afterwards, spellcasting to power levels so high you felt your nerves were on fire. I did that on days we did not have classes.

"But you'd get your second void node sooner," she added.

I bit my tongue. I'd done that a long time ago. Gramps Worrow's training almost never killed anyone, but it for sure made you stronger. You kept reaching for more and more power, and after a while you gained another void node.

"I'll get another node, soon enough," I answered. "How is your forging class doing? Better, I hope?" She'd been complaining about that, so I'd distracted her from her line of thought.

Soon enough, breakfast was over. I marched off to my morning classes. The Perception class with Lab exercises would be straightforward. Metallurgy was fun. I was not at all looking forward to Serene Master Aspen and Diagrammatics. It is not true that Aspen kills students for asking stupid questions, but his glowers would kill a dragon. And I'd done something to annoy him. Nonetheless, Diagrammatics is a critical course for where I want to go, so off to Diagramatics I would be. Diagrammatics was my last class of the day.

"Remember, the exam is this Eightday." Serene Master Aspen gave us his usual unconvincing smile. "Please try to go beyond memorizing your homework solutions," he added. "If you want to pass, anyhow."

Memorizing homework solutions, I thought, never works. How can anyone believe that? I suppose that approach is less dumb that the fellow student who had told me she was sure she was getting an A, because she'd worked each of the homework problems five times – not five different problems, the same problem five times – so she had to know everything she needed to know for the exam. At some point, I had asked her 'why did you multiply by two there?' The answer 'because the Professor's solution says so' seemed inadequate. It was not 'the area of the square is twice the area of the interior triangle', and, surprise, she bombed on the exam, the course, and soon thereafter was rusticated.

I walked up to him as he was packing his lecture notes, the notes into which he almost never looked. "You wanted to see me, Sir?" I asked.

"Ah. Yes. Adara Triskittenion, second year student, major in Practical Magic, recently smashed to flinders an illegal golem," he said.

"Yes, sir," I said. Where was he going with this? The golem was last year.

"I thought I'd identified who was in each of the four homework 'study' groups." He put a deep sneer into the word 'study'. "I realized your answers didn't match any of them, except sometimes there is only one path that takes you to the answer. Joining a study group is perfectly legal, and no secret, but which one is yours?"

"None, sir," I answered. "I almost made that mistake my freshman year, but my brothers had warned me it was a very bad idea. Other people do most of the work, and you don't learn much of anything."

"You're doing all the work yourself, then?" he asked. he looked doubtful.

"And using the library," I answered. "Though finding basic books on diagram magic is a bear. I've paid to copy a half-dozen, including yours."

He nodded politely. "That's what we'd like all our students to do. Use the library. So few do. Where did you find that last solution?"

"It's Marchant's development of triangle diagrams. I just rewrote it for squares," I said. He gave me an odd look. "I had to start at the beginning, basic principles, but the process was the same."

Aspen nodded politely. "Very good. Carry on! Do well on Eightday."

"Yes, sir." I had not done well on the first exam, and needed to make up lost ground. Doing poorly on a second exam would be very bad news. I dropped my carryall over one shoulder and headed back to my townhouse.

It was a beautiful day. There was a pleasant, very gentle breeze, the air sweet as wine. Squirrels chittered in the trees. A lone sheep nibbled at the grass, pruning it short in preparation for the fall rainy season, its path dictated by a groundskeeper's spell. I had two hours before dinner, time enough for a vigorous swim before I dug into homework and note-rewriting. I waved hello to friends. There came an odd breeze and shadow...

Blackness.

***

All at once, I was awake. It was pitch dark. No, I thought, your eyes are closed. I tried to open them. Nothing happened. My lids weren't stuck together. Nothing moved. Time to get up. I tried to prop myself away from the pillow. I couldn't move at all. OK, deep breath. I couldn't. Was I breathing? Yes. I was breathing the shallow inhalations of deep sleep, my heart ticking over slowly. What was wrong with me?

"Adara. Don't try to move." The words crossed my field of vision. "This is Grandpa Worrow's kidnapping script." OK, I'd forgotten that script, something he'd given me years ago, when I legally became a landheir. The script was mostly designed to deal with unmen. Every so often they managed to drug and kidnap someone. Whoever had kidnapped me had managed to trigger it.

I relaxed. All at once, the script gave me awareness of what was happening. Someone had plastered me with wards to keep me unconscious and unable to use my magic. The script eventually put up a skin layer that mimicked my mind, so I appeared to be asleep. It also took complete control over my breathing, heartbeat, and all my muscles, so a medico scanning my body would report that I was unconscious. It recorded what happened to me...no, the script only triggered after I was out cold and in some sort of a box. Whoever moved me used good levitation spells; I didn't feel myself being jostled. How long? The script didn't have a clock. I might have been out for minutes or hours or days. My stomach said hours, a fair number of them. Unfortunately, there are a standard set of medical emergency spells for treating people who are unconscious; they transport food to your stomach and deal with other unpleasant issues. If my captors had used them, I could have been out cold for some time now.

Occasionally there had been people moving near me, but they were scrupulous about not talking. There had been a door opening and closing. My sense of touch said I was lying on a quality sheet wearing more or less no clothing. My arms were stretched left and right, with something cold and smooth around each wrist, covering my void nodes. Shackles, enchanted. They were damping the nodes. More shackles covered my ankles and the nodes there. I tried listening, as hard as I could. I heard nothing. No one coughed or breathed or walked across the floor. I could feel a draft of chill air across my scalp. Enchanted bedsheets and a blanket were keeping me warm. Just as well, because I was wearing absolutely no clothing; I'd been stripped naked.

Grandpa Worrow's script kept my muscles from tensing, but the shadow of terror still crept across my thoughts. Unless I was really lucky, no one except my kidnappers knew where I was. At some point...soon...they would demand I do something, or use spells and torture to break my mind until I cooperated. Then, that being what happens in kidnaps, they would kill me and dispose of the body.

The script recorded noises in the room. I listened to what it remembered. It sounded like two people coming into the room every so often, checking on me, then leaving and closing the door. The last time they'd done that was recently; I had a while to make my escape before they checked on me again.

I'd never prepared for this sort of combat. I could feel their wards pressing against me. There were really heavy-duty spell dampers, shackles on my void nodes that would keep me from drawing on them, and a few spells that monitored my heartbeat and breathing. If I tried doing something active, those spells would trigger. I poked the script so I could risk opening my eyes. The place was dark, but not pitch-black. Light glowed around the top of a door. There had to be a faint night light in one corner. I saw no sign of anyone else in the room.

The shackles were attached to chains leading to wooden four-by-four beams attached to the sides of my bed. The chains were attached to solid-looking bolts that appeared to pass all the way through the beams. The tops of the shackle plates didn't look to be heavily warded. If I could touch them with my fingers...I know some contact spells that could deal with them, except I had no way to reach around and touch. The spell dampers hashed anything I might try to project, not that I could put any power into them, not to mention that they'd warn my guards if I tried anything. They were also visibly set to try to scramble any spell pattern I started to set up around me, before I could set it completely. I'd need to summon a spell, exactly, all at once.

Sometimes, Grandpa Worrow had taught, patience was the best solution. Right now, patience was the wrong answer. I had to escape before they got around to torturing me. What I needed was a spell that would release one of my hands. It had to be truly low power, something that did not vaguely resemble a combat spell, so it wouldn't bother their spell dampers. 'Really low power' and 'escape' didn't appear to match very well.

I tried very hard to think. That's never been my strong point. Some people do that, I'm told. They work their way through a problem step by step to a solution. For me, when I'm doing homework, sketches of answers just appear from nowhere. I started considering the spells I knew. Almost all of them would be damped before I could finish setting them. Finally, I saw the unobvious. The posts holding my chains were wood. The least disturbance I could set was a spell for summoning cardboard out of wood. That spell left in the paper everything that had been present in the original wood. You didn't even put power into that spell. If you did it right, exactly no power was required. Once I transformed a slice of beam to sheets of paper, the beam would be cut in two.

I readied the spell. Then I saw the mistake I had almost made. I needed to make a vertical slice. A horizontal slice would cut the beam in two, meaning that when I cut the beam the top half would fall, loudly, to the floor. Ever so gently, I began to turn a slice of the beam linked to my right hand into cardboard. I had to make haste. If I were caught now, I couldn't defend myself.

I felt the chain begin to sag and pulled, hard.

The chain and the heavy bolt that had been driven through the beam landed on my sheet. At a touch, the spells locking my shackles fell away. My hands were free. Leg irons and a collar I hadn't noticed lasted a few more instants.

I summoned all my void nodes, hard as I could. The wards they'd put on me were wavering. Grandpa Worrow's little trick had its limits, which I was breaking. Very soon the guards would hear alarms going off.

Now what? Sloping ceiling beams and cold air from above showed I was under an outer roof, someplace where the season was not spring. The roof was massively warded, as was the outside wall of the room. Blasting through that looked to be a major project, not something I could do in a few moments. Someone had spent a great deal of time warding the room's door.

Gate out? There were wards blocking shallow gates to the Purple Sea. A Deep Gate? Gramps had warned me. That was a total desperation move, and I was not yet totally desperate.

Trying to move soundlessly, I slid from under the sheets. They'd taken every fragment of my clothing. I spotted my boots under the eaves. Someone looked to have forgotten them. I took a few moments to slip my feet into them. Once I escaped, outside, cold, naked, well, that's why there are weather spells, but running in bare feet with people chasing you was not a great idea.

How could I get out? At a guess, the attic had a central corridor, with rooms to each side. There were doubtless guards beyond the door. One of me versus two adults, probably combat trained and with spellcasters, was a losing proposition.

I had to do something else.

The partitions between those rooms looked flimsy. They weren't warded, either.

I needed to distract pursuers. I faced perpendicular to the corridor and put up hard shields. Screeches in the distance were alarms. Something had finally noticed I was free. My blasting spell took down the partition behind me. A second, third, and fourth blasting spell, each louder than the last, took down the next three partitions, farther and farther back. I heard no screams; those rooms had been empty. Combat spells at the ready, I used a much quieter cutting spell to open a modest gap into the room in front of me.

The next room was a dump for old furniture. Its door was unwarded. I dissolved the door latch, enough it would appear to have rusted shut. Then I dodged around the furniture to cut through to the next room. I slipped through and sent fireballs back to where I'd been imprisoned. My bed, stack of cardboard, floor and walls started burning, vigorously. A shove largely closed the gap I'd opened. I'd set a false trail with the blasting spells. Anyone guessing I'd come this way would first find a rapidly spreading house fire.

If I were really lucky, my last blasting spell had blown open the door to that distant room. Anyone chasing me that way would assume I'd escaped into the corridor. It was time to move vertically. Up was impossible. Down looked to be the right answer. Careful use of a cutting spell let me pull a plug from the floor. Two feet down was the ceiling of another room. The floor beams were ironwood, four-by-twelves, meaning they were decently far apart; I'd fit through the gap between two of them. The wood paneling at the bottom doubtless held lathes for plaster. Was anyone down there? I'd drop a section of that ceiling. Loud protests would be silenced with blasting spells. On silence, I'd lower myself through. My trusty cutting spell dropped a section of the floor down the two feet onto the next ceiling. A repeat dropped the lathe and plaster ceiling into the room below. All was dark. There was no telling what was down there. The falling ceiling was followed by silence, not by outraged shouts. I lowered myself over the edge, set Dance of the Air, and let go.

The drop had to be most of twenty feet. If I'd tried it without Dance, I'd have broken my legs. I summoned light. This was someone's very expensive receiving room. The walls behind me were heavily warded. That had to be the entrance to these quarters. At a guess, I should go the other way until I reached an outside balcony. These rooms must be deserted. No one could have missed the roof collapsing, let alone me dropping though the gap.

A central pair of doors, all deeply carved gilded wood, led me to a modest corridor, perhaps only ten feet wide, with more receiving rooms to the side. The decorations were amazing for their lack of taste. If it was metal, it was solid gold. If it was crystal, it had the oily sheen of diamond. A Triskittenion heir who proposed wasting money on this scale would be disinherited. The thought that these were rooms for landheirs was too dismaying for words. Someplace there were likely to be the his and her bedrooms for the master and mistress of the house. I couldn't check; the side doors were mostly warded.

Here, however, was an open door, a dressing room with closets and all sorts of clothing, including an assortment of bathrobes. I grabbed what looked to be the warmest, cut off the bottom, and made haste. Behind me, smoke was curling down into the receiving room from up above. At the corridor's end were glass-paneled doors. They opened to a balcony overlooking a great room, a room on absurd scale. I had to be thirty feet above the floor, and twenty feet below the ornately painted and gilded ceiling. The center of the room was occupied by a dining table; the expression 'larger than a swimming pool' came to mind. The table had to be a hundred feet long. At its far end was an enormous stained--glass window. Presumably the human figures in the glass were glorious ancestors, people I did not know, shown trampling unmen underfoot. From the light, beyond the glass was outside. No outside doors were to be seen.

"You!" The shout was directly behind me. "Unman serf! Hands high!"

I sent a half dozen combat spells over my back, then pivoted to see what I was facing. The fellows in livery had clearly not been expecting my response. One of them was flat on the floor, one was reeling, and two had set solid defensive wards. I was outnumbered several to one, more adults, at least one drawing a spellcasting sword. I let them have it, targeting not their wards, but a length of the ceiling, walls, and floor. The walls collapsed nicely. The ceiling fell onto their heads. They couldn't see me, and would have trouble pursuing. Still, it was very definitely time to go. I gave myself a moment to focus, summoning more power, and blasted the entirety of the stained--glass wall. I'd made sure to catch the window frames. They all blew outward.

Steel shutters the height of the windows started to slide in from left and right. They slid a few feet, screeched loudly, and ground to a stop. I'd warped their rails enough that they could not close farther. Dance of the Air did not exactly let me fly, but I slid down an invisible ski slope, targeting the center of the window. Outside was a lawn and wall.

As I slid, I summoned flame diagrams, the ones we'd seen earlier this term in Diagrammatics. I massively overpowered them, enough that I saw a bunch of their secondary fillers. Tapestries on the walls burned. The dining room table burst into brilliant flames. Someone had spent centuries oiling the wood regularly. Now it was going up in a blaze of glory. Anyone chasing me had another obstacle in their path.

Crossing the threshold, I soared over a stone patio and its low, decorative walls, then dropped fast to the ground. The patio had been another ten feet up, with a line of arbor vitae masking its foundations. I glanced around. I was facing the house's perimeter wall, something a good twenty feet tall. I could see where that wall turned ninety degrees to head around the house. Each corner had a gods-help-me turreted decorative watchtower. Coming in from the towers, and reaching the house, were a pair of ten-foot-high walls. None of the walls had any doors – or the doors were enchanted to be invisible. There might be doors back into the house, but walking back into the building I had just torched sounded to be a bad idea.

OK, Adara, I told myself, *think carefully. Grandfather Worrow's books on combat magic didn't say much about escaping from prisons. That's why you have barristers and money.* The walls were so heavily enchanted they glowed to the naked eye. There didn't seem to be an alternative. I threw a line of analytic spells, ones I had memorized but never used other than in lab, at the walls. Were there weaknesses?

More alarms wailed in the distance. Were those fire alarms, or had I just told them – whoever they were – where I was? I heard guards shouting, their voices getting louder. Someone was closing on my location.

For once, luck was on my side. Folks who waste money this way sometimes have egos to match, and can't imagine anyone getting into their estate to attack their walls from the defender's side. Almost all the wall wards pointed outward. The control spells were diagrams, an enormous lot of very complicated ones, on the inside, not quite exposed to the weather. I'd need months or more if I wanted to decipher them, but I didn't need to. I could see points from which magic seemed to be leaking from wards under stress. The wards were very complex, heavily overlaid, and had never been quite properly tuned. I drew hard on my void nodes, released the limit stops, and hit the leakage points with ward-breakers.

For a very brief while, everything became very bright. My second sight was dazzled. The released energies had smashed outward, leveling a wide stretch of wall. Beyond the walls was a tangle of trees. I dashed. A trail gave me a choice of directions. I headed downhill, pausing only to tighten the belts on my nightgown. A thousand feet brought me to a road, well-paved, with another woods and hill on the far side. Atop the hill on the far side was a castle, a gingerbread confection of white stone and blue onion-domes atop towers. The image nudged at my memory, but I couldn't quite remember where I'd seen it.

Downhill led to a major street. I could see people crossing the road ahead of me. I told myself that if you carry yourself as though you are in charge, people will give you the right of way, or at least not look askance at your somewhat eccentric but perfectly decent clothing. As I approached, I could read the street sign. Avenir del Pescadores. The glyph by the street name was a mammoth's hoof...I was in Capital. I had just torched a chunk of someone's Hotel de Ville. They were going to be annoyed.

The street was lined with small shops. Patisseries. Household ornaments. Jewelry. Fine clothing. The far side of the street was lined with people looking up at the sky. Rather, they were looking up at a pillar of smoke illuminated from within by lightning flashes, the pillar of smoke arising from the chateau I had just escaped. Every so often, there was a crash as of thunder. My side of the street was quite empty. Here, however, was a bookstore.

Inside the shelves gleamed. There was a faint smell of orange oil from wood polish. Behind the counter was a young man in the traditional long white surcoat of a bookmonger.

"Hello," I said, "Might I please look at a map for a moment? I'm trying to find Staunton's Avenue."

"Two blocks behind you," he said, pointing over my shoulder. "Take a left off Fishing Street. Staunton's runs parallel with Fishing Street here—that's Fishing Street we're on. Any place in particular?"

My pursuers would doubtless guess where I was going. "Triskittenion Bank," I said.

"I walked by there this morning," he explained. "It was all guarded. Outside, to your right, left on the first street, then right on Staunton, two blocks. But you won't get in, even if you're a customer; it's locked up. The kidnapping, you know."

"Kidnapping?"

"Miss Triskittenion, the land-heiress. Someone snatched her out of Dorrance Academy." He put his newspaper flat on the table. "That's her," he said.

It was, too. Me, and the golem from last year. He looked again at the newspaper, and again at me.

I broke into a grin. "I escaped," I explained. "Whose castle was on top of the hill behind your shop?"

"Fourbridge," he answered. "Was?"

"Escape got a bit violent," I explained. "Can you not please tell people I came through, so I can get home, as a favor to me?"

"Happy to, Miss Triskittenion." He pinched his nose. "Favor in return? When you write a good book, I'd like first Capital sale rights."

"Sure," I said, "not that I have a book in me." He gave me a card for his shop, Codfish Books, with 'First Sale' scrawled across it. I pocketed the card.

I was two doors down the street when the ground shook. The release of the Presence, from the direction of Fourbridge Castle, was enough to trigger some of my wards. The crowd across the street was pointing and talking loudly; I'd stay on this side of the street where few people would be close to me. On the bright side, those folks looked to be so distracted they didn't notice my fast-walk by them.

Flashes of light illuminated the cross street; that thoroughfare was Bragg's Crossing. Now I was distinctly curious. What had I wrecked during my escape? Excessive curiosity might draw someone's attention to me, but I risked a glance. The castle's citadel was in flames. Once and again, a ward's anchors released. A burst of flame followed. It looked as though the entire building was wood in its framing, very old and dry wood, and their fireproofing spellwork had failed.

Capital was laid out on a rigid rectangular grid. I could take advantage of that to cover my approach to our bank. I followed Avenir del Pescadores for an extra block, cut left for a block and a half, and took the back alley toward the bank. Once in the alley, mostly out of sight, I called all my combat wards. One did encounter an occasional drunkard hiding out of site, the sort of person who would think he could prey on a young adult. Anyone who tried that on me would get a violent and hopefully fatal surprise.

Triskittenion Bank was much of the way to the far end of the alley. For a factoring operation on our scale, the building was small. Offices were not cramped, but individual offices weren't the area of a small house, either. Our warehouses were well outside Capital, where land taxes are much lower. House Triskittenion prides itself on thrift, a practice reinforced by electing our family council and land-heirs. Heath and Moore knew that they had to perform well, or they would be rusticated. For sure, I'd had enough people tell me that if I only gave up on General Magic in favor of something practical, they'd someday support my bid to join the Family Council.

The bank's shields were up, surrounding the building in a poisonous green haze. I could see a half-dozen sentries in the distance; there were likely more guards inside.

"Here, here," one of them called. "No closer! The bank is closed!" He started to run toward me.

I put one hand firmly against the outer shield and, under my breath, spoke my full name. The wards near me changed color from green to luminous House blue. "I am Adara Triskittenion," I announced, "landheir-third of this House, and this is my bank."

The guard almost tripped on his own feet. "You were kidnapped!" he said.

"I was. I escaped. Brother Heath or Moore might be here?" I

asked.

"Yes, Ma'am! I mean," he stammered. At my age, 'mistress' would have been correct.

"Please notify whoever is in charge inside that I would like to get in," I asked. The 'please' was somewhat pro forma. I could have made it an order, but no sense in getting anyone's back up. Actually, I could probably have ordered the wards to let me pass, but anyone inside might have panicked and started throwing spells in my direction.

"At once, mistress!" he answered.

A few minutes later, I was in Heath's conference room. As I approached, I had heard shouting, but when I entered the room there was dead silence.

"Adara!" Heath said. He was delighted to see me.

"Ady!" Grandpa Worrow always used my baby name.

"Mistress Adara?" Sitting at the far end of the table was someone I did not know, wearing the colors and sigil of the Order of the Axe. "I am OverCaptain Karel Gudmundson. We were just discussing your disappearance."

"Kidnapping," I corrected. "They also seem to have stolen my gnothdiar."

"That and your carryall have been recovered," Gudmundson said. "They were left where you were taken, lying on the ground. Eye-witnesses agree that you and your clothes vanished, leaving your things behind."

"In that case, I have another criminal charge," I said. "I'm wearing the robe I borrowed while making my escape."

"Theft of your clothing, nominal value," Gudmundson said.

"Ummh, no," I corrected again. "When I woke up, after being kidnapped, I was tied face up to a bed wearing absolutely nothing."

Gudmundson looked upset.

"Heath, that's fourth degree rape, isn't it?"

"Third," he corrected. "You have to give evidence that you were naked."

"That's easy. To whom?" I asked.

"Just to the Overcaptain here," he answered.

"You can't take my word for it?" I asked Gudmundson.

"I could have this place, wherever you escaped from, searched for your clothing," he answered. "Where was that, by the way?"

"Fourbridge Hall." I said firmly. "Or so I was told by a bookmonger. The tall hill behind Codfish books. Your search likely fails. My escape got violent. When last I looked, their central keep was a pillar of fire, and their wards were busy collapsing and exploding."

"Fourbridge Hall?" He looked upset. Fourbridge was a major political player. "On fire? I need some evidence that you don't have your clothing, though I agree that robe isn't yours."

"That's easy." Perhaps I was too impulsive. I walked over to him, so everyone else was behind me. The gesture is usually associated with truly little girls, perverts, and raincoats, but the robe fell open very nicely all the way to the bottom, so he, and no one else, saw I was -- as the line goes -- as naked as a jaybird, except for my boots.

"Ah, ah," he squeaked. He choked and turned beet-red.

"Adara!" Heath shouted. Heath was always a bit of a prude.

"The defendant presented irrefutable evidence?" I asked.

"Absolutely!" Gudmundson said, averting his eyes.

I pulled my robe shut and tied it very tight at waist and neck. "None of you are house servants, but this thing looks to have escaped from a second-rate bordello—or a romance novel. Could I persuade someone to buy me some decent clothing? Please? I'll pay you back."

"House will pay," Heath said. "Marjorie, Abstractions, Unlimited? Across the street."

Marjorie, I remembered, was his lead assistant.

"Happy to," she said. "I need sizes."

Fortunately, I had those memorized.

"You had claimed," Gudmundson said, "that you escaped from Fourbridge Hall. But the gown you're wearing has a locator tag, one that tells anyone who finds it where to return it. Of course, wards here obscure its effectiveness, but if that gown were from Fourbridge Hall, it would take us back there."

"It will work on the roof," Heath said. "after she takes it off. After she gets some decent clothing."

"That will also let us confirm her claim that their Hall is burning." Gudmundson shook his head. You would think that after claiming I was wearing no clothing under the robe, and then seeing me prove it, he would have learned his lesson, but no such luck.

Somewhat later, we found ourselves on the top of Triskittenion Northwest Bank. My new clothing even fit. The view to the north was superb. Fourbridge Hall had been built at the top of a steep slope, so it loomed over Capital. Two of its four towers were engulfed in flames, as were the lower buildings around its central spire. Once again, bright flashes and thundering roars signaled that yet another major ward had collapsed. If anyone was trying to fight the fires or stabilize the house wards, it wasn't obvious from here. At a guess, whoever was in residence was trying to evacuate residents and valuables. This being House Fourbridge, I would not have been shocked to learn that the House's unmen servants had been abandoned to their fates.

"While you have all been watching the pretty lights," Gudmundson said, "I have activated the location charm. I can confirm that this robe, well, what's left of it, claims it came from the Fourbridge establishment."

At that moment Fourbridge Hall's central spire collapsed, dropping down almost vertically.

"Where is the Fire Brigade?" Heath asked. "Surely no one in Capital can have missed this catastrophe?"

"Fourbridge is a walled keep," Gudmundson answered. "There's no way for the brigade to get in, so they aren't bothering to try."

"It used to be a walled keep," I said. "While I was leaving, the entire southern wall of that compound was seen to collapse."

"The entire wall?" Heath questioned.

"Perhaps not the towers at its two ends, but, yes, the entire wall. It was seen to fall over," I explained. "By me. It was in my way when I tried to flee."

"You took out an entire wall of a House Hall?" Gudmundson challenged. "One of the most heavily fortified barriers in the Commonality?"

"It appeared to me that it took itself down," I answered. "It exploded through ward failure. In fact, I saw it do that."

"You attacked Fourbridge Hall!" Gudmundson accused.

"I escaped from Fourbridge Hall, incidentally removing a few minor obstacles from my path and using standard methods to obscure my trail," I answered.

"Standard methods?" Gudmundson grumbled.

"Standard methods," I answered. "As discussed in Worrow's *Series On Combat*, in particular pyrotechnics, explosions, and back fires. Notably the back fire that torched a big dining room." I smiled at Gramps.

He grinned like the mythical invisible cat. If Gudmundson didn't know Augustus Primus Worrow was my grandfather, standing a few feet from him, I felt no need to tell him.

"Overcaptain?" Heath intruded into the conversation. Gudmundson turned to face him. "While I need to research the details, I believe that I need to register a House Feud, or perhaps a House War, between House Fourbridge and perhaps its clients, and on the other side House Triskittenion and perhaps its clients."

"Is this necessary?" Gudmundson asked. "Registered Feuds or worse can be unfortunate."

"I'm not sure it is necessary," Heath answered. He was interrupted by another especially loud eruption from Fourbridge Hall. "However, my memory says that failing to notify the Order of the Axe about a potential feud, as soon as possible, is at least severely deprecated."

"Of course it's necessary," Grandpa Worrow interrupted. "That pile of abominations--" he pointed at the pyre that had been Fourbridge Hall, "--assaulted my grand-daughter on her first day at the Academy, tried three times to murder her, once with a stolen illegal Class Four golem on which I have yet to hear of the legally-mandated summary executions, kidnapped and raped her,..and I could go on. My dear grand-daughter is Heir-Third to Triskittenion. The responsible party is the Fourbridge land-heir. This events manifestly constitute an undeclared House War, on which as a Master Combatant and Commander of our House Militia I request the intervention of the

Order of the Axe. I believe you get to start by summoning a Peace Inquiry."

Gudmundson looked wild-eyed.

"Apologies," he said, "but I definitely need to consult with the Order's Council of Chancellors. I've heard of intervention requests, but only as a historical note, and don't know what the rules are."

"There's a time limit," Grandpa said. "A short limit."

"And if the rules so provide, I agree that your timing spell has begun its chant," Gudmundson answered.

"Perfectly fair," Grandpa said. "And if the Chancellors give you a ruling within a day, the chant may legally begin then."

Gudmundson scrambled for the stairs.

"What day is today?" I asked. "I was out cold for a while."

"It's Oneday," Heath said. "You were out for most of three days."

My heart almost stopped. I'd been angry before. Now I was terrified.

"Oh, no!" I shouted. "I missed the Diagrams II exam! Professor Aspen never gives make-up exams!" Suddenly I had to sit down. I was shaking.

"Horatio Aspen?" Heath asked.

I nodded.

"The bastard gave me a C because I misunderstood two of his questions. He never gives make-ups."

"A bit of a difficulty here," Gramps said. "Perhaps I should chat up Chancellor Everbright. Long-time friend of my family, she is. I mean, if Dorrance penalizes you for getting kidnapped, that would make them a co-belligerent in the House War we look to be having."

"Gramps," I managed, "I think maybe I'd better ask him myself, first. Today. Now. He did say he'd let us off if we had truly unique excuses, and since he'd only been teaching for twenty thousand years he was sure there were some still out there."

Heath looked at a wall chart. "It's not yet sun-up at Dorrance," he said. "To be there at the tenth hour, that's the standard first office hour ...You have five hours yet."

"Adara, dear," Gramps asked, "Are you up to a double shield?" I nodded affirmatively. "We'll deep-gate back to Triskittenion house, feed you properly, then advance to your dorm so soon as I round up some more friends."

***

Not quite at the tenth hour, I marched over to Proscenium Hall. Gramps' friends were bodyguards, people from a half-dozen Outremer houses, fully armed and armored. They wanted to be sure I was safe. My own wards were full up. We were followed at a distance by a half-dozen lictors, also heavily armed.

I still wanted to know how someone had circumvented my wards, the Academy Wards, and the Academy blocks against gating on campus. All that had to wait until I negotiated with the Serene Master on replacing the exam. That was clearly more important. I had to do that myself. My heart was pounding. Aspen had a well-deserved reputation for being more than a bit crusty. I could ask for the makeup exam, but he was going to chew my head off.

My bodyguards stopped a polite distance from his office door. I damped my wards, told myself not to be afraid, and marched to the door.

"Ah, Miss Triskittenion." Serene Master Aspen glowered at me as though I were a particularly vile species of mud-dwelling worm. "You missed your examination." He drew out each syllable. "You get to propose a reason why you should be allowed a make-up exam. That has been done successfully before, most recently a little more than two thousand years ago. That time there was an escaped hrordrin. So, propose!"

"I was stunned, kidnapped, raped, and managed to escape. My escape was based on diagram magic," I said.

"Entirely on diagram magic?" he asked. "We'll get to escaped and kidnapped later, for which I need some evidence."

"Well, not entirely," I said sheepishly. "The walls and windows I blew out were just power blasts. But I was in a real hurry."

"So tell me what you did with diagram magic to escape?" He tried to make his question sound interesting.

"First,..." and I described being chained to the bed. "So I set an exact zero-draw diagram to pull a cut through in the wood."

"Hmm. Sugar and carbon black?" He actually sounded interested.

"Umm...oh, I see how that works!" I exclaimed. "I didn't think of that choice. No. I was much less clever. Cardboard, a spell I've been casting for a decade."

"Practice is good! Oh, your House is the papermakers. Making paper is what you do. Definitely the right decision!" he remarked. "I gather it worked." I nodded. "And then?"

"Ran quickly. Set distractions and backfires. I blew out a window, and set a room on fire behind me to end pursuit." I put up a trio of images.

"You torched someone's Greater Ceremonial Hall?" he said. "Someone is going to be annoyed. The flame diagram, lots of power? Excellent! You saw the secondaries? Superb!"

"Then I landed in a garden, with a heavily reinforced outer wall." I put up another image.

"I take it there was no open door?" he asked.

"No. And I heard guards closing on me."

"So you took out the guards, then went to work on the wall?" he asked. "Actually, there was a choice of walls."

"No. I was running. Stop to fight means other people get to arrive and pile on you."

He smiled.

"So I set the tetrachrome analytic diagrams. The outcome was a bit fuzzy; I was pushing them through my wards." I put up one more image, what I remembered of what I saw.

Aspen nodded approvingly. "You tell me what's in that image."

"More layers of spells than I could resolve. Points where things were not set right, and power was leaking." I marked several of those. "Then there were control structures, more than I could trace quickly. So I hit the ones that were leaking! Hard! Including this strange thing that I didn't recognize or see completely, except it seemed to be a control that was leaking badly."

"Vehalno surge disperser," Aspen said. "They're exotic. I'd have been impressed – unless your House defenses have one – if you recognized it."

"If that failed, I'd see if more stuff started leaking, or try brute force against the ground in front of the wall. Some wards take poorly to stuff being driven into them at high speed."

"Very sound. And?" Aspen asked.

"It got very bright all at once. There was no wall, just broken rock. I ran for it," I said.

"Did you try analyzing, later, what else was in the wall?" he asked.

"I will," I said. "I stored my memories so I can later. I've been a bit busy being questioned and checked medically. I still need to reassure relatives I wasn't seriously hurt."

"Questioned?" Aspen asked.

"The Capital Order of the Axe OverCaptain. People from my Family Council. Representatives of the Outremer Council. Others," I ended.

"Capital? Oh, wait, you didn't mention. Where were you claiming you were held prisoner?" he asked.

"Capital," I answered. I pulled from my carryall a copy of the *Capital Intelligencer. EXTRA!* it read on top. "*Fourbridge Hall destroyed.*" Someone had captured an image of the central spire on its way down. "In there. Their wards weren't well isolated, so the building explodi-ated itself." The headlines went on. "*Triskittenion Heir kidnapped! No trace of her location!*"

Aspen spent a couple minutes reading the newspaper. "The Order of the Axe believed you?" he eventually asked. He was now using his normal tone of voice, not his 'you are a living proof of the existence of negative IQ' voice.

"When I finished escaping, I was wearing a pair of boots," I said. "And a bathrobe I borrowed on the way out, a robe with an identity tag, proving it recently came from there. Rape Third is stripped naked and no more. If need be OverCaptain Gudmundson will testify that I had been stripped."

"Definitely a truly unique excuse," he announced. "Write up a complete analysis of their wall wards, as much as you remember, no fair asking for help, and I'll take that as the analysis section of the exam. Your use of the tetrachrome scan shows you understood the recent part of the course. Your path in your homework solutions to solving the square diagram problems was truly clever, enough to prove you are actually understanding the material. If you do the analysis properly, you will get an Excellent on the exam."

Excellent is the grade above A, a grade rarely given. He pointed me at the door. I stood and backed out of the room. I had feared I was bearding the dragon in its den, but he once he discovered I actually had a unique excuse he was entirely friendly.

George Phillies is Professor Emeritus of Physics ("I retired to write full time. So far, so good," he says) and retired politician (on the ballot for US Federal office twice), He lives in Worcester, Massachusetts, with his cat, the world's largest board wargame collection, and large flower gardens. He is also President of the National Fantasy Fan Federation, the world's oldest international SF club and President of AHIKS, the world's oldest and largest intercontinental board wargaming society, He edits four SF fanzines, namely Eldritch Science (fiction), Tightbeam (reviews, all genres), The National Fantasy Fan (club news zine), and The N3F Review of Books Incorporating Prose Bono,

Phillies has to his credit seven SF novels, namely This Shining Sea (tween superheroine), Minutegirls (politics and giant space battles), The One World (Amazon swords against Conquistador matchlocks), Mistress of the Waves (economics), Against Three Lands (not-quite-medieval Japan against not-quite-Europeans), The Girl Who Saved The World (tween superheroine), and Airy Castles All Ablaze (more of the tween superheroine), five textbooks on board game design, four books on political campaign finance, a statistical mechanics textbook, the definitive monograph on polymer solution dynamics, and more than 170 scientific research papers, most on light scattering spectroscopy and polymer dynamics.

THE SCHOOL FOR HIGH FLIERS

BY RHYS HUGHES

I love detective stories and occult stories, and I have long wanted to write a series of stories about an incompetent occult detective. Clumsy Carnacki is the son of a successful occult detective and feels compelled to match his father's achievements, but the truth is that he should have chosen a different line of work. "The School for High Fliers" is his first adventure to be accepted for publication. I have written a few others but they haven't seen print yet, and I am planning more. Of course, the fact he is incompetent at his profession doesn't mean he is an inadequate person. Clumsy seems a rather lovable character to me, and I hope this is the way he will come across to readers.

The School for High Fliers

Clumsy Carnacki was an amateur detective who tried to solve cases that involved ghosts and monsters and demons, but he wasn't very good at it. Most of the ghosts got away, the monsters, too, and the demons weren't even aware that any attempt had been made to 'solve' them. But Clumsy persisted. His father had been a superb occult sleuth, rather famous in his day, and Clumsy wanted to be just like him.

It was a lost cause, but he never gave up. It was the only thing he truly enjoyed. And one evening, as he was returning from a failed effort to put an imp back into a bottle, a shudder ran through him. He stood aside to let the other shudders continue their run without obstruction, and he knew instinctively it was going to be a long night. The shudders were invisible and silent, but he imagined he heard them laughing at him. Depressed, he continued to his house and opened the door.

The moment he stepped over the threshold, he felt that something odd was happening. The rug in his hallway was a tattered thing he had bought in a market on holiday many years ago.

So why did it feel so soft and luxurious beneath his feet?

He stood on it and wondered.

Then he stepped off it and crouched to inspect it more closely. It was much thicker than he remembered. It had turned into a higher quality rug in his absence. This was most curious!

Yet as he extended a finger to prod it, he was astonished when it lifted itself off the floor and floated out the open door. He stumbled after it, but it was already ascending out of reach.

He stood for a few moments with his mouth agape.

Not only was the rug thicker and softer than it should be, but now he saw that the pattern on the underside had changed. Instead of the abstract swirls of faded colour, there was the outline of a strange bird, majestic and beautiful and also somewhat imposing.

Clumsy took a deep breath and reminded himself of his calling in life. This was another chance to solve a supernatural mystery and prove that he was almost as great as his father had been.

He hurried to the shed where he kept his bicycle, unlocked it, wheeled it out, mounted the saddle, and began peddling as fast as he could after the flying rug. The streets were very quiet at this late hour, and there was little traffic. He made good progress. The rug was floating serenely through the air and seemed in no particular rush.

"It's not aware that I'm following it," Clumsy said to himself, and he took care not to give himself away by ringing his bell or pulling too hard on the squeaky brakes. The moon rose, and the rug was illuminated more clearly. It looked just like a big crimson bird that flew without flapping its wings. There was something mysterious about the twinkle in the eyes, and this was especially odd because it wasn't a real bird, only a picture made from threads. Clumsy panted with effort.

He wasn't an especially fit person, but, luckily, his route was flat. At a junction, he almost collided with another cyclist. Both riders swerved and braked sharply and growled in annoyance.

Then Clumsy blinked and cried, "Bounder!"

"Yes, I am," came the reply.

Bounder was one of Clumsy's friends. They both frequented a special club where supernatural matters would be discussed for hours, and all the members would take turns telling ghost stories that were true. "What are you cycling the streets at night for?"

"I was chasing a carpet," answered Bounder.

"That's a coincidence!"

Bounder explained, "My rug suddenly decided to fly out of a window, and I resolved to follow it. But it went too fast, and I lost it. I was thinking about turning back when I caught sight of it again. There it is! Sorry, but I must chase after it. Goodbye!"

"Wait a moment," said Clumsy, spluttering in dismay. "That's my rug up there, not yours. It flew out my door. I am chasing it, and I was doing a good job of keeping up with it, too."

"But it's getting away," replied Bounder.

"Yes it is. Come on!"

Clumsy started pedalling again with Bounder right behind him. It was lucky for both of them that they didn't have too far to go. The carpet flew over a high wall and began to descend.

"Look! It's landing in the grounds of that building."

They stopped next to the wall.

"What is this place?" Clumsy wondered.

"I have no idea," said Bounder before frowning and adding, "But why do you say the rug is yours and not mine? Is it possible that two rugs both flew off on the same night?"

"That's the only logical explanation."

"What can it mean?"

Clumsy shrugged and leaned his bicycle against the wall. He walked alongside the wall looking for a gate or some other means of entry, and his friend followed him. There were no streetlamps here, and it was very dark despite the moon. It was a deserted spot in an area of the city that neither Clumsy nor Bounder had visited before.

The wall formed a vast square around whatever was inside. The bricks were too smooth to climb, and there was no gate or door anywhere. The friends made nearly a full circuit of the square before they suddenly came across a rickety wooden ladder leaning against the wall. A man was in the act of climbing the rungs to the top.

"Yucky!" shouted Bounder.

Clumsy grabbed his arm. "Shhh! Not so loud."

"Hello, my friends!"

The man on the ladder was another of the club members. Clumsy was eager to know what he was doing.

"What does it look like? I'm scaling this wall."

"I can see that. But why?"

"To get over it."

"That's evident. But why do you want to do that?"

Yucky came back down.

"I can't hold a conversation while I'm on a ladder," he said.

Then in a loud whisper he explained that one of his favourite rugs had flown out of his house, and he had followed it here.

"I went back to get a ladder, and so here I am."

"Our rugs also went missing."

"I wonder if the same thing is happening everywhere?"

"Maybe it is. I don't know."

"I bet it is," said Yucky.

Clumsy scratched his head. "If we climb over this wall together, that's one of the things we might find out."

Bounder nodded. "It could be dangerous."

"Supernatural things often are."

They considered the wisdom of this statement for a few moments, and then Clumsy frowned at Yucky.

"There's something different about you tonight."

"I thought so, too," said Bounder.

Yucky smiled and patted his head. "I'm no longer bald. I didn't want the moonlight shining on my smooth scalp to give away my position to anyone inside the building."

"Ah, you are wearing a wig! Where did you get it?"

"It was my grandma's."

This raised new questions, but Clumsy decided not to ask. They had to climb the wall as quickly as possible. The longer they stood around here talking, the more likely they were to be noticed. One at a time, they went up the ladder and dropped over the wall. It was a long drop, but the ground on the other side was extremely soft.

Yucky frowned and asked, "How will we get out?"

"I didn't think of that," admitted Clumsy. "We should have pulled the ladder after us. Too late now..."

"This grass is so luxurious and springy," said Bounder.

"Yes, it's very lush indeed."

They walked over the spongy ground towards the impressive building that stood at the centre of the enclosure. It was a large mansion with more windows and chimneys than they could count. Every time Clumsy tried to count them, he lost count and had to start again from the beginning. There were gables and gargoyles and several entrances, and the whole thing was quite eerie in the moonlight. Most of the windows were pitch dark, but on the ground floor, a series of windows were dimly lit. The friends crouched very low as they approached them.

"Take a peep inside," Clumsy urged Bounder.

Bounder said, "I think Yucky should go first," and Yucky sighed and raised his head over the windowsill.

"It's very old fashioned," reported Yucky.

Bounder was next to take a look. "There's a man in there but I can't hear what he's saying," he said.

Clumsy took a turn, too.

Through the thick pane of glass, he saw a long chamber illuminated by flickering lamps. There were rugs in neat rows on the floor, rugs of many kinds and in a variety of conditions, and at the far end of the chamber on a raised platform stood a tall man.

He noted that this tall man, who was also very thin, held a stick in his hand and he was waving it around like a wand and talking at the same time.

"He seems to be teaching them a lesson," he whispered.

And this was true. The tall thin man was obviously a lecturer but what sane person will lecture a room full of rugs? That makes no sense at all. Was he talking for his own benefit? If so, then why?

"Did you recognise my rug?" asked Bounder.

"Or mine?" added Yucky.

"I don't know what your rugs look like, but I think I saw my own near the middle of the front row."

"We ought to go inside and demand them back."

Clumsy was dubious.

"I am an investigator of the supernatural," he said, "and I am getting a creepy feeling from this. That tall thin man isn't someone we can reason with. I don't know why I think he is so dangerous, it's just a hunch, but I always rely on my intuition and—"

"Your intuition is mostly wrong," said Bounder.

"That's the blunt truth," confirmed Yucky.

"Well, what shall we do?"

Yucky said, "I don't believe that tall thin man is such a threat, thus I suggest we try to get inside anyway but quietly and sneakily. Maybe one of the side doors is unlocked, or possibly we can climb onto the roof and from there slide down a chimney."

Bounder looked up at the roof but Clumsy gripped his arm. "People get stuck in chimneys," he warned.

"Let's find an open door then."

They circled the building, testing the doors one by one. All were shut and locked. At last, they came to a door at the rear of the mansion with a cat flap set into it. Yucky nodded.

"People get stuck in cat flaps too," said Clumsy.

"Let's try it anyway."

Bounder went first, Yucky close behind, then Clumsy got down on his hands and knees and pushed himself through the narrow gap. Halfway to the other side he became wedged fast.

"Pull me through," he said.

Yucky and Bounder tugged at his head.

"Not by the ears please!"

"Why not? They are just like handles."

"They might come off."

"Relax your muscles," advised Bounder, and after ten minutes of work, Clumsy passed right through the cat flap with a loud plopping sound. The three friends froze and strained their ears. Clumsy's ears were sore, and he groaned inwardly as he struggled to listen for sounds inside the building. But no one came to apprehend them.

"Which way to the hall of rugs?" asked Yucky as he dusted himself down and gazed about. Clumsy pointed to a low arch and so they passed beneath it through a series of rooms of various sizes and shapes. It was almost impossible to see anything.

But most of the rooms were empty, and there was no furniture to bump into on this journey. This made the building seem even more mysterious. It wasn't a home for anyone, that much was evident, but in that case, what was it? At least, it was easy enough to move silently through the chambers because of the soft carpets underfoot.

In one room, the moon shone through a window directly onto the floor, and Clumsy pointed at the shape it revealed.

"What's the matter?"

"Look at the pattern! It's a large crimson bird."

Bounder and Yucky understood.

"Yes, the same pattern that was on our rugs when they were escaping through the air. What does it mean?"

Clumsy didn't know, but he noted that the carpet here was roughly the same size as his own missing rug.

It was not feasible to check if the other carpets had the same pattern, but it seemed probable that they did. They pushed on through the gloom. At last, they came to the bottom of a spiral stairway. There was no other way to go. Bounder turned to retreat.

"Where are you going?" asked Clumsy.

"This is clearly the wrong way. Let's go back to the beginning and try a different route," he replied, and Yucky added, "We were foolish to trust your sense of direction," but he didn't say it in a nasty or exasperated way because Clumsy's errors of judgment were something he was used to. But Clumsy began walking up the stairs.

Bounder and Yucky watched him in disbelief.

"Where are *you* going?"

"This way is as good as any other," he said.

"No, it isn't. The hall with the tall thin man and our rugs can be found on the ground floor, not up there."

"I have a positive feeling about these stairs."

"Come back down!"

But Clumsy kept going without heeding their objections. Soon enough, Bounder and Yucky were forced to follow him. The stairway twisted very sharply, and at the top, it deposited them in a narrow and long passage with a solid wall only on one side.

On the other side was a very low railing and beyond the railing empty space. It was a kind of balcony that looked down into the large hall where the tall thin man was lecturing the rugs. He was still waving his wand, and his words could now be heard.

Yucky said, "I think I know what this place is."

"Tell us," said Bounder.

"A school," answered Yucky.

"I don't see many pupils," said Bounder.

"Yes, you do. Look down."

They all leaned over the railing. They felt a little dizzy as they did so but curiosity proved more powerful than vertigo. Now it was apparent the rugs were the pupils, and the tall thin man was the teacher. "He is giving them a lesson on flight," whispered Clumsy.

"How can they hear him?"

"They are only rugs!"

"Yes," said Clumsy, "and rugs don't have ears. I know that. But I told you something supernatural was afoot."

"Whose foot?" Bounder strained to catch his words.

"Shhh!" hissed Yucky.

"I'm sure that one there is my rug," said Clumsy.

"Poor little thing."

"What do you mean by that?"

"Well, it's so worn and thin, clearly maltreated."

Clumsy grew indignant. "I'll have you know that I bought it on one of the best holidays of my life."

"What has that got to do with anything?"

"It was years ago, and I have regarded it with affection ever since; and it's not my fault that wear and tear—"

"Keep your voices down!" squealed Yucky.

But it was too late.

They had attracted the attention of the tall thin man.

He stopped talking and looked up.

And saw them leaning over the railings of the balcony.

"Intruders!" he roared.

Then he waved his wand in a different way and added, in a terrible voice, "Bring them to my office."

"Who is he talking to now?" cried Bounder.

"I have no idea," said Clumsy.

But it didn't take long before they found out.

Flying rugs began converging on the three friends from all directions, from up the spiral stairs and along the passage from both directions, also from the open space beyond the railings.

The friends ran one way, then turned and ran the other. But there was no escape. Finally, they stood still and hugged each other. A large carpet floated gently over the railings and quickly flung itself around them and rolled itself up tight with them inside.

"I feel like a note stuck in a flute!" yelled Clumsy.

The carpet rose and hovered.

"Remove your elbow from my face," said Yucky.

"My apologies," said Bounder.

Struggling and pleading, the friends were carried off by the cylindrical flying carpet down the corridor, under archways, through rooms, then up flights of steps and along more corridors. There were so many bends and turns that Clumsy began to feel nauseous.

At last, the carpet unrolled, and they tumbled over each other, coming to rest on the bare floor of a small room, their arms and legs all tangled together. The carpet retreated but remained hovering near the door of the room, preventing them from leaving.

Clumsy, Bounder and Yucky stood and waited nervously.

The tall thin man reached the entrance of the room, and with a rippling movement, the carpet floated aside to let him in. He strode past the friends and took a seat behind a wide desk.

"This is my office, and I'm the headmaster," he said.

The three friends said nothing.

"You have been very naughty indeed. This is a private school, and you are spies," the tall thin man snarled.

"Oh no, sir," protested Clumsy.

"We just followed our rugs here," said Bounder.

"When they flew away," added Yucky.

The headmaster arched his eyebrows and scrunched up his face into a grimace, and because his face was already sinister, this scrunching actually made it more pleasant, but not very much.

"Flew!" he roared. "Your pathetic little rugs don't know how to fly. I brought them here to teach them that."

"You are teaching our rugs to fly?" blurted Clumsy.

"That's what I said. What else!"

"What else what, sir?"

"What else do you expect me to teach rugs?"

They pondered the matter. There didn't seem to be too many subjects that a rug could ever want to learn.

"But we saw them fly," objected Clumsy.

"No, you didn't. I ordered them to be kidnapped. That's what you saw, and there's a big difference. I arranged for rugs that already know how to fly to enter your houses and slide under your rugs. Then they were able to lift your rugs on their shoulders."

"Do rugs have shoulders?" asked Bounder.

"Metaphorically, I mean."

The headmaster finally let his eyebrows down and continued with his explanation. "My rugs abduct other rugs. That's how this school acquires new pupils. The rugs in the upper grades find rugs that can't fly and bring them here. I teach them to fly."

"But why do you do that?" pressed Yucky.

"Because this is a school for flying carpets!" bellowed the headmaster as if the answer ought to be obvious.

"Yes, I see," said Clumsy.

"And you teach them by yourself?" asked Bounder.

"Yes, I'm afraid I do."

"There are no other teachers in the school?"

"Not one. I am alone."

"Then why is the school so large? One classroom would be enough, I should think. Don't you agree?"

The headmaster sighed. For the first time, his expression softened, and it was plain that, beneath his stern exterior, there were sentimental feelings that had been repressed for too long.

"Yes, you are right. But I wasn't always alone. Once, there were many teachers working for me. Every room in this mansion was occupied by a teacher, and a class of rugs at various levels of flying education. But time passed, and customs changed. People no longer wanted flying carpets, and no one sent their rugs to be educated here. Teachers began leaving to find jobs elsewhere, and eventually, it seemed the school would have to close. That was when I had the idea of kidnapping rugs against the will of their owners. This is the best school of its kind, and I couldn't bear for carpets to be stuck on the ground all the time."

"There are other schools like this?" asked Clumsy.

"Not now. That's why this is the best one. But the world has moved on, and there's no place for me anymore. I know this, but I resist the truth. I don't want to retire just yet."

"I have a few more questions to ask, sir."

"Ask them quickly!"

"How can anyone, no matter how clever, teach a rug to fly? Surely a rug can't hear your lessons?"

"Exactly! That's why they need to be taught how to listen first. But in order to listen, they need to be taught how to think. Rugs are non-sentient objects when they arrive at my school, but when they graduate they have excellent minds. Think, listen, fly!"

"That is the school motto, I suppose?"

The headmaster nodded.

"Rugs are quick learners," he said.

Clumsy asked, "What is the meaning of the crimson bird?"

"You mean the pattern on the rugs?"

"Yes, the big bird."

"It is merely the school symbol."

"Is it stitched onto all the carpets in your care?"

"When they can fly, yes."

"Is it a phoenix?"

"Not quite. That would be a fire hazard. It is the outline of a mythical bird from the fabled east that has grace and wisdom. When rugs graduate from my school, they should also have those qualities. That is my aim, and I am proud of my achievements."

"Are you also from the fabled east?"

The headmaster refused to reply to this question, and Clumsy assumed the answer was yes. His next question was, "But have you been abducting rugs for a long time in this town?"

"No, because I only arrived recently. I have kidnapped perhaps eighty or ninety new pupils since then."

"You are new to our town?" gasped Clumsy.

"Yes I am. I notice that you have stopped calling me 'sir'. I'll make a note of that. It might go against you."

"Sorry, sir! But I am intrigued. If you are a new arrival, what was this building before you turned it into a school? Was it abandoned and empty? How did you claim it as your own?"

"It has always been my school," said the headmaster, but he declined to elaborate on this cryptic answer.

Then he announced, "One final question!"

Clumsy and Bounder exchanged glances. Bounder and Yucky did so, too. Then Clumsy and Yucky took their turn. They all wanted to ask the same question but were scared to do so because the answer might not be to their liking. Clumsy took the plunge.

"What do you intend to do with us now, sir?"

The headmaster rubbed his hands together. He stood up and grinned a horrid grin. "I don't plan to kill you because I am not really a villain. But I can't let you go because you would be sure to report me to the police. I will order one of the larger and more experienced carpets to carry you to a remote island in the middle of the ocean and leave you there. You will be castaways and unable to return."

"Don't roll us up like you did earlier please! I had difficulty breathing inside that tube!" begged Clumsy.

"Very well. You shall balance on top. But don't blame me if you fall off. It will be a long journey."

And he waved his wand, and a very large carpet eased itself through the doorway and slid itself under their feet. They fell down onto it while it reversed direction and raced along corridors at a frightful speed. The headmaster hadn't even bothered to say good-bye! Now they clung onto the fringe of the carpet as they stretched full length on it. The speed was really remarkable. Out through a broad open window, they rushed with barely any clearance on either side.

"Hold on tight," advised Bounder in a shout.

"I intend to," screamed Yucky.

But Clumsy was truer to his name, and he began to slip off. They were now crossing the wall that ringed the building and suddenly Clumsy fell. His fall was broken by the ladder that was still propped against the wall. It splintered and crashed down with him.

The carpet saw it had lost one of its passengers and dipped to reclaim him. Clumsy was bruised and groaning, but he managed to roll out of the way. He called to the others to jump.

They did so, and now the three of them stood unsteadily as the carpet dived down at them. "Beat it," cried Clumsy.

The rungs of the broken ladder lay scattered about.

The friends grabbed one each.

As the carpet came within reach, they lashed out and pounded it with all their might. Dust flew up in a cloud.

The carpet was large and strong but lacked the nerve for this kind of engagement, and it rose and flew back to the house. Doubtless, it wanted to inform the headmaster of its failure and the escape of the prisoners. The friends began limping away from the scene. They intended to inform the police at the earliest available opportunity.

A mighty rumbling noise behind them caused them to pause and look back. The mansion house was rising into the sky. They saw now that the soft springy grass inside the wall was in fact a huge carpet, probably the star pupil of the school, and it was ascending faster and faster towards the star pupils of the night, the actual stars.

The headmaster had no desire to be arrested.

The four walls of the enclosure collapsed inwards, and it was apparent now that they were skirting boards.

"An enormous carpet," said Clumsy.

"Say farewell to our rugs forever," sighed Bounder.

"Good riddance to them!" cried Clumsy.

"What do you mean?"

"Would you really want a flying carpet in your house and run the risk of the thing tripping you up and knocking things over? It would be like a cat but worse, much worse."

"I suppose you have a point," said Bounder.

Yucky squealed and clutched at his head. His wig was floating up and chasing after the departing mansion.

"It overheard the lesson about flying!" he wailed.

"I suppose a wig is a rug," conceded Clumsy, "so it makes sense." He winced and rubbed at his bruises.

"Come on, let's go home and get some rest."

"That's a very good idea."

A few days later, Clumsy was browsing in an encyclopaedia and saw a picture of a crimson bird exactly like the design stitched into the rugs of the flying carpet school. He learned that it was called a simurgh and was indeed of fabled eastern origin. Then he put the book down and went into the kitchen to make a nice cup of tea.

Rhys Hughes was born in Wales but has lived in many different countries. He graduated as an engineer and currently works as a tutor of mathematics. He began writing fiction at an early age and his first book, *Worming the Harpy,* was published in 1995. Since that time he has published more than fifty other books, and his short stories have been translated into ten languages. He is nearing the end of an ambitious project to complete a cycle of exactly 1000 linked tales. His most recent book is the novel *The Pilgrim's Regress,* and he is currently working on *Weirdly Out West,* a collection of short stories, plays and poems. Fantasy, humour, satire, science fiction, adventure, irony, paradoxes and philosophy are combined in his work to create a distinctive style.

DORM WRAITH OUTRAGE

BY BECKY R. JONES

Michael Scaramucci is starting his second year teaching kinetic magic at The Academy Arcane. In exchange for agreeing to be an on-site faculty advisor for the boys' dorm, he gets a rent-free apartment. He has to spend every other weekend on campus, but aside from making sure students follow the rules and keep their magical and non-magical pranks to a minimum, it shouldn't be too much work, right? Right?

This story takes place before *Going Home,* which appeared in *Fantastic Schools Vol. 2.* Michael has not yet met the precocious and talented Moira Donaldson. Right now, he's just trying to get through his first weekend of on-site faculty duties unscathed!

Dorm Wraith Outrage

Michael dropped the last box of books in the middle of the living room. At least the movers had put the furniture where he wanted. Movers, what a concept. They made moving much less of a chore. He reached for his water bottle and gazed around his new apartment.

Not bad at all. And when you considered that it was rent-free, it was positively luxurious.

The headmaster of The Academy Arcane had offered the apartment in the boys' dormitory to Michael when the previous resident faculty advisor had gotten married and moved into a new house with his new wife. Michael had jumped at the chance to live rent-free and enjoy a five-minute walking commute to his office. Of course, he would have to spend every other weekend on campus, but that seemed like a small price to pay.

He moved to the window and gazed at the building, best described as gothic-inspired, on the far side of the gardens. Wilhelmina Solomons Hall housed the girls who boarded at Academy Arcane, while Godfrey Darrington Hall, the building in which Michael was currently standing, housed the boys. While most students at Academy Arcane were day students who either lived nearby or whose parents had the magical means to easily transport their children to and from school every day, about a third of the students were boarders. The combination of more-or-less-local day students and boarding students from farther away was considered to be a good way of insuring that students met peers from a variety of backgrounds.

The two dormitories also contained two apartments each for faculty resident advisors who provided the adult supervision at night and on the weekends. Michael would be alternating weekend and evening duties with his co-advisor who lived in the apartment at the other end of Darrington. Glancing around his new apartment again, Michael sighed happily. He looked forward to starting his second year of teaching kinetic magic at Academy Arcane. Teaching energized him, and watching the students grasp the art behind kinetic patterns was one of Michael's joys in life. Living with his some of his students would definitely be a new experience.

A knock at the door startled him out of his reverie. The apartment had two front doors. One led into the main hallway of the dormitory and the other opened into a small walled garden with a deck, which overlooked the lawn and gardens separating the dorms. The knock was coming from the outside door.

"Ah, Mr. Scaramucci, have you settled in yet? I do hope all your belongings arrived successfully?" Nathaniel Davidson, the headmaster, was a tall, almost cadaverous-looking man who loomed over everybody, although Michael had discovered last year that the headmaster was kind, extremely considerate, and thoroughly invested in the well-being of the students, staff, and the school. He too lived on campus, in a house that was one of the original school buildings.

"Yes, thank you, Headmaster. However, I must admit, I'm tempted to avoid the process of unpacking!" Michael smiled.

"Oh, I quite understand! But kinetics speeds up the process, does it not?" The headmaster laughed.

"True, for some things it does." Michael paused. "I know the boarding students will arrive the day after tomorrow. Is there anything I'm expected to take care of prior to that?" Michael was meticulous and liked to ensure that he didn't leave any loose ends.

"No, no. Just remember, you will need to be available to assist any students who may require it. Of course, as you know, I and other teachers will be here as well to help with move-in day." Headmaster Davidson smiled. "And you and Mr. Noble will need to work out your weekend and evening coverage schedules. It's best if that is taken care of before move-in day, so that the students and their parents have that information immediately. Perhaps you can find Mr. Noble today or tomorrow and start putting that together. And if you would, please leave a copy of the finalized schedule with my secretary."

Mr. Noble was Jonathon Noble, the other resident faculty advisor in Darrington. Michael knew that his co-advisor was not in today as Noble had made a point of telling Michael that he couldn't help him move since he was visiting with friends from out of town. Michael hoped that ducking out was not a normal tactic, but no matter. He wanted to get unpacked and fully settled in as quickly as possible. Two days until the boarding students arrived and three days until the school year officially started meant that there was a lot of work to be done.

The next morning, while strolling around the gardens surrounding the dormitories, Michael noticed that the exterior door to Jon Noble's apartment was open. He walked briskly down the path, through the small private garden that mirrored his own, and knocked on the door frame.

"Hello? Jon?"

"Yes? Oh, hello, Michael. How are you? Get all moved in yesterday?" Jon Noble was tall, blond, and blue-eyed. Where Michael taught kinetics, the art of moving items via patterns, Jon taught elements, the art of controlling and utilizing the base elements of air, fire, water, and earth. "Sorry I wasn't here to help. Old friends came into town at the last minute, and I haven't seen them in a few years."

"Oh, not a problem. The headmaster paid for movers, so the heavy stuff was taken care of by them. But he did say that you and I need to figure out a schedule for the weekend and evening shifts. I thought, if you had the time, we could take care of that now and get it out of the way." Michael smiled.

"Of course. Come on in. You're right let's get this taken care of, and then we can worry about when the monsters...I mean students... arrive tomorrow. Did you talk with the headmaster about move-in day?"

Jon led the way into his living room and gestured for Michael to take a seat in one of the comfortable chairs in front of the fireplace. This apartment was the mirror image of Michael's and situated at the opposite end of the main hallway of Darrington.

"He mentioned helping with move-in day but didn't really give me any details," Michael replied.

Jon returned to the other chair with a calendar, pad of paper, and pen.

"Well, let's get this schedule taken care of, and then I'll give you the general idea of what's involved with move-in day."

They spent a comfortable hour creating a schedule for the weekend and evening shifts that covered the whole school year. Then Jon filled in Michael on what would happen with move-in day.

"Were you here last year for it?" Jon asked.

"No. I'd just gotten hired and was going crazy trying to put together lesson plans. The headmaster told me not to bother," Michael responded.

"Okay. Well, it's pretty chaotic. The older students think they know everything, but always overlook something, while the younger students are still worried about leaving home...especially the youngest ones and those who are boarding for the first time. Most of the parents are pretty good, but there are always a few who seem to think we're the housekeeping staff and not teachers. Or the ones who want to know where the 'guest house' is," Jon made air quotes with his fingers, "so that they can visit Junior every weekend. Sadly for them, but luckily for us, there is no guest house, and the headmaster has already told them that visiting every weekend is discouraged." He gave a wry smile.

Jon painted a vivid picture of how the day would likely unfold, and of the boys and their parents who would all be arriving starting early the next morning. As Jon explained their role in the move-in process, Michael started visualizing the patterns that he expected to see the next day. Students arriving with their parents, unloading vehicles, carrying possessions into the dorm, avoiding collisions with other students, the ebb and flow of students and parents in and out of the dormitory.

He had discovered his aptitude for kinetic magic when he started seeing patterns everywhere. The kinetic mage had to be able to "see" the pattern of movement necessary for an object to move through space. Most of the time patterns were fairly straightforward and didn't require a lot of thought. Moving a box from one side of the room to the other was a straight-line pattern. But moving that same box say, up a staircase and around a corner, required more complex patterns, especially if you didn't know what was around that corner. The complexities of patterns required for even skilled kinetics to move their child's belongings over several miles, much less several hundred, would be exhausting and explained why even the parents who were kinetic mages found more mundane means to move their children into the dorms.

Michael returned his attention to Jon and the details of move-in day. It didn't sound too bad, and it didn't seem like either he or Jon was expected to help with actually carrying in boxes and belongings. It would be a good chance to walk through the entire dorm and get a feel for the patterns that would develop once the students had settled in and the parents had left.

After another hour or so discussing the details of move-in day, Michael left Jon to finish up his own lesson plans and wandered back through the main garden to his new apartment. He took his time and enjoyed the late summer day. The patterns created by the flowers and plantings in the garden caught his interest and he stopped to contemplate them.

"Hello, Michael. What brings you to campus before classes start?" Julieta Ocampo walked down the path toward him. A small compact woman, she had long, black hair that she usually wore pulled back, but today was hanging loose around her shoulders, and skin that looked perpetually tanned.

Michael pulled his mind away from floral patterns. "Hi, Juli. I'm now one of the resident faculty advisors in Darrington. I moved in yesterday. What are you doing here? Are you in Solomons now?" He had met Juli last year, when their afternoon classrooms were next door to each other.

"That's great! Yes, I just moved into Solomons yesterday, too. So, we're neighbors now." She smiled up at him. "Are you enjoying the garden?"

"Yes, I am. I was caught up in the patterns when you walked up," Michael explained.

"You kinetics and your patterns. Try visualizing an entire scene." She laughed.

"Well, there's a reason image mages are called imaginary mages... you only imagine things," Michael teased her back.

Juli laughed. "Okay, good point, even if it is an old joke!"

Michael laughed with her and found himself visualizing patterns that would lead him on walks past Solomons.

"Well, I'm glad we're neighbors, but I need to go buy some food and get back so I can finish unpacking and work on lesson plans," Michael said, wishing he didn't have any pressing tasks.

"Yeah, me, too. I'll see you later," Juli responded.

She turned and strolled back the way she had come.

Michael watched her for a moment before continuing back to his apartment. The school year was definitely looking up.

Move-in day arrived bright and early. Michael was grateful he had made a point of unpacking and setting up his coffeemaker the day before. Students and parents would be showing up shortly, and he needed to be awake. Jon had mentioned that parents of younger students tended to show up earlier to make sure that their child was completely settled before they had to leave. Michael stared out the window overlooking the gardens, coffee cup in hand. A slight movement out of the corner of his eye caught his attention. Did somebody just walk into the side door of the dormitory? He stared at the door but didn't see any further movement. Glancing at the clock he had placed on the mantle of the fireplace, he moved back into the kitchen. Refilling the coffee cup, he made himself a quick breakfast of eggs and toast and wolfed it down.

The day went by without any real problems, unless you counted the senior who joked that he didn't want the haunted room, and the first-year student who overheard the senior and realized the room in question was his room. Trying to reassure an already nervous student and protective parents had been something of a challenge, but not horribly bad. Michael figured that if there were any actual ghosts in Darrington, Jon would have mentioned it to him yesterday.

The first week of classes flew by, and Michael gave in to the sense of relief late on Friday afternoon when he finally walked into his apartment. He would be on campus this first weekend since Jon's friends were still in town, and he wanted to be able to spend time with them. That didn't bother Michael as he was planning on working on the rest of his lesson plans in an attempt to ease some of the mid-year stress that always seemed to sneak up on him.

He made himself dinner and indulged in a glass of wine before settling down to the lesson plans. Several hours of productive work later, Michael stretched his aching shoulders and considered calling it a night. He looked at the clock and was surprised to see it was even later than he'd thought. He decided to finish up the last lesson plan before going to bed. He could sleep in tomorrow.

Loud pounding at the interior front door interrupted those thoughts. Michael sighed, marked his place in the textbook, and pushed back his chair. The pounding on the door became louder and more insistent.

"Mr. Scaramucci! Mr. Scaramucci!" the panicked voice came through the door.

"I'm coming!" Michael called. He opened the door to find a pale, shaking upper classman. Theo Denton was a sixth-year student who Michael knew to be calm, rational, and usually mature. Right now, he was wide-eyed and obviously frightened.

"What is it, Denton?" he asked, slightly alarmed by the look of the student.

"Mr. Scaramucci...th-there's something on the third floor! It went into Tab's and Hector's room...and...um...tried t-to pull Tab through the window! Hector held on to him, and yelled, and the g-ghost, or whatever it was, vanished!"

Michael stared at the student. If Denton was this scared, something had indeed happened. But Michael wasn't quite prepared to buy into the ghost story just yet. First week shenanigans were common, and he suspected the students might be playing him. Nevertheless, Denton looked seriously frightened and Michael didn't think the boy had the acting ability to carry that off.

"Hang on, Denton," Michael went back to the kitchen and grabbed his keys. In addition to keys to the apartment and dormitory main door, he had a master key that opened every room in the building.

Following Denton as the student raced up the stairs, he thought about the patterns in the story. The patterns held together, suggesting Denton was telling the truth. They reached the third floor after a sprint up two flights of stairs that left Michael gasping for air. Several more students were gathered in the hallway in front of the room in question. To a man, they looked immensely relieved to see him. What was going on? This didn't have the feel of a practical joke. There was a strong impression of fear and dread in the air that Michael didn't think could be created by students pulling a prank.

Michael pushed his way through the small crowd of students and into the room shared by Tabata, or Tab, Toshiyuki, and Hector Carvallo. Both young men were sitting on the floor leaning against one of the beds. Both appeared extremely frightened. The one window in the room was shattered, and glass was scattered on the floor beneath it.

"Tell me what happened," Michael sat down on the floor next to a shaking Tab.

Hector cleared his throat. "Well, sir, um…we were both reading. All of a sudden, the room got really cold. Like super cold, and Tab yelled. I looked over and this … thing … ghost … whatever, was trying to push him out the window. The window wasn't open, and it wasn't broken then; but Tab was partially out of it anyway. It was f-freaky, sir. The th-thing was sorta inside and outside at the same time, too. I yelled and grabbed Tab's legs to pull him back in. That's when Theo and some of the others ran in. When they did, the thing disappeared, but Tab was still halfway out the window. We pulled him in, and that's when the window broke. I swear we didn't do it on purpose. But we had to get Tab back into the room!" Hector's voice shook, but he looked Michael in the eye as he finished the story.

Michael looked at the two boys. Tab's face was pale, and his eyes were wide. Michael put a hand on Tab's shoulder.

"Tab? Tab? It's okay. It didn't get you," he said softly.

Slowly Tab's eyes focused on Michael. "Sir? It was so cold. So cold. I couldn't move." His voice was a shaky whisper.

"Tab, I have to ask you…do you think it was a ghost? Or something else?" Michael hated to take the boy back to what was clearly a traumatic incident so soon, but he had to get an idea of what he might be dealing with. If it was a ghoul or wraith, or some other dead creature, it could go after other boys tonight. He didn't want to think about that possibility.

Tab jerked his head in the negative. "I don't know," he whispered.

Michael wondered if Jon was back from his evening out with his friends. He could use some backup about now. He looked up at the boys still gathered in the doorway.

"Denton take somebody with you and go down and see if Mr. Noble is home. Bring him here."

Denton jerked his head at the student next to him, and the two boys raced off. Michael stood and moved to the doorway.

"Before Mr. Carvallo yelled, did any of you see or feel anything? Did you feel the cold he mentioned?"

One of the boys halfraised his hand. "Sir? I think I did. We were playing cards in my room," the student indicated the room immediately across the hall, "and I felt cold all of a sudden and thought the window must have a leak or something. And that was right before we heard Hector yell. But maybe it was...whatever Hector saw?"

"All right. Anybody else? Anything feel strange?" He waited. Feet shuffled and somebody coughed.

"Gentlemen, nobody is getting in trouble tonight. This is too dangerous. Just tell me if you felt something and when and where. I don't want to know *why* you might have been wherever you were," Michael added.

"Well, um...we were coming back in...um...just a bit ago...um...in the, uh, back door..." a voice from the back of the small crowd began hesitatingly.

"Yes?" Michael hoped he sounded encouraging. Right now, he didn't care if they'd been out after hours. "Please just tell me what you saw. I promise. Nobody gets in trouble tonight."

There was more shuffling, and two boys moved up to the front of the small group.

"Mr. O'Hara, Mr. Patel. What did you see?"

"It wasn't so much seeing as feeling, sir. We had just ... um ... opened the back door when Aaka accused me of dumping ice down his shirt. But I hadn't done anything," Brian O'Hara began.

"At first, I didn't believe him, but then I realized my shirt wasn't wet. But it still felt like there was ice running down my back," Aakash

Patel took up the story. "Then the icy feeling just stopped. I didn't think too much about it because we were worried about ... um ... not ... um ... waking anybody up when we came in." Patel at least had the grace to look a little bit ashamed.

"All right. Thank you, gentlemen. I will just say, in the future please try to avoid breaking so many rules in one night." Michael smiled at the two students.

"Michael, what's going on? Is everybody all right?" Jon jogged up to the back of the crowd followed by Denton and the other student.

Michael gave Jon the shortened version of what had happened and included the information he had just received from O'Hara and Patel.

Jon's eyes widened. "This isn't good," he said in a huge understatement.

Michael nodded. "We need to find a place for these two tonight." He indicated Tab and Hector.

"Well, we can pull their beds into a couple of the other rooms for the night. Maintenance can fix the window tomorrow," Jon suggested.

"Good idea," Michael glanced at the students. "Okay. Some of you grab the beds and help Mr. Toshiyuki and Mr. Carvallo with some of their belongings. Pick two rooms. I don't care how you do it; but somebody will take Mr. Toshiyuki, and somebody will take Mr. Carvallo."

Theo Denton moved forward. "C'mon, Tab. Let's get your stuff." He reached out and helped his friend to his feet. Tab was still a bit shaky, but at least he was moving. Brian O'Hara and Aakash Patel helped Hector up and others started pulling mattresses off the beds and grabbing books and some clothes.

Confident that the students had the matter well in hand, Michael looked over at Jon.

"I think we need to talk."

"Yes. I'm assuming you're thinking along the same lines as I am," Jon agreed.

"Most likely. I have some scotch ..." Michael responded.

"Lead the way," Jon said, accepting the implied invitation.

Once back in Michael's apartment, glasses in hand, the two teachers stared at each other.

"Helluva way to begin the school year, eh?" Jon said taking a sip of his scotch.

"No kidding. I'm thinking wraith. You?" Michael fought the urge to down his drink in one gulp.

"Yes. The icy cold feeling described by several boys, and the fact that both Carvallo and Toshiyuki said it put Toshiyuki through the window without breaking it, definitely points to wraith. Any ideas on how to deal with it?" Jon swirled the amber liquid in his glass. The ice cube clinked softly against the side.

Michael stared into his glass. "Wraiths are usually found *elsewhere*. But that doesn't mean they can't cross over to our plane. I don't like it. It means that somebody either brought one with them, or there's some sort of anomaly that allowed this one to cross over."

"I agree. I'm inclined toward the anomaly idea simply because it's too early in the school year for the students to get over-confident in their abilities to safely travel between here and *elsewhere*. End of term is an entirely different matter." Jon smiled wryly.

"Oh, so I have more of this to look forward to?" Michael groaned.

"Not frequently, but it has been known to happen," Jon explained. "We'll need to speak with the headmaster. I think it will take some combined workings to send the thing back to *elsewhere*. And we need to do that tonight."

Michael looked at the clock. It was a bit after one in the morning. The middle of the night was not exactly the best time to be dealing with a wraith, but they didn't really have a choice.

Michael gazed at the moon and reflected that it was a beautiful night. Too bad they were hunting a wraith instead of simply enjoying the beauty of the night skies. After listening to their story, the headmaster had immediately followed them back to the dormitories. He was the one who had awakened Juli Ocampo and Elena Akabueze, her co-advisor in Solomons. They all gathered in the main entrance of Solomons.

"Ladies and gentlemen, we have a serious problem. A wraith attempted to destroy a student in Darrington Hall earlier, and it must be sent back to *elsewhere* tonight. It has already tried to take one student, and we cannot allow it to try again and perhaps succeed." Nathaniel Davidson was not a man to mince words.

Juli was standing next to Michael. She glanced up at him with wide eyes. "What are you guys doing over there?" she whispered.

He shrugged. "I claim ignorance," he whispered back.

The headmaster cleared his throat. Michael jumped guiltily.

"Fortunately, we have one kinetic mage," the headmaster continued pointing to Michael, "two image mages," he indicated Juli and Elena, "and two element mages," he waved a hand at himself and Jon.

Michael swallowed. He had previously traveled to and through *elsewhere*, the area in-between this world and the non-magic world and found *elsewhere* to be an unpleasant experience.In order to travel to *elsewhere* you had to create a pattern that included patterns found *elsewhere*. Since *elsewhere* was its own dimension, those patterns were headache inducing. He understood the theory behind banishing a wraith back to *elsewhere* but had never actually put it into practice. Judging by the looks on the faces of his fellow teachers, they were just as inexperienced. Hopefully, the headmaster was working from experience and not just theory.

As if he'd heard Michael's concerns, Nathaniel smiled.

"I've done this a few times. It's not easy, but it is possible. In essence, Michael will construct a pattern that will create a path to *elsewhere*. Jon and I will use air to push the wraith as that is the strongest means of forcing it anywhere, and Juli and Elena, you will create an image of *elsewhere* that will provide a destination for Michael's pattern. It doesn't matter how it appears, but you two have to have the same image.I suggest you base your image on those found in the textbooks. By separating these two tasks, the pattern and the destination image, we should be able to cut down on the headachest hat inevitably accompany any connections to *elsewhere*." Nathaniel looked around at his teachers to make sure they understood what they would be doing.

Michael glanced at Juli and Elena. "Once you two figure out your image, I'll need to see it so I can create a pattern that leads to it."

Elena nodded. "Okay." She turned to Juli. "Let's go figure out what we're doing."

The two women moved slightly away from the others, heads bent together as they discussed the image they would create.

The headmaster looked at Jon.

"Jon, while they're doing that, we need to work together so that we're familiar with each other's touch when we manipulate the air. We don't want to be pushing in opposite directions when the time comes." He smiled again.

In a relatively short period of time, the four teachers and the headmaster had worked out a plan for finding the wraith and sending it back to *elsewhere*. Michael thought it seemed overly simple, but the headmaster was happy with it, so Michael bowed to experience.

Plan set, the little group moved out of Solomons and went slowly through the garden toward Darrington. The headmaster theorized that, having been driven out of the dormitory, the wraith would lurk in some of the larger bushes in order to ambush the unwary. They spread out and wound their way through the plantings staying alert for the icy cold sensation that signaled the presence of a wraith.

Elena abruptly froze in the middle of the azalea bushes. "Over here!" she called.

The others rapidly moved over to her position. Jon and Nathaniel started the spell that would create the wall of air that would keep the wraith away from the teachers while simultaneously pushing it into Michael's pattern.

Michael stood next to Juli and Elena and recreated the pattern he had previously put together to guide the wraith into *elsewhere*. Suddenly, he felt an icy hand run down his back. He jumped sideways and almost knocked Juli over. She wrapped one arm around his waist and braced herself against him.

"Don't fall! Keep the pattern!" she said tersely.

"Sorry! Wraith touched me. Didn't expect that," Michael gasped.

Nathaniel and Jon were standing shoulder to shoulder. Despite the chilly night, and additional deep chill created by the presence of the wraith, sweat was running down both of their faces.

The icy feel left Michael, but he sensed a great deal of anger in the air. A subsonic howl vibrated their ear drums, and the air temperature dropped precipitously. Michael's head started to pound.

Nathaniel grabbed Jon's forearm. "Keep pushing it!" he rasped. "Michael. Your pattern, now!"

Michael put his hand on Juli's shoulder as she and Elena poured their energy into their image. He made a slight adjustment to his pattern and shot a glance at Nathaniel and Jon.

"Go! The pattern starts in front of Juli!" he shouted.

Both Nathaniel and Jon exhaled explosively. Michael could see the faint outline of something vaguely human-shaped. Two glowing red dots appeared in what Michael supposed was its face. The thing reached one long arm toward Michael. As it was pushed, struggling, into the start of his pattern, Michael took over from Nathaniel and Jon and used his pattern to continue to push the wraith toward *elsewhere*. The wraith was strong, and it clearly didn't want to return. Michael strengthened his pattern and dug deep into his energy reserves. He could feel sweat dripping down his face and into his eyes. He swiped one hand across his face to clear it off.

The wraith chose that moment to surge back against the pattern. Michael staggered and felt control slipping from him. The wraith felt it, too, and pushed even harder. Both arms reached for him, and its eyes glowed brighter. A gaping black hole opened under the eyes. Panic gripped Michael. If he lost control...

Juli wrapped her arm around his waist again. Her other hand grasped Elena's as they worked to maintain their image of *elsewhere.*He felt hands gripping his shoulders. A surge of energy poured into him.

"Keep going! You can do it!" Juli yelled at him.

Michael took a deep breath and drew on the new energy flowing into him, pouring it into his kinetic pattern. The wraith gave another subsonic scream, but he could see it slowly moving through the pattern. Michael directed one more surge of energy into the pattern, and the wraith finally moved through the last piece and into *elsewhere*. He collapsed the pattern, and Juli and Elena let go of their image.

Michael slumped to the ground. The hands he'd felt on his shoulders belonged to Nathaniel and Jon. The other four joined him, sitting in the dirt among the azalea bushes. Everyone was panting as if they'd just run a race.

After about five minutes, during which the panting died down and they started to look around again, Nathaniel smiled. "Well done, everybody! We do have the best teachers at The Academy Arcane!"

"Please tell me that we don't have to do that on a regular basis, sir," Michael managed to gasp out.

"Oh, come now, Michael. You have to admit that was an exciting start to the school year, and to your first year as a resident faculty advisor." The headmaster grinned.

"Oh, certainly sir. Exciting. Yes. Exactly how I would describe it." Michael scrambled to his feet and held out a hand to Juli while Jon dragged himself upright and pulled Elena up. Nathaniel bounced up, showing no signs of weariness.

Juli grinned up at Michael. "Well, with that kind of excitement so early in the year, the rest of should be calmer."

"Oh, don't tempt fate!" Michael returned the grin.

Nathaniel looked up at the sky. "It will be dawn in a few hours. Well, it's the weekend, so at least we don't have to worry about classes tomorrow...er...today. I suggest everybody return home and get what sleep you can. I will contact you later to discuss some steps we should take to prevent this sort of thing in the future."

Juli gave Michael's hand a squeeze. "I'm about to collapse. I'll see you later."

"Sure thing." He smiled.

Juli and Elena headed back to Solomons and Michael, Jon, and the headmaster walked slowly back toward Darrington. The headmaster left them at the main entrance with a cheery wave.

"Is he always that cheerful after fighting wraiths that have invaded his campus?" Michael asked.

"I've never seen him deal with something like a wraith before, so I can't really say. But it does look like he's enjoying himself, doesn't it?" Jon gazed after the headmaster as he disappeared into the shadows at the side of the building.

"Definitely an interesting start to the year," Michael muttered.

Jon laughed. "Get some sleep. We'll talk later."

He turned down the hall toward his apartment.Michaelremembered to lock his own door behind him before shuffling into his bedroom and falling onto the bed. He still had a whole weekend of duty in front of him.

Becky R. Jones grew up in San Diego after spending the first eight years of her life as an Army brat. After college she spent time in banking, building sets for television shows, mobile home park management, and aerospace before going back to school and getting a PhD in political science. That led to 20-plus years in academia. Now, as a newly emerging fiction writer she's changing directions yet again. She currently lives in Philadelphia with her husband and Max, The Wonder Cat.

HANDFASTED TO THE DEAD

BY DENTON SALLE

Because of someone cursed to be a *wawalak*, a type of werewolf doomed to wander for eternity, Alex decided he needs to complete his initiation in the *volkh* path sooner than planned. *Needs must when the devil drives*, Alec will not let her be damned.

But final initiation means facing one of the great powers of the world. His grandfather faced the Lord of Winter. His father faced the Master of Fire, No one knows who you will face or what the cost will be, But for the sake of a bound soul, Alex plans to try.

Turns out the test is more complicated than he knew.

A story from the *Hall of Heroes* series, which takes place offstage from *Black Earth Rises*.

Handfasted to the Dead

The stark landscape of West Texas spread out all around him. The land looked flat from a distance but really was broken up by arroyos and the low, mesa-like hills. Prickly pear cactus grew in massive clumps, surviving even the hottest and driest summer. Small mesquite trees drove their roots deep in search of water and stayed green. The grasses and wildflowers were grey as they slept until the rains came.

Alex could smell dust with tints of the sage and cedar that lived in the lower places or near the beds of seasonal streams. This far onto the Edwards Plateau, you were nearing the desert to the west. Water was scarce, even with the river running though Menard county. When the rains hit, everything would be lush and blooming. Now, it was dusty and dry.

He carefully swept a large circular area clear and, in the center, built his firepit. Normally when they hunted out here, they stayed down nearer the creek. It was sheltered there with water oaks and cotton woods as well as the cedar and sage, Tonight, he wanted to see the stars. It seemed right to see them as he sat vigil.

Vigil. The old word. The New Age freaks would call it a vision quest, stealing the term from a very specific Native American custom. Neither was exactly right. Not enough *volkh* left written notes that it had a name. His teachers did what they could to figure things out from incomplete notes, the old wonder tales, and oral transmission from old men who never thought these things would be needed again. After all, who expected to find the Slavic Otherworld taking root in Texas?

Father Tafesse told Alex these customs still survived in Ethiopia and what his grandfather and father had told him was close to that. So, Alex went to the Pre-Sanctified service, got his blessing, and would spend a night under the stars. He had bread, salt, and vodka just in case, as well as something to break his fast at sunrise.

It was funny how all the fiction books with magic have these strange complex rituals, but the surviving traditions were simple and clean. By morning, he'd have come into his gifts or he'd have laid them down. Or died. Supposedly, others had made the latter choice just as others walked away from the Brotherhood. As much as he didn't want to do this now, he didn't understand that. Why would you leave a tradition dating from the ninth century when so many clamored for meaning in their lives? And why would you want to close yourself off to the Otherworld, the Black Earth, and not see the full glory of Creation?

Well, needs must. He shrugged his shoulders and settled into his hoodie. His jeans and work shirt were enough for the day, but when the sun set, the high desert got cold. He pulled it down to cover the large handgun riding his hip and the long knife next to it. Sitting Vigil was fine, but he really didn't want to get munched on by wild hogs. Or coyotes.

His boots kicked up dust as he prepared the circle. He removed dry grass and brush so the area around his firepit was safe. Then he used a stake and a line to mark out a circle.

The circle was defined. Next, he poured a line of salt around its perimeter. Then he lit the kindling he had collected, using flint and steel. Despite his practice, it took several tries. For some reason, it had to be flint and steel. And no kerosene. *Luddites. What's wrong with a lighter? Like starting the Paschal fire at church. Tradition, or a reflection of something else? So much has layered meaning that might not make sense in the secular world but does on another level.* He shook his head. *It's not like anyone in our family is gonna be a materialist. Not when the house spirits chew your ass in broken English about dirty dishes.*

Alex watched as the fire caught, and settled into a more comfortable position, sitting on his blanket. Dusk fell and he could hear the cries of the nightbirds and the howls of coyotes.

He sat and perhaps nodded off a time or two, watching the fire burn. Suddenly, he noticed the little mesa smelled of roses, and the night seemed brighter, as if someone turned up the dimmer switch on the stars and moon. The full moon gave off enough light that he could have read by it.

Funny, the moon wasn't full tonight according to Google. And roses or myrrh? Somehow, the Black Earth is risen.

He knew that meant the veil had parted, and now he was fully in the Otherworld: part of creation normally invisible to men. He waited. The Otherworld was perilous and marvelous. Time would tell why this had happened. He looked around.

The area about his fire was now white sand and across the circle, he saw a tall figure, dressed in what appeared to be the fur of a bear. Dressed in or... He couldn't tell. It wore weapons like a warrior from the old tales.

"So, Son of Adam, will you strive with me?" a deep voiced echoed. The voice was *basso profundo*, like the deepest voices in Russian music. It sounded like it came from a chest deeper and thicker than a man.

Alex started as memory clicked in. "The Half-Beast Wonder!"

From the old heroic stories of the Court of St. Vladimir the Sun. The half-man hero who killed Annika, the pagan knight who stayed with St. Vladimir even after the prince converted. For the sake of his vow, despite his hatred of Christianity, he kept his oath until he decided to go to Jerusalem and ... There's more to the story, but I don't recall it.

Alex rose, pins and needles dancing in his legs. He felt air on his skin, and realized his clothes had changed. Gone were his hoodie, work shirt and boots. Barefoot and naked to the waist, his jeans had been replaced with the leather riding trousers of a *bogatyr*, In front of him lay a shield and a long sword. The beast man stood watched him. His eyes glowed red in the reflected light. Alex could smell a clean animal musk coming from him, Something nagged at his memory, but he couldn't catch it.

"Arm yourself, man, and show me if the sons of Adam have still courage."

"No spear? Ah well, needs must then." Alex shook his head. He liked spears. Swords meant getting too close to something with fangs and claws.

"No, son of Adam, let us strive like men, not hunt the wild boar."

The Half-Beast Wonder waited as Alex armed himself. Reaching down, he grasped the shield by its handhold. The old Viking-type shield the Rus used before the coming of the Steppes tribes. He picked up the sword. Curved slightly and hilted like the *shasqua*, the old Cossack weapon, but with the cross-guard and partially sharpened false edge of the older styles. He looked at the Wonder and nodded. The Half-Beast Wonder clapped its sword against its shield in salute and rushed him.

Alex fought, using every trick he had learned from his father and from the old men who kept the faith of the Brotherhood when no one believed. The initial clash told him he had neither reach nor strength as an advantage. The Wonder had the strength of a bear.

He cut and slashed, crashed the shield into his opponent's to try and topple him. His blade seemed to dance in his hand, weaving the attacking patterns he had learned. All for naught.

The Wonder stopped his every stroke. His shield punches were redirected, and the beast's blows cleaved pieces off his shield. Stopping them was near impossible. Alex tried to redirect them but still his shield continually took damage.

Cuts came at him as relentlessly as the wind that had whipped up around them. The sand stung his eyes and face. A sense he didn't know he had opened and stilled it.

As it did, the fire flared, and a wall of flame jumped at him. The same sense showed it wouldn't harm him. He reached out and somehow pulled the lightning from the sky. It crashed down around the Wonder, who laughed into the roar of thunder.

The Wonder struck again, and Alex's shield shattered. He dropped the ruined handguard and desperately twisted away from the following cut. He cut back and then used his sword to block the return strike.

Stupid! I know better, but what else can I do.

Then, his sword snapped leaving him with a broken section a quarter of its original length. With only that, he charged with a snarl. The Wonder sidestepped and tripped him. He rolled quickly, avoiding the chop. As he did, he lost the sword.

Coming up he searched for anything to use as a weapon. The sense he had no name for opened, and he reached with it. Grabbing with that sense, he threw what he caught at the Wonder. The ground shook and cracked. Wonder laughed again.

Laughing, Wonder dropped his weapons and gestured. The

ground firmed beneath him. He called to Alex, "Come, young one. If you are too clumsy for arms, let us wrestle."

The Wonder approached him, arms spread, and Alex drove forward to grapple with it. Roughly a man in shape, it had the claws of a beast, a bear with heavy fur. Alex felt another sense open. He started to give a war cry, but all that came out was the growl of a bear.

He froze in shock and looked at himself. He had changed into a grizzly bear.

His pause let the Wonder grab him and start to wrestle. Alex had wrestled in high school and done sambo, but he wasn't a bear then. Despite his best efforts, the Wonder overturned him. He started to change again, but the Wonder pinned him by the throat.

He looked up, changing back into man-shape and saw the Wonder standing over him. Holding him easily with one hand, the Wonder held a sickle in his other. Time froze.

Of course, the half-beast Wonder was Death in disguise. Annika tried to threaten, bribe and finally beg, but it was no use. For Death claims us all at some point.

As Alex realized what he fought, he felt a tap on his forehead. The Wonder had struck him lightly with the back of the sickle. Its eyes, half-human and half-beast, stared into his.

Alex felt his youth falling away. The skin on his hands wrinkled, and the hair on his arms grayed. His joints hurt. The weight of years settled on him. It grew harder to breathe, and his sight dimmed.

He stared at the Wonder, knowing no man escapes death.

His voice, creaking and weak, echoed in his ears. "You win, oh Lord Death."

"You don't beg or bribe, young *volkh*?" the deep voice asked. The eyes continued to bore into his soul.

"Death is but a door to my Lord's judgment. I fear, but I trust in His Promise." Alex shocked himself with the words. He hadn't really considered himself religious. "Besides, I'm of the Brotherhood. We don't always die in bed."

The Wonder laughed and releasing his throat, he stuck his hand out. His half-human, half animal eyes danced with joy. "Then I have no power over you. Rise up, son of Adam." He extended a hand. "Someday I will collect you, and you will know me as an old friend."

Alex took the hand and let the Wonder pull him to his feet. The years fell away. He was again his true age and unharmed, save for the new scars that decorated his chest and arms. Glowing red in the fire-light, he recognized them as similar to what his teachers bore. Marks of the magic freed tonight.

"So," the Wonder said, and its voice had changed to alto. "After striving, let us break bread and drink together."

A dark-haired girl who looked like a twenty-something stood in front of him, still half-beast but exuding a raw sexual appeal that shocked him. She moved toward him and rested her hand on his cheek.

"Come, eat with me," she said, and then smiled. "I think you will find this form more... comfortable than that of many of mine."

She had dark hair that was so long it touched the ground behind her, dusky and tanned skin like caramel, and cat-like eyes as black as the shadows at night, She gestured to the side of the fire. Alex forced his eyes away from her beautiful, glorious nudity, and saw that dishes and cups were set on a blanket by the side of the fire.

He turned back as she took his arm and led him over. They ate, and the taste was something he couldn't name. He cut bread and fruit for her, with a knife she gave him. Fed her grapes and persim-mon. The wine cups never emptied of the strange green wine, and it burned its way to his core. She spoke to him of the magics and powers, of how his gifts would grow, and the prices they would claim.

"You will forget much of what I said until you need it, but now, Son of Adam, I grow weary of teaching. Come and sport with me. Be my lover, young one, and find life in the embrace of death."

Alex shook his head. He struggled to keep his eyes on her face, as she leaned closer and tipped her head up for a kiss. Her breath was like the honeysuckle in summer, and her dark eyes reflected the stars above.

Alex tried to pull back against the passion rising in him.

"Am I not fair among women? Come lie with me and be my lover." Her voice teased and tempted.

"You are wondrous fair, but..."

She leaned back and her eyes flashed.

"But?" she asked.

"They say that to love death leads to a dark end. A bloody one, with insanity and madness."

"Shush," she said and closed his mouth with a kiss. "They lie. I am the other side of life. You must accept me to fully live."

She kissed him again, and he yielded to her charms.

Before dawn, Alex awoke and found himself tangled in her limbs and hair. She was propped on one elbow, watching him. Before he could speak, she smiled sadly and said, "Son of Adam, now we must part, as pleasant as this dalliance was."

She pulled away from him and stood. Still beautiful, still glorious, but also terrible.

The flesh fell from her, evaporating until she was the skeletal Lady of Santa Muerte he had seen in barrio shops. The darkness swirled again, and she was wearing the bright red and gold cowl of those pictures and holding the scythe. The decorated skull looked at him with burning eyes, still somehow feminine.

"So, my young *volkh*, you have now come into your power and yet remain sane," Lady Death said. "Use it wisely, for being given much, much more is required."

Alex nodded.

She offered her hand, and Alex took it. She then looped a long lock of black hair, soft as silk, around their wrists. "Did you ever read Charles Williams?" she asked.

Alex's eyes grew wide. "What? How? I mean yes, I have."

"Then as he said of Talissen, until the doom be handfasted to the dead."

"Are not all of my faith, lady? For surrounding us is a cloud of witnesses..." Alex answered. *Death reads poets? And obscure English ones at that?*

There were no more words. She smiled and vanished as the dawn broke, although Alex still felt her presence.

The birdsong woke Alex from sleep near the remains of his fire. He woke with a start. The sun was long risen. Midmorning from the feel of the air. The Otherworld had settled back, and the veil had retreated from the mortal world. Alex realized he could see it now, shimmering across creation.

He was back in his hoodie and jeans, his boots off and sitting by the dying fire. Nothing remained of last night. He unzipped his hoodie and unbuttoned his shirt. The scars were still there, white lines against his skin like long-healed wounds. Below his collarbone lay marks of teeth, a love bite. And on his left wrist, the image of a braided hair like a faint tattoo.

He closed his shirt up quickly, not knowing when his dad would be back and not wanting him to see the bite. As he stood up to shake his boots out, he saw a glitter by the side of the fire. The silver-hilted knife he had used to cut bread and food for Death lay atop a stone. No other evidence of the duel, the meal, or anything else remained.

He still stood, holding the knife, when he heard the truck coming up the hills.

Denton Salle traveled a lot for business, and when they banned the fun hobbies in airports or on planes, writing took over. It is really just an extension of a strong tendency to tell lies and shaggy-dog stories. After all, the truth can be so confining. Previous works include "Deep

School Tuition" in *Fantastic Schools*, Volume One; *Texas Otherworld*; *Daemonic Mechanical Devices*; *Panda Dreams and Other Hallucinations*; and *Black Earth Rises*, His next book is about a young wizard who randomly turns into a panda. Updates can be found at www. dentonsalle.com

STAR PUPIL

BY PETER RHODAN

Taroniah of Marland—Taroniah was the illegitimate daughter of the King of Marland. Her mother died young, and the King's Master-At-Arms and his wife brought her up. She was not aware of who her father was, and has only vague memories of her mother who died when she was six, She has grown up in a world where the truly great sorcerers and many of the gods killed themselves off in a war two thousand years before. Magic was a thing of no great power in her time, although the number of powerful magicians has been increasing as lost knowledge has been re-discovered.

The court magician detected signs of magic in Taroniah. The King thought it politic to get her out of the capital, where she was being compared to the young and unhealthy son he had eventually sired on his wife. Once at Lightbearer Academy, she quickly became a star pupil while making actual friends, something she had not managed in Marland. She has hidden some of her power to not seem too much better than her friends.

She is in her final year when events elsewhere bring war to where she is and interrupts the graduation of her class.

Star Pupil

Chapter One: The Last Days at School

Taroniah leaned back in the hard, wooden chair and tried to rearrange her posture to ease her aching body. Her mind started wandering as Academagician Lendar droned on. He was one of those teachers that had to repeat each step of each spell construct, over, and over, and over before finally getting to the part where you had to take the full conceptualization and embed the spell in the object to transform it into a magical artifact.

This lesson he was teaching was how to apply a spell of hardening to a china cup so that if dropped it would not break. Not the most exciting of magical objects one could make but she had to admit that the basic spell was not that complicated, and the rest of the class should have no problems doing the practical part. Except maybe Korlah. The spell itself was small and neat, with additional spell work specific to binding the spell to china or at least clay-based objects that was nicely compartmentalized so that it could be modified easily. The same basic spell, once mastered, could easily be modified to harden a sword, a plate, a hammer, and with slightly more modifications, a building or a wall. In truth, masonry hardening was better done with a different type of spell better suited to area effects. Still, heavily modified, it could be used to strengthen masonry and such in a limited area.

Suddenly, she realised Academagician Lendar was standing in front of her. "I see I am boring you, Student Taroniah. Perhaps you would like to demonstrate to the class hardening that cup before I throw it at the wall?"

Taroniah felt herself blush but tried not to look intimidated by his looming presence. He might be her teacher, which meant she had to be at least somewhat respectful, but she had realised some time ago that she was far stronger magically. In some ways she was better-trained because she had extended a lot of the magic she had learned at the Academy far beyond what was taught, mainly due to her having a significantly greater ability at magic than most. Having to experiment carefully and in such a way as to not bring attention to what she was doing had imbued her magic with much greater precision and economy of power than many here would believe.

Now, however, she felt the lure of an interesting idea. "Certainly, Academagician."

She replied brightly and slipped out from behind her desk, stepping briskly forward to his large desk at the front of the room where a row of clay cups had been lined up for the students to practice on. Clay was chosen because it was very porous, which made affixing the spell easier while being essentially a brittle object and one that would reveal a student's failure to embed the spell properly by the simple means of throwing it against the wall.

Wood and cloth were both easier to affect but were not so easy to test to destruction! Steel was the hardest. Taroniah and the other students in this class had watched the Lord of Magic spend more than six hours concentrating on a spell to harden a metal breastplate before finally throwing the conceptualized spell on the armor. A guard had fired a heavy war arrow at the breastplate before the Lord of Magic had started on the spell and although the heavy barbed head of the arrow had not penetrated the armor, it had left a shiny scored line where it had gouged into the metal. After the spell was applied, a similar arrow was fired by the same guard, from the same position, which hit about two finger breadths below the first strike did little except clang loudly. On closer inspection, there was a small mark where the point had impacted.

It had been a good illustration of the advantages magic could provide and at the same time exemplified the inefficient way they were applying their magic. Or so Taroniah believed. And was beginning to prove with her experiments. The Lord of Magic had not just spent six hours but had also been utterly exhausted magically by the time he was finished. And the breastplate had still been marked.

In the meantime, she was going to annoy her teacher!

She conceptualized the hardness spell easily then added the elasticity spell she had developed to apply to swords and such to make them springier and less likely to snap. She modified it on the fly to make the effect stronger and hopefully add some real bounce to the cup! She made a show of struggling and concentrating over the cup even though she had the entire combined spell conceptualized before she reached the desk. A flash of magic, her skill at magical precision and power control making it seem like she applied just the hardening spell. She dramatically slumped her shoulders to try to imply she was done but not confident and turned to the hovering Academagician.

She tried to sound unsure. "There you are, sir. I think I put the spell on properly." She backed away.

Lendar studied her for a moment as if he couldn't decide to believe her then moved over to the desk and picked up the cup. "Hmmm. You have definitely done something to it. Let us see if you have done it correctly."

He threw the cup at the wall, probably a little harder than was necessary, then squawked. The cup not only didn't shatter as it hit the wall, but it also bounced almost straight back at him! He frantically dodged the missile, and the cup landed on the floor on the other side of the classroom before sliding into the wall. Still quite perfectly intact.

Taroniah tried to look contrite. "Oh! I'm sorry sir. I clearly did something wrong. I, I'm not sure exactly what I did, sir." She hung her head while peering up at him through her hair. He looked furious and was a little red in the face.

"Hmmph."

He snorted. He glanced over at the intact cup sitting innocently on the floor across the room and then back to Taroniah.

"Clearly you did do something wrong," he stated sourly. "Yet your cup is intact, so you at least got the idea right." He narrowed his eyes but after a moment simply pointed at her desk. "Go, sit. Watch what the others do."

She turned away and saw that all her classmates were staring at her. She couldn't decide if they were concerned for her fate at the hands of the irate Academagician, or scared of the weird magic she'd just demonstrated. Or maybe they just couldn't decide how to react.

She smiled at Jenna and gave a thumbs-up before sitting down. Jenna gave her a little smile at least.

The others all managed to produce cups that passed the test, only just in Dryden's case as his cup developed a couple of cracks without actually breaking. Except for Korlah, whose cup shattered on impact. Lendar ordered him to stay behind. If he hadn't been such an insufferable snob, Taroniah would have almost felt sorry for the idiot. Almost.

He did have ability, although he didn't pay enough attention to details. He was not popular amongst the senior students partly because of his physical prowess, which he used to intimidate the males, while his arrogant assumptions annoyed the females. He was the nephew of the King of West Dumfordia, about sixth in the line of succession, and knew his worth as the first member of the Royal family to be recognised as having serious magical ability in recent times. He was technically some sort of cousin or perhaps cousin-in-law to Taroniah.

The thought of his reaction to her introducing herself on that basis brought a smile to her lips, and she almost laughed out loud! Being a bastard was interesting, at times.

Fortunately, there were only three female students in the senior class: Jenna, a slightly older woman named Hora, and herself. Having failed to seduce any of them with either his self-proclaimed charm or his Royal standing, he was now applying himself to the females in the next year down. Taroniah was taking the time to advise them all on how to give the idiot the finger. A task that Jenna was happy to help with.

The class was finally dismissed, and they all left the room before heading down to the common room. Taroniah stood talking with Jenna, Hora, and one of the older guys, Jek, for a while before heading to dinner. Academagician Lendar passed down the stairs and out in the courtyard without any sign he saw them off to one side. He was carrying her cup in his hand. Hmmm. That's when she had a brainwave! The problem with the really hard stuff like metal was that trying to embed spells was difficult. Most often the spell failed completely. Sometimes you would get a partial result. It was only now and then that the spell would even work as predicted and often the results were only barely detectable, which was why there was a dearth of incredibly sharp swords and impenetrable armor.

Rough cups and wood were far more porous than iron or bronze, which was why she had just realised she would possibly get better results embedding the spells in metal while it was molten. Or at least red hot, such as when it was being hammered during the forging. The work involved in creating a quality sword from a bar of iron was strenuous and quite tiring for the blacksmith. And that would be the time to embed the spells! Almost certainly.

She would head down to Alcitran on her next free day or days and talk to the blacksmith fellow there. He did repairs to equipment belonging to the Guards stationed at both the town and the Academy and probably could make a sword, or at least a dagger for her. She suddenly realised Jenna was waving a hand in front of her face.

"Hello? Anybody there?" her friend asked, laughing. The other two sniggered. Korlah swaggered down the stairs just then and all four turned their backs on him.

"What were you thinking about?" asked Jek.

Taroniah kept an eye on Korlah, but he made no move in their direction.

"Spells, impressing them in objects, just, well stuff. You know," she ended lamely.

All three sniggered again. They all thought she was some sort of absent-minded genius, she was sure. All of them knew she was the most capable magician of the group, the entire class did for that matter, but she was prone to vagueness when distracted. She had once, only once mind, walked into a wall because she was thinking about something else. None of them let her ever forget it, either.

They all glanced at each other. Hora shook her head as if in sadness. "Thinking about class stuff, after class. Sad. Very sad."

The others sniggered and even Taroniah had to smile.

"So, what did you do to your cup?" asked Jenna, grinning.

Taroniah was already the tallest of the women and nearly as tall as Jek. She did an obvious look around as if making sure no one was listening before she bent her head a little downward and spoke softly towards the floor. "I added elasticity to the spell so the cup would not only remain in one piece but bounce well, too."

She giggled. The others all giggled as well.

"Damn. I wish I could combine two spells on the fly like that!" Hora said enviously. The others nodded.

"With old Lendar glaring at you too. I can't think when he's staring at me," Jek offered.

"Oh. Do you actually think?" Jenna asked, gripping her chin with her hand in a thoughtful manner.

Jek glared and offered violence, but they all knew he was kidding. Jek and Jenna had a thing going. Taroniah wasn't sure if they'd got to the real intimate stuff yet, but she fully expected wedding bells in the not-too-distant future. This thought brought home her own lack of suitable swains. Not that there was anyone here that appealed to her. The only person she had ever really had a thing for had been Olli Marteen, Captain in the Royal Guard and second son of Kern Norgart. That had been an early teenage crush and it hadn't really survived her coming here, fortunately. Looking back, she was glad she had never had the opportunity or the gumption to approach the twenty-something Captain when she was only fourteen. It would have been embarrassing. Probably very embarrassing!

The rest of the evening passed pleasantly with her friends, though of course Korlah tried his hand at chatting to some second-year girls. Jeez, he was a slimeball! Taroniah made a note to have a word to them. The group broke up early and headed to bed.

One thing about magic school, it sure was tiring. Jenna, Hora, and she shared a dorm with four bunk beds, the other remaining empty, as there were only three senior girls. She settled down to think some more about her sword-embedding idea and fell asleep almost immediately.

Chapter Two: New Skills Today

Taroniah struggled through Advanced Magical Theory the next morning and was much happier doing Fourth Year Physical Exercise after lunch. The powers-that-be at the school felt that being physically fit aided mental fitness. Taroniah wasn't sure herself, but she enjoyed the physical training two afternoons a week. As with magic itself, the school made no differentiation between male and female students. They all ran. They all did unarmed combat. They all practiced with bow, sword, and spear. In this, the school was all on its own as far as treating students equally. Her real father's court would be appalled to see her wrestling with fellow students. To be fair, the instructors avoided opposite-sex matches where activities required close physical contact, generally. All the women were entitled to enter the end-of-term open tournaments the Guards oversaw although few women entered either of the two physical combat contests, these being wrestling and boxing. But the instructors certainly encouraged the girls to not hold back with each other!

Jenna was easily the best of the three senior girls at hand-to-hand combat, apparently because she had several brothers. Taroniah had never been taught that sort of physical combat at home; it wasn't something even a bastard female was allowed to engage in, being too unladylike by far. Strangely, her foster father had allowed her to learn to use weapons such as swords, spears, and shields as well as to master archery. Archery, at least, was something noblewomen were allowed to engage in although the more martial training she had received was kept out of sight of the court ladies. And even from the other girls at court, most of whom ignored her at best and verbally harassed her whenever they were able. Coming to learn here was in many ways a relief.

Here at Lightbearer Academy, she was allowed to train under the martial arts instructor without many restrictions. Wooden swords and blunt spears were used of course, with heavy padding, when engaging in training drills or combat bouts. She was the best swordswoman and probably best with a bow as well, although Jenna was her near equal. Of the male students, Korlah was easily the best at everything, except archery where some fellow from the back of nowhere was almost unbelievable. Largen was quite a pleasant young man, as far as young men go. He'd asked her to go to town with him once and taken no for answer without any problem. He hailed from a small coastal village on one of the islands West Dumfordia claimed called Extell, a village that no one had ever heard of, including Korlah!

Running around the training ground a few times and swapping wooden sword blows with her fellow students made a nice change from boring lectures. She was actually fascinated by Magical Theory and had enjoyed the class immensely back in her first year. She found the Advanced level course, on the other hand, absolutely boring. Apart from the occasional discussion of small things that either didn't fit within accepted theory or were so odd no one had managed to define them at all, the Advanced course was in practice nothing more than the Basic course in more detail. Sheesh.

She had begun making notes in class early on about various aspects of magical theory that interested her and which were either barely covered or simply ignored. Academagician Khast had a particularly nasal, high-pitched voice that grated on Taroniah's nerves, just to make the class even more enjoyable! During the first half of the semester, she had thought Khast simply had little understanding of magical theory himself, but as the class continued, she had eventually realised that, while his voice was annoying and his teaching methods tedious, the lack of theory being taught wasn't really his fault. A discussion with him in town one day when she had chanced to run into him at the wine shop had opened her eyes to the realisation that most advanced magical theory had been lost. A lot of stuff had been destroyed in the Great War, and what survived in the way of magical texts and inscriptions was eradicated by the Revilers in the century following.

Khast, himself, was not a powerful magician and had trouble conceptualizing some of the more advanced spells the students were learning in their last year, but he did have a much better grasp of theory than she had realized. The problem was it took years to test, refine, and then write up magical theory, especially if one wasn't a great sorcerer oneself. He had a new text he was working on, covering several more advanced theories, but he doubted it would be finished until the year after next. And then he had to persuade the Lord of Magic to approve the text and have copies made for future classes to be able to reference.

The conversation had left Taroniah with a different view of both Khast and the state of magical theory, and she had surprised him by offering to help him over the mid-year break, once she had visited home and returned. This offer had been almost gratefully received, and she resolved to be less critical in his class. His admission about the state of magical theory had been eye-opening and given her a new insight into the limits of spell conceptualization taught at the school as well.

That afternoon, when they had finished their Physical Exercise Class, which had involved mostly running, wrestling, and boxing, Taroniah had asked to do a little archery practice with the end of the year tests coming up.. The instructor let her have an extra half hour.

She made sure she was on the range by herself before trying out an idea she had been mulling over for a few weeks. She had tried affecting the course of an arrow in flight with magic to limited results, but now she had a different idea. She had come up with a spell that made an object hit the spot the magician visualised. Or so she hoped. She rolled out the spell mentally, conceptualized it, studied it. Made a couple of minor changes. Memorized them. Conceptualized it again, and laid it on five arrows in a row. Hard.

Then she stood, lined up at the shooting mark, and studied the targets. The furthest was three hundred paces, almost beyond the range of the bows even with the strongest man drawing one. She could reach the two hundred pace targets, just, and with limited accuracy, being right at the limit of her strength. Now she sighted down-range on the three hundred pace target before raising the bow to what she felt was about the right height to reach that range if she'd had the strength to draw the bow back far enough to impart sufficient force. Then she focused on the bullseye which she could only just see, held that vision in her head as she released the arrow, magically releasing the spell at the same time.

A faint thunk. Yes! The arrow was standing out proud from the bullseye in the centre of the target. Right!

She sent three more arrows down range and all hit the bullseye! She kept the last arrow for future reference and then wandered down to view her handiwork. All four arrows were crowded in the bullseye, but she found that each of them had hardly penetrated the cloth-covered straw at all. As she stood in front of the targets somewhat surprised, one fell out even as she studied them. *Ah,* she thought. *So, I can make arrows shoot right where I want, but because the range was so long there was no force behind the impacts. Interesting.* A lot of food for thought there.

She headed back to the equipment shed where she deposited the bow and then had another thought. She felt the arrows and realised that the spell was still embedded in the wood. She had better not put them back with the ordinary arrows! She went in search of the instructor and found him sweeping out the area where the wrestling and boxing took place. He nodded to her and then cocked his head when he saw she still had the arrows in her hand.

"Yes?" he asked.

She grinned sheepishly. "I was trying an idea out and impressed a spell into these arrows so I thought I better give them to you so you can keep them apart from the others."

He looked at the arrows, looked at her. "What did you do?"

It wasn't as if this was the first time she had experimented on school equipment. She had probably spent more money on replacing equipment her spell experiments had broken than she had on good food in the town. Not that school food was bad. It was just, well, limited.

She held the arrows up.

"I put a spell of targeting into the shafts. If the archer has any magic, focuses on the spot she wants to target, and then triggers the spell as she releases the arrow, the arrow will hit the target."

He looked startled.

"Just like that?"

She shrugged. "Pretty much. It was something mentioned in some of the accounts, you know. Kern Martane and his magical arrows that never miss."

He nodded. It was one of the few stories that had survived the Great War and it was included in any number of the common ballads that had spread around the lands of Ithria. Over the centuries it had morphed and changed a great deal. The version you would hear way up here would be rather different from the version common in, say, the Republic of Witon. Even the names and events were changed in some versions, but the basic story remained.

He stared at her steadily.

She stuttered a little.

"S-so, I, um, impressed this spell I worked out into these five arrows and fired four of them at the centre target of the three hundred pace targets."

"You don't have the strength to shoot that far," he offered.

She shook her head.

"Well, yeah, magic, you know. All four hit the bullseye in the centre of the target. They didn't penetrate far; in fact, one fell out as I reached them to have a look, but the spell meant they went where I aimed. All four."

He held out his hand and looked at the five arrows she handed him. "Right. I won't go and test them just now but I will put them under lock and key. They are very dangerous objects to have laying around."

"I know. That's why I brought them to you," she offered with a small smile. At least he hadn't yelled at her this time.

"I shudder to think what you will come up with next!" he said, a bit melodramatically. She could tell he was putting it on a bit from the crinkling around his eyes.

"I could tell you," she offered, trying to look innocent.

He threw up his hands.

"No! I don't want to know! Go have dinner, you horrible girl."

He pointed at the main building, but he was smiling as well. She smiled as she nodded and headed inside. She rather thought the next thing she'd scare him with would be the sword she was going to get the blacksmith to make, that would have properly embedded spells. She was almost certain her idea would work.

Fronday brought Advanced Spell Notation, an interesting subject. Spell notation was the method of writing out a spell on a clay tablet, waxed board, or even, horrors, parchment while you fiddled with the various aspects and values of the spell. Most people found it easier to grasp a new spell by studying it in written form first before trying to conceptualize it. And those that were developing new spells always wrote them out as they went. It was too easy for most people to miss something if they tried to develop a complex spell just in their head. Instead of turning water into wine, you could just as easily turn it to acid.

The original Spell Notation system went right back to a couple of small scrolls that had somehow survived the Great War and the purge by the Revilers in the century following. The school had copies, and so did several Royal libraries in the area, specifically the four kingdoms that supported the School. These consisted of Marland, Metonia, Pickantia, and West Dumfordia, and with their support, over the centuries the Academagicians at the school had slowly expanded the notation to cover new things they had developed. This was helped by the odd scrap of notation that turned up now and then and the occasional reference in an old tale that something could be inferred from. There was nothing intrinsically magical about the notations, but it was useful, if limited.

Taroniah had already come up with a dozen variations of standard notation forms for various tweaks to spells she had developed, and she had also devised a dozen new notation forms to cover spell aspects she had already created and she now needed to define a couple more. So far, no one had asked about her strange spell notations, but then she didn't wave them around in front of everybody.

After lunch was the mundane History and Geography class where the Known World was studied and the supposed history analyzed.

That night, she thought about how there were no sorcerers anymore and why that was so, but didn't come up with any fresh insights before she fell into a restless sleep.

And then it was Bedinday.

Chapter Three: Words of Power

Taroniah left her friends to enjoy the town of Alcitran, and headed up the street to where the temple of Emilar stood opposite the temple of Teshar. Both temples were small and were attended by only a few priests or priestesses most of the time. Emilar was one of the old gods that had fought in the Great War where many of the gods and most of the sorcerers had died. In the century that had followed, the Revilers had destroyed the remaining temples and shrines wherever they had found them, conflating the gods with the magic they were determined to stamp out.

As a great many of the gods appeared to have died in the Great War, most lacked any worshippers these days. Once the Revilers had lost their drive to destroy almost all signs of magic in the world, the worship of the old gods had begun to pop up again here and there. At first, it had just been small wayside shrines, untended, which the occasional passerby might choose to say a prayer at. With the reign of the Revilers over, along with a gradual rediscovery of magic, the centuries that followed saw a gradual increase in the worship of some of the old gods, mostly the ones purported to have survived the Great War.

These days, the religions were once more gaining in power and influence as their carefully husbanded wealth compounded slowly over the centuries. There was still prejudice and some realms didn't allow the worship of some gods while others were bound to the worship of different gods. Emilar and Teshar were two of the more common gods worshipped and their temples were found in most towns and cities.

The small temple of Emilar consisted of a raised platform that was three steps above ground level. In the centre of the platform was a rectangular building, although the rear two corners were actually rounded in form. At the front, the roof extended forward from the building resting on three plain stone columns. There was a simple doorway that led into the front part of the temple. There was the traditional alcove for offerings to the right and on the left were the hand and feet basins where supplicants could wash.

In the front centre against the wall that ran across the width of the building stood a statue of the goddess. This was reputed to be the likeness of the real goddess taken from before the Great War and carefully reproduced ever since. To the right of the statue was a small wooden door that led into the further part of the temple building where the priestesses lived. Taroniah dropped a silver coin in the curved stone basin for offerings, then moved across and quickly washed her hands and feet before moving forward and kneeling before the statue of the goddess.

She had always felt an affinity for Emilar, and as she knelt in front of the goddess she felt it stronger than ever before. She reached out and touched the carved foot of the goddess and prayed.

"Oh, Goddess Emilar. I ask you to grant me wisdom in the use of the great powers I have been given. I ask for your guidance that I may not succumb to the vanity of pride, to the slippery slope of hate, and that I restrict the use of my powers to when they are truly needed and not just arbitrarily to satisfy my personal greed and whims."

As she paused to consider her words it felt as if the stone had warmed to her touch. "Let me not succumb to the temptation to treat others as lesser beings than I am, as many of the great sorcerers appeared to have done in the time before the Great War. Grant me the ability to see when I must use my powers fully or when mercy and restraint are the better courses of action. Hear me, goddess Emilar as I supplicate myself before you."

She was about to continue when she heard a gasp to her right. Opening her eyes, she saw that the statue of the goddess was glowing in a pale mauve light. She glanced to her right where the sound had come from and saw a priestess standing there with hands to her face, apparently shocked.

"I meant no offense," Taroniah said defensively.

The priestess jerked slightly as if she had just come awake and stared blankly at Taroniah for a moment. Taroniah could see out of the corner of her eye that the mauve glow had dissipated and the statue was back to its normal appearance.

"How did you do that?" the priestess demanded, moving towards her.

"I merely prayed to the goddess. I did not even see the glow until you disturbed me," Taroniah replied.

The priestess halted a pace from her and looked her up and down. Whatever she saw caused her to change her manner from one of concerned annoyance to a softer, puzzled expression.

"I have never seen the statue of the goddess glow before. I have heard a couple of rumors that a statue had glowed here or there, but nothing ever certain; and only ever in front of one person, never with a witness." She looked again at the statue and appeared to mumble something that Taroniah couldn't make out. Whatever it was, the statue remained inert.

"In the time before the Great War, the statues of the Goddess would glow frequently whenever a true worshipper prayed to Her. That's a sign that the Goddess was indeed listening. Now I have seen something I never expected to see... who are you, that the Goddess would listen to your prayers when she ignores even her own priestesses?"

Taroniah studied the priestess for a moment but the annoyance appeared to have disappeared from the woman's face and had been replaced by a look of inquiry. "I am Taroniah of Marland. I am in my final year at Lightbearer Academy."

The priestess muttered something which Taroniah decided was a simple spell of some type and not one that was inimical so she ignored it. A look of surprise appeared on the priestess's face. She took a step back.

"You are powerful for one so young."

Taroniah nodded.

"Yes. Which was why I sought guidance from the goddess." She decided it was time to get back to Harkon, so she bowed to the priestess. "I have other tasks perform this afternoon so I will be leaving now."

The priestess considered her for a moment, then nodded slightly.

Taroniah turned on her heel and left the temple. She headed for the smithy, where she sought the permission of big Harkon the blacksmith to watch him work as she had an idea.

"An idea, young lady?" He laughed. He had made her a sword a couple of years ago which she had been unable to turn into a magical sword, but she had an idea.

"Yes, big man. I won't trouble you today if you let me watch for a while and also think on a price for a new sword, one I will help you forge."

Harkon looked at her for a moment but then nodded and went back to his work. She watched for a while and thought her idea had some chance of succeeding. After some time, her stomach started complaining so she headed to the inn where the food was good. Jenna and Jek were just leaving, ready to head back to the school. They were surprised she was just heading in to get something to eat as it was getting fairly late in the day.

"Don't take too long, Taroniah." Jenna said. "You need to get back to school before the night monsters come out."

"Ha. They're just old wives' tales." She grinned and headed into the inn. The food was as good as usual, not fancy but different from the school fare so it made a nice change. The innkeeper looked worried as she left, admonishing her to hurry back to school.

She waved and headed up the road out of town towards the Academy. As she traipsed up the road, she thought over the strange business in the temple. Why was she so powerful? Why had no one else been able to duplicate the targeted arrows of Kern Mentone? And while her sword idea was not fully viable, she was almost certain she was on the right track. If so, they would produce the first magical sword to be made in two thousand years.

But it didn't seem that hard to her.

Was it perhaps that all the powerful sorcerers had been killed in the Great War and it had taken this long for a new generation of powerful sorcerers to arise? Well, one powerful sorcerer. She grinned. It was very strange. None of her teachers were anywhere near as powerful as she was. She wasn't entirely sure about the Lord of Magic, though she rather suspected he wasn't much more powerful than any of the other academics at the school.

She thought of the court magician at home and realised that he probably wasn't as powerful as most of the lecturers here. She hadn't considered that aspect before. The lack of knowledge was perhaps a large part as well. It would be hard to be a powerful sorcerer if you had no idea of how to go about it.

Which brought her back to Kern Mentone, and the arrows that never missed. Yes, it had taken her some months of thought, planning, and writing out innumerable versions of the spell before she was happy with the version she had finally used. But, in all the centuries since the Great War, was there no one else that had been able to think up the same spell?

Apparently not.

It was completely dark as she neared the Academy gate. She was sure something was moving parallel to her in the scrub off the trail to her right. Tales of night monsters ran around inside her head and she was starting to feel a little nervous. Then she slapped herself, mentally. She conceptualized another spell she had been working on for months and which she had only tested slightly but was sure would work. She thought, *All right, night monster, come on out and we'll see who the monster is!*

Having the spell ready made her feel much better, and she picked her way along the road far more relaxed despite the darkness. The movement to her right seemed to speed up and angle in towards the road as if it was trying to get ahead of her. *I'm ready for you,* she thought. She actually saw the bushes beside her move as something passed through them and onto the road, She heard a hissing sound.

There was some sort of beast standing in the road. It had a strange glow, and she realised with a start that it was some sort of magical beast!

Well, doh! she thought. Everyone said the night monsters were magical. She put one foot forward and raised her arm for spellcasting with power.

"Piss off or die!" she commanded. Not that the thing would understand her words, except, well, it *was* magical.

It hunkered down like a cat preparing to pounce while the magical glow intensified. She had never seen a magical glow on a living thing other than a fellow human before, only on objects in class that had been magically impregnated. Hmmm.

Right, it was going to pounce.

"Piss off!" she yelled and threw the spell.

She had only half-tested it in a small way, but although untested she was sure her spell would work. What she hadn't expected was *how* it would work.

Her small experiment had resulted in a small pile of leaves bursting into flame like someone had doused them in oil and then dropped a lighted taper on them. There had been a sort of soft puff; a hot air halo had formed around the leaves; and then, the leaves burst into flame and started burning like, well, leaves. All very unexciting, and not really like the firestorm spells spoken of in stories. Still, she at least knew she could set things alight. It was something that wasn't in the list of spells available to be learnt at the Academy, let alone amongst the small sub-set of spells that were actually taught.

Her previous small test meant she was totally unprepared for the rather different effect of the spell when thrown, hard, with her very strong magical ability. The beast literally burst into flame, incredibly hot flame, that lasted maybe three or four seconds before the beast was reduced to ashes and the flames subsided and went out. Parts of the woods and bushes behind where the beast had stood were also smouldering, although they soon went out as they hadn't really caught fire because she had concentrated the spell on the beast.

Taroniah sank down on the ground, sitting cross-legged, and contemplated instant incineration. Shit! She had modified the spell to affect only the beast but she had put too much into it not expecting it to work so well. She felt quite drained, and doubted she could throw it again for a good while, or any other major spells for that matter!

Right, up and at them, uppity Royal female bastard, she thought. She stood up and immediately saw stars before her head cleared. She wobbled around the charred patch of ground where there were just a few ashes to show where the beast had stood and headed unsteadily up the road.

The Academy was reached without further incident.

After knocking on the gate to rouse the no doubt sleeping guards, she was finally allowed inside. The other girls all fussed over her once she reached the breakroom, wanting to know why she was so late. Wasn't she afraid of night monsters? And why had she spent so much time at the smithy? Wasn't Harkon a little old for her?

She brushed off their concerns without mentioning the real night monster she had dealt with, laughed at the quip about Harkon, and after a quick meal headed off to bed. In truth, she was utterly exhausted.

She awoke the next morning feeling like she hadn't slept hardly at all. Somehow, she got herself up and moving. By the time she sat down for breakfast, she felt almost human.

The next week's lectures crawled past. She got into trouble a couple of times for not paying attention, but whenever put to the test she had no trouble performing the magic she supposedly hadn't been listening to the instructions for. Her mind kept swirling around with ideas for other spells for weapons, for spells to reinforce castle walls, for all sorts of ideas. She spent most of her free time re-reading the few tales that had survived from the Great War and before with their amazing tales of magical feats that most people thought had to be exaggerated.

The week ahead would mark the end of formal instruction. The week after that, there would be a series of magical tests, supervised by the Lord of Magic and the two senior lecturers, Academagician Lendar and Academagician Horren.

Chapter Four: The Sorcerer is Revealed

On Fronday, there was a stir as a soldier came galloping to the Academy and headed straight for the Lord of Magic's office. That evening at mealtime, the students gathered together and the Lord of Magic came to speak to the whole body.

"Students. The King of Shoveria has launched a surprise attack on Kinder Island, which as you should all know is owned by the Kingdom of Metonia. They landed troops north of Watfield, which allowed them to take the town by surprise. As you should also know, the Metonian possession of the island has long been a bone of contention between the two realms." He paused and looked around the room.

"We have two students from Shoveria and one from Metonia, I want no trouble between the three of you. What your kingdoms do is not the business of this Academy. Take due heed of my warning."

He held up his right hand and a small ball of fire appeared in the air above it. As a show of magical power, his ability to do that had always been seen as very intimidating by Taroniah's fellow students. Even she had been intimidated in her first year, but since then, not so much.

"No one is to leave the Academy for the next week at least. The exams start on Ashday, so I expect you all to spend the next two days studying." He nodded severely and left.

The students returned to their meals and the hubbub grew enormously as the students discussed this sudden turn of events. Korlah was holding forth about how it would mean war as West Dumfordia was allied to Metonia. Taroniah rather thought he was right, just for once. Her own land, the Kingdom of Marland, would almost certainly join in as well, although that would depend on the attitude of their long-time rivals, Bovil and the much larger Kingdom of Padmouthia on Marland's southern border.

The exams were more important than a possible war at this stage. She spent the next two days practicing various things she was likely to need to be able to do in the tests. The hardest part would be not showing off! Being more powerful than most, if not all, of your tutors was quite awkward. Sick of study, late on Urday she took her bundled sword outside and around behind the building where she was unlikely to be seen. Here she practiced wielding it in either hand, trying to build up her muscles. She was much weaker in her left arm than her right and she worked hard on it until she could barely lift the sword at all.

"You're going to be sore tomorrow," a voice said quietly behind her.

Taroniah spun around. Jenna stood at the corner of the building, watching her.

"I got sick of study." She began bagging her sword as Jenna approached.

Jenna nodded, then peered at the bag now that she was closer.

"That bag has magic applied to it. Or inside it. Or something."

Taroniah quickly considered the fact that her friend was quite strong magically as well and decided to test her. She closed the bag up and wrapped the excess cloth around the sword and scabbard. "Yeah. I impregnated the cloth with hardness like the cups we did in class last week, so hopefully, the cloth won't rip too easily."

Jenna looked at the bag, then at Taroniah. "Oh. Interesting idea." And although she sometimes looked at the bag again as they walked inside, she never said anything else about the bag, the magic aura, or anything.

The next day was the first exam day, but the senior students had no tests. Most spent the day quietly studying in their dorms.

The day after, Taroniah's first test was Spell Notation. The Academagician put four incomplete spells on the board and they had to write the full spell out. The first two were straightforward. The third was tricky in that the spell section on the board was missing the first part of the spell, as well as some of the end. The fourth was just the end part of a common, but complicated, spell that purified water.

In the afternoon she had martial arts. The archery was easy; she slapped her accuracy spell on each arrow as she fired and scored three nicely clumped bullseyes at two hundred paces. The sword drill was harder, but she lasted long enough against the instructor to pass. The hand-to-hand combat was much harder as she was put up against one of the shorter and slighter male guards. Surprisingly, her speed let her win three to two, so an easy pass in the end as the girls only needed to get one fall against the male guards. Her opponent got ribbed mercilessly by his mates after their match!

History and Geography the following morning was straightforward, and although she didn't get a great score, it was high enough.

Spell Casting after that was a test of how many spells they could get through in a limited period of time. The Academagician had five wooden boards, each with a basic spell on it. He held them up randomly as quickly as you cast the previous spell. She topped the class, she thought, although nothing was said.

Strangely, Korlah did very well at this test. Interesting.

Emilday, they had the morning free then Spell Conceptualization in the afternoon. Taroniah entered the room she was assigned to and found herself facing the Lord of Magic. Lord Margary was the brother of the Kern of Kenshire in the Kingdom of West Dumfordia and a personal friend of the King. She had always been rather intimidated by him and seeing him here to give her the test was no different. Suddenly, she had butterflies as she walked forward.

"Ah. Taroniah of Marland. I have heard a lot about you in your four years here," he said in a deadpan voice from which she couldn't gather whether he meant good things or bad. Her butterflies began to be replaced by anger. "The test will consist of you conceptualising and casting three very complicated and difficult spells. You have two hours, so it shouldn't be about the time limit with only three spells."

He paused and studied her.

"Do you understand?"

"Yes, sir." She was puzzled. Only three spells?

He turned over three boards on the table in front of him. Apply a spell of hardness to a glass pane so it wouldn't break: apply a spell of light to a candle that would illuminate the room brightly while causing the candle to continue to burn normally: and finally to apply a spell of force and knock over a small brick wall. She looked around.

Ah. There was a wood-rimmed pane of glass, a candle on a small table, and over there behind where she had come in, a small brick wall, cemented several days ago by the colour.

"Tricky, sir," she said.

He looked slightly puzzled by her comment. She concentrated, calling up the hardness spell and double, then triple strengthening it, the brightness spell, and finally a spell of force. It was hard mentally organising and balancing the three sets of spells and she lost the concept twice before she bundled it all together and could cast the combination.

The Lord of Magic had sat down behind the desk and was starting to look rather bored by the time she cast her combination conceptualization. The candle brightened and the bricks were not just knocked over but thrown violently against the stone wall.

"Oops. Sorry. Too much force, sir," she offered at his startled reaction.

He had sat up with a start and now looked sharply at her before walking over to the bricks. He looked at the mess for a moment, picked one up, and threw it at the pane of glass. The force of the blow sent the wooden framed glass pane flying, yet despite being hit by the brick andlanding hard on the floor, the glass didn't break.

He stood and stared.

She shrugged. She'd done what he'd asked.

"I didn't mean perform all three tasks simultaneously in one big spell," he said at last.

What? Oh.

"Sorry, sir. I misunderstood."

"Obviously," he said shortly, then shook his head. "Well, you passed this test, Student Taroniah. In a most astonishing manner, too. Well done." He actually smiled and shook her hand!

It was so unexpected, she left the room in a daze and didn't even realize she was back in the common room till Jenna shook her.

"Hello?"

Taroniah started and smiled.

"Oh, hi,"

"What happened? Did you mess up?" her friend asked, looking concerned.

"No. No. Well not exactly. The Lord of Magic shook my hand." Her voice sounded odd, even to herself.

"Really?" Jenna looked stunned. So did Korlah, who happened to have walked in just then.

"You're not serious?" he asked.

Taroniah just nodded.

Before they could question her further, there was some noise outside. Armed men entered the room. Two wore West Dumfordia green, but the lead man wore Marland blue and Royal Guard blue at that. They marched over to the Academagician, Lendar as it happened, at the far end of the room, and had a few words. Whatever it was, Lendar looked surprised, then nodded. He moved to the area at the front and rapped the gavel on the lectern there.

"Students. You are all to immediately retire to your rooms, pack everything you can carry, and assemble in the courtyard. We are evacuating the Academy!"

This brought immediate noise and confusion. Taroniah looked at Korlah.

"Shoveria," she pronounced.

He nodded, as did Jenna, and the three left the hubbub behind. She packed everything she had quickly. To help make her seem like a normal student, she hadn't come loaded with chests of fancy clothes which meant she had all her possessions in a pack that could be worn on her back. Only the sword wouldn't fit, so she carried it, still in the bag, downstairs.

The courtyard was utterly chaotic, but the regular guards and the small force of West Dumfordian troops from the town, as well as the three Marland Royal Guards in evidence there, soon had the students organised and marching to the town. She couldn't get a good look at the Marland fellows, but the tallest one did seem familiar. The Academagicians stayed behind to hide everything they couldn't carry. Most of the ordinary staff joined the march to Alcitran.

Even though it was late in the day, they arrived before full dark.

They were herded into two of the temples. The girls were sent into the Temple of Emilar, and the boys into the Temple of Teshar.

Simple pallets had been laid out by the priestesses and the girls were made welcome. Taroniah had barely put her pack down before there was a commotion at the door. Two men in Marland blue entered. The taller one she could now clearly see was Olli Marteen, Captain in the Royal Guard. As she stood up erect, he came straight over.

"Captain Marteen. A pleasure to see you again," she said, suddenly all lady-like.

He gave her a small bow.

"Lady Taroniah. Your father sent us to escort you home after you finished your exams, but it appears we will be delayed."

Taroniah nodded.

"So, Shoveria?" At his nod, she continued. "How many and how far away?"

If he was surprised by her questions, he gave no sign.

"Upwards of two thousand, horse and foot. They will be here tomorrow according to the Dumfordian fellows."

She nodded.

"I wonder if they have any sorcerers?"

He laughed.

"Not bloody likely. Maybe a couple of magicians who went to your school, but there aren't any real sorcerers anymore."

Which was indeed the common belief and no doubt probably true up until now.

"Well, they are in for a world of hurt tomorrow then." She waved at her fellow senior students. "We can all do serious magic, magic with military application, I might add. And the senior boys are just about as good." She saw Jenna snicker out of the corner of her eye.

"I can't let you risk yourself, Lady." He tried to look stern.

She stuck her chin up just a little, held out her hand, and produced a ball of fire like the Lord of Magic used to illustrate his power.

"You will find it almost impossible to prevent me, Captain," she said imperiously.

He stepped back a little and frowned at the small fire floating above her hand.

"My orders are to keep safe, Lady."

"Well then, Captain, I have no objection to you and your men forming my bodyguard on the morrow when we fight the Shoverians." She stared at him as if daring him to say otherwise. She let the fire disappear.

"If it wasn't for the two Shoverian ships off the port, I'd drag aboard our ship and sail tonight," he countered.

She laughed.

"I doubt you'd have much luck trying that, Captain. Now, if you will excuse us. We ladies have to get cleaned up before going to bed." She made swishing motions with her hands. "So, shoo."

Glancing around at the numerous giggling female students and the glaring priestesses, he decided discretion was in order.

"Very well, Lady. We will continue our discussion tomorrow."

He bowed, turned on his heel, and led his still silent companion out of the temple.

The next morning, Taroniah got dressed quickly. After a short breakfast put on by the Priestesses, she headed for Harkon's smithy. From things overheard in the street, she gathered the Shoverian force was still a couple of hours away. Given the panic in the streets, it probably wasn't far enough. Harkon's was packed with fellows wanting their weapons sharpened, armor repaired, and a host of other things. All at once! He had his apprentice and another young fellow helping, but even that wasn't keeping up with the demand.

Taroniah pushed her way into the smithy more by force of will than anything, along with the fact she was a female whom the men were reluctant to lay hands on. She managed to catch Harkon's eye.

"Any armor for a girl?" she yelled.

He looked at her blankly for a moment then pointed to the other small shed.

"Check in there. Take whatever you want. We can sort it out later."

She blew him a kiss and pushed out of the crowd. The shed held a lot of junk, cast-offs, broken swords, spears, along with God knew what. There were two wooden boxes against the side wall and one held all manner of leather bits and pieces. She found some shin guards, arm guards, and one leather helmet that were serviceable. In the other, there were all sorts of armor, mostly bits of mail or mail armor with holes in it. She found two serviceable coifs, two mail tunics that were on the small side, one with a hole in the front and the other with a hole in the back. The other tunics were way too big for her, but she took them with her for the guys.

Somehow, she managed to pick up the enormous pile of junk and stagger into the street. One of the West Dumfordian guardsmen spotted her and took two-thirds of the load from her and helped carry it all back to the temple.

Captain Marteen and his two offsiders were already there and looking quite irate, probably because she wasn't there! Ha!

She and the guardsman plonked all the gear down on the steps outside the temple. She saw Korlah over on the steps of the Temple of Teshar.

"Korlah. Come get some protection!" she yelled.

He glanced at her, saw what she was carrying, and started nudging the other boys to head this way. Taroniah purloined the mail tunic with the hole in the back, a couple of leather braces for her forearms, and two leather shin guards. Captain Marteen looked to interfere, but she held up her hand.

"There is nothing to discuss, Captain. Now I am going to get my sword. Don't go away." With that, she marched into the temple. The armor was heavy but should serve. She was more concerned about the blow she didn't see coming than any opponent in front of her.

"Come." She led the captain back outside. She wandered around and finally found where the Academagicians were congregated with the Lord of Magic. Walking straight up to him she gained his attention by the simple expedient of stepping in his space, right in front of him.

"Sir," she said,

He blinked. Ignoring several other Academagicians talking at him, he looked at Taroniah.

"Yes?" he asked.

She held out the scroll she had made up with the arrow spell. "This is a spell of targeting. The spell needs to be impressed into an arrow, then the magician draws the arrow, visualises the target and where he wants the arrow to hit, lets fly, and then activates the spell. Done correctly, the arrow will hit the target exactly as aimed provided the target is in range."

She pressed the scroll into his hand.

"Really, Taroniah—" Lendar started.

The Lord of Magic held up his hand, bringing silence. He indicated Taroniah should continue.

"The spell is difficult to conceptualize, but I think all the Academagicians should be able to at least impress the spell on a dozen or more arrows before they tire, the senior students maybe less. The other magical students and any guards with magical ability should be given bows so they can use the magic arrows in the defense of the town."

The other Academagicians all waited to see what the Lord of Magic would say or do. He opened the scroll and studied it. And studied it some more. He looked up at Taroniah.

"This works?"

"Yes. I tried them out on the archery range a couple of weeks ago."

He frowned.

"I see." He studied the scroll again. "Kern Martane and his magical arrows?"

She smiled.

"Maybe. It is what inspired me."

He nodded.

"I see. We will talk more after this is over."

She nodded, whereupon he swung 'round and addressed the Academagicians.

"Find the senior students. We will make as many magical arrows as we can before the Shoverians arrive." He turned to a West Dumfordian soldier who had been hovering, obviously trying to listen to what the magical types were up to. "We will need bows for us and the students and all the arrows you can find."

The man looked blankly back at him.

"Now, soldier!"

The soldier jerked upright.

"Sir!" And ran off.

The Lord of Magic handed the scroll to Lendar. "Study it. See if you can conceptualize it. Give to one of the others while you start making magical arrows."

"Um. Yes. Of course, Lord." He took the scroll as though it was a poisonous snake.

Satisfied her work here was done, Taroniah headed for the main gate and the short tower that over-topped it. There was a ladder up to the parapet which she climbed, found a spot, and sat down to rest. Captain Marteen loomed over her.

"What are you doing?" he asked.

"Resting."

"I will not let you fight in this battle," he said.

She looked up at him.

"You don't get to choose. The Shoverians aren't going storm the town and then point at us and go, 'Oh. Marland people, leave them be,' while they sack the rest of the town, now, are they?" she asked sarcastically.

He shook his head, but before he could say anything she continued.

"Besides. These people are my friends." She waved at the town. "As are my fellow students." She closed her eyes for a moment, then opened them again. "I'm not about to let a bunch of Shoverian misogynists rape and pillage their way through here."

"So you're going to stop them all by yourself?" he asked, being equally as sarcastic as her earlier tone.

She stared at him for a moment.

"No, I won't be alone. There will be a bunch of magical students firing magic arrows at the stupid bastards, but more importantly, we'll have the only sorcerer on the battlefield."

She closed her eyes again and heard him snort, but he offered no further commentary.

She may have managed to doze off at some point, because suddenly she could hear yells and shouted orders and it was clear the Shoverian army had arrived. Standing up awkwardly as she worked the somewhat painful kinks out of her body she turned to look out over the scene to the south of the town. The Shoverian soldiers were lined up in six blocks, most about six ranks deep and around fifty men wide. A force of mounted men, maybe two hundred or a bit more was on one end of the line and another, smaller mounted force at the other end. Quite a few of the infantry at the front appeared to be holding one end of wooden ladders to be used to scale the town's walls, no doubt.

Forward of the army, there was a gaggle of officers, mostly nobles by the look of the fancy outfits. Captain Marteen must have been shielding her in her position on the wall because the whole battlement above the gate was full of people. The town Mayor and Royal Governor stood looking at the Shoverians just a little further along the parapet from where she was. The senior West Dumfordian Guard, Captain Killew, was with him, as was the Lord of Magic and one of the other Academagicians (although that worthy was on the far side of the group and she couldn't see who it was).

Several soldiers filled up the available space. The nobles at the front of the Shoverian force broke up and three rode forward, the gaudiest in the lead. When about a hundred paces from the town gate, they halted and the leader scanned the walls before speaking.

"I am Sharpe of Aveham, sent by my King to restore this land to the rule of Shoveria," he bellowed.

Larinet, the Governor, gave this claim no standing immediately.

"This is not Shoverian land and never has been. West Dumfordia gained it by driving out the Wigian barbarians many centuries ago. We have held this land ever since."

Sharpe waved this away.

"Long-standing occupation of our land does not give ownership," he retorted.

"Nor does loud claims by fancy upstarts!" Larinet replied.

Taroniah presumed there was something about Sharpe's pedigree she wasn't aware of. Never having heard of the fellow before, this was understandable. She could see the Shoverian was upset by this retort.

Sharpe pointed at the walls.

"You have maybe forty or fifty soldiers and I have two thousand. A few old magicians are not going to help you as I have some of my own." He pointed back at the four fellows who hadn't ridden forward.

"Harve's pretty good. The others not so much. They all studied here," the Lord of Magic commented.

"Surrender, and all will be spared and treated honorably," Sharpe continued.

There was something to be said for this course of action. If the Shoverians could be trusted. Taroniah wondered which way Larinet would jump. He was some sort of cousin to the King of West Dumfordia and had been a successful Admiral if she remembered correctly. But he was not that important in the Kingdom of Shoveria, or he wouldn't have been assigned way out here.

"I think not," Larinet replied. "My king gave this land into my charge. I will not give it up without orders from him."

Well, that's done it, Taroniah decided.

"Very well. On your head be it," Sharpe bellowed and went to turn away.

"Hey. You. Shoverian fellow." Taroniah yelled out, much to the surprise of those on the battlements.

Sharpe turned back and looked up at her.

"I am Taroniah of Marland. Do you have any sorcerers amongst those magicians back there?"

The man frowned. Shoverians were very patriarchal so he probably wasn't used to a woman yelling at him.

"No, you stupid girl. Everyone knows there are no sorcerers anymore." The dismissive tone was well done, she had to admit.

"Well then, Sharpe of Aveham. I suggest you turn your army around and head back home, thus saving your men's lives. And your own, for that matter. Because we do have a sorcerer."

Sharpe looked at her for a moment then scanned the wall before turning back to her.

"And where is this mighty sorcerer?" he asked, his voice dripping sarcasm.

"Perhaps I should have said sorceress. You're looking at her," she replied boldly.

There was no response for a moment. Then he and his fellows burst out laughing.

"You are a child," he managed at last. "I hope you survive the assault because I am going to enjoy playing with you." He turned his horse and led his fellows back to the magicians.

The people on the battlement were all looking at her.

"Really?" Larinet asked?

She shrugged.

"We'll soon see. There are lots of those magical arrows?" she asked the Lord of Magic.

"Yes. We divided up the students and those of the staff who have some skill with a bow and placed them along the wall under the command of a couple of the guards who have sufficient magical power to set off the spell themselves."

She nodded.

"Good." She looked at the Shoverians, who had begun to advance. "Okay. I am not sure how this will go, but I suggest you all stay below the wall of the battlement."

Having said that, she focused on the fire spell she had used on the beast. The one she had modeled on the tall tales of the great sorcerer battles from the Great War. She conceptualized it as big as she could and readied herself. A deep breath, two, and then she focused on where Sharpe and his fellows were. Refined the spell wider rather than deeper and raised her hands, concentrated, and launched the spell.

The air in front of her began to shimmer like a heat haze. The closer to the enemy, the stronger the shimmer became.

Then the air burst alight into a spreading, roiling mass of fire that slammed into the Shoverian troops and incinerated them. A massive firestorm swept over the centre of the Shoverian army blasting over Sharpe and his fellows and continued into the distance before finally petering out maybe a mile away. The troops directly in the path were reduced to ashes, the metal in their gear warped and deformed if not melted. Trees and bushes were just dissolved by the heat. On the edges of the firestorm there were half-incinerated bodies and beyond that men were screaming and dying as their clothes burned them alive.

Most of the Shoverian mounted forces were galloping into the distance, with those riders still on their horses desperately trying to rein the panicked animals in. Probably half the Shoverian army was dead or dying.

Taroniah saw stars and sank down until she was sitting on the ground with her eyes closed, leaning against the parapet desperately trying to not pass out. She didn't see the horrified looks cast in her direction by all those on the wall area above the gate. Her dazed state was interrupted by something hard being pushed into her hands. She opened her eyes and found a ceramic water bottle. She glanced up and saw Marteen's worried face looking down at her.

Her head was belling like a temple gong and she started seeing stars again. Closing her eyes helped and she moved the jug to her mouth and swallowed some very welcome and surprising cool water. The water helped her feel better. When she opened her eyes again she didn't see stars.

"Thank you." She put a hand on the ground and levered herself up.

"Stay down," he ordered.

She halted, kneeling. "What's happening?"

"Each surviving half of their army has halted their advance. They appear to be sorting out who is in command. Your magical arrows are taking a toll, even at this range."

"Good," she whispered. Her head was improving. Another gulp of water made her feel even more the thing. "Help me up."

"No. You can hardly stand."

"Doesn't matter," she replied. "Get me up and they will run."

She tried to stand. Seeing she was determined, he helped her up.

"Press against my back so they can't see you're holding me up," she whispered. She moved forward until her front was held up by the parapet. The Captain pressed against her back as requested and she was able to remain standing.

Her re-appearance caused a stir amongst the nearby defenders, which in turn caught the attention of the Shoverian troops. She steadied herself and took a couple of deep breaths, then projected her voice as well as she could.

"Go!" she yelled. And then raised her hands and made some movements directed at the troops on the right. The officers might have had other ideas, but the troops there simply broke and fled. She lowered her hands and turned towards the troops on the left. She had hardly started to raise her hands when they fled as well.

"Good," she whispered, and found that putting both her hands on the top of the stone parapet let her stand a bit longer. Eventually, the Shoverians passed from view.

"They're gone," Marteen said in her ear.

"Yes." She promptly blacked out.

She awoke in the temple with a priestess sitting in a chair nearby reading a scroll.

"Oh." She felt somewhat refreshed, and her head was back to normal although she felt very weak.

The priestess rose and brought a mug with juice in it,

She took it gratefully, feeling weak and hungry. She downed the juice and looked up.

"How long?"

"Two days," the priestess replied.

Oh, Taroniah thought.

"The Marland Guardsman carried you in here. He felt you would be safer here, quite rightly," the Priestess added.

There would be war, Taroniah felt. Maybe,

The priestess looked her over then made to leave.

"I will summon the Senior Mother. She wished to speak with you when you woke."

Taroniah nodded acceptance to this. She wasn't sure she wanted to talk to anyone just yet, but she didn't fancy trying to stand up. This limited her options. There was no point in being stupidly stubborn. She must have dozed a little because suddenly the lined face of the Senior Mother was looking down at her.

"Ah. My trip was not wasted," the old woman said, smiling at Taroniah.

"Senior Mother," Taroniah acknowledged the older woman. She hadn't believed in the old gods before she came here, but she was starting to change her mind. If the fanciful stories of the great magics the sorcerers of old could do were still possible, perhaps the gods were more real than she had believed.

"Well. You have certainly stirred things up, young lady. No matter. You are safe here. At least for the moment." The old woman sank onto the chair the priestess had occupied when Taroniah had awoken. "The real question is, what do you want to do?" Her pinched face made her glinting eyes stand out. The Senior Mother might be old and frail, but her brain was still sharp and her personality remained strong.

Taroniah looked off into space for a moment.

"I want to explore more magic. Teach, even. I will have to go home and see my parents and my real father but after that, I think, I would like to return to Lightbearer Academy if the Lord of Magic will allow me."

The old woman studied her for a moment.

"It is long since there was a true Sorcerer in the world. Even my Lady feels more alive to me now that you have shown yourself. Very well. You may stay here until you feel able to leave, either for your home or back to the Academy.

"It will be interesting to see what you cause to transpire, Lady Sorceress, Taroniah of Marland."

Peter Rhodan grew up in Sydney, Australia but has lived on the Gold Coast, Australia for over thirty years. His working career has spanned a lot of things, having been a courier driver, retail sales assistant, casino croupier, small business owner, graphic designer, and most recently Uber driver.

He lives with his wife and a border collie cross dog who thinks she's a human, their two great kids having both flown the coop.

The first fiction book he read that he liked was *Eagle of the Ninth* and the first Science Fiction book he read and liked was *Foundation* by Asimov. At one stage, his library held over 1600 dead tree books, but he has barely 100 now, having pruned a lot in various moves and replaced most with electronic versions.

His favorite authors, at the moment, are David Weber, Lois McMaster Bujold, Christopher Nuttall, and Pam Uphoff.

Chris Nuttall and Pam Uphoff both inspired him to "have a go, mate," and so he has. His books are on Amazon only at present.

He runs a blog, which he updates periodically: https://rhodanblog.wordpress.com/ or on Facebook. (Be warned though, he posts funny and politically conservative/incorrect stuff regularly there.)

UNDER THE SUBLIME MOON

BY AARON VAN TREECK

This may be most readers' first foray into Xianxia fiction. It's a modern form of Chinese storytelling about heroes who cultivate some form of energy in order to reach enlightenment and immortality. This is typically accomplished through meditation, the practice of martial arts, and the use of magical treasures and medicines. Fans of *Dragon Ball* will recognize the idea of Qi granting superhuman abilities.

Stories like these are often bound up with traditional Confucian and Taoist principles. Very strict adherence to certain codes of behaviors is common and, in my opinion, can make for somewhat stuffy reading at times. So, when I realized that this was the type of story I wanted to write for this magical school anthology, I decided to liven things up by throwing a magical Celt into the mix. If you enjoy this story, I highly recommend Will Wight's *Cradle* series.

***

Under the Sublime Moon

Cu MacDann

"Qi is the energy that lets you live and move and breathe. For most, this energy allows them to live ordinary lives and nothing more. But, for those of you born to the higher castes and the special few who find a Natural Treasure, it can be your door to a world the average man will never see. A world of wonders and power." I stopped to look out at my students, feeling the slight pressure that they exuded while cycling their Qi through their bodies. It was like feeling a faint drumbeat vibrate the air, or a dozen drumbeats, as the case happened to be. Wait, a dozen and one? A moment of concentration allowed me to find the extra student.

There were always servants moving about the Sect's grand hallways and open courtyards, cleaning, organizing, and bringing supplies when needed. Standing in a shaded corner of the courtyard was a girl, nearly a young woman, wearing the drab brown robes and head covering of the maids. Her drum beat louder and faster than the rest. My own Qi shivered in excitement. She wasn't sitting in a meditative pose on the ground like my students were. She was standing and moving around. She was plucking withered leaves from the shrubs that surrounded the small courtyard and putting them into a bag to be disposed of. It was an accomplishment worthy of a senior student, and it was being done by someone who should not have been capable of performing even so well as the children before me taking their first real instruction in the Art.

"Someday, this Qi cycling technique will become second nature to you. If you choose to begin a Path, you will eventually advance your will to the point where it is possible to cycle while you sleep. Now, Li," I called the name of one of the students. "Tell us what a Path is."

"Teacher." He rose and bowed to me.

His Qi vibrated with disdain and anger. Clearly, this son of a Prefect considered me, a foreigner to the Kingdom of Mirrored Water, unworthy to be an instructor in the Sublime Moon Sect. His notion of social strata and status were unsuited to a student of the Art, so I decided to give him a glimpse of what a Master could truly do. But not yet. First, he had a question to answer.

"A Path is the beginning of true power. It is forged by the one who walks it, and each is unique. The First Step is the ritual by which a student becomes a novice in the Art."

"Technically correct. How many of you have witnessed one of the Masters here practice their path?"

No student answered me. A person's Path was not some party trick to be casually displayed. Or, that was how the people of this land thought of it. They were the Sine', people of the steppe, and the tundra. Frivolity was foreign to them. I was from a different place and a different people.

"Then watch closely. Bear witness to the Path Under the Hill."

I dropped the veil of still Qi I maintained around myself to prevent my own drumbeat from deafening or outright killing those with less power than myself. My red hair began to glow with power, and my green eyes would be like twin flames. Every muscle in my body sang with pent-up energy begging to be put to use. I pushed my Qi out of my body, reaching out to that particular energy that my spirit had bonded to. Behind me, reality became thinner, and wild colors, inhuman colors, began pouring out.

"Come, Gwyn Pukah." I turned to the hole in the world and pulled through a large creature, an unsettling mix of man and beast that bore a passing resemblance to a rabbit.

"What manner of monster is that?!" Li cried out.

"This is Gwyn Pookah. He is a creature from the Land Under the Hill, a world like and unlike our own. My Path allows me to open roads into and out of that land, which has allowed me to make deals with its native creatures. Witness."

I pulled three small clay jars from the box I'd brought with me for this lecture. One was honey, one was cream, and one was a very valuable spirit from my homeland, Tua'De. I handed them over to the large bipedal rabbit with three simple instructions, things that could be interpreted in a number of ways, but I had trust in this particular creature to understand and follow my intentions. To be sure my students wouldn't hear me, I spoke in my native tongue, something far more flowing and lyrical than the sharp consonants and precise vowels of the Sine language. *"Humble the proud one, aid the one who hides, and bring danger here."*

The Pookah didn't answer me, merely took my bribes and vanished. A few of my less reserved students gasped, startled, as my Fey friend vanished from sight and their fledgling senses.

"What demon or monster was that?" Li demanded.

"Neither. Check your registries of demons; his name is not on it. Now, return to your place, Li."

The boy's scowl deepened, but he obeyed. As he was taking his seat, the cushion in his place was suddenly jerked away. The dull thud and pained grunt of the young man drew the eyes of his fellow students. None turned their heads, nor did their expressions change, but their opinion of Li would drop after such a display of clumsy behavior. His long, braided black hair shook as he clenched his jaw, a display of emotion equivalent to shouting and screaming in my homeland.

"Everyone, stand!" I barked. All of the students obeyed quickly, except for Li who took several moments to comply. "For those of you who believe what happened to be humorous or a good show, watch closely."

I picked up a piece of wood and held it to my side. A blade made of sharpened stone drove into and through the wood, burying itself in the wooden beam just behind me. Every eye in the room went wide.

"I chose to have my friend Gwyn play a small joke on your fellow student to prove a point, but none of you were intelligent enough to understand. A pulled pillow could just as easily be a knife across your throat. Now, I will show you how to guard yourselves against an invisible enemy. As Li reminded everyone, there are demons and monsters who can make themselves unseen." The student in question looked less angry now, but still glared at me. "Li will be the first to learn this technique."

I spent the next several hours walking the young man through the internal movements needed to force Qi out of the body and into a kind of fog. This field of energy would be like a second set of skin, sensitive to change or disturbance. Once every student was able to perform this technique for several seconds, I allowed them to leave for their evening meal. The maidservant snuck out only a moment before my student left.

"Uncouth dog." A short, slender man with squinting eyes stood at the entrance to the garden where I prefered to instruct students.

"Master Feng, join me for a drink?" I offered.

"The sun has not even reached its peak, degenerate outsider."

"You are far too free with your compliments." I took a gourd of water from my bag and started drinking from it. The gourd exploded into steam, lightly-scalding my skin. I dropped what was left and gave Feng a bored look.

"And you are a stain that I will burn from this world." He threw something at my face. I didn't bother to move or catch the object. A bundle of cloth hit me and draped over my head. My muscles tensed as I realized what this was. "Three days from now, on the night of the Gate Rituals. We will meet in the Arena of the Sixth Gate. If you flee, I will hunt you down. Your promised decade of hiding behind the Grand Elder's robe is over."

When I heard Feng leave, I pulled the fabric from my head and looked at it to confirm what I already knew. That son of a donkey had torn my banner from the Master's Hall as an insult and a formal challenge. I was honor-bound to meet it, and when I did, Feng would do his best to kill me.

Shui Lan

There were wonders unimaginable to behold in the vaunted halls of the Sublime Moon Sect. People who could shape the elements into weapons, heal with a touch, make drawings take on a life of their own. There were sacred weapons, unearthly icons, miraculous medicines, and trees that glowed with the light of the heavens. My first task today was cleaning the bathrooms. There was nothing wonderful or miraculous about them, except for the self-warming seats. Crap is still crap.

I scrubbed the floors and seats with herb water to clean the marble and purge the smell. Rosemary smelled strong enough to linger for a few days so I wouldn't have to do it again for a little while. I got off my aching knees and breathed deeply. Some smell of filth still lingered from the rags and soiled water, but the room was clean once again. I breathed deeply, this time to move the Qi from my belly into my limbs, refreshing them for the tasks that lay ahead. I pictured the lines of energy woven through my body and guided the pure life energy through them, bringing relief to my aching muscles and beginning to heal the scrapes and light bruises that came from working on one's hands and knees for hours.

"Shui Lan!" The voice cracked like a whip. I spun around, eyes carefully kept low, and head slightly bowed.

"The maidservant greets the honored Master," I said, pressing my hands together one atop the other in front of me then bowing more deeply. I didn't have to look to know who had spoken to me. Master Feng of the Path of Wandering Flame, one of the instructors in the Sublime Moon Sect. His large green eyes would be narrowed to chips of emerald color, his irritable nature and need of glasses giving him an almost eternal glaring expression. His black beard hung elegantly down to his waist, accented by the robe of sparkling stones he wore.

"The Grand Elder has called for all to attend his demonstration. That includes you. Hurry up, girl. It would not do for the greatest of us to wait upon the needs of a mere maidservant."

My Qi burned cold for a moment.

"As the honored Master wishes." I bowed more deeply and listened to his steps tapping their way toward the entrance of the massive pagoda that housed the Sect. I took a brief moment to breathe and try one more thing. I sped up the circulation of Qi in my body, forcing it outward and into my skin. Sweat poured out of me, pushing ingrained filth with it. I continued to force my Qi outward and after a full minute of effort, the stench was eliminated from my body and clothes. A quick sniff told me I would still smell like sweat, but it was a definite improvement.

Master Feng gave me a slight glare when I arrived outside, my simple bamboo sandals making far too much noise for me to join the crowd unnoticed. But I didn't care. Sage of the Sublime Moon, Khan Yue, stood in a simple white robe facing an oncoming thunderstorm. Atop a platform of raised earth nearly a thousand paces removed from us, he stood alone before a force of nature. The students and instructors were murmuring to each other about the nature of the demonstration. Apparently, the Grand Elder hadn't told anyone much of anything other than where to stand.

A peal of thunder shook the ground we stood on, and an animalistic cry shook the souls of the crowd. Something not quite a tiger and not quite a bird burst through the clouds trailing lightning. It was large enough to swallow a man whole with a long snake-headed tail with eyes that burned like embers.

"A Yao Nue." Master Feng gasped.

The word ran through the crowd like a line of fireworks. One student, no more than twelve summers old, tripped on his own feet trying to run and bowled into his friends. Master Yi of the Path of Shimmering Stone quickly disciplined the boy, cuffing him on the ear once he was on his feet. The slim Master could have taken the boy's head off with such a blow, but his self-control let him strike with a merely human amount of strength.

The Yao beast roared again, and lightning crashed to the earth in a dazzling flash. Dirt was churned and stone shattered by the awesome natural energy the creature had called from the storm. Not a bit of it harmed Khan Yue. Not a speck of debris touched his white robes. The Yao beast, a creature born of either evil sorcery or corrupted natural energy, was surrounded by storm clouds that looked more like an artist's portrait of clouds than the real thing. That was where the power of the creature was leaking into reality, seeping out to disrupt the natural weather and create that massive thunderstorm.

The Grand Elder stood on the raised plateau as a serene counterpoint to the chaos around him. The students were terrified, and I was right there with them. Wind buffeted my clothes and had blown my hair-wrap to the other end of the Kingdom by now. Rain washed over us in a sheet. I could see the Masters of the Sect pushing the rain away from themselves with a minor outpouring of Qi. A few of the more-enterprising students tried, but even those talented enough to replicate the technique quickly exhausted themselves. I thought about trying it myself, but the rain was washing away the sweat, so I shrugged and let the rain wash me clean.

The Yao Nue must have seen the Sage's defiance because it roared and ran through the air toward him, rain and lighting following in its wake. The ancient man stood tall in the face of a living natural disaster. Then, so fast it was difficult for my eyes to follow, he set his feet in a martial artist's stance. His arms, still thick and strong, were thrust out at the invading monster, and I saw the air around him stir. He moved in a fluid motion turning his body clockwise with his arms moving in wide sweeping arcs. His right arm swept up toward the sky, and the clouds parted as if cut with a god's sword. Moonlight, bright and beautiful, spilled onto the rain-drenched ground.

The Nue screeched in inhuman rage as the rain and lighting were stripped away from it, but still it charged at the Sage. Again, the old man seemed to dance in a circle. This time, his right hand swept down at the ground. The world around the beast distorted, and it fell impossibly fast. All of us felt the impact of the monster when it slammed into the stone of the mountain, and all of us heard the sound of shattering rock. The monstrous creature had been pulled out of the sky and broken on the mountainside by a single technique of the Sage of the Sublime Moon. The entire gathering was dead silent, awed and terrified by the power of the wise old man.

"Three cheers for the Sage's great victory!" one impertinent student shouted.

Many began to clap or cheer once the silence was broken, but none of the Masters even breathed as far as I could see. Master Feng, a proud and self-satisfied man if there ever was one, looked far paler than his ruddy complexion should have allowed. I wasn't as well-learned as any Master, not even as much as most of the students, but I thought I understood. That hadn't been a fight, it had been butchery. The Sage had crushed a beast of mythical proportions with less effort than it would have taken one of the Masters to beat down an unruly student.

"Immortal," Master Feng breathed.

Had I been a few feet further away I wouldn't have heard him. I was preoccupied with something else. The Sage's dance had felt wrong. The arrogance of that thought struck me like a rock to the back of the head. He had just decimated a Yao Nue, a herald of destruction for cities, and I was thinking I knew Qi techniques better than he did. But still...

No, it wasn't something I could afford to spend time on. I'd lost half an hour of time, and I still had so much work to do. I rushed back inside ahead of the students and instructors and began wiping down the floors in the auditorium with a rag wetted in cinnamon-infused water. Rosemary was more common and far less expensive, but Master Cu MacDann said rosemary reminded him too much of his lost home.

"Well, that was quite a sight, was it not?" Master Cu, a large man with pale skin and green eyes said, turned me around to face him. "You don't see a Nue killed in single combat every day."

I didn't know him, but I knew of him. He was the only Master at the sect from outside the kingdom, possibly the only Master to have come from across the Tempest Sea. He was infamous in the Sect for ignoring anything resembling rules of decorum or social strata. I was a maidservant. Conversing with someone like me as a friend or acquaintance was an act that would cause most to lose face. I wasn't sure he understood the concept of social honor. If he did, then he chose to ignore it entirely.

"This lowly maidservant has never witnessed such a sight, Master of Fey Roads."

Master Cu let out a deep sigh.

"You Sine', so formal. My former countrymen sometimes said

that your people know neither how to laugh or smile. They are not far wrong based on my time with the Sect."

My Qi twisted in my core. What did I have to laugh about? I stilled my mind by regulating my breathing. Calm. I needed calm.

"It is not my place to correct the Honored Master."

"Song and drink, girl! Can't you even get mad and insult me openly?"

"It is not the place of one as lowly as myself." I bowed deeply and held that pose until the temperamental Master got sick of me.

"Very well. Go back to your cleaning, maid. But don't assume I am as blinded by my own genius as the others. I see you."

My reaction to those words was too strong to hide entirely. He'd noticed something. Either my own increasing mastery of Qi, or my eavesdropping on the lectures and demonstrations of the Masters of the Sect. No one ever paid attention to the cleaning servants! I swallowed down the lump in my throat. No one, except a foreigner with no concept of social hierarchy. Curse his ancestors to the eighth generation!

I made the mistake of meeting Master Cu's eyes. He was grinning at me, at whatever expression of fear had crept into my face.

"And I don't mind."

"Will the honored Master keep this lowly one's confidence?" I dared to ask.

"I will, if you do one thing for me." He waited until I was forced to ask the question he'd left hanging in the air.

"What does the Master require of this one?"

"The Ritual of the First Step is happening in three days. The students require attendants as they are put to the test. I would like you to be one of those attendants." My heart and my Qi stopped for a moment. The Ritual was one of the closely-guarded secrets of the Sect. Most students were sent back to their families before the Ritual. A basic mastery of Qi was enough to strengthen the body and provide the student with a lifetime of good health and a youth almost certain to span half a century. But to pass the first Gate meant beginning a Path. A Path leads to power and status. There was only one answer to give.

"I humbly accept the Master's request." Despite the trembling in my hands, I dared a further question. "Does the Master have any words of wisdom for this humble maidservant?"

"Now that is almost a smile," Master Cu said, grinning like some fool child who won a footrace. "Seek the will of Heaven" he intoned.

I stopped and pondered that simple statement, but he was not done.

"All that resides on Earth reflects the heavens. Man stands above the Earth but below Heaven. Think on this as you practice."

I did not understand, but I was not willing to make another request of this strangely generous man. The secrets of Qi and Paths were closely guarded. The entrance fee for the Sect was equal to the wages of a farmer over a fifty-year period. Only the sons of wealthy merchants or high government officials could afford it, assuming they could manipulate Qi at all. Even then, if you did not show talent or catch the eye of a Master, basic mastery of Qi was all you could ever hope for.

"The maidservant thanks the Master for his generosity." I bowed deeply.

For the first time, my bow was honest. It felt better than I thought, being genuinely thankful. Or maybe that was the hope. Hope that I could reach beyond the life my parents had sacrificed me to. I hadn't even fetched a year's wages. Old bile crept up my throat, but I forced it back down.

"One more thing." Master Cu's words caught me halfway out of his lecture hall. I stopped and turned back, hoping for more information. "All the power in the world doesn't amount to much if the person holding it doesn't know how to smile."

My disappointment must have shown on my face because he began to laugh at me.

"Truth can be a bitter pill, but it is still medicine."

I didn't bother with the bow this time and left as quickly as was polite. I had work to finish and I wanted, no, I *needed* to finish early tonight. I was so focused on working fast I began circulating my Qi without realizing. I only noticed when the water on my hands began steaming away from the excess energy.

"Careful, dear," Head Maidservant Mei Liang warned me.

I slowed the flow down to just enough to keep the chill from the stone floor from numbing my skin. Two years, I guess that was how long it took to start moving Qi by reflex.

"Never let a Master know you've been working with open ears. They might take you for a thief." It was an admonishment, but it was a soft one. Too bad it was a day too late.

"Yes, Matron Mei." That earned me a gentle knock on the head.

"Keep your ears open to me, too, Shui. Just because I'm not a Master doesn't mean I have nothing valuable to teach you." Mei was older than she looked, nearly a century old if the rumors the other servants whispered were true. Tales of how she lived so long, while looking like a woman in her late third decade of life, were many and colorful. My personal favorite was that a Master had fallen in love with her and given her a Natural Treasure. An herb or gemstone overflowing with naturally-occurring Qi that was safe for ordinary people to use. A single leaf from an Orous Tree or a cluster of berries from the Trueblood Vine could add a century to someone's life.

"I will do as the Lady commands." I bowed deeply to her and redoubled my efforts at cleaning.

Cu MacDann

There is nothing like alcohol from your home to make you feel nostalgic. Gwyn had returned and offered me a small portion of his payback. In Tua'De, refusing such a gift was as good as insulting a man's mother. Typically, because mothers made such spirits for their favored sons.

"You always play the best games, MacDann," the Pookah laughed.

"In this land of dour faces, I need a bit of excitement now and again." I raised the mostly full jar to him after taking a generous swallow of the strong liquor.

"The girl. She is an interest of yours?"

"Of a kind. She's still just a girl, but I see so much potential for someone so neglected by the wise and powerful of this land. I want to give her a chance to shine. The other Masters would never agree to it. No benefit to the Sect to waste resources on some poor servant girl."

"An old story, and a common one," the Pookah said, gravely. "You wish my help?"

"I paid for it," I reminded him. Friend or not, you needed to hold the Fey Folk to their bargains. They wouldn't respect you if you didn't.

"And handsomely. Do your students know that the spirits of Tua'De are a Natural Treasure? Or that it is made by common farmers?"

"My students? One of them might try to murder me for what I have left if they knew that. The Sage knows. I gave him some as a gift when he gave me sanctuary. And he's of the Rosh. They have a monopoly over most of the Natural Treasures in the Kingdom. One more isn't going to pique his interest."

"How do you wish me to help the girl?"

When I told the Fey creature what I had in mind. he laughed uproariously. As his laughter echoed on the stone outer wall of the Sect building, I sipped more of the Silver Water and tried to uproot my uncertainty.

"And you believe this will give the Sage of the Sublime Moon reason to keep you under his protection indefinitely?"

"Maybe. But it might also give me a powerful ally once she advances down her Path. If she doesn't die first." I opened a jar of the rice liquor made by the people of the Kingdom. It was far sweeter than I preferred, but it had Qi refining properties of its own that were useful in quieting anxiety. "I know I asked for you to bring trouble, but you nipped a tiger's tail. Had I been the one to fight the Nue, I don't know that I would have survived. The Sect might have suffered serious damage. Lives would have been lost. Where did you even find such a beast?" I demanded of the trickster drinking with me.

"Far closer than you might expect. This Kingdom is blind to at least one enemy."

"What-?" I cut off my question.

Information worth the life or death of a kingdom was worth far more than I could pay without becoming a slave. I examined the creature I'd long called a friend. He'd made a ploy against me, trying to strip me of my freedom, maybe my life. Yet, he'd made me alert to a threat to my current home. He'd done as the Fey do, been both friend and foe within the span of a few words.

"Nevermind. I'll deal with that when its time comes. One last thing." I took a piece of stone from my robe. It was small, jagged, and outwardly worthless. But for those who knew the legends of the Tua'De, it was a near priceless treasure. A fragment of the Hearthstone of Scathac, the founder of my homeland. It was a piece of the key to the Land of Shadows where one might speak with the dead. For me, it was something far more precious. "Three days from now, I am to do combat with Master Feng, a master of fire. Bring that stone to me the next morning."

"You believe you'll lose?"

I gave the Fey a flat look. "Those who enter a duel to the death and do not plan for a loss are fools. And fools tend to die badly."

Shui Lan

"Curse his ancestors to the ninth generation!" I hissed through my teeth.

That damn foreigner had shifted the servants' schedule, and now I was assigned to his instruction area every day. And on the day of the Ritual, as well! I did not need this kind of disruption on such an important day. Besides, I'd been practicing my version of the Grand Elder's dance, and I almost had it perfected. I just needed more time.

I walked quickly down the wood-floored hallway, being careful to keep my eyes down and dodge both the students moving around and the priceless works of art sitting on pedestals. My bucket of scented water and pack full of cleaning tools shifted as I went. After two years, I was an expert at moving with that shifting weight while keeping the water in the bucket.

"—when you have nothing left." Master Cu glanced toward me as I entered his teaching area, a stone garden. I quickly busied myself raking bits of leaves and twigs from the soft white sand of the garden, staying far from any of the students. "Senior student Tong, what is the next thing you must do in the situation I just described?"

"Pull inward, as powerfully as you can manage." Tong was one of the Rosh and was far more relaxed in his expressions than the Sine'. His pitch-black eyes gave away his national origin, as did the brightly-colored green robe he wore. If he wore such a thing on the steppe, he could be seen for a mile. An easy target for a predator, whether of the human or monstrous type.

"Why?"

"There is a chance you can pull in the Qi of other things in order to fuel a technique for a moment."

I hadn't known that. What's more, it made no sense. Qi was produced within the body and dissipated the further it got from the body. Natural Treasures were natural concentrations of non-toxic Qi, and they were incredibly rare. Was he lying? Or wrong?

"Very good."

My eyes snapped over to Master Cu. If he was teaching this to senior students, it had to be correct.

"Keep that in mind this evening. It may save your life. Dismissed."

The students filed out. I stood behind one of the large stones near the exit and waited with my head bowed and eyes looking safely at the floor, until I noticed a pair of feet that paused for a long moment at the exit of the open garden. A slight glance in that direction showed me that Tong was there, and he was looking at me. I snapped my eyes back down and prayed to whatever god or spirit might be listening that he was not actually looking at me. A dozen frenzied heartbeats later, he left.

I let out a breath I hadn't realized I'd been holding. I did not need more attention. Bad enough a Master knew what I was doing. But a student? And a Rosh? The rumors would be spread to every person in the Sect by nightfall.

"I think he's interested in you."

That lilting, mushy voice belonged to Master Cu. Even if he spoke my language enough for me to understand, his accent made him sound as if he was constantly drunk. Si, the language of the Sine', was precise and orderly. Cu MacDann was not orderly by any human standard.

"The maidservant is unworthy of such attention."

"Never underestimate the desires of men. Wars have been fought over such lingering glances."

I dared to look at the Master, still sitting in lotus position at the center of the garden. His eyes were closed, and he was obviously in some meditative practice. So I started cleaning the garden of debris and raking the sand into proper evenness. The sensation of dense Qi hit my shoulders like a week's worth of the Sect's laundry, nearly crushing me to the ground. Everything was suddenly too heavy. I couldn't move, couldn't breathe. My own Qi was being compressed toward my stomach. So cold.

"Maybe you are just a maid."

I went from cold to red hot in an instant. I forced my Qi to run through my chest and my limbs, pushing back against the oppressive weight trying to crush the life out of me.

"If you can't walk over here and strike me, I will find someone else to attend the students at the Ritual tonight."

May thirteen generations of his ancestors rot in the hell of the bloody lakes! I cycled my Qi, pushing, driving it into my limbs and back to my stomach. I breathed. It was harsh and labored, but I did. Then I took one step forward.

It was the hardest thing I'd ever done in my life. I wanted to collapse. I glanced at Master Cu and saw the mocking grin on his face. I took another step toward that son of a promiscuous toad. Then another. For the next few steps, I forgot how badly I wanted to fall and only thought of how badly I wanted to slap that look off his face. One eternity later I stood in front of him and struggled to raise my hand.

"Poor little girl."

My vision went red and I blanked out for a minute. The next

thing I knew I was standing without effort and cradling my throbbing right hand. A real, genuine smile was lighting up the Master's face, along with a slight pink tint on one cheek.

"I-" I suddenly realized that I, a maidservant, had physically struck a Master of the Sect. People had been flogged to death for less. I dropped to my knees and put my forehead to the floor so quickly I saw stars for a moment. "This unworthy servant begs the Master's forgiveness!"

"I haven't been struck by a woman in thirty years," the Master mused with a smile still on his face. "Far too long, don't you think? Perhaps I should find myself a wife." He sounded amused, but I didn't believe that. The moment I offered anything less than pure contrition he would drag me out by my hair and throw me down the side of the mountain.

"Mercy," I begged.

"Look at me, girl." I did as he asked and saw a happy smile.

"You did fine. I just needed to be sure. Now, the laws of the Sect prohibit me from teaching someone who has not paid their tribute to the Grand Elder. But there are no laws prohibiting someone from observing what I do. Understand?"

I nodded.

He put a hand on the top of my head and patted me as if I were a favored pet. "Good. Go get cleaned up. You'll find ceremonial robes for you in your quarters. Once you're ready, come to the Gate of the First Step. The head maid will tell you what to do from there."

"Will you be there, Master Cu?"

"Sadly, no." He tossed me something small. A wooden token with a tiny gem set in the center. "If I don't come back, take that token to the Clerk, Mu Gon."

"I will do as the Master commands." I hurried back to my tiny room in the servant's quarters and found beautiful white silk robes and a chain covered in semi-precious stones. I quickly washed in a small basin, pulled on the robe, and belted it with the chain. I pulled my hair into the simple bun that the servants always wore beneath their head wraps. Then, I walked to the entrance to the second ring of the Sect's building. The place where those who practiced a Path would take their first Step.

Cu MacDann

The Gate of the Sixth Step was a bit more menacing than the First. The bones of humans, monsters, and great beasts adorned it. It was not an accident, nor was it mere symbolism. The Sixth Step was the Gate of Death. To pass it, a Qi Master must offer the body of a mighty enemy. For Master Feng, I was going to be that enemy—assuming he won our duel.

"Foreign dog!" The small man approached wearing a formal set of combat robes. All of the ornamentation of a Master was gone. The only ostentatious element to it was the gold thread embroidery in the image of a roaring dragon.

"Short-sighted rat." I nodded toward him.

My own robes were as simple as ever, dull green cloth tied with a simple rope. I dropped the shell of Qi around me and brought forth a gate in the air above my hand. Into it dropped a long spear of living wood and a head made of crystalline metal native to the Fey realm. A dull red light shone on the tip, a reflection of the bloodlust that inhabited the weapon. Gwyn had told me the name long ago, but I called it Gore. I thought it fit better than Gae Lug.

"Today, you die, and I ascend to the Sixth Step."

"Still one Step short of perfection, and two short of immortality. And your fellow Masters will always see you as a man without respect for his peers. Are you sure you want to do this?"

"You even talk like a coward."

That was a word I would not take lightly. The light of the spear grew brighter with my anger.

"Then come; let's get this done."

I slammed the butt of the spear into the ground at the base of the Gate, and a field of energy formed around us. It would limit the damage to our surroundings. I leaned back and angled my spear forward, preparing for a thrust or parry, depending on the weapon

Feng had chosen. Fire rose about the Master and encased him in a suit of flickering armor. From his right hand extended a lash of liquid fire, blazing like the sun. He planned to do battle with weapons and armor forged purely from his own power. It was one of the great advantages for those who found their strength in the physical elements. Those like me, whose strength was manifested in unusual ways, found direct combat far less simple.

I opened a gate behind me and shattered a small stone that hung around my neck. Seven creatures of the Fey realm answered my summons. Humanoids, far taller than any man and bearing the antlers of a stag, walked through my portal and pointed their primitive weapons at my enemy. The Udlach would be enough to destroy a small village of normal people. Against someone like Feng, I expected them to last a minute or less.

"Pathetic, to lean on strength not your own." Feng lashed out with his whip, and I swung Gore to deflect it. The technique shattered on my spear, and a portion of the power was pulled into it. I advanced, commanding the Udlach to advance with me and strike when they found a target of opportunity.

When two Masters, those on the Fifth Step or higher, clashed, it tended to be loud and incredibly destructive. When I moved, the ground cracked under the pressure of my feet. I moved forward so quickly that the air shrieked in my ears. The tip of my spear was pushed aside by a gauntleted arm, and I was forced to twist aside as Feng followed up with a fist aimed for my face. As I dodged, Feng lashed out and split one of the Udlach in two before they were even within weapon range.

I spun Gore over and drove it back toward him with a similarly poor result. But this time, I followed with a punch to his exposed face. He ducked aside, and we locked together for a moment. My skin, toughened by my Path to withstand the energy of foriegn realms, started to cook within seconds. I kicked at his back foot, widening his stance and forcing Feng off balance. I pushed off him using the haft of my spear the moment before two of the stag-men brought a sword and club crashing down on my enemy. Fire exploded outward and cooked them where they stood, but the blast of power was costly for Feng.

I forced Qi into the spear, and it blazed, both with my power and with the power stolen from Feng. I opened a gate between us and thrust the spear through it. Feng cried out in pain as the spearhead emerged from the portal I'd opened at his back and punched through his armor. Fire and heat washed back out of the portal, blinding me and driving me back until I collided against the barrier, several dozen yards from where I'd been. Even with a body strengthened by a Path, and Qi circulating to numb the pain, I was hurting.

I heard the screams of the remaining Udlach as Feng cut them down in a flurry of whip strikes before he turned back to me. His eyes were stars, burning white with power he'd channeled back into his own body to reinforce his strength and resistance to pain. I must have hurt him badly with that spear thrust.

I opened a gate in front of me, warping the flat plane until it surrounded me, though doing something so contrary to the natural laws taxed my strength severely. Straining, I opened another portal in the air above my enemy. A bare moment later and thousands of gallons of water poured down, swallowing him and dousing his fire. The boiling steam that exploded from the point of contact was safely diverted away from me by the twisted portal, as was the wave of sea water that tried to sweep over everything within the barrier. I closed both a moment later, gasping for breath like a man who'd spent the last two days running.

Feng screamed in rage from the opposite side of the domed arena. He was all but immune to his fire, but the steam had cooked portions of his skin.

"You cheating bastard!"

I picked up Gore and circulated my depleted Qi to give me enough strength to move effectively. I leaped, my movements covered by the fog that now hung thick in the air. Feng lashed a fiery whip wildly in the air around him, either trying to hit me or simply searching randomly for his target. When I was several yards away, one of the lines of flame swept toward my head, and I shattered it with the spear. Feng felt it, and an inferno of flames flowed along the line his whip had followed. It was an unpolished attack, unfocused in its rage. I spun Gore in a sweeping arc, and the pillar of fire was scattered, more of it being pulled into the blazing spearhead.

It was a perfect moment. My heart was beating so hard that I felt my blood rushing through every inch of my body. Any hunter can recognize the anticipation and pleasure of the moment before a kill. Your world narrows down to you and your prey. The moment of ultimate power, being able to choose life or death for another living creature. I loved it, and feared it. When my spear pierced through Feng's slender chest, the rush peaked, and I screamed my elation to the heavens.

Then I was unceremoniously blasted through the air by an explosion of fire. My spear went flying from my grip and stuck into the glowing boundary of the barrier nearly twenty yards off the ground. I hit the stony earth like a bag of potatoes and tried to stop the world from spinning.

"Arrogant barbarian. I walk the Path of Wandering Flame. You only killed an Inferno Sculpture." His foot slammed hard into my ribs and tossed me another dozen yards through the air.

Feng had sculpted a likeness of himself out of fire-natured Qi and hidden it in the steam. It was a clever move. Pain, all the pain I was dulling with my Qi, surged up, and my body locked into a rictus of agony. I forced the cycling to begin again, but the pain lingered. I dropped myself through a portal, appearing a dozen yards above where Gore was stuck in the barrier. My momentum let me pull the spear free and I threw it, putting all the Qi I could manage into the weapon to power its flight toward my enemy. As it flew, I shouted a word in the language of the Fey.

Iridescent flames caught along the head and haft of the spear, looking as if it was a burning rainbow. Feng saw it coming and tried to dodge, throwing up a hardened screen of flame to deflect my throw. It was for naught. Gae Lug was a spear forged by a being very close to a god. Once commanded to slay an enemy, it will pierce any defense and unerringly hit its target. But there was a steep price.

Feng didn't scream, even with the Fey weapon pinning him to the ground. He sneered at me with bloodstained teeth and glared with eyes that still burned like fire. He spat blood at me.

"Don't feel too bad. You did kill me. That spear is cursed. The moment I tell it to kill, I am destined to die by it. Let that be a solace to you, as you fade into the Land of Shadows."

He died sneering.

The moment his spirit departed, the barrier fell, and his body was pulled off the spear and onto the Gate of the Sixth Step. His flesh melted away until only bone remained. As the last drop of blood was pulled into the wood of the gate, the bones locking it shut began to move, and the Gate opened to me.

"I should have known."

Every Step on my Path got me more and more tangled up in the world and business of the Fey. Why would this step be any different?

"A pleasure to make your acquaintance, Queen Titania."

Shui Lan

The Grand Elder was overseeing the Ritual of the First Gate. In the courtyard between the outermost ring of the compound and the second most ring was a massive gate made of shimmering light. Outside it stood two dozen students. Around us were physical representations of every element in nature and every natural force I could think of. There was even a glass bottle full of twisting lighting.

"Tonight, some of you will advance to the First Step and the First Inner Court. The rest of you will be sent back to your families, your training having gone as far as it could." The Grand Elder's voice was low and gruff. The age of a Master was almost impossible to know. The Sage might have been a hundred years old or a thousand. But he sounded like a man near the end of his life. "You will each be given a small artifice. Keep it on your person at all times during this test. Anyone who removes it will fail and be expelled from this Sect in disgrace."

A group of students who had Passed the First Gate last year

walked through from the other side and began handing the younger students small tokens, just like the one I was carrying. *Oh no, did he set me up?*

"The test begins now." The Grand Elder waved a hand, and my world went white for a moment. The world snapped back, and I was being held up by one of the other maids, a girl who'd only recently been purchased by the Sect. The students were on their knees or on the ground, a few of them weren't moving at all.

"Are you alright?" the girl whispered. She had green eyes, so I assumed she was Sine'.

"I'm at the end of a double shift."

The girl nodded sympathetically and let go of my arm. I was able to stand, but not very easily. I tried to circulate my Qi, but when I did I felt a tug toward the token in my robe's inner pocket next to my heart. It made me feel sick, like I had a parasite stealing the strength and health from my body.

To the thirteenth generation! And the hell of endless stinging gnats! I cursed Master Cu in my head again for putting me in this position. I had come here to learn the secrets of the ritual, but he had made me a participant without my knowledge or consent. If I ever advanced past him on a Path, he would do well to keep his back to a wall.

"Now, fight until you feel your spirit is about to leave your body. Then continue fighting." The Sage, his eerie white eyes roving over the students, clapped his hands, and the older students began attacking. Noses were quickly bloodied. and I heard at least one bone break inside the first minute. "Now now, if you cannot last until your Qi is exhausted then there is no point."

"When students fall unconscious, pull them away and give them medicine," Matron Mei instructed us. "Bandage any open wounds with a poultice of Evergreening Leaves."

We went to work. I was losing Qi fast, but I had to keep cycling to pull the boys clear of the fighting. One, two, three. The less hardy of the students fell quickly, then there was a surge in the air, like some massive beast pulling in a deep breath. One of the younger students suddenly glowed with energy. Then a clap of thunder blasted back everyone near him as lightning crackled around him for an instant.

"There we are, the first of the new Paths to be discovered this night," the Sage said, no longer looking dispassionate or bored. "Lightning and thunder. Some wind as well. Jin Xiao, Path of the Shattering Sky." I stopped and stared. That was it. That was the secret. Exhaust your Qi completely and pull in natural energy which will mix with the Qi that maintains your body. That was the First Step.

"Keep up, Shui Lan," Mei hissed under her breath.

Two more students were on the ground, and we hauled him to the wall behind us, dripping a medicinal tea into his mouth and binding cuts with sticky green leaves. I was sweating profusely under my robe, and my vision was getting blurry. I think I was beginning to see things as well. For a moment, I thought I saw a rabbit the size of a man. Worse, I felt like I recognized it. Another feeling of being pulled toward the group of students, and another flare of power. This time, the earth shook beneath our feet, and small bits of glass began to form in the sand.

"Gu Mori, Path of the Clear Sands."

Two more students had the same life-changing surge of power. One created a shearing gust of wind that had sliced deeply into the ground around him in a circle. The other caused frost to form over everything within ten yards.

There were only two students left standing. One painful sounding punch to the stomach later, and there was only one standing. Tong, the student who had been looking at me this morning. He threw a desperate punch at one of the older students. The more experienced fighter stepped aside effortlessly. Another deep breath pulled me slightly forward, and Tong radiated blazing flames. Then those flames sprang forward like an arrow shot from a bow.

Before anyone could react, the arrow of flame bent toward me, as if some invisible hand had altered the path of its flight. I was so tired that I didn't even feel fear. In that moment of exhaustion and danger, something clicked inside my head. The Sage's dance, it was a dance that moved things. That was what I'd been missing. I stepped forward, spinning my arms as I turned in a smooth circle. The flames seemed to curve, no longer a straight line. I turned faster, feeling something new and bright fill me from head to toe. The arrow turned with me until I reached the end of the dance and thrust my hand out, pointing at the Gate's capstone. The flame detonated in a shower of red sparks that rained down onto the group of older students, Tong, and the Sage.

They were all looking at me. The SAGE was looking at me. I felt a hand push on the back of my neck.

"Down, foolish girl!" Mei whispered in my ear. "The head maid-servant takes full responsibility for this foolish child, Grand Elder. Please, have mercy on her."

Silence hung over us like a sword waiting to fall. Then the whispering started among the older students.

"Was that-?"

"That Path..."

"A mere servant? How?"

"She did seem different. I've seen her watching Master Cu instead of cleaning." That was Tong.

I started shaking. Everyone would know now. I would be cast out, or killed. They would kill me for stealing their secrets. Tears wet the backs of my hands. Hands that still shimmered with dim white light.

"Tong Su, Path of the Burning Spear," the Sage said, cutting off the whispering. "Matron Mei, introduce this... unusual girl."

"Please, show her pity. Her parents sold her to pay their debts to the Sect. She is an ignorant child of farmers."

"Humble beginnings do not a fool make. Stand, both of you."

"Merc-" Mei was suddenly flattened to the ground. There was a perfect circle of sand being depressed around her. It lasted for several fast heartbeats, then Mei was no longer being crushed.

"I do not accept backtalk from my servants, Mei. You should know that by now. What. Is. Her. Name?"

"Shui Lan," I said, hoping to spare the kind woman more pain.

The Sage looked at me with his strange eyes, and I felt something move inside me. It was like I was being pulled in, pulled toward the Sage.

"Shui Lan. Path of the Sublime Moon."

Not even a cricket broke the silence then.

Suddenly, I wondered if I was having a dream, or a nightmare. Unreality settled over everything. I wasn't really here, I was sleeping on my pile of straw, dreaming of success that would forever be beyond someone of my station.

Before I could over-breathe myself into unconsciousness, the Sage spoke again. "Seven students have taken the First Step this year. An auspicious beginning. You six may enter the Gate. Mei, take the others back to the outer ring dormitories. Shui Lan, I will speak with you privately."

I stood where I was, struggling to breathe easily as I waited to be alone with one of the most powerful men in the kingdom. I counted the grains of sand at my feet.

Curse every generation of Cu MacDann's ancestors! Curse them to the hell of eternal darkness and cold!

I wanted to run. No, I wanted to shrink to a particle of sand and disappear among the thousands of grains at my feet.

"Student Shui Lan. Hand me the token tucked away in your robe." The Sage held out his hand.

I pulled the tiny thing from my inner pocket, doing my best to wipe the sweat from it first. The Sage looked at it for only a moment before sighing and crushing it as if it were a sugar cube. "You have my condolences, girl. It seems you are deeply in the debt of Cu MacDann. But that is bad news for another day. Welcome to the Path of the Sublime Moon, apprentice. I have much to teach you." He bowed to me.

It was only a slight incline of his head, but the Sage of the Sublime Moon bowed to ME! I bowed deeply, trying not to start crying from relief and joy.

"The apprentice greets her Master. I wish to learn all you have to teach."

"That is good. Your first lesson: Do not trust those who traffic with the Fey. They look after their own interests first and always. May I ask a favor, apprentice?"

"Anything you wish, Master."

"Punch Master Cu in the face when next you see him."

"Gladly."

This is **Aaron Van Treeck's** second published short story, as the first was published in Volume 1 of the *Fantastic Schools* anthology series. He has a Master of Arts in Political Science and an (imaginary) Ph.D. in fantasy world-building. He's currently working as a number cruncher for whatever business is willing to pay the bills but aspires to be more than just his day job. He is supported by his parents, brother, and many encouraging friends.

THE CUNNING MAN'S TALE

BY CHRISTOPHER G. NUTTALL

It is rare, in the world of *Schooled in Magic*, for a magic-less mundane to enter a magic school, let alone study there. Even the very best of the theoretical magicians—the ones who design spells they could never cast—do their training elsewhere, well away from magical elitists who'd look down on them and magical bullies who'd turn them into frogs. It is simply not possible to be a magician without magic.

But, at Heart's Eye University, founded by Emily on the remains of the school she liberated in *The Sergeant's Apprentice*, magicians and mundanes mix freely. Science and technology and folk wisdom is studied alongside charms, alchemy and all the magical arts. And one young mundane will make a name for himself, if he survives his first weeks in a magical environment without magic ...

(Note—in-universe, this story takes place at roughly the same time as *Little Witches*.)

A CUNNING MAN'S TALE

CHAPTER ONE

I had barely rested my head on the pillow when I was awakened by a terrific banging.

I jumped awake, half-convinced I'd overslept and my master was furious. Master Pittwater was decent and easy-going, as masters went, but he had every right to be upset if I'd overslept. The apothecary didn't run itself, as I knew all too well. If Master Pittwater had to work the counter himself, he would be mad. He needed to restock a dozen potions before the rush began ...

My head spun as I sat up. Where was I? It wasn't my garret above the shop. It wasn't the bedroom I'd shared with my brothers, back in Beneficence. It was a small room, barren save for an uncomfortable bed, illuminated by a single glowing crystal. My bag lay in the corner, where I'd left it ... I blinked as memory returned. I'd been so tired when I'd finally reached Heart's Eye that I'd had very little awareness of being shown to a room and collapsing. Master Pittwater had warned me about portal lag, about the body being convinced it was in one time zone while actually being in another, but I hadn't believed it. Not until now. The clock on the wall insisted it was ten bells, but it felt like the middle of the night.

There was another hard knock on the door. I cursed as I stumbled to my feet and staggered towards the sound. I honestly had no idea who was out there. Master Pittwater had promised he'd make the arrangements and advised me to check in with Master Landis as soon as I arrived, but I couldn't remember if I actually had. Everything—the portals, the train—was a blur. I wondered, as I turned the doorknob, if I actually *was* in Heart's Eye. It was quite possible I'd been in such a state that I'd gone to the wrong place.

"Well," a feminine voice said, as I opened the door. "It's about time."

I blinked in surprise. A girl—young woman, really—was standing on the far side of the door, eyeing me as if I was something particularly unpleasant under her foot. She was striking, in a way that most female magicians are striking, and yet the sneer on her face made it hard to like her. Her eyes narrowed with contempt as she looked me up and down. I looked back at her, noting the long red hair and magical robes. Her skin was unmarked by life, her hands lacking the scars of mine. She looked like a person from another world.

"I trust you have been getting ready to attend upon us?" The girl sounded as though she didn't believe it. "Or have you been lollygagging around in bed ...?"

She looked past me, as if she expected to discover that I wasn't alone. I felt my temper flare. I didn't know who she was, or who she thought *I* was, but I didn't like *anyone* talking to me like that. I was a free citizen of Beneficence, not a serf or a slave or a runaway peasant. I might be an apprentice, but I had rights. They didn't include having to take such ... disdain ... from someone who was clearly as immature as someone half her age.

I cleared my throat. "Who are you?"

"Lilith," the girl snapped. "Don't you know me?"

"No," I said, in honest bemusement. I was supposed to know her? She wasn't a customer at the shop—my former shop—and I was fairly sure she didn't live in Beneficence. Even the snootier magicians at least *tried* to be polite. Mostly. "Am I supposed to know you?"

Lilith gave me a nasty look. "I am" —she paused, clearly

rethinking what she was about to say— "I am Master Landis's apprentice. And I have to take you to the lab."

She looked me up and down. "And you're not even appropriately dressed!"

"I only got in last night," I said. The urge to just slam the door in her face was overwhelming. "You woke me up."

"That won't do at all," Lilith said. "Get dressed in lab robes and meet me there in ten minutes and ..."

"I don't even know where the lab is," I said. "I can't ..."

Lilith scowled. "Get dressed," she ordered. "I'll wait outside. Hurry."

I scowled back as I closed the door, opened my bag and dug through it for the apprenticeship robe. Master Pittwater had given it to me as his farewell present, along with a handful of printed text-books and tomes. My skin felt grimy as I shucked my trousers and shirt, taking time to change my underwear before pulling the robe over my head. I had been far too long since I'd had a proper shower, let alone a bath. Master Pittwater had been insistent I shower every day, if I lived above the shop. I'd grown used to the luxury.

Gritting my teeth, I dug out the letters of introduction and slipped them into my pocket. Master Pittwater had assured me that every-thing had been sorted, that Master Landis would give me a fair shot at an apprenticeship. He hadn't mentioned another apprentice, a girl no less. I wasn't sure what to make of that. Female apprentices were rare, outside the magical community. And Lilith clearly had a massive chip on her shoulder. If I'd shown that sort of attitude, I would have been in deep trouble.

"You're not an apprentice," Lilith said, when I opened the door. "You shouldn't be wearing those robes."

I glared at her, feeling pushed to breaking point. "I came here for an apprenticeship," I said, sharply. "Shouldn't I be dressed for the part?"

"You're not a *real* apprentice," Lilith countered. She held up her palm. A spark of light danced over her skin. It was a trick magicians often used to identify themselves. I tried not to wince as I looked at the reminder I would *never* be a magician. "All you're good for is preparing the ingredients. Menial work."

She turned and marched down the corridor, then stopped. "Did you even think to have something to eat?"

"No," I said. I was used to hunger—my family had never been wealthy enough to be sure of putting food on the table—and I could have gone on for quite some time without making mistakes, but I wanted to irritate her. Just a little. "Is there something to eat?"

Lilith snorted and turned to walk down a staircase. "Follow me," she snapped. "And stay a step or two behind me."

I ignored the insult as I peered around with interest. Heart's Eye was *big*, easily larger than anything I'd seen in Beneficence. The corridors seemed like giant mazes, although someone had helpfully hung signs and markers everywhere. There were no paintings on the walls, save for a handful of strikingly-realistic portraits. I frowned as I ran my eye over the names below the portraits. MISTRESS IRENE, LADY EMILY ... *the* Emily, I assumed. CALEB. MASTER LANDIS ... I stopped to study his face, wondering just how closely the painting matched reality. He looked very different to Master Pittwater. A pale face, neatly-trimmed goatee, green eyes ... I couldn't help thinking he reminded me of someone, although I wasn't sure who.

"That's your new boss," Lilith said. She seemed in no hurry, all of a sudden. "We don't want people forgetting who runs this place."

I gave her a sharp look. "Do you even want to be here?"

Lilith looked thoroughly displeased. "I have no choice," she said. "You do. Why don't you leave?"

She turned and strode down the corridor before I could think of a reply. I glared at her back as I started to follow her. I didn't have a choice, not if I wanted to be something more than an apothecary's assistant. Master Pittwater had made that clear, when he'd told me I could go no further in his employ. I could either accept being a lowly assistant for the rest of my life or take a chance on Heart's Eye. He hadn't promised me it would be easy.

I heard people talking as we reached the bottom of the corridor and stepped into a large hall. It was crammed with people, ranging from students to older men and women wearing worker's overalls and protective outfits. The tables seemed to be scattered at random, although I could tell there were dozens of groups and subgroups already. I glanced from table to table, noting youngsters who were clearly magicians and men who looked like proud craftsmen. I felt a tinge of envy. I'd thought about becoming a craftsman myself, but I hadn't been able to get an apprenticeship.

Lilith pointed to the table at the front of the hall, raising her voice so I could hear over the din. "Take what you want," she said. "Don't worry about paying for it."

"Really?" It sounded as if she wanted to get me in hot water. "Are you sure?"

"Yeah," Lilith said. She walked beside me, the crowd parting in front of her. I couldn't help noticing that she—and I—were getting wary looks, even from the magicians. "Right now, the food is free."

It was also very basic, I decided, as I filled a bowl with porridge and dried fruit. Oats were easy to grow, if I recalled correctly; they were probably shipped in by the ton through the portals. Or something. Heart's Eye was in the middle of a desert, but I'd been told the land was slowly becoming fertile again. I put the matter aside for later consideration as we sat down, Lilith nursing a mug of Kava. I couldn't help thinking we were in a bubble. The others gave us a wide berth. Even the magicians seemed wary of her.

"Eat quickly," Lilith said. She didn't seem pleased with her seeming unpopularity. "We don't have much time."

I nodded and tucked into the porridge. It tasted bland, but I knew I should be glad to have it. My stomach growled warningly, suggesting I should go back for seconds. There was dried fish, too, as well as meats I didn't recognise. I wanted to go for more, but Lilith was clearly impatient. I drank my Kava—stronger than anything I'd had back home—and stood, carrying the plate and bowl to the collection point. It looked as if the staff had a full-time job.

"Who does the cooking?" I asked, as Lilith led me out of the hall. "And everything else?"

"Depends," Lilith said. "The cooks do the cooking" —she wasn't looking at me, but I could *hear* the sneer— "assisted by students who are working their way through the university courses. They do the labour and, in exchange, are allowed to attend courses. It is *quite* the arrangement."

I stared at her back. "What's wrong with it?"

"They cannot use it," Lilith said. "What's the point?"

I couldn't put my feelings into words. Lilith didn't seem to notice as she walked down two flights of stairs and along a long corridor. I felt a tingle passing through me, my hair threatening to stand on end, as we crossed the wards. Silence fell, noticeably. I hadn't really been aware of the background noise until it was gone. A pair of young girls walked past, going in the other direction. They both gave Lilith a wide berth. I frowned. Lilith wasn't that bad, was she? I'd met people who were worse.

"This is the lab," Lilith said, as she pushed open a door. "Master Landis will key you into the wards, once you prove yourself."

"I proved myself to Master Pittwater," I protested. "I know ..."

"An apothecary," Lilith said, in a tone that suggested Master Pittwater was one step above a gutter rat. "This is an *alchemical* lab. The rules are different."

She muttered a word as she stepped inside. The air glowed with light. I felt a thrill, despite myself, as I looked around. The chamber was massive, a dozen wooden tables—neatly spaced, in line with the rules Master Pittwater had drummed into me—dominating the room. The walls were lined with shelves upon shelves of potion ingredients, alchemical textbooks and everything an alchemist needed, from cauldrons to glass vials, jars and bottles. I stepped closer, admiring the collection of ingredients. A number were so expensive that Master Pittwater had rarely, if ever, used them. I couldn't help shuddering as I saw a pickled frog in a jar.

"That was a boy who tried to kiss me," Lilith said. I couldn't tell if she was joking. "I turned him into a frog and pickled him."

I felt sick. "Do you think that's funny?"

Lilith shrugged. "There's a washroom through there," she said. "I take it you know how to wash your hands and put on a proper apron?"

I didn't bother to dignify that stupid question with a stupid answer. I hadn't worked a *day* in the shop before I'd learnt the dangers of cross-contamination and injury. It was very easy to get seriously hurt, even if one couldn't brew the more dangerous potions. I'd helped Master Pittwater clean the wounds, after one of his previous apprentices had splashed himself with cockatrice blood. It wasn't as lethal as basilisk or manticore venom, but it had still done enough damage to terminate the poor man's career. I had no idea what had happened to him afterwards. I hoped he wasn't starving on the streets somewhere.

Lilith rattled around in the lab as I washed and dried my hands, then donned an apron. It wouldn't provide *much* protection, if a cauldron exploded, but it might give me a few seconds to tear it off before the boiling liquid burned my skin. I tested it lightly, making sure I could pull it free, then headed back into the lab. Lilith had laid out a set of ingredients, and a small collection of tools. I felt a thrill when I looked at them. I knew how to use them all.

"To work," Lilith ordered. She jabbed a finger at the pile. "Ready these for use."

I frowned as I stared at the pile. Some were common, so common a child could prepare them properly. A couple required almost no preparation. The remainder were tricky. I couldn't prepare them unless I knew what we were going to brew. The Darkle Roots needed to be sliced one way for a sleeping potion and quite another way for a purgative. The Candy Seeds needed to be left intact for a shape-change potion and crushed for a healing potion. And the daisies ... Master Pittwater had joked about a vile old witch who found daisies soothing, but—as far as I knew—they had no real magical applications. They were useless.

"Interesting," I said, as neutrally as I could. "What are we going to brew?"

Lilith sniffed. "A simple painkilling potion," she said. She hadn't said which one. There were over fifty different recipes, with varying levels of potency. "Prepare the ingredients."

I kept my face under tight control as I considered the recipes I'd memorised. There were only four that involved all but one of the ingredients. The daisies were a mystery. I shrugged, resisting the urge to ask about them as I started to work. I chopped up the Darkle Roots, being very careful to avoid mixing them with the Hawthorne Thistles. They didn't go well together unless they were blended in a cauldron. The Jigger Stems were of too poor quality for two of the four recipes, so I angled my work towards the remaining two. Lilith watched, occasionally tossing in a question. I was almost insulted. I'd covered most of them within the first two months of my time in the shop.

"I've done everything, but the daisies," I said, finally. "What are we going to brew?"

Lilith snorted. "We? I'm going to brew ..."

I felt my temper snap. "I just prepared the ingredients for you," I said, sharply. A thought struck me. "Did I just help you with *your* work?"

"It's your job," Lilith snapped. "You prepare the ingredients. I turn them into potions!"

"I came here for an apprenticeship, not to be a servant," I snapped back. I didn't mind preparing ingredients. It was part of the job. But I didn't want to be *just* a preparer. "I need to learn to brew and ..."

"With what?" Lilith turned to face me. "You have no magic. You can toss this lot into a cauldron and get what? Sludge! You cannot do anything with this. All you're good for is preparing the ingredients!"

"I can learn," I said. "I can ..."

Lilith jabbed a finger at me. My entire body froze. I could neither move nor speak.

"I learnt that spell before I went to school," Lilith said. She tapped me on the head. It sounded as if she'd rapped her knuckles against solid metal. "You are powerless against it. You cannot defend yourself against even the merest touch of magic. You have no place here, save as a servant to your betters. And the sooner you learn it, the better."

I struggled to move, but I couldn't. My entire body was locked solid. I couldn't even move my eyes. I watched, helplessly, as Lilith took the ingredients I'd lovingly prepared and started to turn them into a potion. She was good, I admitted grudgingly; she was far better than the other apprentices I'd met. Her fingers moved with easy skill, her magic sparking with life as she worked. And yet she thought of me as a servant ...

My heart sank. *How the hell did I get into this mess?*

CHAPTER TWO

A week ago, Master Pittwater had asked me to come into his office after I'd finished clearing up for the day.

"You're in trouble," Matt said. My fellow apprentice carefully emptied the cauldrons as he spoke. "What did you do?"

I shook my head. I hadn't done anything. Nothing worth mentioning, anyway. I'd gotten involved in a big apprentice fight two weeks ago and had to refuse service to a customer who was clearly too inebriated to make good decisions, but neither one would have landed me in real trouble. Matt and I had a habit of bickering, yet that had been resolved months ago. We might never be friends—he had magic, I didn't—but at least we'd come to a mutual understanding.

"Nothing," I said. I wiped the tables, then discarded the cloths. "Maybe it was something *you* did."

Matt smirked. "He wouldn't be summoning you if *I* was the one in trouble."

That was a good point. I decided to ignore it as I straightened up and looked around the shop. It had been a reasonably peaceful day, all things considered. I'd spent the morning assisting our master to prepare his potions, then the afternoon tending to customers.

Nothing had gone particularly wrong. I certainly wasn't even *planning* for it. My friends had invited me out for drinks, after work, but I wasn't sure I'd be going. I intended to catch up on my reading as soon as I had a free moment. I'd borrowed a handful of books on magic theory from the local library, and I planned to read them before we started work on a new selection of brews for the shop.

"I'll see you later," Matt said. He lived in one of the apartment blocks on the far side of the city, rather than above the shop. I'd often wondered if he preferred a little space between him and his master, or if he was just unwilling to share a garret with me. It wasn't as if there was enough room for *two* young men. "Good luck. Try not to make it worse."

I made a rude gesture as he donned his cloak and left the shop. I wasn't in trouble and yet ... my stomach was churning anyway. Master Pittwater wouldn't have asked me to see him after hours unless ... I shook my head. My master wasn't the sort of person to wait if he wanted to bawl me out for something. He'd certainly shown no hesitation in scolding his apprentices in front of the other apprentices. I finished sweeping the floor, directed the dust into a bag for disposal and washed my hands before heading to the office. The door was firmly closed. I raised my hand to knock, then hesitated. What if I was in trouble?

"Come in," Master Pittwater called.

I flushed. The door was heavily warded. He'd probably known I was there the moment I walked up. I schooled my face into a calm expression, then pushed the door open and stepped inside. Master Pittwater's office was smaller than I'd expected, for a man of his status, crammed with books and papers ... some of which he'd let me read. I couldn't help staring at the titles, wondering if I could convince him to let me see some of the older tomes. There were no copies of *them* in the local library.

"Master," I said. "What can I do for you?"

"Take a seat," Master Pittwater said. "I'll be with you in a moment."

I sat and studied him as he read a parchment scroll. He was old, although I had no idea *how* old. Rumour had it he'd lived in the city since before we'd freed ourselves from the leech of Zangaria. He was certainly old enough to be my grandfather and looked it, too, with white hair framing a wrinkled face and a body that was slightly heavyset for a magician. I knew very little about his past, save for the fact he'd studied at Heart's Eye long before the school had fallen to the necromancers. He rarely talked about it. I had the feeling his time there hadn't been entirely happy.

It was hard not to feel a twinge of envy. I'd have done anything in my power to attend a magic school. It wasn't easy to make a career in magic if one didn't *have* magic, but I was sure I could do it. I could climb to the very top, if only I could reach the very first stair. Matt and the other magical apprentices didn't know how lucky they'd been, let alone the opportunities they'd had that had been denied me. It was hard, sometimes, to remember that it had been nothing more than the luck of the draw.

"Adam," Master Pittwater said. He straightened up, fixing me with a stare. "We have things to discuss."

I nodded, racking my brains. What had I done? I couldn't think of anything ... unless he'd changed his mind about something and forgotten to tell me until it was too late. No, it couldn't be something like that. Master Pittwater was quite reasonable, unlike some of the other masters in the city. I'd been told there were masters who beat their apprentices bloody for the slightest mistake, even when it had been the *master* who'd committed the mistake. If I was in trouble ...

"There's no easy way to say this," Master Pittwater said. His fingers played with the scroll. "I think you've gone about as far as you can with me."

I blinked. "What?"

Master Pittwater looked sympathetic. It didn't help. "You have mastered reading and writing," he said. "Both Old Script and the New Learning. You have passed through several levels of theoretical magic, even though you've had little formal training. I'd say you actually have more skill at theory than Matt, despite the fact Matt went to Whitehall. If you had the proper training, you could go far."

"I ..." I swallowed, hard. This ... this wasn't what I'd expected. "Master ..."

"The problem is that you don't have any magic yourself," Master Pittwater said. "If you did, I would have no hesitation in taking you as a formal apprentice. If you did" —his eyes met mine— "I think you would have completed your apprenticeship very quickly and moved on to better and brighter things. As it is ... you will never rise any further. You *cannot* rise any further, not here. The best you can hope for is to remain in the shop, after Matt or a later apprentice takes my place."

I felt as if I'd been slapped across the face. "Master, I ... Master, are you dying?"

Master Pittwater shrugged. "I am old," he said. If he was offended by my stunned question, he didn't show it. "We must face facts. As long as my life has been, it won't last forever. I have already started to slow down and make mistakes, Adam. There's a very good chance Matt will be my last apprentice. The Guild has already been giving me pointed hints that it's time to retire and pass the shop to someone new."

"I could run it," I said. I knew I was pleading, but it was hard to care. My world had turned upside down. I'd once dared to dream I'd take his place. Now ... that dream was dust and less than dust. "Master, I could take the shop and ..."

"You couldn't," Master Pittwater said, flatly. "The Guild would never allow it. Even if they did, even if you somehow convinced them to make an exception, you simply couldn't hope to run the shop successfully. You would need to hire Matt, or someone like him, to make the potions, and very few magicians would agree to work under you. Anyone who did ... they might spend a year or two with you and then petition the Guild to give them the shop. And even if they didn't ..."

He shook his head. "Right now, the best you can hope for is working for Matt," he said. "And you might not like that very much."

I bit my lip. Matt and I had reached an understanding, based partly on the fact we were both apprentices ... in a manner of speaking. I didn't think things would go so smoothly if Matt was actually running the shop. Master Pittwater was right. It was rare, very rare, to find a magician who was comfortable serving under a mundane. They had to be very rich and powerful if they wanted willing service. Matt might, or might not, tell me to leave. He certainly wouldn't treat me as anything like an equal.

"No, Master," I said. Hopelessness welled up within me. What good *was* I? I'd spent my teenage years in the shop. Even if I tried to find another master, in a mundane field, I'd be competing against younger boys who weren't so aware of their rights. I couldn't think of anyone who'd take me. "What ... what am I going to do?"

My mind raced. There were other apothecaries and potion houses, but they wouldn't want me as an apprentice. They'd just want me to slice and dice the ingredients, leaving the actual brewing to the magicians. I didn't mind the menial labour, and I knew I was good at it, but I didn't want to spend my entire life supporting others. I wanted to do something for myself.

Master Pittwater raised the scroll. "I have an old friend," he said. "Master Landis. Have you heard of him?"

"No, Master," I said. I knew very little about my master's social life. He rarely left the shop, as far as I could tell. There'd been a big conference a couple of years ago about *something* and he'd had to attend, but he'd grumbled so extensively about it afterwards that I'd had the feeling it hadn't been pleasant. If he had friends, I'd never met them. "Who is he?"

"We were at Heart's Eye together, in a manner of speaking," Master Pittwater said. "He's younger than I, with more ... interest in innovation. And he's gone *back* to Heart's Eye."

I blinked. I knew the story, of course. Everyone did. Heart's Eye had been occupied by a necromancer until the Necromancer's Bane had kicked his ass in single combat and killed him. Since then ... I'd heard all sorts of crazy rumours, from her turning the school into a giant super-fortress to the school preparing to accept new students. I wasn't sure what to make of them. I'd been in the shop, too busy trying to accomplish the impossible to pay much attention. In hindsight, that might have been a mistake.

"Heart's Eye is becoming something new and different," Master Pittwater said. "Lady Emily believes that magic and mundane *technology*" —he stumbled over the unfamiliar word— "can mix. Or so Landis tells me. I have communicated with him, and he has informed me that he would be happy to take you as a prospective apprentice or, at the very least, provide gainful employment long enough for you to find your feet. Heart's Eye has only been open for a few months, but it is already expanding rapidly. I think you'd do well there."

"I ..." I stared at him. "I don't know what to say."

I shivered, torn between hope and fear. I'd admired the steam engines as they made their way between Beneficence and Cockatrice. I would have applied to work as a driver if I hadn't been so obsessed with theoretical magic. The gods knew that nearly every young man —and at least half the young women—in the city dreamed of driving an engine. I also knew very few would make it, at least at the start. It would be years before the railways reached all the way to Alexis and beyond. Vesperian, damn the man, had put the brakes on investment.

"It's like this." Master Pittwater met my eyes. "Matt has two years to go, at his current rate, before he's ready to take the exams. Once he does, I intend to retire. Matt will probably take the shop. I'd certainly prefer to let him have it, rather than surrender it to someone I didn't teach personally. And once that happens—and it will—your career will be curtailed. You will certainly not get any further."

He let out a breath. "It is unlikely that any theoretical magician will take you on," he added, stiffly. "Very few of them have the resources to take on an apprentice. Those who do are connected to magical families and probably wouldn't want someone like you, who has neither magic nor connections. My recommendations only go so far. I cannot guarantee that you'll get anywhere at Heart's Eye, Adam, but I don't see any other option. If nothing else, you will be no worse off."

I tried, desperately, to think of an alternative. Nothing came to mind. The Apothecaries Guild had always looked down its collective nose at people like me, mundanes who worked in magic shops. Matt might have a claim, if Master Pittwater died unexpectedly; I certainly did not. I eyed Master Pittwater, wondering if he was on the verge of death. He was the oldest person I knew, old enough ... I shook my head. That line of thought wasn't remotely productive.

"Master," I said. "How long do I have to decide?"

Master Pittwater glanced at the scroll. "He needs an assistant," he said. "I'd say you have a week, no more. If you agree, I'll pay for your trip through the portals to Farrakhan and railway journey to Heart's Eye itself. They seem to prefer newcomers to travel via railway, at least for the first time. I have no idea why. I'll also give you a stack of references, if you need to find employment somewhere else."

He frowned. "If you accept, I can write to him now and say so. That should ensure you get the post."

I nodded, slowly. "And he would teach me?"

"He'll give you a very basic apprenticeship," Master Pittwater said. "What you make of it, afterwards, is up to you. If some of the wilder concepts work, you might manage to build an entire career on it. If not ... you'll be in a position to make a place for yourself. Heart's Eye doesn't have a small army of guilds, not yet. You won't have to bow and scrape in front of them for employment."

"That sounds wonderful," I said, weakly.

I sat back and forced myself to think. Master Pittwater was right. I hated to admit it, but he was right. My career really wouldn't go anywhere if I stayed here. I didn't want to spend the rest of my life working for Matt or another alchemist who didn't see me as anything more than a servant. And there was nowhere else to go, not really. Sure, I could get a job at the docks, but it would be hard, dangerous and poorly paid. Otherwise ...

"I'll have to speak to my parents," I said. "But ... yes. I'll go."

Master Pittwater smiled. "I'll write tonight," he said. "And hopefully make arrangements for you to go as soon as possible."

"Thank you," I said. "I ..."

"Thank me afterwards," Master Pittwater said. "I don't know if I'm doing you any favours at all."

I stood and bowed, then hurried out of the shop. The streets were already heaving with people as apprentices, workers and visitors headed back home after work or went straight to the pubs. It was traditional for apprentices to go out drinking and carousing every night ... I felt a sudden pang of regret that I wouldn't be doing that any longer. Drunken fights were always fun, although the hangovers weren't remotely pleasant. One of the advantages of working for an alchemist was that there was always a hangover potion on hand.

My parents were not pleased when I told them what was happening. I wasn't surprised. Two of my brothers had already left, leaving the family shop in my sister's hands. She did it perfectly well, in my opinion, but my father had always been an old-fashioned sod. He feared her husband, when she married, would take the business for himself. I doubted it was going to happen. My sister was tough. She'd come pretty close to breaking *my* jaw once, and I doubted she would hold back if she had an overbearing husband. I almost felt sorry for whoever she married.

And besides, I hadn't wanted to inherit the business anyway.

Master Pittwater might have been old, but he moved with commendable speed. The following day, he told me he'd booked my trip through a pair of portals, gave me a pouch of money and a small collection of books and proffered his formal blessing. Matt slapped me on the back, wished me luck and promised there'd always be a place for me if I wanted to return home. I wondered, as I waved goodbye, precisely what Master Pittwater had told *him*. I'd never thought Matt would stay and run the shop ...

The trip would have been enjoyable, if the sudden shift in time zone hadn't caught me by surprise. The portals might have taken me halfway across the world in the blink of an eye, but the railway was slow and bumpy and extremely uncomfortable. I was already tired when I reached Heart's Ease and made my way to Heart's Eye. I was barely even awake when I was shown to my room—Master Landis had told the staff I was coming—and didn't even bother to undress before I hit the sheets. And then Lilith woke me ...

And that, more or less, brings us back to where we were.

CHAPTER THREE

I stood, frozen solid, and waited.

There was nothing else I could do. The magic held me still. Lilith didn't pay any attention to me as she took the ingredients I'd prepared and turned them into a potion. She moved in and out of my field of vision, as if I was nothing more than the statue I so resembled. The helplessness gnawed at me as I waited, mocking me. She was younger than me—probably—and yet she'd overpowered me effortlessly. My sister had clobbered me once, but that was different. I could have clobbered her first, if I'd tried.

"Good," Lilith said, more to herself than to me. The potion was bubbling merrily as it settled down. "Very good."

I wanted to scream. I wanted to ... I wasn't sure what I wanted to do. There was nothing I could do. Master Pittwater had been right. I could run the calculations and plot out how best to turn a collection of ingredients into a potion, but I could never do it myself. Lilith could ... and more, much more, beside. I felt a surge of pure hatred, mingled with bitter regret. I'd been assured Heart's Eye would be different. So far, it was shaping up to be worse.

The door opened. Master Landis stepped into the room. His eyebrow raised as he saw me, then looked at Lilith. She glanced at him. I couldn't see her face, but ... Master Landis gave her an indulgent smile and waved a hand at me. The spell broke. I dropped to the floor, like a puppet whose strings had been cut. It was all I could do not to scream. I didn't want to give Lilith the satisfaction.

"He was very cheeky to me," Lilith said, in a tone one might use to talk about the weather. "I had to put him in his place."

"Good, good," Master Landis said. There was a hint of exasperation in his tone, rather than anger. "I'm sure he won't do it again."

I tried not to glare as I picked myself up, Matt had used magic on me. Once. Master Pittwater had strapped him so hard he hadn't been able to sit down for a week afterwards. I'd seen the welts. After that ... we might not have been close friends, but at least we'd managed to work together. Lilith ... I couldn't believe she'd simply been allowed to get away with it. I had to bite my tongue to keep from snitching. The little ... *witch* ... deserved it and worse.

"Come over here," Master Landis ordered. "Pittwater spoke highly of you."

"Thank you," I managed. I could *feel* Lilith's gaze boring into my back. "He spoke highly of you, too."

Lilith made a spluttering noise behind me. Master Landis didn't seem to care.

"What do you get," he asked instead, "if you mingle Tostada Powder with Raymore Oats at room temperature?"

"A mess," I said. It was true, although it was hardly precise. "The two simply don't blend at room temperature. Worse, they clog up the rest of the potion and expend the magic too early. You have to put the powder in water and bring it to the boil before you add the oats."

"Good, good," Master Landis said. "Why can't you use preservation spells on regeneration potion?"

"Because the magic within the spells triggers a reaction within the potion," I said. It had been one of the very first things I'd learnt as a shop assistant. "The potion goes sour very quickly and becomes useless."

"Any fool knows *that*," Lilith put in.

"Yes," Master Landis agreed. "How do you compensate for the effect?"

I hesitated. As far as I knew, there was *no* way to compensate for the effect. Regeneration potions were incredibly difficult to produce, even for trained alchemists. There'd been times when they simply couldn't be brewed in time. The best of them needed blood, skin and even bones from the patient ... I frowned. Was there something I'd missed? Or was it a trick question?

"I don't think you can compensate for the effect," I said. "Stasis spells, preservation spells, even basic freeze charms ... they'd all have an effect on the potion. You could freeze it the mundane way, but it would take too long and ..."

"Impossible," Lilith said.

Master Landis held up a hand. "It might work, but keeping the potion stable would be impossible," he said. "You're right. As far as we know, it cannot be done."

I had no time to enjoy the moment. Master Landis bombarded me with questions, ranging from easy to extremely difficult, including a couple I had to work out before I dared open my mouth. I had no idea how well I was doing, although Lilith snorted a couple of times at some of my more uncertain answers. Master Landis seemed inclined to ignore her, something that annoyed me. Lilith's attitude was going to get her in real trouble if she mouthed off to someone *really* dangerous.

"Very good," Master Landis said, after what felt like hours. "You have a good grounding in basic magical theory."

"But almost no practical skill," Lilith put in. "I told him that ..."

I promised myself I'd find a way to get a little revenge as Master Landis showed me around the lab. It was even bigger than I'd thought, with a small kitchen next to the washroom and a preservation cabinet humming with magic in the next room. I was impressed, particularly with the library. Master Landis passed me a handful of papers and told me to check his work, forcing me to go through the calculations one by one. They looked accurate, but not precise. A skilled brewer could easily compensate for any weaknesses as he prepared the potion. It was only people like me who needed to be perfectly precise.

Except I can't even get started, I thought, sourly. *There's no way I can trigger the reaction myself.*

The day wore on. Master Landis had me slicing, dicing and otherwise preparing ingredients as he and Lilith turned them into potions. Lilith shot me snide looks every time I brought her a tray of ingredients, to the point I was tempted—very tempted—to make a mistake that would ensure the cauldron exploded in her face. Master Landis would have fired me on the spot, if he didn't kill me outright ... I ground my teeth, meditating on the value of patience. I'd find out what was actually going on first, before I did anything. I had never known a master to put up with such behaviour from an apprentice. There had to be a reason why Master Landis was letting her get away with it.

I studied him, thoughtfully, as he brewed. Master Pittwater had been cool and calm and very precise. Master Landis seemed much more of a performer, practically dancing as he placed the ingredients in the cauldron and triggered the reaction that turned them into potion. It was impressive, although I couldn't help thinking Lilith found him rather *embarrassing*. She cast sidelong looks as he worked, as if she couldn't quite believe what she was seeing. How long had she been his apprentice? It had to have been quite some time if she was confident he wouldn't punish her for bitchiness.

"Done," Master Landis said. He put out the flame, then nodded to me. "Bottle it up and label everything, then put it in storage. We'll take it to the infirmary later."

"Yes, Master," I said.

Lilith shot me a nasty look. I ignored her as best as I could. Master Pittwater had made sure I understood precisely how to label the vials, noting everything from the potion name to the precise time and date it was brewed. The basic healing potion would last for weeks, as long as it wasn't exposed to the air. I wondered, suddenly, just how many people got hurt at Heart's Eye? I'd heard enough horror stories about magic schools to know the answer might be terrifyingly high.

Master Landis didn't seem to tire. Instead, he tossed more and more questions at me as he worked his way through his books. It was strange to realise just how much I didn't know ... just how much I could never know. Matt had tried to explain magic to me, and how it felt to use it, but I hadn't been able to follow his explanation. It was like trying to imagine myself a girl, only worse. There were spells and potions to turn boys into girls—and girls into boys—but there was no way to become a magician. If there had been ... I was sure Master Pittwater would have made it for me. There were certainly plenty of rich mundanes who would have paid through the nose to become magical.

Lilith's disdain seemed to grow with every successive answer. I rapidly came to realise she was more annoyed by correct answers than mistakes. Did she feel threatened? I found it hard to believe. She had magic, and I did not; and that was the end of it. I could plot out how to produce a potion, but I couldn't brew it. She'd get the credit if she took something I plotted and actually made it work. I wouldn't have faulted her, either. It was a great deal easier to plot how to do something—anything— than actually doing it.

I allowed myself a sigh of relief as Master Landis seemed to run out of questions. He really did remind me of someone, although I wasn't sure who. Master Pittwater? My imagination suggested that Master Pittwater could be Master Landis's father, but it didn't seem likely. They were very different. I wasn't a carbon copy of my father, yet we were very clearly related. Besides, I'd never seen any sign that Master Pittwater was interested in women. Or men. How had they even met? Unless Master Landis was a lot older than he looked, they were from different generations. I wasn't sure I dared ask. It would be better to wait long enough to figure out what would offend him before I tried.

"Work on this," Master Landis said, finally. "Let me know if you can make it work."

I took the parchment and stared at it as Master Landis and Lilith returned to their brewing. The spell notation was odd, strangely imprecise ... I glanced at them, unsure who'd actually prepared the parchment. The very first section was so badly aligned with the rest that I found it hard to believe they'd been written by the same person. Matt had made some howlers, when he'd started his apprenticeship, but nothing as bad as this. I allowed myself to hope that Lilith had prepared the parchment, as I started to straighten it out. Fixing the first section ...

My heart sank. Fixing the first section threw the rest of the spell out of alignment. I was suddenly *entirely* sure that Lilith had sketched it out. She had the power to hold it together long enough to make it work ... to make it do whatever it was supposed to do. Anyone else ... I shook my head. It felt more like a very crude piece of spellwork than anything else. I honestly couldn't tell what it was intended to do. No matter how I looked at it, there just didn't seem to be any reasonable endpoint.

I waited for Master Landis to finish his brewing, then cleared my throat. "I can't figure out what it's meant to do," I said. "The first section draws on a great deal of power, but the second and third sections pull in different directions. What is the spell trying to do?"

"It was devised to split the potion in two, then brew each section separately before allowing them to recombine," Master Landis said. "Does that make it any easier?"

"No." I was too puzzled to pay proper respect. "Wouldn't it be better to brew them in separate cauldrons?"

Lilith snickered. "What an idea!"

I glared at her. "And what's *wrong* with the idea?"

"Tell him," Master Landis said.

"Of course." Lilith smiled at me. It would have been sweet if it had been anyone else. "The first part of the brew needs to be perfectly balanced. That means you cannot brew two separate batches, even if you make it as precise as possible. You have to produce one batch and split it into two. And *then* you have to let them merge as equals, once you have prepared the second stage. You cannot simply pour one into the other. You have to let them blur as equals."

I scowled as Master Landis gave her an approving look. It was the sort of explanation, I felt, that only made sense to magicians. What did it matter if one batch was poured into the other? Why did it matter if they were equals? What happened if they weren't? And wouldn't it be easier, the nastier part of my mind wondered, if the cauldron was designed with a physical partition? One could separate the two batches without using magic, thus avoiding the risk of accidental contamination. Or was there something I was missing? I had no way to know.

Make a note of it, I told myself. The spell was an order of magnitude more complex than anything I'd seen in the old shop. Master Pittwater had never used anything like it. *And follow up on it later.*

I looked back at the spell notation, feeling my heart sink once again. There was no way to tighten it up, not really. It needed to be cast by someone who was perfectly attuned to both the potion and the spell ... a magician, a very experienced magician. There was no way *I* could even begin to make it work. I could fix the problems so someone else could cast the spell ... no, I realised suddenly. I could only make them worse.

"It can't be fixed," I said, pushing my notes aside. "I mean ... it's cumbersome and stupid, but there's no way to improve upon it without making it impossible to brew the potion. It simply cannot be done."

"No," Master Landis agreed. "Well-spotted."

I didn't need to look at Lilith to know she was sneering. She knew I hadn't really done anything. Hell, all I'd *really* done was waste time. I'd thought the problem could be fixed ... if not by me, then by someone. But ... I shook my head. There was always a cost. One couldn't make money without spending money, as Master Pittwater had said. It hadn't taken me long to realise it applied to magic too.

"Thank you," I said.

Master Landis nodded and turned away. Lilith snapped her fingers at me. I felt a burning pain on my hand, as if I'd splashed myself with hot water. She smirked at me as I glared helplessly at her, daring me to do something. I knew there was nothing I could do. She could freeze me in my tracks, or worse, before I could lay a finger on her.

"Prepare me some Kava," Master Landis ordered. "And then you and Lilith can go on your tour."

Lilith smiled. "Prepare me some, too," she said.

I made a face as I turned and headed into the kitchen. It was surprisingly big, the walls lined with cupboards crammed with everything from powered grains to potion ingredients and supplies. I lit the fire under the stove, filled the kettle with water and started to dig through the cupboards for supplies. A handful of inactive potions rested above the sink, including one I knew from the shop. Inactive dogbreath potion was useless, unless it was given to a magician ...

The kettle started to boil. I took it off the stove, poured water into the mugs and added the grains, then hesitated. I'd had more than enough of Lilith's attitude, but my apprenticeship was at stake ... I took a little of the potion and added it to her mug. I'd pay for it, I was sure, but it would be worth it. If nothing else, it might teach her a lesson.

I took the mugs back into the workroom and passed them out. Lilith sneered as she took hers and drank. I watched, wondering if she could taste the potion. It wasn't supposed to taste of anything, but everyone knew magicians had a sixth sense for magic. I waited, sipping my own drink. Master Landis said something to Lilith ...

... And she started to bark.

I couldn't help myself. I sniggered. Lilith glared at me, a stream of barks and growls coming out of her mouth. Master Landis seemed unconcerned. She glanced at him, then raised a hand and pointed it at me. I got ready to jump to one side. Maybe I could make my escape before she managed to zap me into a frog or something equally humiliating. Or ... traditionally, a master couldn't punish an apprentice if the apprentice had already been punished. It dawned on me, too late, that the rule might not hold fast here.

Master Landis cleared his throat. "Lilith, you are obliged to give Adam the tour," he said, curtly. He dug into his pocket and produced a handful of coins. I tried not to notice he'd just given Lilith more money than I'd ever earned in a week. No wonder she was such a spoilt brat. "Take him for lunch in town, then show him around."

Lilith growled and barked. Master Landis passed her a vial. She drank it, then scowled at me. I tried not to smile. She looked murderous. I'd embarrassed her in front of her master.

"And behave," Master Landis added. His eyes moved to me, then back to Lilith. "Both of you."

"Yes, Master," I said.

Lilith just glared.

CHAPTER FOUR

There'd been times, when I'd been younger, when going for a walk with a pretty girl had been fun. Everyone had understood that it was a way to be alone without ever quite being *truly* alone. The girl could talk to her suitor without compromising her virtue or—if the suitor proved to be a wolf in sheep's clothing—being in a position where he could compromise her beyond repair. Normally, I might have enjoyed going for a walk with a pretty girl. But now ...

I was all too aware of Lilith's brooding anger as we walked through the university—she showed me the dorms, the library, the lecture halls and the small studies—and out of the main doors. The air outside was uncomfortably hot, the tang of sand and tainted magic brushing against my tongue. It smelt as if something wet was burning, a stench that lingered long after the fire was out. If Lilith noticed, or cared, she gave no sign. I did my best not to glance at her too openly as we started to walk down the road. It looked like a well-beaten dirt track, with people and carts hurrying up and down. I would have enjoyed it more if the air hadn't smelt so bad.

Lilith let out an angry snort. I decided I didn't want to know what she was thinking, although it seemed he was trying to devise something truly horrible to do to me. King Randor had put his enemies through a series of tortures so unpleasant I found it hard to believe any of them had survived the first stage. Lilith probably thought that turning me into a slug and stepping on me was too good for me. Or something. I shivered, trying not to edge away. Back home, girls were vulnerable. Everyone knew it. Here, I was the vulnerable one. It didn't sit well.

The strange smell grew stronger as Heart's Ease came into view. It was a sprawling mass of a town, expanding so rapidly it probably counted as a small city. I hadn't seen many cities, beyond my hometown, but ... I couldn't help thinking Heart's Ease looked *odd*. It struck me as ramshackle, as if it had been thrown together without any forethought. Old buildings, marked by time, stood next to rickety-looking apartment blocks and tents large enough to hold a whole circus. I saw row upon row of smaller tents, with men sleeping on the streets or lining up outside the more solid-looking buildings. A row of signs invited me to seek employment as everything from a craftsman to an ironmonger or a shop assistant. I wondered, morbidly, if I could find a job here. The air was so full of energy that it was easy to ignore the smell.

Lilith guided me through the edge of town and past a string of stalls. People seemed to be buying and selling everything from paper books—*lots* of books—to food, drink and basic potions. I blinked in astonishment as I saw a fishmonger, his prices so high that I couldn't believe anyone would even *look* at his shop. And yet he had customers ... I stared, remembering—suddenly—that we were hundreds of miles from the sea. The nearest kingdom was almost completely land-locked. A sign in front of the shop informed his customers that the fish was fresh. I doubted it. Unless the fish were preserved by magic, they would probably be on the verge of going rotten ... I looked away and stared as a man led a line of wild pigs down the street. No one seemed to care.

The sense of life only grew stronger as we reached the centre of town. It was bustling with activity, from people running around to horses and carts pushing their way through the crowd. A steam engine tooted in the distance, coming into view briefly as it made it way along the tracks, I stared, remembering just how bumpy the ride had been. It was hard to believe the railway line was remotely solid.

"There are too many people here," Lilith said. She sounded uncomfortable. "How do they live like this?"

"They don't have a choice," I said. I'd heard stories from people who'd fled the aristocratic estates and made their way to the cities. Their new homes weren't perfect, but at least the locals weren't slaves. "Where were you born?"

Lilith gave me a sharp look as she led me into a small cafe. I took one look at the prices and blanched. It would cost me nearly everything I had to eat there. I wanted to suggest we went elsewhere, but Lilith was already heading to a table. The waiter eyed her nervously. I had the feeling she'd made a name for herself and not in a good way.

"Order what you like," she said, curtly. "He's paying."

I glanced at the menu, feeling my heart skip a beat. Master Pittwater hadn't been *poor*, but he couldn't have afforded to eat at the cafe. I didn't know anyone who could ... no, that wasn't true any longer. I eyed Lilith as she ordered without looking at the menu. How could she afford to spend so much money on a single meal? I could have kept myself fed for an entire month on what she was insisting we spend.

"I don't know what to order," I said. The menu was useless. I didn't recognise any of the names. "What should I have?"

Lilith shrugged. I scowled and picked something at random, then looked around as the waiter collected the menus and hurried off. There weren't many other customers in the cafe and the handful I could see looked older and richer than anyone I'd encountered back home. They didn't seem remotely interested in us. A man wearing colourful livery, suggesting he was the sworn servant of a king or powerful aristocrat, was having dinner with a man in magical robes, Two rows down, there were three women in fancy dresses that showed off their breasts. I found it hard not to stare. Anyone dressed like that, back home, would almost certainly be a whore.

"The town gets bigger every time I come," Lilith said, darkly. It struck me, suddenly, that she might be agoraphobic. One of Master

Pittwater's apprentices—he hadn't lasted long—had never managed to adapt to city life. He'd found crowds terrifying. "They put up new buildings overnight, and then wonder why they fall down."

I stared at her. "Do they really fall down?"

"Yes," Lilith said. "This place isn't called the Desert of Death for nothing. The storms are *nasty*. Those tents out there? If they're not charmed just right, they'll be picked up and thrown all the way to the Great Ocean when the wind blows. Those buildings? They're too big to be safe. And most of them aren't anchored properly either. The gods blow, and they come tumbling down."

I shivered, then looked up as the waiter returned with a tray of food. I'd ordered lobster with butter, boiled potatoes and green peas. I shook my head—my mother could have cooked a dozen lobsters for the price of one—and started to eat. It wasn't cooked very well. Lilith snorted, just loud enough for me to hear, then tore into her own meal. She had something with meat, rice, and strange-smelling sauce.

"You can find anything here," Lilith said, between bites. "People are coming from all over the Allied Lands. Students, craftsmen, traders ... and people who want to get rich scamming them. You can find a place to eat anything you like, if you go poking around in the right places."

I smiled. "Isn't this place scamming us?"

"It's fancy," Lilith said. "Of course, it's expensive."

I smiled. It seemed to annoy her. She honestly had no idea how much things were actually worth. I was sure she wouldn't last a week on the streets. Traders would see her coming and mark up their prices, sure she wouldn't lower herself to haggle. The lobster in front of me had been marked up so badly ... maybe it had been transported hundreds of miles. It was still massively overpriced.

"I think we'd better eat somewhere else, next time," I said. "There have to be cheaper places."

"But none so important," Lilith said, firmly. "And what makes you think there's going to be a next time?"

That effectively killed conversation, at least until we'd finished our meals and headed back outside. The air had grown even hotter, somehow, but the crowds hadn't abated. If anything, they'd grown worse. I tried not to look too closely at the buildings as we walked past, dreading the thought of having to live in them. Lilith might have been a witch—as well as something that rhymed with witch—but she was right. The majority of buildings looked as if they'd been thrown together in a hurry. I had the feeling they weren't remotely secure. The railway line didn't look as if it had been solidly pinned either. I supposed the desert wasn't the easiest place to lay railway tracks.

Lilith led me on a long walk around the town. I followed her, staring at all the life. Giant warehouses, each one thrown up so quickly they looked about as solid as the housing. The Foundry was a massive complex of factories and industrial facilitates that pulsed with light. I saw a steam locomotive, gleaming dully under the sunlight, chugging out of the shed and into the lines for the first time. In the darkness, I saw three more in various stages of construction. The craftsmen milling around them looked happy and confident and certain, very certain, that they were important. I knew they were right. A trained craftsman was worth his weight in gold.

A man ran up to us and shoved a leaflet into my hand. I read it as he hurried away again, frowning. The very first line read LEVELLER MEETING, 2100 HRS. I glanced through the rest of the text, including promises that a number of prominent Levellers would be there and quotes from others, including Lady Emily herself. I'd known Levellers back home, but I'd never paid too much attention. It was harder for them to gain a following in a city where everyone, at least in theory, could influence the council.

"They think we're all equal," Lilith commented, sardonically. "And that we are all one and the same."

I glanced at her. "And you don't think so?"

Lilith gave me a cold smile. "Do you know what I could do to you?"

"Yes," I said. A shiver ran down my spine. Matt had told me students played horrible pranks on each other. If a freeze spell was a first-year spell, nothing more than a joke, I shuddered to think what might be considered genuine malice. "It doesn't make you better than me."

"Keep dreaming." Lilith snorted. "If it makes you feel any better."

She didn't bother to lower her voice as we walked back towards the town. "If you had something I wanted, I could just take it. Who could stop me?"

"My sister is weaker than me," I said. "She still nearly broke my jaw."

Lilith ignored me. "The Levellers can protest all they like. They can build all the fancy toys" —she waved a hand at the steam engine, sitting on the track— "they like. It won't make any difference. If they cause too much trouble, we'll crush them like bugs."

She paused,then looked into my eyes, "We'll turn them into bugs and crush them. So *what* if they're smarter? So what if *you're* smarter? I still have power beyond your comprehension."

I winced, She grinned. "You have no power over me, and we both know it. Your sister is on the same level as you. I am so far above you that the gap simply cannot be put into words."

"The last time I heard someone say something like that," I said, "he took a massive pratfall because of his overconfidence."

"But my overconfidence is justified," Lilith pointed out. "Was his?"

I tried not to clench my fists. The idiot had bragged he could kick my ass at Strategy. He'd been so overconfident that I'd wiped him off the board, after he'd committed the sort of mistake no one would make when facing someone with half a brain. Or even a working knowledge of the rules. Lilith ... sure, I could beat her on the game-board. She could still slap me down any moment she wished. I wondered, suddenly, if she was connected to someone powerful. Or if she was more powerful than I'd thought. It was hard to believe that any magician would put up with her, if there wasn't a very good reason. Master Pittwater had certainly not put up with arrogant or snooty apprentices.

I was tempted to ask. But I doubted I'd get a straight answer.

We kept walking, circumventing the edge of the town. Lilith hadn't been too far wrong about the building practices, I decided as we passed a block of new flats. They were nothing more than a shell, being put together at terrifying speed. The workers looked surprisingly slapdash, compared to the ones I'd seen back home. But then, the guilds kept construction workers firmly under their thumbs. Here ... I had a feeling there simply weren't any guilds. I certainly hadn't seen any advertised.

Lilith glanced at me. "You could live here?"

I frowned. It was tempting, if I couldn't go home. There was no shortage of work. I'd seen enough advertised to know there simply wasn't enough labour to go around. The wages would be higher than anything back home, with demands for qualifications and experience correspondingly low. I still had the money I'd been given, enough to find lodging long enough to start earning. It would mean giving up the dream, but ...

"Lilith," I said. "Can I ask a question?"

"Of course." Lilith spoke like a haughty monarch bestowing a favour on a courtier. "You may ask anything you like."

"You didn't like me from the start," I said. It was true, but I didn't know why. Oversleeping hardly deserved the death sentence. "You disliked and resented—perhaps even hated—me. You cursed me and ..."

"Hexed you," Lilith corrected, coldly.

"Why?" I stopped and stared at her. "Why do you hate me?"

Lilith said nothing for a long moment. "I don't hate you," she said. "You simply don't belong here."

She started to walk, heading back up the road to the university. I followed her, a dozen questions running through my head. I didn't belong ...? Master Pittwater had asked Master Landis to take me, and he'd agreed. Lilith ... Lilith didn't have a say in it. Was *that* what she resented? I found it hard to believe. Apprentices were, legally, children. Lilith could no more boss Master Landis around than I could.

I paced her. "What makes you say that?"

"You have no magic," Lilith said, flatly. "You cannot do even the simplest spells. All you can do is prepare ingredients and write spells, both of which I could do. Anyone could do, if they had magic. You just" —she scowled— "you just exist on our sufferance. You should not be here."

"Heart's Eye is for mundanes as well as magicians," I said. "Lady Emily ..."

"Lady Emily is an idealist," Lilith said, flatly. "I met her once, just before she left to take up her own apprenticeship. She doesn't realise just how incompatible magicals and mundanes actually are. She has no grasp at all of the realities of the world."

"And I suppose you do?" It was hard not to sound mocking, even though I knew *just* what she could do to me. "You know better than the Necromancer's Bane?"

Lilith glared. Her hand raised—I braced myself to dodge—before she calmed herself. "What can you do," she asked, "that I cannot do better?"

I tried not to say something like *father children*. Lilith would not have taken that calmly, if I'd dared. Instead ... I tried to think of an answer. I knew plenty of magical theory, but Lilith presumably knew plenty herself. And she understood how magic worked on a level I'd never be able to match. What little I could do would be easy for her to match, if she put in the time and effort. I was quite sure she knew precisely how to prepare potion ingredients. Master Pittwater had drilled Matt as well as me.

"I can find out," I said. "Let me try."

"You're wasting your time," Lilith said, darkly. A shadow crossed her face. "And Master Landis's, too."

"It's his time to waste," I said.

"He isn't sure himself," Lilith said. "You know why you have a bedroom, instead of one of the dorms? He doesn't know you'll be staying. He's waiting to see if you're truly useful ... or not."

I winced. I wanted to believe she was lying, but ... it sounded true. Lilith didn't strike me as a very good liar. It didn't feel as if she'd ever had the need to learn.

"Let me prove myself," I said, finally. "Give me time."

Lilith smirked. "You don't stand a chance."

I met her eyes. "You want to bet on it?"

"Very well," Lilith said. "I'll give you two months. You impress me, and I'll withdraw all objection to your presence. You don't" —she leaned closer— "I'll turn you into something small and slimy and drop you somewhere you'll never be found."

She turned and walked off. I watched her go, feeling sick. What had I got myself into now?

CHAPTER FIVE

It didn't take me too long to realise, as the first week of my semi-apprenticeship sped by, that impressing Lilith might be extremely difficult.

She was an odd duck, even by magical standards. The male magicians, including the ones who looked around the same age as Lilith, went out of their way to avoid her. It was hard to be sure, as we were hardly confidantes, but it seemed to wear on her. She appeared to be almost completely isolated, to the point we hung out together a couple of times since our first visit to Heart's Ease. I would have felt sorry for her if she hadn't spent half of her time reminding me that I had only a few weeks to impress her, or else. Part of me was tempted to throw in the towel, tell Master Landis that I'd made a dreadful mistake in coming, and find somewhere to stay in the town. The rest of me was just too stubborn to quit.

The hell of it was that I *liked* the university. It was bigger than I'd realised, with classes and lectures on every subject under the sun. I attended a speech on royal politics one day and a lecture on farming practice the next; I listened to a talk on how best to enchant objects from an enchanter and an explanation of how water was turned to steam to power a steam engine. The woman who gave the speech was a craftsman in her own right, according to Lilith; a formidable woman who looked tough enough to face down an army. Lilith sneered that the only reason she hadn't been taken down a peg or two by a magician was that she was in a relationship with a powerful enchanter, but I didn't believe it. A woman who became a full-fledged craftsman was clearly formidable enough to look after herself. If I hadn't been so worried about proving myself, I would have loved to bury myself in the university and never come out.

Lilith had been right about one thing, I realised dully. I hadn't been assigned to an apprentice dorm and wouldn't be unless I was taken on permanently. I wasn't sure what to make of it. I liked the idea of having my own room—I'd never had any privacy before, even in my garret—but it was a sign that I might not be there long. Perhaps that was another reason why I found myself alone when I wasn't with her. No one wanted to befriend someone who wasn't going to stick around. I'd seen that before, as an apprentice. It stung more than I remembered.

I spent most of my working hours in the lab, assisting Master Landis and Lilith. He wasn't a bad master, at least to me, although he showed no interest in curtailing Lilith's misbehaviour. I didn't understand it. An apprentice's behaviour reflected badly on her master and yet ... it made no sense. No one would question him if he punished or dismissed her. Or would they? Who was she, really? A person with powerful connections? I found it hard to believe after the first week. In my experience, anyone with powerful connections would find themselves surrounded by sycophants and fair-weather friends. Lilith was practically alone.

No wonder she spends time with me, even if she hates me, I thought. *I don't pretend she isn't there.*

The thought mocked me as I chopped ingredients for the two magicians. It was important work, I knew, but it wasn't what I wanted to do. And yet, what else could I do? I couldn't brew anything but the most basic potions. Lilith reminded me of that, time and time again. I'd watched her put a handful of ingredients in her cauldron and produce miracles, while I couldn't produce anything beyond sludge.

It was immensely frustrating. I wanted to claim credit for half the work, but I couldn't. Lilith could replace me overnight, if she wanted. I couldn't replace her.

"Done," I said, once I'd finished preparing the roots. "There's enough to produce two batches of potion."

"Good, good," Master Landis said. "You appreciate the importance of cutting them perfectly?"

I nodded, stiffly, as Lilith examined each and every root in cynical detail. She wanted to get me in trouble, I was sure. Perhaps Master Landis was quietly encouraging her. She wouldn't slack on the examination if she thought the slightest problem would land me in hot water. She could be relied upon to rub my nose in any mistakes. I scowled as she finished her task, then passed the roots to her master. The look she gave me was sour. I wondered, idly, if she thought I was wasting her time.

She's not lazy, I thought, as Master Landis took the roots and started to line them up. *She's just ... unpleasant.*

I put the thought aside as Master Landis directed me to fetch the rest of the ingredients, weigh them out and line them up for use. Master Pittwater had taught me the importance of making sure everything was on hand, before one started to brew, but Master Landis took it so seriously it was practically a religion. I supposed it made sense. He worked with far more dangerous ingredients. Master Pittwater hadn't had more than a tiny handful of dragon scales, while Master Landis had entire *bags*. A mistake with *those* could result in utter disaster. The university's wards should be able to contain the blast, if my calculations were correct, but the three of us would be blown straight to the gods. I wondered if they'd be pleased to see me. It had been a long time since I'd made an offering at the family shrine.

Master Landis bombarded me with questions as he checked and rechecked the ingredients. I tried not to sigh as I answered them, knowing it wouldn't get me anything more than a sneer from Lilith. She leaned against the wall, pretending she wasn't paying attention. It would have been more convincing if her green eyes hadn't been boring into me. I did my best to ignore her as I struggled to answer the questions, silently noting aspects of magical theory I'd have to study. Lilith had shown me where to find the library. I could go there after I'd been dismissed for the day.

"Very good," Master Landis said. "You would have gone far, if you'd had the gift."

I didn't let myself look at Lilith. I knew she'd be sneering. Instead, I watched as Master Landis heated the cauldron and started to brew. The memory potion was tricky—and dangerous. Master Pittwater had flatly refused to brew it, although I'd seen him brew far more complex potions. I didn't understand his reluctance. It wasn't as if the potion was beyond him.

Master Landis glanced at me as the liquid started to simmer. "You have a question?"

I blinked. How had he known?

"Yes, Master," I managed. I wished Lilith wasn't there. I was sure she'd find a way to make fun of the question. "Why did Master Pittwater refuse to brew memory potion?"

"Perhaps your master wasn't as good a master as he claimed," Lilith said. "Perhaps ..."

She broke off as Master Landis skewered her with a glare. I stared, surprised. It was the first time he'd shown her anything beyond mild annoyance. I just didn't understand it. Why didn't he react to her prodding me but shut her down the moment she insulted Master Pittwater? Perhaps they really had been close friends, despite the age gap. Or Master Pittwater had taught Master Landis. I supposed it was possible.

"Memory potions live up to their name," Master Landis said. He returned his gaze to the shimmering liquid, his fingers beating out a timing pattern on his hand. "If you drink the potion, you will remember—in perfect detail—everything that happens while the potion is within your system. You will never forget. Go to a complex lecture and everything you hear will be recorded within your mind, allowing you to recall and think about it later. On the face of it, the potion is very useful indeed."

I nodded. I could have used a memory potion, when I'd been studying. It would have saved me trying to remember all the letters and sigils, all the runes and ingredients and everything else I'd been forced to commit to memory. Matt and Lilith didn't know how lucky they were. They had an instinctive grasp of something I'd had to force myself to comprehend. It would have been easy, so easy, to simply dismiss it as something completely beyond my ken and find something else to do with my life. But I hadn't.

"The downside is that you will remember *everything*," Master Landis said. The potion started to bubble. He reached for a jar of powder and poured it into the liquid. "Everything, and I mean *everything*. Break up with your partner? You won't be able to forget every last cruel word. Get a lecture from your master? The words will linger in your mind until the end of your days. And if you're unwell? You will never be able to truly get over it."

"I see," I said, although I didn't. "Why do *you* brew it?"

"Because there are students who feel they need it," Lilith said. "And they're old enough to understand the risks and accept them."

I frowned as Master Landis kept working. It didn't make sense. Master Pittwater had sold all sorts of potions, from simple contraceptives to healing balms. There was no reason he couldn't sell memory potions. I could easily see scholars and engineers drinking the potion and using it to make sure they memorised something before the exam. Why had it been considered too dangerous to sell? It wasn't as if it was a shape-changing or a love potion. They were banned, with good reason. Master Pittwater had called the City Guard on a lovesick young woman whose paramour had not returned her feelings.

"There must be another downside," I said. "Why ...?"

"Good question," Master Landis said. "Lilith?"

Lilith gave me a look that promised vengeance. Painful, humiliating vengeance. I made a mental note to duck out of the lab as soon as working hours had ended for the day and head straight to the library. It would give her time to cool down and think better of whatever she intended to do. It wasn't the bravest thing I'd ever done, but

... I scowled. It had been a lot easier dealing with Matt. He hadn't been quite so difficult in his early days.

"You cannot replace the memory," Lilith said. "Whatever you learn, you cannot replace it."

I gave her a questioning look. "Replace it?"

Lilith glared. "Suppose I told you that I was twenty, which is true," she said. "You would believe me. You know it's true. If you drank the potion, that fact would remain stuck in your head. But next year, I'll be twenty-one. Right?"

"Yes," I said. I resisted the urge to point out that she was acting like a toddler. There was only a year between us, physically, but mentally we were worlds apart. "Unless something happens between now and then."

"Yes." Lilith's glare deepened. "But you wouldn't be able to ... think of me as someone older than twenty. The fact—that I am twenty— would be so stuck in your head that you'd still think of me as twenty, even when I was two hundred. Logically, you'd know I couldn't possibly be twenty. Emotionally, you would still believe me to be twenty."

"The problem is worse than that," Master Landis put in. "You might memorise a recipe for a potion, then find yourself unable to replace it with a superior recipe."

I shook my head. "If that's true ..."

"Of course, it's true," Lilith snapped.

"If that's true," I asked, "then why are we brewing it?"

"Because the students here are supposed to be old enough to understand the dangers," Master Landis said. "And there are certain fields of study that have enough ... *near*-certainties ,, for the potion to be quite useful. A healer, for example, needs to memorise a vast array of facts about the human body. They can use the potion to remember the details. They're generally isolated during the lecture and afterwards to limit the amount of accidental memorising they do."

The cauldron started to steam. Master Landis motioned to Lilith. She came forward, holding a silver knife in one hand. I stared, unsure what they intended to do. I'd already sliced and diced everything he needed to brew the potion. Master Pittwater had taught me that there were some potions that required the brewer to perform all the steps himself, preparing him as well as the ingredients, but memory potion wasn't one of them. Master Landis wouldn't have asked me to help if it was. I frowned as Lilith held her hand over the cauldron, then blinked in shock as she pressed the knife against her bare skin. A droplet of blood fell into the liquid. It started to hiss ominously.

I grabbed a cloth and held it out to Lilith. She shot me a nasty look as she snatched the cloth and pressed it against the cut. It had to have hurt, but ... she hadn't made a sound. I was almost impressed. The blade probably wasn't charmed. They didn't want the blood tainted by outside magic ...

My heart skipped a beat. *Blood*?

I found my voice. "Master, why ...?"

"Wait," Master Landis snapped.

I tried not to stare as he stirred the cauldron, muttering a spell under his breath. Blood magic was *dangerous*. Master Pittwater had warned me that anything involving blood was risky, even if it didn't cross the line into dark magic. A sample of someone's blood could be used against them, if they didn't take the right precautions, And yet ... I stared at Lilith, wondering what the hell she thought she was doing. Blood magic? She was mad. She had to be.

The cauldron blazed with light. I threw up a hand to cover my eyes. Lilith looked, just for a moment, as if she was caught in a storm. It struck me, as the light pulsed against the walls, that her senses weren't such an advantage now. If the light was bright enough to hurt me, what was it doing to her? It snapped out of existence so quickly I was convinced, just for a second, she'd hit me with a blinding hex. The lab was suddenly very dark. Multicoloured spots drifted in front of my eyes.

"Lilith, bottle up the potion," Master Landis ordered, curtly. He turned and headed for the door. "Adam, make sure to label every vial properly."

"Yes, Master," I said.

Lilith looked pale, even in the dimmed light, as she carefully ladled the potion into the vials and pushed the stoppers into place. I watched her, wondering just what she was doing. There were rules covering apprenticeships, magical and mundane alike. I found it hard to believe Master Landis had the right to demand her blood, certainly not when *she* wasn't the one brewing the potion. It was ... I shuddered. I'd heard horror stories about bad masters, but none of them involved *blood*.

I cleared my throat. "What ... what was *that* about?"

"My blood has powerful magic." Lilith sounded a little more like her old self. I was almost relieved. "It gives the potion a boost."

"Your blood?" I gave her a sidelong look. "Why couldn't he use his?"

"Because the potion would have interacted badly with his magic if he tried," Lilith said, curtly. "Using mine was a risk, but ..."

She broke off. "Yours is useless, of course."

I scowled. "How so?"

"You have no magic in your veins," Lilith said. "It's just ... *blood*."

"And yet, I got told to take care of my blood, too," I said. "Why would anyone bother if my blood was useless?"

Lilith snorted. "Your blood is linked to you. Someone could use it to brew you a healing potion, if they felt it worth the effort, or they could use it to curse you. They could put a spell on you from the other side of the world, if they had some of your blood. Mine? My blood can be used to power spells, because magic runs in my veins. There are magicians out there who sell their blood for money."

I raised my eyebrows. "What *else* do they sell it for?"

"You don't want to know," Lilith said. "You really don't."

"I'll take your word for it," I said. I'd look it up later, as well as a few other things. "Is your blood *that* powerful?"

Lilith smirked. "I can perform spells that would leave you gasping in awe," she said, as she finished sealing the vials. "What do you think?"

Master Landis stepped back into the room before I could come up with a snappy comeback and headed for the kitchen. "Lilith, stay here," he ordered. He picked up the vials, one by one, and checked the labels. I breathed a sigh of relief he didn't find any fault with them. "Adam, I want you to go to the library after dinner and dig up some books for me. I'll give you the references."

"Yes, Master," I said. I'd planned to go to the library anyway. "Potion recipes?"

"Among others," Master Landis said. He produced a sheet of paper and held it out. I took it and glanced at the list. The references included a list of names I knew by reputation, but never actually seen. "Read them carefully. I'll be wanting your opinions afterwards."

Lilith sneered as I headed to the door. "Don't forget you have to impress me," she said, making a show of looking at the calendar. "How much time do you have left?"

"Enough," I said. It was a lie, and I feared she knew it. "Bye."

CHAPTER SIX

The library was a wonderful place.

I couldn't help staring as I walked into the giant chamber and looked around. The library was huge, far larger than the library I'd visited in Beneficence. There were giant shelves, row upon row of books; I found my eyes trailing from freshly-printed books to ancient tomes so old they were stored in glass—and presumably warded—cabinets. I wanted to drool as I saw a set of new potion books, including reprints of textbooks I'd had to borrow from Matt and his predecessors. There weren't any warning signs, banning me from so much as *looking* at certain textbooks. Heart's Eye was open to all.

A young man sat at the desk, studying a ledger. He wore a simple grey tunic, rather than a robe, but I was fairly sure he was a magician. It was something about his attitude, although I couldn't have put it into words. I had the impression he was a few years older than me. It was hard to be sure. Lilith was twenty—she'd said—and she looked and acted like she was eighteen.

"Welcome to the library," the librarian said. "Have you read the rules?"

He held out a parchment before I could answer. I took it and ran my eyes down the list. It was fairly basic. No books to be taken out of the library without being signed out. All books to be returned or renewed before their due date ... or else. Borrowed books were to be returned upon demand, or else. Patrons to be as quiet as possible, particularly in the main chamber, or else. I had the feeling the consequences were likely to be dire. The library represented the greatest collection of knowledge and books within a thousand miles. It would be heavily protected.

I met his eyes. "Or else what?"

He smiled at me, coldly. "You don't want to know."

I passed him the sheet of references. "Where do I look for these?"

"Potion books are stored in Room Two," he informed me. "Or I can have them brought out for you."

"I'll look first," I said. "I can ask if I need help."

The air was oddly silent as I made my way through the stacks and into the rear chambers. I guessed the wards were designed to keep the room as quiet as possible. The handful of students at study desks were quiet, even though they were clearly talking. I couldn't hear a word. They gave me odd looks as I passed. I ignored them as I ran my eye along the giant shelves. There were so many books in view that I found it hard to understand how anyone could find anything. I doubted the librarians were experts in each and every magical field.

And technological field, I thought, as I passed a stack of books on steam engines. It was hard to resist the temptation to stop and browse. A couple had fanciful pictures of giant flying sausages and bat-winged flying ... *things. The librarians can't hope to keep the system in order, can they?*

I put the thought out of my head as I walked into Room Two. The chamber was empty, save for a pair of younger girls who didn't look up. I felt oddly dismayed as I turned to study the giant stacks. It would have been nice to talk—or at least make eye contact—with someone who wasn't Lilith. And they were quite attractive ... I dismissed the idea as I raised my eyes. The really dangerous books had been placed well out of reach. I guessed they'd been placed there to make it harder for someone to get them without magic.

Cheek, I thought. *It isn't as if I could do anything with a book on dark magic.*

I picked a table for myself, then started to hunt for the books. Master Landis had named a dozen ancient tomes, each one old enough to have been written by my great-grandfather. The world had been a very different place, or so I'd been told. It was hard to believe that *people* had really been that different. They lived and died, loved and hated ... I wondered, idly, what my great-grandfather would have made of Heart's Eye. Would he have seen it as a chance for me to rise high? Or as a newfangled idea that would never get off the ground? Who knew?

It was surprisingly easy to find the books, once I figured out how the system worked. The volumes were dusty and old, but whoever had bound them had charmed the leather to ensure the text remained legible and the pages remained intact. I gathered them, one by one, and started to dig out the references. They were nothing more than a set of recipes, all of which I thought had been superseded long ago. I had no idea why Master Landis was looking at them. They looked inefficient, compared to their modern counterparts. And yet ... I frowned as I realised it would be easier to get the ingredients. The modern recipes relied on supplies from all over the Allied Lands.

Odd, I mused. *If it's cheaper to make the older recipes, why didn't they stay in use?*

I mulled it over as I worked my way through the books, carefully copying the recipes into my notebook. They weren't that hard ... if one had magic. My heart clenched as I realised there was no way I could simplify them to the point I could brew them myself. I'd be readying the ingredients for Master Landis or Lilith, not ... I groaned in dismay. It was suddenly very easy to believe I was wasting my time. There was no way I would be anything more than a glorified assistant.

And she said I had to impress her, I thought. *I agreed to an unwinnable bet.*

The thought mocked me as I pushed the books aside and stared down at my powerless hands. I was deluding myself. Perhaps it was time to surrender, to admit I couldn't make it. Master Landis had promised me two years of work as an assistant, if nothing else. I could use the time to search for a new position, then move on. Lilith would be pleased, I was sure. She might even let me go without a final taunt. Or hex.

I remembered the memory potion and frowned as I made my way back to the shelves. There had to be a book on blood-based potions *somewhere*. Master Pittwater had never let me study *those* potions, but ... I smiled as I spotted a book on blood magic and cracked it open. It wasn't as detailed as I'd hoped—the writer constantly danced around the issue, as if he expected his readers to read between the lines—yet it was clear Lilith was right. Blood carried magic. Blood could be used to power a spell. Not for long, if I was reading the text correctly, but long enough. And yet ... it carried dangers. Lilith had to be very trusting or very stupid.

She's not stupid, I thought. It hurt to make that admission, but I couldn't deny it. *She has to have some reason to trust him.*

The thought nagged me as I kept looking through references. Apprentices traded their services for their education, but ... their blood? I didn't think it was smart. I wasn't even sure it was legal. I'd certainly never seen Master Pittwater claim blood from anyone. There was no point in trying to claim blood from *me*. Lilith had been right about that, too. My blood didn't hold any magic. It was point-less. Anyone who wanted to curse me didn't need to go to all the trouble of getting their hands on my blood. They could just walk up to me and turn me into a toad.

I stopped, dead, as a thought struck me. *Could my blood store magic?*

My eyes searched for more books as the concept danced through my mind. Once I'd had it, it refused to go away. Storing magic wasn't easy. Even the strongest wards didn't last forever. Master Pittwater had once commented that the simplest way to get into a sealed and warded tome was just to sit back and wait for the wards to fade. I'd heard a rumour that *someone* had found a way to store magic perma-nently, but nothing concrete. Lilith's blood had magic. Did it have magic because Lilith was a magician? Or because it had absorbed her magic?

I rubbed my forehead. I had to be tired. That had almost made sense.

The books didn't provide any clear answer. Everyone agreed that magical blood could be used in potions—mundane blood was far less useful—but no one agreed on why. It was almost as if they'd carefully *not* thought about the question. I thought I understood why. If you looked at something too closely, it stopped being wonderful. And yet, understanding how a steam engine worked didn't make the locomotives any less fantastic. I still felt the urge to walk up to the railway manager and beg, on bended knee, for the chance to drive one of his trains.

I smiled. *Kings don't want their people asking too many questions about how they and their ancestors became kings in the first place*, I thought. I'd read a hundred pamphlets about King Randor and his daughter, ranging from the practical to accusations of incest, rape and crimes I hadn't known were even *theoretically* possible. *If someone realised the king became the king because his ancestor bumped off the previous king, they might start planning to bump off the* current *king*.

The thought drove me on as I worked through the textbooks. Perhaps people hadn't looked too closely because they were afraid of what they might find. Perhaps people hadn't wanted to think about the implications, when they figured out the answers. Perhaps ... it was certainly hard to believe in the divine right of kings when kings regularly assassinated each other. I snorted. Lilith and her fellows had magic. It wouldn't go away if they looked at it too closely, would it? The thought was absurd.

I read my way through a section on storing blood, frowning. The unknown writer insisted that blood lost its potency, if it wasn't stored very carefully. It reminded me of the lectures on storing potions, although blood seemed to be less sensitive to magical taint. And it could be held in stasis for years, if necessary. And that meant ...

Her blood stores magic, I thought. *Does mine?*

I started to put the books on the trolley—there was a sign warning patrons not to try reshelving the books, or else—as I considered it. One of the books had insisted that, with the right sort of magic, a man could carry a child to term. It struck me as absurd—female bodies were designed to carry children, while males could not —but the writer insisted it was possible. And that meant ... my mind raced. If I could find a way to get a magic charge, could I do magic?

Be careful, I told myself. *You want to believe it.*

I yawned as I finished putting the books on the trolley. I *really* wanted to believe it. The gods knew there'd been times when I'd thought—when I'd deluded myself into thinking—that I had magic. And yet ... the theory was sound. Or was it? Lilith didn't just generate magic. She channelled it, too.

The librarian stepped into the chamber. "Did you have a good time?"

I glanced at the clock and blinked. It was nearly midnight. I should be in bed. I was going to pay for it tomorrow. Lilith was going to rub my nose in it if I overslept again. Master Landis ... I yawned, again, as my stomach growled. Perhaps I could grab a bite to eat and then go straight to bed. It wasn't as if there were strict dining hours in the university. Lilith had assured me that I could get something to eat any time I wanted, as long as I didn't mind basic grub.

"It was very interesting," I said. "Can you help me find something?"

"It *is* what we do here," the librarian said, dryly. "And if we don't have any books on the subject, we might be able to order them from somewhere else."

I was interested. "What happens if they refuse?"

The librarian smiled. "The magical community keeps an index of old, rare or restricted books," he said. "Their current locations are a matter of public record. Only a handful of them are truly unique. If one place refuses to either send their copy here, or let you read it there, we can look elsewhere. There's even a project underway to copy the rarest volumes so everyone can read them."

"I see," I said. I wasn't sure *that* was a good idea - Master Pittwater had told me stories of dangerous books—but it wasn't my problem. "I'm looking for books on channelling magic. Ambient magic."

"Interesting question," the librarian said. "Background magic? Not a magical aura?"

"Background magic," I said. I didn't have an aura to channel. Lilith wouldn't help me, and I didn't know anyone else, not at Heart's Eye. "I thought it might come in handy for potions and alchemy."

"It can," the librarian said. "You'd want to look up subtle magic. I think."

He led me through the darkened stacks and into a smaller room. "There aren't many printed books on subtle magic," he said. "It is not a commonly-discussed subject. Alchemists generally learn a little at school, then sharpen their skills in their workrooms. Be extremely careful if you experiment, as the results can be ... unpredictable."

I raised my eyebrows. "Dangerous?"

"That, too," the librarian said. He found a textbook and pulled it off the shelf. "This is a good starter book. There are references in the back if you wish to continue your studies later."

I took the book, let him sign it out to me and hurried back to my room. The corridors felt as busy as always, even though it was midnight. The students didn't seem inclined to go to their beds. I felt eyes following me as I walked: curious eyes, hostile eyes. I felt singled out, even though I'd barely been at the university for a week. Lilith seemed to have made me guilty by association. But guilty of what?

I could ask her, I thought, *but I doubt I'd get a straight answer.*

I showered quickly—I was going to miss the washroom, when I moved to the apprentice dorms—climbed into bed and opened the book. It was fascinating, revealing a whole new field of magic. Master Pittwater had carved runes into his desk and chairs—and brewing tables—but he'd never revealed why. I understood now. He'd been trying to redirect the magic around the shop, steering it away from his work. The runes were easy. Too easy. I could have used them myself, if I'd known it was possible.

It was hours before I managed to put the book down and get some sleep. The internal logic haunted me. It was easy enough to channel magic ... harder to direct it to a useful purpose, but I didn't really *need* to direct it. If I was right ... I wanted to take the idea straight to Master Landis and ask for his advice and support, yet ... I didn't know what he'd say. I knew what *Lilith* would say. She'd say it was too dangerous for a mundane like me. It certainly wouldn't impress her.

And that means I have to try the idea myself, I thought. *If I can get hold of the right tools.*

It felt as if I hadn't slept at all, when I jerked myself awake in the morning. The textbook—and my notebook—rested on the bedside table, waiting for me. I was tempted to skip breakfast and go straight to work, but my growling stomach reminded me that I hadn't bothered to eat anything last night. I certainly didn't want to faint midway through the day. Lilith didn't need more excuses to make fun of me. Instead, I headed for the dining hall for breakfast. I'd put my plan into action later.

Lilith met me when I reached the lab. "Master Landis has been delayed," she said, holding out her hand. "You've got a bunch of preps to do."

I smiled. "And how many of them are supposed to be done by you?"

She snapped her fingers at me. "You're not allowed to talk anymore," she said. I found my lips sealed together. "Get to work."

I shrugged. She clearly wasn't in a very good mood. I watched her stamping about the lab, digging her way through books and notes as she waited for her master. I wondered why she wasn't doing something more useful with her time. She'd be able to look at a recipe and know why it was useless, something I couldn't do without a great deal of time and effort. Instead, she was sulking. Perhaps something bad had happened, last night. Or perhaps she was just in a snit. It seemed to be her default mood. I honestly had no idea how I was going to impress her. My idea might not work ...

You don't have to impress her, I reminded myself as I started to cut up the foul-smelling fruit into tiny chunks. *You just have to impress Master Landis.*

I sighed, inwardly. Lilith would complain if she had to be partnered with me for much longer, I was sure. And who knew who'd listen to her? I might find myself kicked out just for existing ...

Put your idea into practice, I told myself. *And then see if it will work.*

CHAPTER SEVEN

"I'll see you in the entrance hall at five," Lilith said, when working hours had finally come to an end. My lips had unsealed themselves long ago, but we'd worked in silence anyway. "We're going to the town."

I gave her a sidelong look. Anyone else would have *asked* before deciding we were going out. I was fairly sure I knew what she'd say— or do—if I presumed to tell her we were going to the town, let alone go somewhere else. Lilith might be lonely, to the point she was prepared to put up with me rather than be alone, but ... I sighed, inwardly. It wasn't the right time to pick a fight.

"Sure," I said. I tried to sound like it was nothing, even though I felt weird being with her and oddly guilty about spending our master's money. So what if he could afford it? It wasn't *my* money. "I'll see you at five."

I turned and hurried down the corridor, feeling eyes on my back. Again. Lilith was up to something ... I was sure of it. Or maybe Master Landis thought romance had reared its lovely and terrifying head. That was naïve of him, if he thought so. Lilith and I were from different worlds. She was unlikely to think of me as a possible partner, and I found her personality too grating to tolerate her for any longer than I absolutely had to. I snorted as I made my way further and further into the building, heading down to the workshop. The air smelt faintly of molten iron and oil. It was almost appealing.

A young man stepped out to block my way. "Can I help you?"

I hesitated. "I need to speak to a craftsman," I said. It struck me, suddenly, that I hadn't thought my approach through very well. "Someone who can make a decision."

He looked at me for a long moment. "Come with me."

I followed him through a set of workshops, each one larger than the library. Craftsmen and their apprentices worked on all sorts of machines, from guns to steam engines and things I couldn't even begin to understand. The din was deafening. I saw young women working with the men, wearing the same clothes ... I wondered, suddenly, just how well they worked together. Female apprentices were rare, outside the magical community ... I shook my head in irritation. It wasn't my problem, not now. My companion stopped outside a door, tapped it once and then pushed it open. I found myself stepping into a room that looked like a cross between an office, compete with desks and filing cabinets, and a workshop. Senior Craftswoman Yvonne sat behind the desk, studying a set of blueprints. She looked up as we entered.

"Yes?"

"Senior Craftswoman," I said. I realised I didn't know how to address her, either. It was hard not to stare. She was at least a decade older than me, and far from classically pretty, but she had a presence that was hard to ignore. Her bare arms bore the signs of a career spent at a blacksmith's forge. "I ..."

"Craftswoman is fine," she said. She nodded to my guide, who left. "What can I do for you?"

"I need something forged for me," I said, as I dug my notes out of my pocket. "I ... it's part of my apprenticeship."

"Runic tiles, made of iron?" Yvonne's face betrayed nothing of her feelings as she studied the notes. I cringed, inwardly. I was no draftsman. She probably found it hard to read my handwriting. "What do you intend to do with it?"

"Channel magic into a potion," I said, carefully. I didn't intend to talk about blood to her. Not yet. "I don't have magic, you see ..."

"So I heard." Yvonne gave me a sharp look. "What do you think you could achieve?"

I swallowed a pair of nasty answers. She was a woman in a male-dominated field. She should understand how hard it could be to make one's way when everyone else was different. And had power ... I put the thought aside. Yvonne was a craftsman. She wouldn't appreciate an argument based on raw emotion, let alone emotional blackmail. And she'd probably clobber me if I tried. Her fists looked big enough to knock me into next week.

"I can't muster the magic to turn a cauldron of ingredients into an actual potion," I said, curtly. She'd be familiar with the problem, I was sure. "But this should let me charge the potion without magic."

"I see." Yvonne's expression didn't change. I couldn't tell if she thought I was right, if she thought I was wasting my time—and hers, too, probably a mortal sin—or if she thought I was hiding something. "We could stamp out the tiles for you."

I breathed a sigh of relief. "Thank you."

"You'll have to pay for this, somehow," Yvonne added. "Am I correct in assuming you haven't told your master about this?"

"... Yes," I said. I didn't dare lie. "I want to prove it works first."

"Understandable," Yvonne said. I had the feeling she wanted to say something else, but refrained. "We can have these ready for you tomorrow. If they work, we'll discuss payment with your master. If they don't" —she smiled— "I'm sure we can find a way to make you pay for it."

I bowed. "Thank you, Craftswoman."

"An interesting thought," Yvonne said. "We have worked with runes before, but nothing quite like this. We'll discuss it further if you succeed."

Her tone made it clear she was dismissing me. I bowed again, then left the room and walked back through the workshop. It was fascinating—I stared at a young man carefully fiddling with a piece of clockwork—but, at the same time, it wasn't *me*. I wanted to be there, to be one of them, and yet I didn't. I felt cold, despite the heat, as I made my way back up to my room to change before dinner. Lilith had made it clear I had to look presentable, when we hung out. I was tempted to point out, more than once, that we weren't friends. I didn't want to know what was going through her mind.

"You still haven't impressed me," she said, when we met. "What have you done that I couldn't do?"

"What have you done that no one *else* could do?" I turned the question around and tossed it back at her. "Why are you so special?"

Lilith looked, just for a moment, as though I'd slapped her. I was surprised. Lilith was a magician, and a powerful one, but she was hardly unique. There were hundreds of other magicians, including some her age who were far more powerful than she was. Lady Emily had battled a dozen necromancers in single combat and torn them to shreds. Lilith wasn't anything *like* that powerful. I certainly hadn't seen people crawling over broken glass and potion spills to be her friend. It was depressing to realise that *I* might be the closest thing she had to a friend.

She said nothing as we walked down the road and into the town. It never seemed to sleep. There were buildings, clearly visible, that I was sure hadn't been there the last time we'd visited. Lilith led me to another fancy diner, despite my suggestion we went somewhere cheaper, and ordered the most expensive thing on the menu. I tried not to point out it would probably be cheaper to use the portals so we could eat out somewhere on the other side of the world. The diner was probably teetering constantly on the edge of bankruptcy.

It was an awkward dinner, even by our normal standards, and I was quietly relieved when we made our way back to the university and parted in the entrance hall. Lilith had been quiet, unusually so. She hadn't even made snide remarks about drunken apprentices singing in the streets, something that was almost always the precursor to a brawl back home. I eyed her, worriedly, as she headed back to her room. I'd never visited. I had no idea where she slept.

She probably has an entire suite to herself, I thought. I couldn't see her sharing a dorm, even with her fellow magicians. *Or she might even sleep somewhere outside the castle.*

I dismissed the thought as I went back to my own rooms, slept the sleep of the exhausted and headed back down to the lab in the morning. Master Landis, looking disgustingly bright and cheerful, directed me to spend the entire day preparing ingredients for his latest experiment. I did my best to ignore his cheer, and Lilith's silent glower, as I worked, pausing only for a quick bite to eat at lunchtime. It was a relief, when working hours finally came to an end, that Lilith left without speaking to me. I was torn between being worried about her and being grateful she hadn't hexed me on her way out.

"I checked your notes," Master Landis said. "You did well."

I blinked, caught by surprise. "My potion notes?"

"Yes. The recipes you copied for me." Master Landis held out the papers. "There are a few minor additions, but I think your improvements are solid."

"But not solid enough to let me brew them," I said, regretfully.

"You've helped a great many people," Master Landis said. "They can't take that from you."

If they ever gave it to me in the first place, I thought, as I bowed to him. I knew I was acting like Lilith, but ... it was hard to feel anything, save for bitter resentment. I'd done well —his praise made me swell with pride— yet hardly anyone would know what I'd done. Lilith and her ilk would use my work and take the credit. *Is it really worth it?*

I sighed, inwardly, as I made my way back to the workshop. I wanted fame and fortune, although I'd settle for fortune. It was unlikely I was going to get it. I'd lost my chance to be a craftsman, I'd probably lost my chance to make my mark in the magical world ... what did that leave? Go sailing, in hopes of discovering unknown lands rich in treasure? Sign up with a mercenary band? My parents would disown me. They'd probably prefer I worked in a brothel.

There weren't many occupations less reputable than being a mercenary ...

"Welcome back," Yvonne said, when I reached her office. "What do you think?"

I took the box and looked down at the runic tiles. One of them quivered slightly when I ran my fingers over it. It was designed to detect magic. I felt a flicker of hope, quashed by cold reality. The university was practically glowing with magic. The remaining runes were dead and cold. I had no way to know if they were doing their job or not. It was hard to tell how well they actually worked. I'd checked and rechecked my calculations, but it was quite possible I'd missed something so fundamental no one had bothered to write it down.

"I discussed the matter with Praxis," Yvonne said. It took me a moment to connect the name with her lover, the enchanter. "It was his considered opinion that the magic charge wouldn't last long enough to do more than warm the tiles, if that. It won't trigger off a potions cascade."

"I know," I said. I still didn't want to talk about the blood. "I have an idea."

"I hope you know what you're doing," Yvonne said. "Good luck."

I took the tiles and headed back to my room. I hoped I knew what I was doing, too. The risk of causing an explosion was very low, unless my calculations were so off they were on the other side of the globe, but the chances of making a complete and total fool out of myself were a great deal higher. If I was wrong, nothing would happen. I would almost prefer an explosion. It would be proof I'd stumbled onto something, even if it claimed my life. I wondered, as I closed and locked the door behind me, if I should leave a note for Master Landis. If I died ...

Don't be an idiot, I told myself. *The worst thing that can reasonably happen is nothing.*

I put the box on the table and carefully unpacked the tiles. Yvonne and her apprentices had done a very good job. The runes were perfect. I hoped. It was hard to be entirely sure without magic. And who could I ask to test them? Lilith? I snorted as I dug through the small collection of tools I'd brought with me. Master Pittwater had given me the traditional set, back when I'd hoped I'd turn my time at the shop into a career. In hindsight, I wondered why he'd bothered. Perhaps he'd had hopes, too.

Or perhaps it cost him very little, I thought. The silver knife was worth its weight in gold, literally, but I knew how much money the shop had taken in every week. *For all I know, it cost him only a tiny sliver of his fortune.*

I felt my heart starting to pound as I placed a glass dish in the centre of the table, then carefully pressed the knife against my bare skin. The pain stabbed through me. It was all I could do not to scream. I reminded myself, sharply, that Lilith had done the same and shown no sign of pain. Perhaps she'd used magic. Her blood was magic, as she'd reminded me. It was hard to believe a little more would hurt. I let the blood drip into the dish, then kicked myself mentally as I looked around for a cloth. I'd forgotten to have a bandage within reach. Master Pittwater would have beaten me for such an oversight. It would have been hard to blame him.

Gritting my teeth, I wrapped a cloth around my palm and clenched my fist as I started to put the tiles into place. They would not only gather the magic in the room and channel it towards the blood, but also—if my calculations were correct—keep it in place long enough for the blood to absorb the magic. If my calculations were correct ... I sat back on my bed, clenching my fist tightly until the blood stopped flowing. I didn't dare go to a healer. There would be questions I didn't want to have to answer.

And if I leave the blood here, I asked myself, *will anyone notice?*

I didn't know. Lilith had told me that magical students regarded breaking and entering as a harmless prank. She'd even insisted she'd broken into the headmistress's office, although I wasn't sure I believed her. Here ... I sat up and stared at the blood, unsure what would happen if someone sneaked into my room. Lilith never had, as far as I knew. Why would she? I supposed the fact I hadn't found myself zapped into a frog the moment I sat on the bed was proof she hadn't. It was just the sort of puerile joke that magicians considered the height of humour and everyone else considered utterly horrifying.

If someone asks, I decided, *I'll tell them the truth.*

I went for dinner, ate alone—Lilith was nowhere in sight—and returned to my room to sleep until the following day. It was my off-day, but Master Landis had given me permission to use the lab as I saw fit ... as long as I was careful. I took the blood— the magic-sensing rune vibrated when I held it over the dish—and hurried downstairs, trying to make sure I didn't bump into anyone who might ask awkward questions. It was a great deal easier to ask forgiveness than permission. I breathed a sigh of relief as I stepped into the lab, the lights coming on automatically. Lilith wasn't there. I hadn't been looking forward to trying to explain to her what I was doing.

Muttering a quiet prayer under my breath, I started to gather the ingredients to brew a basic potion. It wasn't anything like as complex as some of the potions I'd seen Master Landis make, but it needed magic. *Real* magic. I could do everything as perfectly as possible and yet fail because I couldn't ... I looked at the blood as I put the mixture together, resting everything within the cauldron. I needed a magic surge ...

Bracing myself, I dipped a spoon into the blood and let a droplet dribble into the cauldron.

The liquid glowed with light. I jumped back, torn between delight and fear. The light was clear proof that *something* was happening. I'd made magic. It might not be *my* magic, but ... it was *mine*. I'd done something no one, not even Lilith, could take away from me. The light grew brighter, then faded. I inched towards the cauldron and peered inside. The potion was ready.

"I did it!" I jumped in the air, nearly knocking over the cauldron. "I did it!"

I laughed. Lilith would have to admit I'd impressed her now. Wouldn't she? I'd made magic! Well, I'd tapped into the background magic, but ... I'd made it work! Master Pittwater had spent hours complaining about how hard it was to convince brewers to focus on the simple potions. I'd just solved that problem for him. And yet ...

My heart sank. *What if she isn't impressed?*

I looked at the cauldron, and then at the vast collection of ingredients, and then back at the cauldron. Steam was pouring out of the mixture, slowly reducing as it cooled down. Steam ... something nagged at my mind. I knew how to make steam and ...

... And I had a very good idea.

CHAPTER EIGHT

It took me longer than it should have to work up the nerve to brew the next potion.

I was no coward. I knew that for a fact. I'd grown up in a rough area, where turning the other cheek meant getting slapped twice, and I'd been an apprentice since I grew into adulthood. I'd taken part in my fair share of drunken brawls, when apprentices would go out on the town and start fights with the other apprentices; I'd done plenty of stupid things that, as I matured, I'd probably look back at and groan. And yet ...

It wasn't easy to check my calculations. I honestly wasn't sure if I wanted the idea to be workable. Perversely, it wouldn't have worked at all if Master Landis hadn't made me look at the old recipes. The newer ones would have been quite beyond me, with or without the charged blood. I concentrated on working out the details, then prepared the ingredients and started to brew. The stench was almost unbearable. I was fairly sure I knew why so many alchemists wanted apprentices—and why so few apprentices stayed. *Someone* had to prepare the ingredients. Why not someone who couldn't reasonably object?

I glanced at the clock as I put the ingredients into the cauldron. It was late morning. I had no way to know if Lilith or Master Landis would come to the lab. Lilith might even come looking for me, despite everything. The thought made me frown as I finished the preparations and lit the flame under the mixture. Who knew what was going through that girl's mind?

The mixture heated slowly. I kept a wary eye on it. The brew shouldn't turn magical until I inserted the rest of the charged blood, but it was hard to be sure. Master Pittwater had cautioned me to watch for tainted ingredients, pointing out that the slightest hint of excess magic could cause an explosion, but I had no way to sense it. The rune hadn't vibrated when I'd held it close to the ingredients. I had a nasty feeling that proved nothing. The background magic wasn't so strong in the lab. In hindsight, I understood why it had been steered away from the chamber.

I smiled as the liquid started to smell, then stirred four times and added the blood. The stench grew worse, immeasurably worse. I swallowed hard, trying not to gag as the magic worked its way through the brew. Durian fruit was supposed to be good to eat, but it would be a brave or foolish man—or one without a nose—who actually put it in his mouth. I'd been in washrooms and toilets that smelled better. The liquid shimmered, boiled and started to glow. I breathed a sigh of relief as I put out the flame. It had worked.

Grinning, I lifted the cauldron off the heat—just to ensure it cooled quicker—and put it to one side, then walked into the kitchen to make a cup of Kava. The kettle whistled as it boiled, the water steadily turning to steam. It looked like a miniature steam engine, vibrating frantically on top of the stove. I picked it up, poured hot water into the mug ... and stopped, dead, as a thought occurred to me. If water became steam, and steam was a type of gas, what *else* could become a gas? What else ...

The idea stuck in my mind and refused to go away. I knew how a steam engine worked. I also knew that boiling water purified it, that steam was effectively purified water that would—eventually—condense back into water droplets. What if I found a way to turn a *potion* into a gas? What if ... I stared at the collection of equipment, from beakers to tiny kettles and heating globes. If I turned the potion into a gas, what would happen if someone breathed it in? I took a breath, tasting the stench in the air. To me, it was just unpleasant. To a magician ...

I knew I should take the idea to Master Landis. There were strict limits on just how far an apprentice could go, without his master's permission. And yet, I was too enthused to care. I took some of my potion, a potion I knew might not work properly, and started to experiment. It wasn't easy to turn the liquid into gas without causing the ingredients to separate. If it hadn't been a potion, I wasn't sure I could have done it at all. The magic I'd used to turn the ingredients into magic was holding it together, even as it became a gas. I felt my heart pounding as the air slowly filled with steam. It would probably smell terrible, I decided, if the air didn't already stink. And ...

She wanted me to impress her, I thought. I was gambling everything and yet ... I thought it would work. It was worth a try. I didn't have *that* much time before I had to leave or Lilith carried out her threat or ... or whatever. *Let me see if* this *impresses her.*

I headed to the door and peered outside. There was a messenger station positioned at the top of the corridor, manned by a pair of students who paid for their education by fetching and carrying for magicians. They eyed me worriedly as I beckoned to them. I had the feeling they didn't know what to make of me. I was no magician, they knew, and yet I worked for one. Their eyes looked past me as they approached. I guessed they were afraid Lilith was right behind me.

"Here," I said. I held out a coin. We didn't have to tip, but I'd been a shopboy long enough to know that tipping ensured better service. "I want you to take a message for me."

The messengers exchanged glances, then one stepped forward. "Yes, sir?"

"Go to Lilith," I said. They'd know where to find her or they'd ask someone who could check the wards. "Tell her to come to the potions lab."

The messenger looked reluctant—I guessed he wasn't too keen to go to Lilith's bedroom, wherever it was—but took the coin and hurried off anyway. I smiled as I went back into the lab and closed the door. The wards should keep the smell from getting into the corridors, but there was no point in taking chances. There would be so many complaints if it did get out of the lab, that Master Landis would probably dismiss me on the spot. Who could blame him for throwing me to the wolves? He'd be the one facing the wrath of his peers.

I waited, hoping Lilith would come without an argument. The messenger might not tell her who'd sent the message. Perhaps she'd assume Master Landis had summoned her. I hoped so. She'd probably make a point of being late, or not coming at all, if she knew it was me. I felt the seconds ticking by, the air growing warmer as the steam continued to boil. It was impossible to even *guess* at the concentrations of potion hanging in the air. It was quite possible I'd overdone it.

Or that the concentrations aren't high enough to have any real effect, I thought. *If this goes wrong ...*

Something cold settled in my heart. If it worked ... I looked at the empty dish and winced. I'd proven blood could be used to store magic, at least for a few hours. Perhaps that would have been enough to secure my apprenticeship. If not, I could have taken the concept back to Master Pittwater or sold it to the Alchemical Guilds. The secret wouldn't stay that way for long—it wouldn't be hard to work out what I'd done—but I might be able to parlay it into a secure place in one of the guilds. Or somewhere.

The door opened. Lilith stepped in, wearing a dress. I blinked. I'd never seen her in anything other than magical robes. Her face twisted in disgust as she took a breath. I'd grown used to the stench, but she'd walked into it blind. The look she gave me suggested that hanging, drawing and quartering was too good for me. I knew how she felt. The sudden stench was enough to put anyone off their lunch.

"Adam." Lilith coughed and started again. "Adam, what are you doing?"

"An experiment," I said. I waved a hand at the cluster of equipment on the table. "What do you make of it?"

Lilith glared. "Did you just call me here to show off a mess? I should ..."

I held up a hand. If this went wrong ... I was doomed. "You should turn me into a frog?"

"You ..." Lilith raised her hand. "You ..."

She jabbed a finger at me. I braced myself. Nothing happened.

Lilith stared in incomprehension. The look on her face ... I couldn't help myself. I sniggered. She blinked, then jabbed her finger at me again. Nothing happened. She looked at her fingers in shock. They were powerless, as powerless as my own. She stumbled back as she raised her eyes, looking at me in horror. I could see the question she didn't want to ask, written all over her face. What the hell had I done?

I felt a surge of ... of something I didn't want to look at too closely. Lilith was smaller than me and a girl besides. I could knock her down, as easily as she'd once been able to freeze or transfigure me. A wave of sheer rage washed through me. I could beat her. I could put her over my knee. I could teach her a lesson she would never forget. I could ...

Shame overwhelmed me. I wasn't going to do that. I couldn't even *begin* to do that. It wasn't me.

Lilith stumbled back until she hit the wall. I could see panic in her eyes, panic and fear and a grim awareness she was powerless. I could do anything to her, and she knew it. Guilt warred, in my mind, with a sense she needed the lesson before she picked on someone much more powerful than herself. I'd knocked her down, but only for a few seconds. The next person she picked on might blast her into little pieces and scatter them over the entire world.

"What ...?" Lilith forced herself to stand up, despite the fear in her eyes. "What have you done to me?"

"I made Durian potion," I said, waving a hand at the table. The stench should have tipped her off, if nothing else. There was *nothing* that smelt quite like Durian. "And then I turned it into a gas."

Lilith blinked. "You *made* Durian potion?"

"Yes," I said. For an instant, I thought I saw a keen alchemist peek out from behind her eyes. Lilith didn't *have* to be an alchemical apprentice. She could easily have done something else with her life. There were plenty of careers open to magicians—and, I supposed, she could always get married. If she could find someone willing to marry her ... "I made it myself."

Her eyes narrowed. "Liar."

"I'm not lying," I said. "Listen."

I outlined everything I'd done, from the moment I'd realised that blood could be used to store magic to actually using my blood in a potion. Lilith's face kept twisting, as if she was unsure if she should be impressed or horrified. I wondered, not for the first time, if I'd made a terrible mistake. I could have taken my insight away from the university and worked on it in private, without the risk of making an unrelenting enemy. And ... I went through the calculations, showing her how I'd woven my blood into the potion. It had worked. *That* was the important thing. Everything else was gravy.

Lilith muttered a word I didn't catch as she forced herself to go through the calculations. Her dress was stained with sweat and potion ... I wondered, grimly, if I'd interrupted something. Why *had* she put on a nice dress? It was her day off, but she didn't have anywhere to go. Or did she? Magicians could teleport. I had no idea if *she* could, but it was possible ...

"And you made me breathe the potion," Lilith finished. "You ..."

Panic filled her eyes. "How long does it last?"

"Not long," I assured her. I wasn't sure *how* long. There'd been no way to calculate the dosage, let alone how quickly the gas would lose its potency. Lilith might regain her powers the moment she went back to her bedroom, had a shower and changed into something less comfortable. Or it might be a few hours before she could use magic again. She was still breathing in the gas. "An hour, a day, a week, a month, a year, a decade, a ..."

"You don't know," Lilith said, flatly. "Do you?"

It wasn't a question. "No," I said. "But it shouldn't be longer than an hour or two."

Lilith sat down at the table. I wondered what was going through her mind. I'd asked her, only a day or so ago, what made her special. Nothing, as far as I could tell. And now I'd stripped her of the one thing she could hold over me. I remembered how I'd felt when she— and Matt—had used magic on me and told myself I shouldn't feel guilty. She felt helpless and vulnerable ... she'd made *me* feel helpless and vulnerable. I told myself that time and time again, but it didn't work. I'd stolen her confidence in herself ... no, in her magic. I didn't have to do anything else to her for her to know I *could.*

I sat on the other side, keeping my distance. Girls didn't like to be crowded—my mother had drummed that into my head when I'd been a child—even when they weren't feeling weak and helpless. I'd give Lilith that consideration, even if she didn't give me any in return. It was the right thing to do.

"You challenged me to impress you," I said. "Have I?"

Lilith said nothing. I wondered what was going through her mind. She was very far from stupid. The longer she breathed in the gas, the longer it would take to regain her powers. Probably. She could take a purgative, I supposed, but it would be a thoroughly unpleasant experience, with no guarantee it would speed things up. I tried not to think about it. I'd taken one once, when I'd swallowed something I really shouldn't have, and it had been enough to convince me I really didn't want to do it again. She should go ... did she think I'd stop her? Or was she reluctant to leave the room without her powers? She was hardly the most popular person in the university.

"Yeah," Lilith conceded, finally. "I guess you have."

I smiled. "And you think I can do more?"

Lilith grinned. I think it was the first time I'd seen a genuine smile from her. "I suppose you can."

I stood and started to clear up the mess, pouring the remains of the potion into the vat for disposal and putting the caldrons, tubes and kettles in the sink. They'd have to be cleaned carefully, just to make sure there was nothing left to contaminate the next batch of potion. I'd never met an alchemist who wasn't a real stickler for cleaning, even the ones who liked pushing the limits as far as they'd go. Lilith watched, unmoving, as the air started to clear. I wondered, suddenly, just how long it would be until we could breathe freely again. The spells Master Landis used to clear the air wouldn't be any use if we didn't have magic ...

Lilith picked up my calculations and frowned. "You're good at this."

"Thanks." I hoped it was a peace offering, of a sort. Lilith would regain her powers and then ... she might set out to take revenge. "So are you."

"I don't have a talent for theoretical magic," Lilith said. "I can cast spells. I can brew potions. But I can't improve on them."

"We can, if we work together," I pointed out. "I'll devise the spells, you cast them."

Lilith shot me an unreadable look. I had no idea what was going through her head. The idea of working with me wasn't that bad, was it? It wasn't as if she had anyone else who might work with her. She was isolated, alone in a crowd. I opened my mouth to ask why, then thought better of it. Lilith would tell me if she wanted to tell me.

"Father won't be too pleased," Lilith said. "He wants me to follow in his footsteps."

Something clicked in my mind. "Master Landis is your *father*?"

"Yes." Lilith looked surprised. "You didn't know?"

I kicked myself, mentally. It was rare for a male magician to have a female apprentice. People would talk. Rumours would start to spread. I should have realised. The only reason someone hadn't asked hard questions about the apprenticeship was because they were closely related. Father and daughter ... no one could question *them* being alone together. I wondered, suddenly, what had happened to the mother. And why Lilith was so isolated.

"No," I said. I was sure I was missing something. If Lilith was Master Landis's daughter, why wasn't everyone sucking up to her? "I never realised ..."

The door opened. Master Landis stepped into the room, followed by two strangers. One was an old woman, with cold grey eyes and greyer hair. The other was a young man with floppy brown hair and scars on his hands. He waved a hand in the air, casting a spell to remove the remnants of the potion. Good thinking on his part, I noted. And quick, too.

"Well," Master Landis said. It was suddenly impossible to miss the resemblance between him and his daughter. "Adam. Lilith. What are you doing?"

I swallowed and started to explain.

CHAPTER NINE

"Blood," Master Landis said, when I'd finished. "You used blood."

I swallowed. His tone suggested I was dead. I tried to think as he looked at his two companions. Blood ... using blood wasn't illegal, just highly dangerous. And the only person at risk had been me. It wasn't as if I'd stolen blood from a genuine magician and worked it into a spell. I wondered, suddenly, if that was even possible. One didn't *need* a sneaky potion to render a magician helpless. A quick blow to the head, followed by steady doses of sleeping potion, would be quite enough.

"Indeed," the older woman said. She looked thoughtful, rather than angry. "Did you understand the risks?"

"I believed there was minimal risk," I said, carefully. "And if there had been risks, they would have fallen on me. It was my blood."

"Experimenting with blood is not something we want to encourage," the older woman said, tartly. "The risks are often unpredictable."

"Mistress Irene, it was *his* blood," the young man said. "I think Emily would approve."

I blinked. If the older woman was Mistress Irene, *Administrator* Irene, did that mean the young man was Caleb? I'd heard stories about him, although most of them had grown in the telling. Had he really been Lady Emily's lover? And had they broken up because he'd wanted to ... to do what? The stories had grown in the telling, to the point it was hard to believe the young man in front of me was the same person. He didn't *look* like a creature out of myth and legend. He certainly didn't look anything like his painting. I hadn't recognised him.

"I dare say she would," Mistress Irene said. She looked at me. "You do realise you have made a *real* breakthrough? The concept of storing magic has been discussed extensively, but using blood— mundane blood—as a storage medium has never been considered, let alone tried."

I felt a thrill. "I'm the first?"

"Yes." Caleb smiled. "Well done."

"As far as we know," Mistress Irene corrected, coldly. "There are plenty of unanswered questions about how certain things were done in the past. It is possible that you have rediscovered something that was lost, rather than being the first person to so much as *consider* the possibility."

"However, none of us know that," Caleb said. "Even if he wasn't the first, he might as well be."

Mistress Irene speared me with her eyes. "Your achievement will be discussed extensively during the next board meeting," she said. "It will be taken as proof, one hopes, that the idea of merging magic and mundane concepts is not as foolish as some believe. However" —her eyes hardened — "you will also study the risks inherent in blood magic. You could have hurt yourself quite badly, if something had gone wrong. You could not have been *certain* your blood was untainted."

She nodded to Master Landis, then turned and marched out the door. Caleb winked at me—I had a feeling he intended to talk to me later, when we were alone—and followed the older woman, closing the door behind him. Master Landis paced around the room, inspecting my papers and calculations as he calmed himself. I forced myself to wait, not daring to speak first. On one hand, my achievements reflected well on him. On the other, I'd broken at least nine different rules and bent dozens of others. And I'd rendered his daughter powerless. He would be quite within his rights to give me the boot, if he wished. I wondered, sourly, if I'd managed to impress Lilith only to lose her father's regard.

Master Landis turned to face me. "Why didn't you ask me first?"

He sounded calm. I wasn't reassured. "It was my idea," I said. "I had to be the one to test it."

"You tested it on Lilith," Master Landis said. His tone was so flat I knew I was in deep trouble. "And you could not hope to predict *all* the effects."

"I ran the calculations," I said, "and I brewed the potion myself. It worked."

"Yes," Master Landis agreed. He glanced at my sheet of calculations. "Your brewing was masterful. The technique might not be *easy* to adapt to more complex brews, but ... it certainly opens the door to more research. It will change the world."

"Thank you, sir," I said.

"Master Pittwater said you had potential," Master Landis added. "I see he was right."

I beamed. "Thank you, sir," I repeated.

"That said, I do *not* want you carrying out any further experiments without my permission," he continued. "Blood is a dangerously volatile substance. You could not be *sure* your blood was untainted, as Irene pointed out. You work in a potions lab. You work next to two magicians. The risks were quite high, higher than you seem to realise. I do *not* want you to repeat the same mistake. Do you understand me?"

It was hard not to feel chastened. I didn't dare look at Lilith. "Yes, Master."

"I think you can consider yourself a formal apprentice from this moment on," Master Landis said. "If, of course, you wish to do so. We'll perform the formal oaths on Monday. That'll give you a day to decide if you want to stay. If not ... I look forward to hearing what you make of yourself."

It was hard not to jump for joy as he turned and walked out the door. I was an apprentice! A *real* apprentice! If I charged more blood, under his supervision, I could brew! It was going to be great! I sobered as I looked at Lilith, who'd been oddly silent as the older magicians spoke. If she didn't want me to stay ...

"You did well," she said, tonelessly. "Congratulations."

I sat down facing her. "Do you want me to stay?"

"Yes. No. I don't know." Lilith stared at her hands. "You won't find it easy."

"You didn't make it easy," I pointed out. "Why not?"

"Father believes in this place," Lilith said. "He thinks ... he thinks the future will be born here. Not everyone agrees. Lots of people think he's a traitor for coming here. They think he sold out for sunshine and rainbows."

I nodded in understanding. Magicians joked about sunshine and rainbows in the same way mundanes joked about fool's gold ... and sneered at those who took it for *real* gold. If Lilith was right, Master Landis's enemies saw him as selling out for nothing. They would probably have been a little more understanding if he'd sold out for a big pile of gold. And yet ...

"They don't seem to like you," I said. "Is that why?"

Lilith looked pained. "Yeah."

I was tempted to point out that probably wasn't true. Or not entirely true. Lilith was pretty enough to have suitors prepared to overlook her personality. And some of those suitors would have enough power to protect themselves. And yet ... I could understand why she might have few friends. It wasn't easy being related to a teacher, even when said teacher wasn't held in high regard. I had a feeling there were political issues I was missing.

"Well ..." I made up my mind, although in truth there had never been any real doubt. "I'll stay."

I stood and held out my hand. "Adam, Son of Don and Martha," I said. "Pleased to meet you,"

Lilith blinked, then shook my hand. "Lilith, Daughter of Landis," she said. "But then, you knew that already."

"I didn't," I said. "It never crossed my mind."

"Here's something that should cross your mind," Lilith said. She pointed a long finger at the potion I'd bottled for later. "What you've accomplished, here and now, is a game-changer. A world-changer. You've unlocked something no one knew how to do, until now. And word is going to spread. Father is going to tell everyone about his *brilliant* new apprentice and what's he's done."

She stood, brushing down her stained dress. "And what's going to happen," she asked, "when the world realises what you've done?"

"I don't know," I said.

"Nor do I," Lilith said. "And that scares me."

I watched her go, feeling the ground shift under my feet. Lilith had a point. There was no way the technique would remain secret. It was just too useful to be buried in a vault and forgotten. Master Landis had probably gotten a lot of sharp and sarcastic comments about his willingness to take me as an apprentice. His own uncertainty about the situation had probably been why he hadn't put Lilith in her place long ago. Unless I missed my guess, he'd be delighted to show off what I'd done—and what he'd achieved, through me. Anyone could use the technique. Who knew where the chips would fall?

And yet ...

I grinned as I returned to tidying up. It didn't matter. The future could take care of itself. I'd made it! I'd become an apprentice, with a genuine chance of making my mark on the world and ... hell, I'd *already* made my mark on the world. I could do nothing, for the rest of my life, and my name would still be hailed and cursed as a world-changer. The first mundane to serve as a true alchemical apprentice, perhaps; the first mundane to prove that technology and magic could not only co-exist, but work together. And I'd managed to prove myself to someone who'd loathed me just for existing.

My smile grew wider. The future looked bright and full of promise.

I couldn't wait.

ABOUT THE AUTHOR

Christopher G. Nuttall is the author of the *Schooled in Magic* series, the *Zero Enigma* series and many others, covering everything from high fantasy to alternate history, military science-fiction and thrillers, He currently lives in Edinburgh with his wife and sons.`

Website: http://chrishanger.net/

Blog: https://chrishanger.wordpress.com/

AFTERWORD

If you enjoyed this volume, please consider leaving a review.

Also check out:

Fantastic Schools, Volume 1— Follow a girl trying desperately to find her place in a school of dark magic, a band of witches desperate to prove they can be as good as the wizards, a school of magical monsters standing between the evil one and ultimate power, a businesswoman discovering the secrets of darkest evil ... and what happens when a magical education goes badly wrong.

Includes stories by: Christopher G. Nuttall, Thomas K. Carpenter, Mel Lee Newmin, Emily Martha Sorensen, Aaron Van Treeck, Steven G. Johnson, George Phillies, Benjamin Wheeler, Frank B. Luke, G. Scott Huggins, Bernadette Durbin, Roger D. Strahan, Erin N.H. Furbym and Denton Salle.

Fantastic Schools, Volume 2—Follow a mundane teacher striding into a world of magic, a spy on a mission, a guided tour of a magical school, a school dance for monsters, a dangerous reunion ... and many more.

Includes stories by: Christopher G. Nuttall, L. Jagi Lamplighter, J.F. Posthumus, Christine Amsden, James Pyles, Becky R. Jones,

Morgon Newquist, Tom Anderson, Patrick Lauser, James Odell, Misha Burnett, Audrey Andrews, Paul A. Piatt, David Breitenbeck.

For more books about Fantastic Schools, check out the *Fantastic Schools and Where to Find Them* website and the *Fantastic Schools Book List*:

https://www.superversivesf.com/fantasticschools/fantastic-schools-book-list/